Master

The Sanctuary Series
Volume 5

Robert J. Crane

Master
The Sanctuary Series, Volume 5

Copyright © 2014 Midian Press
All Rights Reserved.

1st Edition

This book is a work of fiction. Names, characters, places and incidents are products of the author's imagination or are used fictitiously. Any resemblance to actual events or locales or persons, living or dead, is entirely coincidental.

The scanning, uploading and distribution of this book via the internet or any other means without the permission of the publisher is illegal and punishable by law. Please purchase only authorized electronic editions, and do not participate in or encourage electronic piracy of copyrighted materials. Your support of the author's rights is appreciated.

No part of this publication may be reproduced in whole or in part without the written permission of the publisher. For information regarding permission, please email cyrusdavidon@gmail.com

Dedication

This book is dedicated to my grandfather, a retired factory worker who read thousands of books in spite of not going any further in school than eighth grade. He had a love of reading that was handed down through the generations to land on me. Thanks, Papaw. I'll miss you.

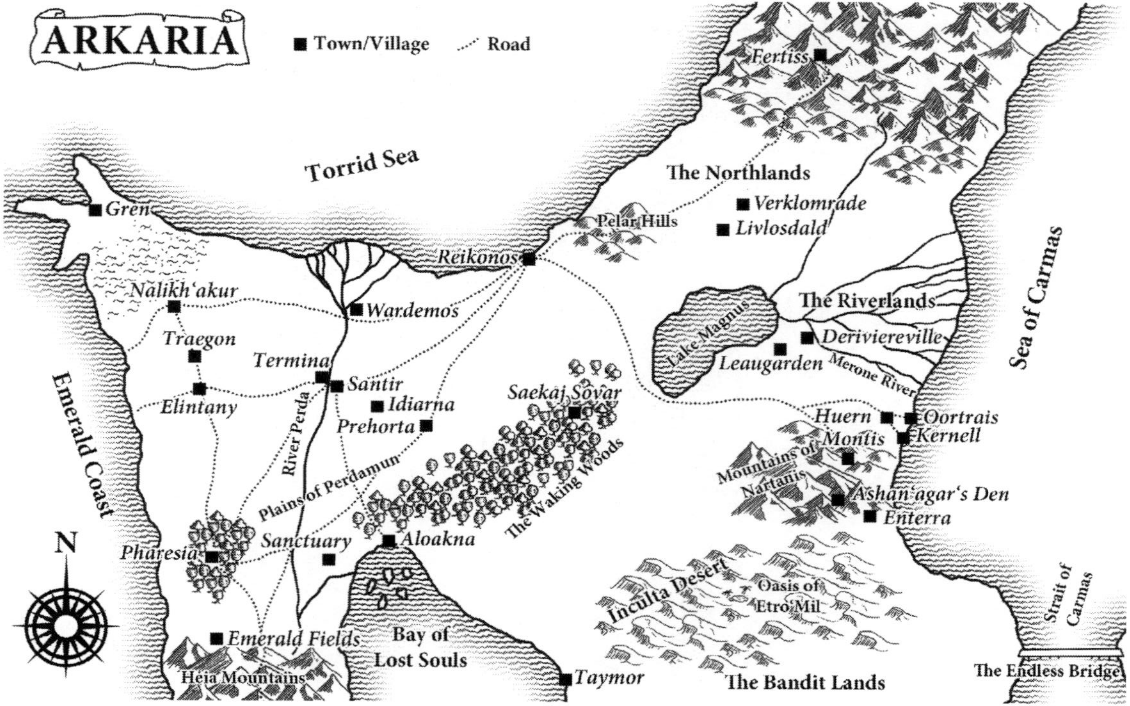
ARKARIA
Town/Village
Road
Torrid Sea
Gren
Nalikh'akur
Traegon
Elintany
Emerald Coast
Wardemos
Termina
Santir
Idiarna
Prehorta
River Perda
Plains of Perdamun
Reikonos
Pelar Hills
The Northlands
Verklomrade
Livlosdald
Fertiss
Lake Magnus
The Riverlands
Derivièreville
Leaugarden
Merone River
Sea of Carmas
Saekaj Sovar
The Waking Woods
Sanctuary
Aloakna
Pharesia
Emerald Fields
Heia Mountains
Bay of Lost Souls
Taymor
Huern
Oortrais
Montis
Kernell
Mountains of Nartanis
Ashan'agar's Den
Enterra
Inculta Desert
Oasis of Etro Mil
The Bandit Lands
Strait of Carmas
The Endless Bridge
N

SHEKAI SOVAR

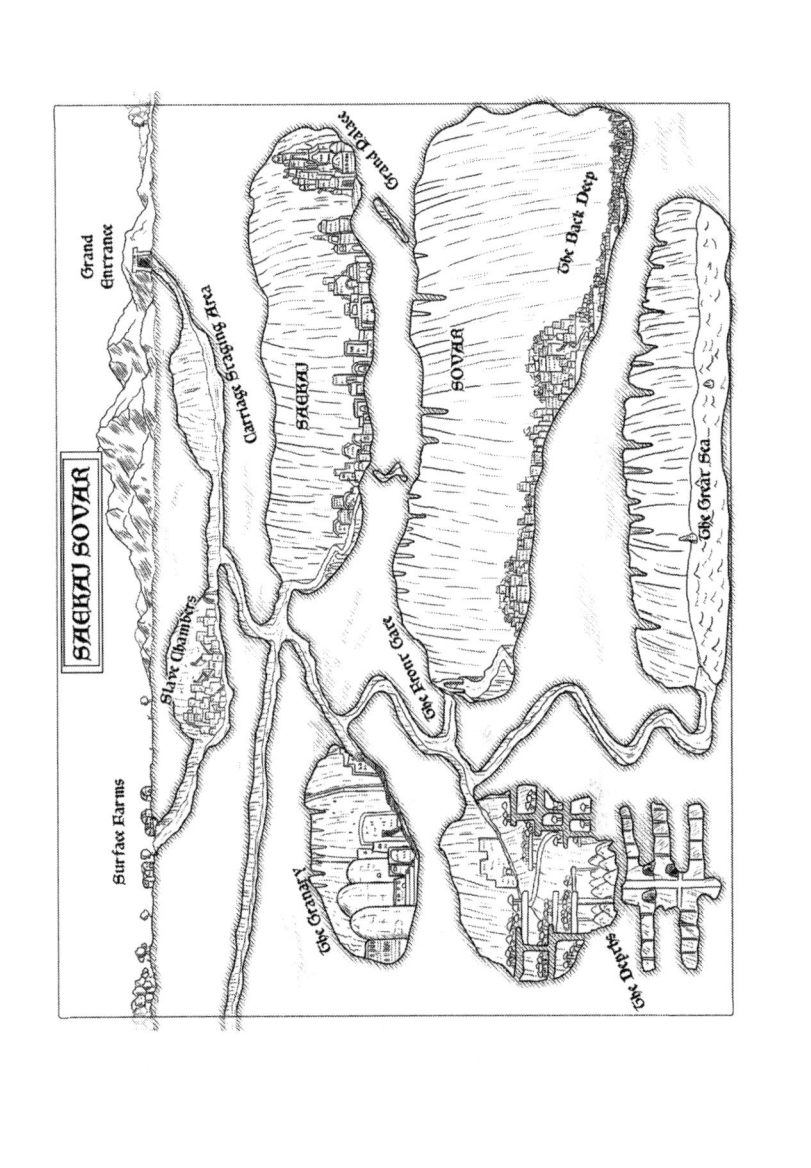

Grand Entrance

Grand Dalak

Surface Farms

Carriage Staging Area

Slave Chambers

SHEKAI

SOVAR

The Back Deep

The Great Sea

The Front Gate

The Granary

The Depths

NOW

Prologue

"I thought she hated me at first, you know," Cyrus Davidon said as he stared out the window. Darkness had descended upon the Plains of Perdamun, a light rain falling on the already saturated ground. "When we met, I mean. I thought she acted the way she did because she hated me." There was a seeping chill around him, even as the fire crackled in the hearth at his back. "I was sure of it the first year, and I never really reconsidered it after that." He shrugged, his black armor clanking as he moved his broad shoulders. "I just thought she hated me. All the way until … Nalikh'akur, I guess."

"Was that the place she tried to drown you?" Vaste's dry voice crackled with wit. Cyrus turned to see the troll sitting in a chair, pulled up next to the fire. His frame was enormous, even taller than Cyrus's seven feet. The troll's teeth were pronounced, catching the glare of the dancing flames. Even still, there was no menace about Vaste. The sweet smell of the burning wood wafted under Cyrus's nose.

Cyrus felt himself laugh, unintentionally. "Yes. But it was bit more complicated than that. I had a fever, you see—"

"I've heard this story before and it bores me," Vaste said, shaking his great green head, blurring his dark eyes as he moved. "Tell me a fun one—like that time she came to your quarters when you got back from Luukessia—"

"That's not a fun one," Cyrus said darkly.

"Tell it anyway," Vaste said. "I never get tired of that one." His glee was palpable, as it often was, but there was a hint of hesitancy as well, a kind of velvet touch that his sarcasm seldom held. *Waiting to see how I react*, Cyrus thought.

Cyrus felt a sigh building. He stared at the troll, but he sensed no intentional antagonism there. *This is who Vaste is, how he relates to the world.*

How he deals with ... what we're dealing with here.

"All right," Cyrus said, and inspiration struck. "I have a better idea."

"First, I'm shocked you have an idea—"

"Quiet, troll," Cyrus said and fumbled with the leather-bound diary at his side, lifting it up with a flourish. "How about I read you Vara's impressions of that night?"

Vaste arched a black eyebrow. "Proceed."

Cyrus flipped through the diary, searching for the date. When he found it between the careworn pages, the delicate, flowing handwriting was easy to read.

"I walked to Cyrus Davidon's quarters in a fit of annoyance. We'd had a conversation in the Council Chambers when he returned, and it had been deeply unsatisfying, like eating a meal in a gnomish tavern."

"What was it with her and the gnomes?" Vaste asked. "So much hate."

"Hush," Cyrus said. *"Apparently in a bid to devalue myself further, I made a decision in the night that proved to be ridiculously fateful. I walked to the door of his quarters, and I knocked.*

I stood there in the dim light of the torches, their flames dancing on the wall, and counted all the reasons I should go back to my bed. It was waiting for me, it was warm and inviting—and I was sure to toss and turn for the rest of the night. I was wearing something rather scandalous, I realized a moment after I knocked, the type of thing I wear to bed, with its curls and lace—"

"Tell me more," Vaste said.

"I'm about to tell you a whole lot less," Cyrus said, giving Vaste the eye. *"I stood at his door in my grossly inappropriate attire, worried for the half second before I heard his movement within that I would be thought a slattern for certain. Then, once I heard him coming to answer it, all thought of panic at how I was dressed fled me and was replaced by a much more sweeping, general sense of panic.*

He opened the door—quite nude, I might add, which thus soothed my concern about appropriate attire.

"You," he said.

"Me," I replied, not really sure what to say. He looked as if I'd woken him from a good sleep. His dark hair was tousled, and he was months—or years—unshaven. A thick scar ran across the base of his neck, a horrible, jagged mark that came from a tale that made me quite ill in the hearing. "May I come in?" I asked, then flogged myself mentally for the stupidity of my question. He was nude, after all, that much was obvious from what was visible in the half-open door.

He squinted at me in the dim light of the hall, shrouded in the darkness of his own room. He had a vacant expression that was not usually present upon his face, no matter how much I might wish to convince him otherwise in moments of ire. "Didn't we already have this conversation?" he asked, blinking the sleep from his eyes. With that, he turned to look over his shoulder to the bed, uncomprehending. "Oh. Ohhhhh … oh, damn."

It took me slightly less time with my superior elven eyesight to make out the shape in the bed, of course. Her blue skin was slightly at odds with his light sheets, but her white hair shone quite well. I saw the blink of her eyes, as well, while she watched the whole exchange. I doubt he caught it, of course, but it was there and I saw it.

Saw it and let it boil my blood as though a dragon had breathed into my veins.

"Vara, wait!" he called, stepping out into the hall to give chase as I made to leave.

"You are naked and have just bedded a dark elven thief," I said to him without turning back. I am certain that 'dragon-like' would have applied to my attributes in that moment as well. I was hot, furious—at myself for being too late, at him for sinking so bloody low as to dive back into bed with that. "I think our discussions are at an end."

"But—I—" Had it been in different circumstances, I might have thought his sputtering adorable. Yes. Me. I might have. This was, after all, a commanding General, an incredible leader, and I had just reduced him by my presence and his guilt to an incoherent mess.

As it was, I simply found it contemptible. "I need no explanations from you, General." I said it, I meant it, and I emphasized it as I gave him a pitiless gaze.

He said nothing, and I left him in his naked shame, standing there in the hallway like the fool he was as I stormed back into my quarters to scream my bloody rage into a pillow until I had no more voice left to give it."

Vaste's chuckle was low. "She tells it better than you do."

"You're an ass." Cyrus scowled and snapped the diary shut. "It was late, I was half-asleep, I had spent days in battle and I had a yearning for—"

"You thought with the wrong head," Vaste said. "That's my conclusion. Every man has done it, though, in your usual attempt to be the undisputed master of everything, you did it in a rather more spectacular fashion than the rest of us would have."

"I am glad this tale tickles your fancy," Cyrus said, moving back to the window.

"At this point, I'm glad to find anything that tickles my fancy," Vaste said, and Cyrus heard him lift himself off the chair as the wood protested at the troll's weight. He held his distance, his slow, heavy breathing audible over Cyrus's shoulder. "It's been dark times for a while, after all."

"The darkest," Cyrus said.

"Thank you," Vaste said. "For humoring me. It was ... surprising to me that you did. You could have balked."

Cyrus glanced back at him, watched the orange glow play over his green skin, turning it yellow. "You're just being you."

"But you're not yourself anymore."

Cyrus bowed his head and pursed his lips. "Got no cause to be."

Vaste let that silence linger for a moment. "Let's change that." His voice took on a hint of life. "With what you told me ... I mean, this could be ... enormous. And coming from a troll, that means quite large indeed." The flicker of amusement fled his voice with the next sentence, turning to earnestness. "Others would come, and gladly."

Cyrus felt the frown crease his forehead, weigh it down and squint his eyes nearly shut. He turned to look at Vaste. "What do you think is going to happen here?"

"You called me back," Vaste said, staring back at him. His expression was guileless, almost innocent. "We're going to begin again, aren't we? To rebuild? We need a leader." Cyrus could see him about to burst with the floe of excitement that was cracking loose in him.

Cyrus just stared at him and felt the mixed emotions roll through—regret, for leading his friend astray. Concern. Worry that he might have said the wrong thing in his letter. *He doesn't know,* Cyrus thought. *It's not quite time to tell him, either. Soon, though. Still, that misperception he's carrying ...*

"Well?" Vaste asked, and his dark eyes were alive, dancing in the firelight. "When do we start again?"

"We don't," Cyrus said. The words were so heavy that he had trouble getting them out, as though they were an immense boulder lodged in his soul. As soon as he said it, though, he felt the burden lift, and he was light and free again. He watched Vaste's face fall, and even though he knew his point was made, the blow was dealt, he said it once more, lower, for himself. "We don't."

Four Years Earlier

Chapter 1

Cyrus Davidon thrashed about, the water pressing in on him. There were walls in the middle distance, not far. He was in a passage that extended ahead, blue with the tinge of the water around him, his eyes enhanced by a spell a druid had cast so he could see in the dark. Another spell allowed him to swim without breathing. The briny water was held at bay just outside his nose, but he could smell it, the salty, despoiled flavor lurking like a distant whiff of bread baking in the distance.

The water was cool against his skin, his armor conspicuous by its absence. He was in deep water now; the metal weight would have been an impediment to his ability to navigate, so he'd left it behind, and he indeed felt weightless as he swam. A grey corridor of stone swept ahead of him, leading beyond his line of sight. He followed it, one hand on his sword and the other alternating between swimming to propel him forward and touching the stone that surrounded him. He could hear noises in the distance through the water, a faint sound of rumbling like a rushing river.

Next time I get the bright idea to run an expedition that involves a sunken temple, someone should stab me repeatedly in the head, he thought, the water forcing him to blink his eyes. *I think Vara would do that rather gladly*. His eyes burned just a little, as if he'd held them open far too long. Straining to see ahead through the passage, he could make out shapes in the murk, faint lines that blurred as though he were looking through his own tears.

He swam forward as the passage disappeared ahead. He emerged from the tight hallway to find himself in a wide, open chamber. His eyes strained to take in the whole thing. It was a little smaller than the

Sanctuary foyer, complete with statuary that stretched from floor to ceiling. He estimated the height of the building would have been something approaching three floors. The statue resting squarely in the middle of the room was familiar to him: Ashea, the Goddess of Water. There was a darkness below, something his vision couldn't quite penetrate, and he realized it was a bed of seaweed, growing out of the bottom of the temple.

He saw motion in the murk, something rising from the field of green seaweed that waved in the currents of water like grass swaying on the Plains of Perdamun. Heads were moving, followed by long necks, snakes ascending out of the seaweed. They swayed out of time with the vegetation around them, at least eight of them by Cyrus's count, lining up with their eyes squarely on him.

He floated there, feeling the sword in his hand as he pondered how to go about it. *This wasn't part of the deal.* There was a pounding in his head, a desire to have this over with so he could leave this magic behind and draw a breath on the surface. He longed for it, for the open sky and the boat he knew waited far, far above and out of the temple. *The sooner I go through them, the sooner I can get out of here.*

He darted forward, using his legs to churn through the water in powerful strokes. He was aided by the mystical power of his sword, Praelior, which augmented his strength and speed. Even with the increased resistance of the water, it still made him fast.

He came at the first snake and sliced through the water with his sword. It dodged back, avoiding his motion, mouth open as though it were hissing at him.

Two more of them came at him, and Cyrus tried to backpedal but found his coordination off in the water. One caught his left arm midbicep, and he felt the sting of its teeth. Blood clouded the water as he brought the sword around and buried it in the neck of the thing. He barely got it back around in time to catch the other one in the throat.

Two down. Six to go. He would have sighed, but the water made it impossible. *Where's my army when I need them?*

He spun in the water, scissoring his legs to push him back out of range. Four of the snakes waved in the seaweed ahead, waiting for him to get closer. *It has got to be down in the grass, dammit. Somewhere. No more water expeditions; the Realm of Purgatory and that gods-damned eel are bad enough, but this is just intolerable.*

Also, where is my army?

He knew they were somewhere above, but he'd gotten separated from the expedition while chasing one of the Mler, a fish-like creature, one of hundreds that were the guardians of this temple. *Other than these snakes, that is. The servants of Ashea align against us, we plunderers of their birthright.*

Cyrus dodged the attack of another snake, this one barreling at him with mouth open. *That one was coming for my throat; they're plainly serious about keeping whatever is down there safe.*

He rolled in the water, spinning himself over and feeling the turbulence in the water at his maneuver. Bubbles rushed all around him as he threw his sword arm forward just in time to catch another of the snakes on the sharp tip.

Three down. Five more, now.

He pushed himself forward, dipping low into the grass. The snake closest to him tried to adjust but was already out of position. Cyrus went low and churned through the water, landing a strike that neatly cut it in half. He grinned and looked back at his foe, but the grin didn't last more than a second.

Liberated from the ground, the snake was oozing blood from its stump, but it was moving through the water unrestrained, now. *Aw, shit. Now I've got a mobile enemy instead of a tethered one!*

Cyrus swam upward, toward the top of the chamber, removing himself from the threat of the last four snakes in the seaweed. They snapped at him impotently as he dodged away. The last snake followed, moving more slowly than an eel, but pursuing nonetheless.

Cy reached the top of the chamber and caught himself on the stone top of the pyramid. He see could the other snakes far below, resting in the shadow of the massive statue. *First things first.*

The snake came at him, and he launched himself off the wall at it. It dodged surprisingly fast. *It's holding out on me, faking me out!* He felt the pain in his left hand as it caught him on the wrist with a fang, then it darted away before he could counter.

Next time remind me to bring a shield. A thin line of blood seeped into the water from his wound. *Oh, right, I'm not doing this again.*

The snake readjusted, hanging in the water a few feet away from him. It was coiled, blood clouding the water from its wound and his.

Cyrus threw himself forward and sliced Praelior horizontally. The sword dug into the foot-thick snake and cut through, even with the reduced speed of Cyrus's swing. Blood clouded the water, blinding Cyrus momentarily.

He turned his head, trying to confirm that he'd killed it. *It'd be just my luck if I hadn't.* He swam out of the cloud and saw the snake writhing, cut in half. It fell to the seabed below, just outside of the field of its brethren, and then remained still.

Four down. Halfway home.

He churned the water as he swam now, racing down at the ones that remained without preamble. The steady, burning pain of the bites from his other foes was nagging at him, but minor compared to countless other pains he'd felt before. He went straight at the nearest snake, saw it coil, waiting for him.

It struck, nearly too fast for him. He threw his sword up just in time and positioned it perfectly. The snake ran its head at him as he raised the blade, catching it just under the jaw and sending the head spiraling away into the seabed.

Cyrus flashed a grin at the next snake. *Let's see if your timing is any better.* It lunged at him, and he caught it a little further down, severing the head along with a foot of neck; it thrashed ineffectually against the water, unable to gain any sort of momentum from its movement. It fell in a wash of red blood back into the seaweed bed.

Six down. Cyrus let himself smile, feeling the confidence return. *Two to go. And now I know how to deal with them.*

He turned to go after the remaining two snakes but found them already coming at him. Their bodies were lengthening, withdrawing from the seabed, and he realized with a start that they were either growing much larger or they had never truly been tethered to the ground. As one of the tails swished free of the green, dancing seaweed, he realized that it was the latter.

Shit.

Cursing the damned things for their fakery, he threw himself into an immediate sideways roll through the water as one of them came at him head-on. He dealt it a glancing blow as it shot past, enough to cloud the waters a little more.

The second struck him from underneath seconds after he'd finished his roll. The disorientation worked against him, vision impaired by bubbles, and the snake buried a two-inch set of teeth in his ribs, anchoring itself to his side..

Cyrus brought Praelior down and lopped the head neatly off the creature. The body fell back into the seaweed, but the fangs remained tightly clenched on his side, a searing agony rolling through him even as the water there turned dark with his blood.

Son of a bitch. He grimaced, trying to focus on the last of them. He turned in the water and caught a flash of motion. It was around him, a coil spiraling out a couple feet away from his face. He started to raise Praelior to deal with it, but it was too late.

The snake closed the coil tight in an instant, wrapping around him and trapping his sword down at his side. Cyrus tensed, feeling his bones and ligaments resist as the snake began to squeeze. Together, they fell back toward the seaweed below.

Cyrus felt the world turn upside down as they took a slow, drifting path to the bottom of the temple's chamber. The squeeze tightened, and he flexed his muscles to resist the force of the snake's enclosure. It darted at him and buried its teeth in his scalp after Cyrus dodged his head to the side at the last moment. *Better the scalp than the neck*, he reasoned. He could feel the teeth, halted by bone, slide across his skull with a grinding pain, ripping the skin and hair from his head.

He worked at his sword, trying to move it up into position, but it was trapped, the snake coiled around his upper body to pin his forearm in place, leaving just enough space between coils for it to jut out impotently. *How the hell did I get into this situation? Damnable water, slowing me down. I'm used to being faster than my foes.*

He felt the popping of his joints as the snake squeezed tighter, and there was an unbearable pain at his ear as the snake ripped into it. *Recrimination later, killing first.*

But as an aside, leaving your army to chase a fleeing Mler? Dumb. Really dumb, Cyrus.

He reacted to the popping sound of his shoulder leaving the joint by twisting his hand as far up as it could go and poking the tip of Praelior as sharply up as he could. There was a faint cracking sound as one of the teeth of the snake found purchase in his skull and his world went red. He stabbed harder and felt the grip of the mouth on his head tighten.

Dumb. Worthy of every insult Vara ever leveled your way.

Reaching the limits of his ability to push, he forced the blade a little further up with his fingertips, pushing it to the maximum distance his digits allowed. Something gave, and he felt the snake loosen just a hair, even as his skull cracked in his ears and his vision clouded with blood. *Well, of course, it couldn't just get better; it had to get worse as well ...*

He pushed up on the coil securing his arm and wriggled free of it. He pulled his blade out, and the water grew even redder. He pulled his sword and shoved it up, aiming blindly over his head. He felt the impact of his thrust, felt the snake's mouth slacken its grip on him, and he pushed it free. Feeling woozy, he pulled a fang out from behind his ear where it had broken the skin and the bone.

I may pass out. Need to find the Sanctuary army before that happens. But first ...

He dropped the corpse of the snake. It did not even flail as it fell down into the seabed, brown skin disappearing under green grasses. He swam down, down to the base of the massive stone statue of Ashea, and sent her a single-fingered gesture of insult. *Here's what I think of your water-dwelling worshippers, and if I could make Bellarum's own brand of war on them, I damned well would.*

His skull seared with agony, alternating between sharp, knife-like pains and a low, throbbing one. He pushed aside the pain like he pushed aside the seaweed as he descended, looking for something, hoping it was here ...

Ah! His eyes caught sight of it in the shadow of Ashea's garish figurine. It was a chest, the wood dark and shadowed to his eyes. In truth, he would not have seen it without the spell Ryin Ayend had cast upon him that allowed his vision in this dark place. *It is only that and the breathing spell that allow me to tread these waters at all. And in the future, I would be wiser to remember that and remain only in places that require no magic, especially when it comes to fighting battles.*

He reached the treasure chest and laid a hand upon it. The wood was slimy, as if it had been under the water for decades—which he knew it had. He fumbled with the lock and found it unwilling to give. Sighing an unbreathed sigh, he jammed the tip of Praelior into the chest and pried it open. The locking mechanism broke with an unheard sound, and he forced the wet wood lid up and stared down into the darkness of the chest.

The key.

Cyrus clutched the ornate metal object in his hand, his eyes following the twists and curves of it. It looked like someone had taken a string and knotted it in a bizarre attempt to imitate a key. *This will gain us access to the treasure of the Mler, to things lost to the memory of men.*

He turned his eyes up toward Ashea and the entrance to the chamber. *Now all we need do is to pacify the Mler.*

But first … I need my army.

He kicked off the sandy bottom of the seaweed bed, ignoring the still-aching pain in his head. A healer's spell would be a welcome remedy. He felt the seaweed kiss him goodbye, tendrils drifting across his arms and chest as he swam upward past Ashea's lean and haunting face toward the square hole at the top of the temple.

Hard to believe this place was built in such a way. Why construct a temple on the surface and then sink it to the bottom of the sea? Truly, the Ancients had wonders at their command.

He entered the passage above and felt the constraint of the four walls around him, the tightening fear of the confined space creeping in on him. He swam along to an intersection and wondered which direction to go. He looked for signs of passage, trying to remember which way he had come. He had last seen the Mler he was chasing in an intersection like this, but they all looked damnably similar.

He swam right on a whim, clutching Praelior in anticipation of trouble. When he rounded the next corner, he found the corridor ahead as bare as the one he'd just left. It stretched off into the dark distance past the limits of his vision. *This place is monstrous, a labyrinth.*

He looked back and realized that he could no longer see the intersection from whence he had just come. A stir of unease grew within him. *This could be … difficult.*

Salt water seeped into his nose, a cold shock that caused him to gasp in surprise, drawing more water into his sinuses. *The spell … it's fading!* He lurched forward, toward the darkness, and blew the water out of his nose as best he could. He felt sudden, deep pressure on his ears, like someone was jamming their fingers deep within them. His head wound flared with agony as he swam on, and his lungs felt tight and painful, like the snake had his chest in its grip once more. His eyesight flickered red, then faded, and he was left utterly in the dark.

I guess my time ran out, he thought, rather more wistfully than he would have expected. There was nothing in his vision but faint spots, like the colors a bevy of torches would leave on a dark night when he closed his eyes. He tried to thrash forward but hit a wall. He opened his mouth in shock and the salt water flooded in, the strong taste washing over his tongue as he forced down the temptation to yell.

His chest was so tight it was as though the temple had collapsed on it, the desire to draw a breath so strong he knew he would take one in seconds, whether he wanted to or not. He reached out with his hand and touched the smooth stone wall as his instinct took over and he breathed in the seawater, the rush of it down his throat and into his lungs filling him with a flailing panic unlike anything he'd ever known.

Cyrus thrashed mindlessly, his limbs no longer in his control, sightless, blind to any world around him. The cold water surrounded him, held him in its embrace, and he knew with its kiss that he was done. *I've seen no one from Sanctuary in the better part of an hour ... how likely is it they'll find me before my hour is up, and my soul is lost to death for good?*

He felt his body settle, the movement strangely gone from his arms and legs, his weight carrying him peacefully down to the stone floor of the tunnel after long moments of painful thrashing. He pictured in his mind a blond-haired girl on a background of white, just for a beat, and wondered why he was thinking of her at a moment such as this.

His eyes burned from the salt water, and as he looked at the stone wall, he felt himself fade, the darkness closing in on him utterly. One last thought ran through his mind before consciousness fled him.

Is this how Alaric felt when he ...?

Chapter 2

"—feels like he weighs a literal ton," the surly voice said as Cyrus awoke, sputtering and choking on water.

"Catch him, hold him!"

Cyrus's eyes were pressed tight as he heaved, flopping against a hard surface. His hand brushed against uneven planks of wet wood. Beyond the spots in his vision, all the world was light. His head was aching, but the searing agony was gone. His eyes sprang open and he gurgled, unable to get his breath. Warm liquid dribbled down his cheeks and his chin, too much to be spittle.

"His lungs are full of water!"

Every attempt at breath was sheerest agony, struggling for air. He slapped his hand down on the wood planking he lay upon.

"I apologize for this in advance," came a voice, soothing, quiet, and terribly familiar. He had a sense that this had happened before, this voice soothing him just before a horrendous pain was visited upon him. A piercing stab caught him in the right side. Cyrus gasped and gurgled as hot liquid dribbled through his back in fiery agony as he was lifted up. Another sharp, searing stab caught him in the other side, on the left, and he writhed in strong arms as they held him steady.

He could not scream, much as he wanted to. All that came out was a gurgling, and more warm, soupy, blood-smelling liquid. He felt the pressure in his chest lighten, but the pain did not recede. The sound of dripping came even amidst the other noises that reached his ears—gulls calling, waves lapping, the roar of sea foam and crashing water. The sun shone down on him and warmed his skin even as the pain wracked him. He squinted and opened his eyes just a little, and the bright sun nearly blinded him. The salt was still heavy on his tongue, which felt like it had dried out like a slug in the sun.

"You might want to heal him before he dies," came a voice of concern at his right. Cyrus jerked his head to look and found himself staring at a man in dark steel armor, almost blued. His helm was a most peculiar contraption, and he had a worn look about the eyes. *Samwen Longwell*, Cyrus's mind told him.

"Can't do it too soon," came another voice, forcing Cyrus to look over and see another familiar face, this one attached to a man with bronzed skin and long blond hair. He was naked to the waist and slick with water, but Cyrus knew him. *Odellan.* "We need to let as much of the water drain out of him as possible."

"And all his blood too, I suppose?" The next voice was choked with emotion, near hysterical and high pitched. He rolled his head to look to his side and saw a man with a long, dripping dark beard and sopping hair that was slicked back behind him. His white robes were drenched and clinging to him, revealing just the hint of a belly sticking out. *Andren.*

Cyrus coughed and tried to roll, but Longwell and Odellan each had a shoulder and did not yield it. He pulled at his legs again, futilely, feeling the blood bubbling up in his mouth with the salt water, the strange metallic taste combining with the salt as it flooded out of him and ran down his chin.

"Don't kick me," came a voice from near his feet. Cyrus arced his head to look. A mountainous figure of a man stood down there, similarly soaked, but his robes were black and his skin was flushed green in the sunlight, like the grass of the plains. "If you hit anything important, I'm going to be forced to rip your leg off and beat you with it as a warning to everyone else in Sanctuary that I'm not to be trifled with."

"Even by a drowning man as his lungs are pierced to let the water out?" Cyrus's head rolled to the last figure, a man in red armor with half of it stripped off, his breastplate hanging loose and his hair wet. *Thad Proelius.*

"Especially by such a character," Vaste replied. "Otherwise all the drowning men with pierced lungs will take it as a sign to kick me."

"Figure you'll run into that problem a lot, do you?" Thad asked.

"I didn't think I'd have to deal with it ever," Vaste said, "but with Cyrus Davidon in charge of your expedition, one should be prepared for anything."

"I'm healing you now," Curatio said, the healer in white, wet robes just beyond Vaste and Thad. "You'll try and take a grand breath when I'm finished, and that will be a mistake. Go slowly, Cyrus." He waved a hand, and a glimmer of light brighter than the sun burst from his palm.

Cyrus felt the pain in his chest subside, and he let out a long, racking cough that dredged up blood and horror to run down his hairy chest.

Vaste dropped his leg unceremoniously, and Cyrus felt it hit the wood below him. "That's gratitude for you. I let you kick me, and now you've spit blood and ocean water in my face."

"Didn't ... mean ..." Cyrus gargled the foul stuff in his mouth, the blood and salt water, and nausea swept over him. He expelled the contents of his stomach all over the wooden surface below him, and it took a moment to realize it was the deck of a ship. He turned and heaved again, twisting now that Vaste was not counter-balancing his feet, and his sick hit Thad squarely in the breastplate.

"Ugh," Thad said, gagging, "you might have warned me that was coming!" He retched.

"Don't be such a baby," Vaste said dryly, from a few steps behind Thad. "You've been around resurrection spells long enough by now to know what effects they bring. You had to know it would be even worse when the victim was spitting up salt water from drowning."

Thad shot the troll an injured look. "You knew he would do that?"

Vaste shrugged. "Of course. I've been around resurrected people before."

"You could have warned me!"

"Sorry," Vaste said, keeping his expression even, "I was too incensed from being kicked."

Cyrus felt his lips still bubbling and let out a wet, hacking cough that dredged up watery phlegm. Tears stung his eyes. A second coughing fit came hard on the heels of the first.

"Well, meathead," came a sour voice from behind him, "I hope you're happy."

Odellan and Longwell lowered his upper body slowly to the deck, and Cyrus sat there in a puddle of his own sick, nearly naked but for the cloth breeches he habitually wore under his armor. He cast a look upward and saw Erith Frostmoor lingering over the shoulders of Longwell and Odellan, peering down at him with ire on her navy blue face. "Of ... course," Cyrus said before coughing again. He took a sniff and caught a potent dose of his stomach's returns as they puddled about him. "I'm covered in vomit, I just came back from death ... I feel like I'm coughing up the entirety of the Torrid Sea ... while a disapproving dark elven princess glares at me like I ... just stole her tiara. What's not ... to be happy about?"

"It would appear his faculties remain undamaged," Curatio said with a little humor from near Cyrus's feet.

"That would be more impressive if he had faculties to begin with," Erith said a rough snort of annoyance. The sun caught her white hair and made it gleam at Cyrus, reminding him of something he'd seen whilst drowning. It tickled at the back of his mind, something he'd thought in the moments before he'd died.

"Well, at least he found the key," another voice rang out, more melodic this time. Cyrus looked to his side, past Andren, to see another dark elven face. *Terian?* his mind called out, just for a brief moment. *No. J'anda.* The enchanter's dark blue robes were soaked, and he wore his own face, the deeply entrenched wrinkles still a shock. His long, greyed hair was back in a slick ponytail. *Looks old.*

"No illusion, J'anda?" Cyrus asked, feeling a slight smile coming on. "You must have been worried."

"You have figured me out," the enchanter said, his own smile wan. "But, now that the moment of crisis has passed and you appear to be alive and well, I can resume my more stylish and less ... shall we say, 'drenched' mode of appearance." He waved a hand and was suddenly a tanned human, muscular chest displayed for all to see.

"Are you all right?" This faint voice came from his other side, and he turned his head to see another dark elf. *Aisling.* She stood above him, oddly at a distance, like she was almost afraid to touch him.

"I think I will be," Cyrus said and coughed again, a long, racking series of coughs. "No, really."

"I think your adventures for today have come to an end," Curatio said, and the firmness in the healer's tone was unmistakable.

"I'll be fine in a few minutes," Cyrus said, and then was racked with spasms once more. "Well ... maybe more than a few."

"Your lungs may swell with sickness in a few hours," Curatio said. "If that comes, it will not be a pleasant recovery. In fact, you may not recover at all." The healer's quiet voice cast a pall over the sunny deck of the ship. "As I said, your adventures are done, at the very least for today, and most likely for the better part of the week."

"We have spent ... months tracking down the clues and putting together this expedition," Cyrus said, clearing his throat in a wet rasp. His hand found its way into the warm mess of liquid by his side. "I can't just—"

"There are plenty of other warriors," Thad said, looking at Cyrus from the ground. "And you will not be of much use in any further action today, especially facing the Mler in their underwater environs."

Cyrus could hear the reason in the warrior's words. He looked at the faces around him, from Curatio's—most stern—to Vaste, whose scarred visage looked a little pinched. His eyes fell on Andren, who still looked stricken and said nothing. Then he came to Longwell and Odellan, twin bastions of disapproval and concern. Erith still remained behind them, glowering at him with reproach. There was another figure in the background, a glimmer of blond hair from just over Erith's shoulder, and he caught sight of an emotionless face, watching him all the while.

"You," he called out to her, and she slid forward with slow steps, still neutral. "Will you take over for me?"

"Of course," she replied coolly.

"And you'll make certain," he coughed, "that they finish the expedition? Capture the Mlers'—"

"I said I would take over," she cut him off. "Success of the expedition was implied after that." There was no frost in the way she said it; it was a simple statement of fact.

"All right," Curatio said, nodding. "I'll accompany Cyrus back to Sanctuary, and the rest of you lot—"

"I'll go with him," Andren said, stepping up to stand over him. "I'll take care of it. Your hands are steadier for healing in combat anyhow."

Curatio raised an eyebrow at the bearded elven healer. "Are you certain?"

"Aye," Andren said, looking down at Cyrus with a worn and lined appearance. "I'll take care of him."

"I could come with you," Aisling said, and Cyrus looked up at her. She felt oddly distant now, hovering a little out of arm's length of him, as though she were afraid of his sick.

"No," Cyrus said. "Stay. Help them finish."

"All right," she said after only a moment's pause, then leaned down to kiss his wet forehead before stepping away again just as quickly.

Cyrus looked at the crowd that had formed around him as Andren knelt next to him. "I'll cast the return spell," Andren said. "Just brace close to me."

"I'm covered in my own expulsions, drenched wet, and nearly naked," Cyrus said, eyeing Andren. "I remember a time when you wouldn't cast the return spell on me when I was fully clothed, dry, and smelled considerably better."

"Disagree on the last point," Vaste said. "You have a lovely aroma now; stomach bile adds some very pleasant cover to your typical smells of lust and shame."

"I'm truly growing as a person," Andren said, kneeling next to Cyrus and slinging an arm around his shoulder.

"Must be all that ale you consume," Vaste added. "Does wonders for the firmness of your stomach, too."

"Ready?" Andren asked, ignoring the troll again.

"Sure," Cyrus said, and tilted his head back again. She waited, looking on, still as expressionless as ever he'd seen her. "Take care of—"

"I will handle it," she said to him, no trace of anger in her reply, none of the hostility she would once have breathed upon him like dragon's fire. Vara stepped up, her armor gleaming in the sun's light, her ponytail wet and dripping on the silver metal breastplate. "You need not worry."

Cyrus started to say something else but stopped himself. It had been six months since their encounter in the doorway of his quarters—six months of near silence. She stared at him flatly, no emotion. The return spell took hold of him and he felt himself go insubstantial as the light of the sun faded before his eyes, replaced by the thousand sparkles of light as the magic consumed his body.

His last vision of the deck of the ship was Vara, still expressionless, watching him as he faded away.

Chapter 3

Cyrus reappeared in the foyer of Sanctuary, the stone walls fading into view around him. The smell of the wide hearth burning across the room filled his nose. Light streamed in from the circular, stained-glass window above the mighty doors, which were open, sunlight flooding the room.

"Davidon?" The voice that greeted him was an old, dry one, filled with sound of age. Cyrus turned his head to see Belkan Stillhet standing just a few feet away, sword in hand. Martaina Proelius was at his side, her brown hair colored by the flecks of light from the stained glass window's shine. "What the blazes are you doing?" Belkan's eyebrow twitched. "And where's your armor?"

"Left it on the boat," Cyrus said with a watery cough. "I'm sure someone will bring it back to me when they're done."

"I'm beginning to see how you've gone through three swords in four years," the old armorer said, his leather armor creaking as he turned to look at the force of guards huddled around him. A hundred of them stood in a rough circle, spears pointed at the center—at him and Andren, splayed upon the great seal carved into the middle of the foyer.

Andren slipped an arm around his chest and helped Cyrus to his feet. "How goes the defense of Sanctuary, Belkan?" Cyrus asked, sniffling. He could feel water run down his nose and onto his lip as he got to his feet.

"Better than it looks like your expedition treated you," Belkan replied.

Martaina Proelius stared at Cyrus with undisguised disgust. "You smell like you draped yourself in seaweed and sunned yourself in a desert for a week." She sniffed. "And then vomited all over the place."

Cyrus gave it a pause before nodding. "Sounds about right."

There was a sound as loud as a thunderclap from the entry to the Great Hall, and Cyrus turned to see Larana Stillhet standing in the door, staring at him, a pot of stew fallen to her feet. Liquid spilled out, darkening the stone as it spread in a puddle. Her hands were over her mouth as she stared at Cyrus then turned and ran back into the Great Hall, disappearing behind the wall.

Cyrus looked down at himself. "I look that bad, huh?"

"I've seen more lively-looking corpses," Belkan opined.

"Which is no great coincidence, since I was one of those only a few minutes ago," Cyrus said. "Absent the liveliness."

"He needs rest," Andren said, and his voice took on an aura of urgency. "He's at a high risk of developing a great malady of the chest."

"I believe Curatio called it lung sickness," Cyrus said, bringing up a wad of something with a racking cough. "Pneumonia, I think it is?"

Andren shot him a look of irritation. "Whether you know its name or not, it will kill you all the same. You need to be taken to bed, immediately, and we should get one of those 'natural' healers in here, the ones that practice without magic, only herbs and such."

Belkan exchanged a look with Martaina, whose tanned face wore a look of greatest amusement. "By oddest coincidence," Belkan said, bringing his lined face back around to look at Cyrus, "one of those has already showed up, looking for you."

"For me?" Cyrus asked, a little dumbstruck. The taste of salt was still strong on his tongue, mingling with the bile.

"Indeed," Belkan said.

"Why would a natural healer be looking for me?" Cyrus asked, taking up a little of his own weight.

"Because I so missed the sight of you shirtless before me that I could not wait another minute to come rushing to your side," came an amused voice from the stairs. Cyrus turned to see a woman standing there, dark hair falling around her shoulders, which were bare, as they had been when last he had seen her. The rest of her upper body was fairly covered, which was not how it had been when last his eyes had graced her.

"Arydni, High Priestess of Vidara," Cyrus said, bowing formally as best he was able to.

"Ary!" Andren cried out.

"It is good to lay eyes upon you again, Andren," Arydni said, crossing the stone floor in her sandaled feet, her pure, white robes barely touching the stone floor as she walked, almost gliding, toward them.

"It's not bad looking upon you again, either," Andren agreed, letting his word become literal as he stared at the priestess, lowering his gaze to her chest. Cyrus watched as Andren stared at her. "All of y—"

"That's enough," Cyrus whispered to Andren, whose arm was still draped around his shoulder, helping him keep steady. "How we can we assist you, m'lady?"

"She used to be my lady, you know," Andren said under his breath.

"Not now," Cyrus hissed.

Arydni broke into a gentle laugh. "I expect I could do you the courtesy of helping to look after you for a space of time before imposing upon you with any requests." She crossed the distance between them with palms upturned, hands at her sides.

"It is no imposition to have you ask anything of us," Cyrus said.

"Still and all," Arydni said, now only feet away from Cyrus, "your guild has hosted me these last days, and to earn my keep would be a welcome task."

Cyrus exchanged a look with Andren, who nodded, his shaggy, frizzed hair and beard looking particularly wild now that they had dried. "You might not want to get too close to me right now," Cyrus said, glancing back at the priestess. "I don't smell all that wonderful, I've been told." He cast a look over his shoulder at Martaina, who shrugged and gave him a look in return that told him, *Obviously*.

"I am a Keeper of Life," Arydni said, sliding next to him on the side opposite Andren and placing his arm over her shoulder. He felt only the lightest touch from her. "Let us get you settled so that I may examine you. All else can wait."

"Are you certain?" Cyrus asked, looking down at her. "I don't know too many people who would travel all the way here from Pharesia for a problem that wasn't important."

"Oh, be assured," she said, looking up at him, face lit with a tiredness he had not seen in her, not even in the days after the fall of Termina, "what I come to you with is neither trifling nor some matter I will simply forget or fail to bring up out of politeness—when the moment arrives for us to discuss it." She ran a hand across his shoulder; her touch was as smooth and soft as velvet. "But for now, let us tend to your malady."

With slow, halting steps, she and Andren helped him up the stairs to his quarters. Cyrus felt every one of them, his body resisting him out of fatigue, his pace slowed by frequent coughing fits. Still, in the countless floors between the foyer and his quarters near the top of the center tower, Arydni never once looked at him, keeping her silence the entire way.

Chapter 4

"Do you have any lef'tres grass on hand?" Arydni asked after they had gotten Cyrus to his quarters. She bustled about while Andren stood near the hearth, fidgeting and watching her hover over Cyrus. "Also, I need honey and a basin of clean water."

"There's running water in there," Cyrus gestured to the door at the far end of his quarters. "I keep a basin in there as well."

"Andren, would you be a dear and fetch that for me?" Arydni looked over her shoulder at him. "And then light a fire in the hearth."

"Ah, yeah, easily done." Andren snapped his fingers at the hearth. It promptly caught on fire, filling the air with a lovely aroma of light wood smoke, though there was no haze from it. He ducked into the bath and emerged a few moments later with a tin basin a little larger than a dinner plate. A cloth was hanging from the side.

"Wait," Cyrus said, and was halted by a cough. "I can bathe myself. There's a tub in the bath."

"You need rest," Arydni said, taking the proffered cloth from Andren and soaking it, then wringing it out in the basin. The sound of splashing water reminded Cyrus faintly of the ocean when he was on the deck of the ship. Before, on the way to the temple's site, he had found the sound peaceful. Now it simply made him ill. "I will cleanse you, then you will lie down for a time." She looked over at Andren. "Lef'tres grass? And honey?"

"Ah," Andren said, thinking it over, "Curatio keeps some of both on hand in the Halls of Healing, I believe."

"I need it," Arydni said, running the wet rag over Cyrus's matted chest hair, cleansing the residue of the salt water sick off him. He sat on the edge of his bed, the discomfort from being bathed by a woman he scarcely knew – *who was married to my friend, no less* – keeping him frozen in place.

"Right then," Andren said after a moment's hesitation, "I suppose I'll uh ... go and get that, then." Cyrus met the healer's gaze and caught his reluctance. "I'll ... be back in just a sparrow's flight, that's all." Andren smiled weakly. "Before you even know I'm gone."

"Go on, then," Arydni said, not looking back at him. "Hurry."

Andren stepped sideways toward the door and then backed out of it, as though afraid to take his eyes off of the two of them. He didn't shut the door, leaving it partially open as his footsteps faded down the corridor toward the stairs. Cyrus could hear them echoing faintly over the sound of Arydni squeezing water out of the rag and into the basin.

"I believe he still has a little bit of a torch for you," Cyrus said after the footsteps had faded.

"I believe he has a burning lust," Arydni said, looking at him sideways, "and little else in the way of feeling for me at this point."

Cyrus coughed. "So ..."

Arydni did not say anything for a moment, moving the rag in a rhythmic pattern up and down his chest. Cyrus could feel the rough cloth against his skin, scrubbing some of the smell off of him. "How have you been since last we met?"

"I've been ... busy," Cyrus said.

"Oh?" She did not look up. "Doing what? Tell me all your news."

Cyrus chewed his lower lip for a fraction of a second. "Are we really going to do this?" Her eyes met his, and he saw the knowing look within them. "This talk of small things, ignoring the large ones?"

"For just a bit longer, yes, I think," Arydni whispered.

Cyrus nodded after a brief pause. "After we parted ways last time in Pharesia, I helped kill the God of Death. Then I fought in a war over the Endless Bridge in Luukessia—ever heard of it?" He waited until she nodded to proceed. "I witnessed that entire land die in the maw of a beast of my own creation—the souls of Mortus's dead, loosed from a portal in the northern reaches of that place. Only by the sacrifice of his life was my Guildmaster, Alaric Garaunt, able to stop them." Cyrus felt his face cast into a stiff mask, free of expression. "We never even found his body. It was lost to the sea. In the half year since then, I've been helping to build a new home for the Luukessian refugees in the Emerald Fields and trying to build my guild's fortunes."

"These are not small things." Arydni dabbed the cloth upon his chin. "But I had heard rumors of much of this. You have my deepest sympathies for the loss of your Guildmaster. I shall say a prayer in his name to the Life Giver this very eve."

"Thank you," Cyrus said, resisting the temptation to add anything sarcastic. He sniffed the fresh smell of the water, gradually cleansing the salt from his flesh. "And you? How goes life in the land of the elves in the interval since last we met?"

"It goes as it has for roughly an age," Arydni said. "We are at war with the dark elves, and little is happening. Termina is free once more," she said with a slight smile, "thanks to your efforts in bleeding the dark elves dry in the defense. The King's army stares across the River Perda at the unrelenting faces of the dark elven scourge—"

"I wouldn't use that word to describe them, exactly," Cyrus said.

Arydni's eyebrows rose. "Oh? Well, their army, then. We continue to engage in the least-fought war in our history, at least since the last of the dark elves was expelled from Termina over the bridges."

"As it should be," Cyrus said, feeling a quaver in his voice that he hoped was related to the drainage running down his throat. "Your people are in no condition to mount a major offensive against the Sovereignty."

"Someone should," she said, watching him carefully.

Cyrus watched her in return, carefully studying her face. It was still youthful; he would have guessed late thirties in human years, and her full lips did not move in the slightest. "You heard about it, didn't you?"

"So it's true?" Arydni asked.

"Depends on what you heard," Cyrus said. He felt the cool touch of the rag, this time upon his shoulder.

"A rumor reached my ear that Sanctuary accepted a mercenary contract," Arydni said, looking up at him with careful consideration. "From the Human Confederation."

Cyrus tried not to blink and look away. "It is true, after a fashion."

"You've become a paid army," she said.

"It's not like that," Cyrus said, and he felt his face redden and not from where the sun had kissed his flesh on the boat ride. "We accepted an offer from Pretnam Urides and the Council of Twelve for a one-time action against the dark elves, and fought to free Prehorta from the enemy garrison that had been left there."

"You had never done this before," Arydni said softly. "Sanctuary, I mean."

"No," Cyrus said with a shake of the head. "But the pay was exceptional for little risk to our people. And we are already enthusiastic enemies of the dark elves." He glanced toward the window, which was shut. "Perhaps you saw some hints of their siege here only six months ago? Admittedly, the southwest tower is reconstructed and we've patched the holes in the outer curtain wall, but the scarring from what they did is still there, I think."

"I didn't really notice," Arydni said. "I was more interested in the news about Sanctuary going out for hire."

"We have a whole city's worth of refugees to support," Cyrus said, biting back the hostility that threatened to enter his voice. "The Emerald Fields are not yet self-sufficient, and this is the manner through which we have to earn enough gold to support them. I suspect you've heard, but after what the dark elves did to the Plains of Perdamun, there's more than a small famine going on in Arkaria, and the price of food everywhere but the Elven Kingdom has gone to ridiculous heights—"

"You misunderstand me," Arydni said, dropping the rag in the basin and folding her hands in her lap, smoothing the edges of her robe as she did so. "I do not judge you for what you have done. I know you to be an honorable man, and not some rudderless brigand who turns solely in the direction of coin." He watched her hands clench on the soft cloth of her robe. "Which is why I am here."

"Not to judge or sway me from the path of the mercenary?" Cyrus said with only slight amusement. "Not to discourage me from involving myself in the wars and skirmishes of the day in exchange for gold?"

"No," she said with a slow shake of her head. "Not at all. I came here after I heard the rumor because I ... I have a problem. A rather sizable one." Her eyes met his, and he could see within her lively irises a faint hint of hope. "I came ... because I wish to hire you."

Chapter 5

"You want to hire me?" Cyrus asked. He felt himself slump a little and adjusted to lean against the headboard of his massive bed. It was made of dragon bones, with elephant tusks for each of the posts, and he lay back and stared at the elven priestess sitting upon the edge. "Hire me ... or hire my guild?"

"Perhaps both," Arydni said, facing the door.

Cyrus let the quiet fill the room for a moment. "You seem to be taking great pains to twirl your way around this without providing any detail."

She turned her profile so that it was visible to him, and a wistful smile curved on her mouth. "I have always enjoyed a dance from time to time."

"Unfortunately, I'm not very light on my feet at the moment." Cyrus gestured to his legs, splayed on the bed. He could feel fatigue setting in, a weariness from the sick feeling the resurrection spell had left him with. "Why not just tell me?"

"I am not sure how to say it," Arydni said. "What I would ask of you—I am not certain it can be done, that you could do it, that anyone —" She sighed. "It is uncomfortable to even put into words."

"So long as you're not asking me to father your children," Cyrus said, wondering where the hell those words had come from even as he finished the sentence, "I think we'll be all right."

Arydni gave him a sidelong look, and her smile went from wistful to amused all in one. "How old are you now?"

"Uh ... I am thirty-one."

"Oh, you're as green as the first blooms of spring," Arydni said dryly.

"I ... uh ... I am seeing someone in any case," Cyrus said, clearing his throat.

"I hope it's Vara," Arydni said, watching him for a response.

"I'm afraid it's not," Cyrus said. He suppressed a desire to cough, and loudly.

"What foolishness is this—yours or hers?" Arydni asked.

"It's more complicated than that," Cyrus said. "I'm sure you weren't just here to talk about her, though. Or her and I."

"I am not," Arydni said and glanced back at the door. "Where is Andren with the lef'tres and the honey? You need to inhale some of the grass, mixed with the honey and burned, in order to help keep the affliction from growing in your lungs." She tapped on the stone floor with a foot and Cyrus's mattress moved, giving him a slight feeling of queasiness.

"Tell me what you need from us," Cyrus said. "No more dancing, no more evasion."

She turned her head and gazed at him. "You're in an odd position to make demands. Flat on your back, weak like a baby goat. You look more likely to fall asleep than have a discussion about what I'm after. Take your rest, we can talk after you're better."

"I'd like to know," Cyrus said, reaching over and taking her hand in his. He cupped it and she looked up at him, all seriousness. She was warm and soft, but there was strength in her fingers. "Please. I'll help if I can."

Arydni sighed. "It is against my better judgment to burden a man as potentially ill as you, but as it seems you are fixated on knowing, I will explain. You may ask me questions for a few minutes, and then you will take your inhalation and sleep. If this is something you wish to pursue further, we can discuss it once you are mended."

"Your terms are acceptable," Cyrus said. "Go on."

Arydni hesitated, pulling her hand from him. "I need ... someone found."

"'Someone'?" Cyrus gave her a small smile, indulgent. "And this someone has a name?"

"Indeed they do," Arydni said, smiling at him. *She's dodging again; nary a blade could land upon her in a battle of words.*

"All right," Cyrus said. "Are they missing? From the war, perhaps? You can't find them after the battle of Termina?"

"Not exactly," Arydni said.

"You're going to make the sick man guess, huh?"

"I will tell you, if you give me a moment." Arydni smoothed her robes again, fidgeting. "This ... person ... has gone missing. They are not to be found where they were before. They were not in Termina, nor in Pharesia, nor in the Elven Kingdom at all, so it has nothing to do with the war, so far as I know."

"Where were they?" Cyrus asked, trying to keep his patience. The fatigue was settling on him, and he struggled with his eyelids, fighting to keep them open. The line of questioning was providing entertainment enough to stave off the desire for sleep, but he was wearying of it.

"Elsewhere," she answered.

"If it's not to do with the war, I'd ask if they were in the Dwarven Alliance, the Goblin—"

"Not there."

"Where in Arkaria?" Cyrus asked.

Arydni pursed her lips. "Not in Arkaria."

"Now you're just tormenting me for fun," Cyrus said. "A different land? Because I don't think we possess the means to go across the Torrid Sea, or anywhere much beyond a few weeks' travel of one of the portals—"

"No," Arydni said. "Not terribly far."

"All right, I give up," Cyrus said. "Where?"

Arydni hesitated and stood up, taking a few tentative steps around the bed to the window, where she drew the curtain shut, shrouding the room in darkness. The lamps lit around him of their own accord, giving him enough light to see her by. "I am looking for someone ... who has vanished from her home. Someone that some would not even have dared believe existed until recently." She turned her head. "And yet I always knew it was true, even before I met her. Now she is gone, and I feel lost without her light."

Cyrus waited, saying nothing, and after a pause Arydni continued. "I need you to find Vidara."

Cyrus felt the dull, slow sense of a joke being played on him coming to rest in his mind. "This is perhaps the oddest attempt at converting me to a life-worshipper that I've ever heard. You want to pay me—and my guild—to 'Find Vidara'?" His hand came up to his face and he rubbed his temples. "Look, not that I don't appreciate your religion, I just don't think it's for me—"

"The priestesses have been making regular pilgrimages to the Realm of Life since the gateways to the higher realms opened four years ago," Arydni said, calm and slow. "We have been greeted by her servants, ushered into her presence, been given wisdom and fellowship and guidance by the Goddess herself over the last years." Arydni turned and clutched at the seam of her robes.

"Wait," Cyrus said, "this isn't metaphorical, is it?"

"No," Arydni said with a slight shudder, "it is quite literal." She took a step closer to the bed and fell to her knees. "We went on an expedition only weeks ago to the Realm of Life. Every other time we have gone, the atmosphere has been serene. There are guards, there are servants. There is respect. There are greetings and pleasantries." Her face looked suddenly lined, as though she were aging before his eyes. "This time, they were in disarray. They threatened us, and it was only when we were about to leave that one of the servants who knew us well stopped the guards from throwing us out unceremoniously. He took us aside." She shook her head. "The realm was in turmoil, that much was obvious from just looking around. It was …" her voice trailed off. "No matter. The servant told us one crucial thing, though. Vidara is gone. No one has seen her enter or exit the realm, but she has vanished as surely as the bread we leave outside for the poor disappears after morning worship."

"She's a goddess," Cyrus said. "Surely she can leave her realm anytime she wishes—"

"She has never left her realm in such a way before," Arydni said with a strong shake of her head. "Her servant was most emphatic. She does not leave in this way—and to disappear for weeks now? Out of the question. She is missing."

A dull certainty settled in Cyrus's stomach. "So you want me … my guild … to …"

"Find the Goddess of Life," Arydni said, bowing her head. "Find Vidara, and restore her to her place in her realm—before the very balance of life itself is disrupted in our world."

Chapter 6

"Oh, good, involving ourselves once more in the affairs of gods and monsters," Longwell said, leaning back in his chair just to Cyrus's right in the Council Chambers, a sullen look marring his handsome features, "because that surely won't have any long-term negative consequences. You know, again."

"Agreed," Vaste said, just beyond Longwell, deep voice ringing through the Council Chamber. "This time it will surely be a rollicking, fun occasion, filled with rainbows, roast mutton, and perhaps—if we are very lucky—delicious pie."

Cyrus looked around the chamber. It had been a few days, and the consumptive illness that had been feared for him had not manifested. He considered that fortunate but chafed under Arydni's ministrations and had been relieved when she had pronounced him healthy enough leave her care and present her offer to the Council. He was also pleased to be back in his armor with Praelior at his side. *Being without a sword for days is an unpleasant business for a warrior of Bellarum.*

The round table felt surprisingly empty, as it had for months. Curatio and Vara sat in chairs flanking Alaric's high-backed, empty seat. J'anda was to Curatio's right, followed by Ryin, then Terian's old chair, also empty. Erith sat just to the other side of that, next to Cyrus. Her face looked blank, disinterested in the discussion at hand.

"Arydni promised payment if we can discover the whereabouts of the Goddess," Cyrus said, looking to Longwell. "Gold is gold, and it could help our people."

"Aye," Longwell said after a moment's pause, his harsh look softening slightly, "it could at that." The young former King was prone to fits of moodiness of late, his visage habitually much darker than it had been before the Luukessia nightmare. *I don't expect I'd be handling it quite so well if it were me*, Cyrus thought.

"The Goddess of Life being missing is more than a simple mercenary job," Vara said. "At least for some of us."

"Are we always going to take money for our services from now on?" Ryin asked, looking more than a little weary himself. "I had thought hiring ourselves out was to be a one-time-only thing. At least that was how it was proposed when we undertook the Prehorta assault—"

"Which you voted against, if I recall," Vaste said.

"Not because I disagreed with the ends," Ryin said, clearly irritated, "but because I dislike the thought of hiring Sanctuary out as a mercenary company. We are a guild of adventurers, and if we believed that strongly in their aims, we should have done the job for free."

"Like we did in Termina?" Vaste asked, looking innocently at the druid. "Because I believe you vetoed our involvement in that as well."

"I simply do not wish to see us traverse the road of losing our identity as a guild of adventurers because we have become focused on gold to the exclusion of all else," Ryin said. "Do any of you care for the idea of becoming a regular army in the service of the Human Confederation, for example?"

"So we come back to this again," J'anda said, wearing his aged dark elven features for the Council meeting. "I accept that we have principles, but I also recognize that we have a rather large obligation to the refugees of Luukessia. Accepting jobs which carry monetary reward does not seem out of line. It seems practical."

"And they will continue to seem reasonable as we take step after step away from our original mission, which was to be a guild of adventurers, not soldiers for a particular religious group or nations," Ryin said. "This missing goddess is not our problem."

"Except for those of us who actually worship her," Vara said, her cheeks flushed red. She rarely said anything in Council anymore. *Clearly a banner day for her.*

"As a guild, Sanctuary is religiously neutral," Ryin said, avoiding Vara's gaze. "We have believers of all religions here—"

"Except for the God of Death, for some bizarre reason," Vaste said. "No one seems to believe in him anymore. Not sure why."

"—and we should remain neutral," Ryin said. "Going on some hunt for the Goddess of Life is us begging to take another step away from our principles at a time when are experiencing enough slide as it is."

"I think it's another case where principle intersects with opportunity," Cyrus said at last. Heads turned, and a hush fell over the chambers. "No, we don't all follow Vidara, but some of our number do. No, we don't love the idea of taking gold in exchange for our services, but we are experiencing a rapid drain of our treasury because we're trying to make good on our commitment to the Luukessians, whose lives and well-being are in our charge." Cyrus shrugged. "I'm not a Vidara worshipper, but I don't have anything against her, either. Why not go searching? Why not try and find out what happened to her? It's not like she's Yartraak, God of Darkness," he said with a smirk, noting that J'anda and Erith, the only dark elves at the table, soured at the mere mention of the name. "She's not one of the evil ones, the ones that inflict pain and sorrow and suffering. She's either neutral or good, depending on your view of things, and her followers are benevolent for the most part. Why not give comfort to some of our guildmates who believe, earn some gold from a group who has given us aid in the past, and do some right in the process?"

"Because it's another step toward making us a gold-grubbing band of mercenaries who are constantly looking for a higher bidder," Ryin said, sighing in exasperation. "Do you not see what evil can come from this? Do none of you acknowledge that whatever footing we were on before the day we went to the Realm of Death has slipped away and we are falling down a steep and rocky slope? Every choice we have made since then has been in a vain effort to undo the wrong we did by that decision, ignoring that we continue to find ourselves in a worse predicament following each such action." He folded his arms and sighed. "But you wish to traverse this road again."

"It's not exactly the same road," Cyrus said.

"As Longwell indicated, you want to mix the affairs of men with those of gods," Ryin cut him off. "There are places we do not belong, and this is one of them."

"I thought your argument was that you don't want us to accept money for our services," J'anda said.

Ryin took a breath. "Are you incapable of seeing the complexity of my argument? I am opposed to both taking money for our services and further engaging in any sort of dealings with gods."

"I understand your argument," Curatio said, finally speaking up. Cyrus looked to him, the regal elf who was as close to a Guildmaster as they presently had. "But I think you are outnumbered in this instance, as before." He gave a quick look around the table. "Does anyone stand with Ryin in this matter?" When no nods were forthcoming, he turned his attention back to the druid. "Your intentions are noble, your objections are understood—"

"I don't understand them," Vaste said, "but then again I'm a troll, and perhaps your complexity is just a little too much for my simple mind to comprehend."

Erith snickered, and J'anda echoed her. A look from Curatio snuffed it in a moment.

"Yes, I can tell my opinions are well tolerated here," Ryin said sourly.

"Be that as it may," Curatio said, "it would appear we are going to undertake preliminaries in this matter of investigation." The healer looked around the table once more. "May I suggest we only commit to an investigation at present? No action of any sort? I would hate to see us take this on in haste and land ourselves in further trouble." There was a murmur of agreement, and Cyrus looked at the healer to realize something for the first time—Curatio looked as though he'd aged. His eyes were a bit sunken, with dark circles underneath them. The smile that had so defined him was absent and had been for some months. "All right, that seems agreed. Any other business?"

"We need more officers," J'anda said.

"Why?" Ryin asked.

"To make fun of your blatantly stupid opinions," Vaste said. "I try to do it all myself but it's exhausting, as each meeting you seem to come up with new ways to trump your previous stupidities."

"If you don't care for my oppositional ideals, even though I present them in a loyal manner designed to produce thought before reckless action—" Ryin began.

"You desperately need some action right now, I think," Vaste said.

"Was that a personal remark?" Ryin asked, face pinched in anger.

"Yes, I was suggesting you need to have relations," Vaste said, straight faced. "Ever since you and Nyad parted ways, you've been a particularly grim son of a bitch." He glanced at Nyad, who reddened but said nothing.

"I am not ... grim," Ryin said, sputtering.

"Not as grim as Vara, it's true," Vaste said, "but we've all given up hope that she will ever get laid and lighten up. You still have some potential."

"Oh, gods," Cyrus muttered under his breath.

Vara said nothing. Gradually every head turned to her. Her face remained expressionless, but her eyes turned to take in every looker. "I have nothing to say in this matter."

Cyrus looked over at Vaste, who mouthed the words *No hope* before Curatio cleared his throat in the silence.

"If we might come back to the matters at hand," the healer said, his voice a little thin and raspy, "and steer clear of the personal?"

"Sure, give it a go," Vaste said.

"We need more officers because we now have somewhere in the neighborhood of fifteen thousand members," J'anda spoke up, looking over at Ryin and keeping his voice smooth while he spoke. "When we had sixty-eight members just three and a half years ago, we had seven officers. Now we have nine officers and fifteen thousand members, with more applicants flooding in all the time. The Halls of Healing are in disarray because Curatio—as acting Guildmaster—no longer has time to run them with his focus on keeping the guild going day to day." The enchanter leaned forward and placed his hands onto the table. "We need more help. All of us are feeling the pinch."

"I just don't know that we need to expand the Council just yet—" Ryin said.

"Almost all of us are feeling the pinch," Vaste corrected. "The lazy are apparently quite fine, doing nothing as always."

"I am not lazy," Ryin said, reddening again. "I, too, have more work to be done than time to do it, but I am hesitant to grow the numbers in Council before we are ready, because it is a potentially dangerous exercise that could eventually cost us control of the guild. Does anyone recall only a few short years ago when Goliath nearly manipulated us into a merger? Only the Council's united will kept us from a momentous mistake."

"Ah, yes, I remember your strong leadership in that matter," Vaste said, stroking his chin. "Oh, wait, weren't you the one leading the charge for Goliath?"

Ryin glared at him. "I don't mind using my mistakes to make a point. The Council was right and I was wrong, but the only reason you were successful in thwarting their intentions was because the Council was small enough to avoid fragmentation while they held us together."

"He has a point," Erith said, and everyone looked to the dark elven woman, who stared back with smoky eyes. "Double the size of the Council, and you potentially lose our identity. There are some ten thousand fighting Luukessians in Sanctuary now; I'm sure they'd love to have a proportional say in how things are run." She looked at Longwell. "Why, they could dominate the elections and pack the Council with their own people."

"No, they can't," Longwell said, shaking his head. "The charter states that one can only become an officer of Sanctuary after a minimum of one year's membership."

"Not that they've thought of it, clearly," Vaste said.

"Not that it matters," Longwell said, giving the troll a look of near-indifference. "The Luukessians are as fragmented as anyone else in this land. The cavalrymen are largely from Galbadien, it's true, but we have others that are from Actaluere and Syloreas, and they have no loyalty to me any more than to any of you. Most of our discipline problems remain internecine quarrels between soldiers of the old kingdoms. I wouldn't worry about it if I were you; in the short term, they're simply a voting bloc, and in the long term, they'll be true members of Sanctuary."

"Said the hawk to the fieldmouse," Vaste said.

"You are more than a bit hectoring today," Ryin said with a frown.

"It's my job," Vaste said, "much as yours is to make randomly contrarian pronouncements like, 'Instead of swords, I think we should arm our warriors with garden snails'!"

"Some of them would do more damage with the snails," Vara said. A hush fell over the Council, and every eye turned to her. She merely shrugged, as expressionless as ever. *That was a hint of the old Vara. But only a hint.*

"Anything else before we adjourn?" Curatio said, after the silence had been steady in place for a few more moments.

"I have something I'd like to bring up again," Vaste said. "Can we please talk about—"

"No," Vara said, her voice steely, the silence falling afterwards as complete as if she'd pulled out her sword and driven it into the Council table.

Vaste hesitated, and after a moment he spoke up again. "It's been six months—"

"No," Vara said again, and this time she stood, the first hint of thunderclouds gathering over her brow, which was stitched in a downward line.

She stood there, unmoving, staring down the troll, who looked back at her, unblinking. "When can we finally discuss it?" he asked.

"Not yet," Cyrus breathed, and Vaste looked left at him. Vara looked at him, too, but in the same way she would have glanced at a wall in order to avoid walking into it.

"Some other day, perhaps," Curatio said with a faint smile, clearly forced. "I think that'll be all for now."

"So says the interim Guildmaster," Vaste said then looked at Vara again. "If only we could talk about electing a permanent one without breaking down into emotional hysterics."

Vara stared back at him, and the storm breaking across her face expanded, turning her cheeks red with fury. "Not … today."

"Fine," Vaste said, unintimidated by her rising fury. "Pick a date and let's schedule it. I'll get a calendar."

Vara's hard expression did not break. After directing her furious stare at him for a moment more, she turned and walked out of the Council Chambers, her metal boots clanking against the stone with each step. She slammed the door behind her, rocking it on its hinges and causing Erith to flinch next to Cyrus.

"Perhaps it was something I said." Vaste's tone was light. "Still, now that she's gone, perhaps we can finally at least discuss—"

"You heard her," Cyrus said quietly, looking at the door. He stood and adjusted his armor, placing his helm back on his head from where it had rested on the table during the meeting. "Not today." Without waiting for a response, he turned and walked out the door, taking care not to slam it behind him.

Chapter 7

The halls of stone echoed with his steps, and Cyrus paused at the door to his chamber, listening for any noise down the hall. He wondered if Vara had returned to her chambers, but he heard no sign of her. *Not that I had heard much sign of her before.*

His hand rested on the doorknob, and he gave it a slow turn, eyes still watching the door two down from his, wishing almost unconsciously that it would squeak, that its hinges would announce its motion as it opened. He sighed, filling his ears with a sound like regret. He stepped into his chambers and shut the door behind him with a click.

"How did the Council meeting go?" The voice came from the bed, shrouded in the darkness cast by the curtains blocking the sun from the room. The hearth was dark as well, the torches unlit, and he struggled to place the voice for a moment.

"Arydni?" Cyrus asked.

"Hardly," the smooth voice returned, and he saw a shadowed figure slide from the bed, navy skin catching the sheen of the barely-there sunlight peeking in through the edges of the curtains.

"Aisling," Cyrus said, a little more tautly than he might have under other circumstances. "I didn't expect to see you now."

She crept up to him, her white hair catching a thin shaft of sunlight and sparkling as Cyrus's eyes struggled to adjust to the room's dimness. "You should know I always show up sooner or later." Her hands found his face, and he realized she was nude. Her hands fell down his breastplate, skin squeaking as she rubbed the dark metal.

"You've been absent for a few days."

"You were being tended to by an elven priestess." Aisling's eyes flashed at him, he could see it even in the dark. Her hand went to his belt, loosening it until it clattered to the ground.

"Is that a hint of jealousy?" Cyrus asked.

"No," Aisling said. "A statement of fact. You were in no condition to accept my ... ministrations ... while you were under hers."

"That makes it sound a little untoward," Cyrus said.

"I don't assume she did anything untoward," Aisling said, unfastening his breastplate and backplate. "That's my job."

Cyrus felt a curious stirring within. "Right now?"

"I'd wait, but it's hard to find a time when you're idle nowadays." She unfastened his gorget and let it clink to the ground as she leaned up and into his neck. She kissed him, and then the pressure increased as she leaned in, her tongue working against his skin. He'd dispensed with the beard when he'd returned from Luukessia, and since then she'd left him with enough bruises on his neck that he pondered growing it back again. *It feels good, though, I can't deny that.*

"Not in the mood?" Aisling said, taking her mouth away from his neck for just a heartbeat. "Give me a minute and you will be."

She took his plate armor off with practiced ease, and he let her lead this dance, as he so often had of late. She took him to the bed and ministered to him there. He kept eyes tightly closed save for once, when he saw a flash of her astride him, her deep blue skin even more shadowed in the dark. Her white hair moved as she gyrated, and then he closed his eyes again, and envisioned himself somewhere else—only two doors down.

Chapter 8

"So …" Cyrus asked the assemblage before him, "how do we find a missing goddess?"

His words were followed by a rough sort of quiet punctuated by the sound of pots and pans slamming together somewhere in the distance. Cyrus sat in a wooden chair in a room behind the Great Hall, staring at a small group he'd summoned together to consider the problem at hand. Since many of them were not officers, he'd opted to hold the meeting in a different place than the Council Chambers, deciding on an unused conference room at the back of the first floor of Sanctuary. The smell of dinner filled the air, the aroma of fresh meat wafting down the hall and causing Cyrus's stomach to rumble.

"I'm sorry," Vaste said, "I couldn't hear you over the sound of my belly screaming for Larana's cooking."

"This is quite a serious matter—and disheartening, I might add," Odellan said, leaning forward in his chair, elbows upon his knees and face in his hands.

"It does seem bad," J'anda said, a goblet of wine in his hand, his appearance that of a dark elven longshoreman of the sort Cyrus had seen in Reikonos. "I'm a bit unsure of why you've asked for my aid in this, though."

"Or mine," Mendicant spoke up, his green, scaly skin pulled back to reveal his fearsome teeth. Cyrus tried to decide if the goblin was smiling, then realized it was probably more of a grimace. "Not that I don't appreciate being called in to strategize with the great Lord Davidon—"

"Oh, there went my appetite," Vaste said.

"—but I don't think I can be of much help to you in this matter," Mendicant finished, his grimace now faded. *He looks almost ... regretful,* Cyrus decided.

"I asked all of you here for a specific reason," Cyrus said, turning to the last member of the group, Martaina Proelius. She had said nothing thus far, preferring to stand near the door, tall and lithe, surveying the meeting with a watchful eye as though something—or someone—were about to burst through the door at any moment. Her green cloak covered her hands and arms as well as her body, and she stood stiff and still, taking it all in. *Or napping with her eyes open, for all I know.* "You are some of the smartest and most experienced people in Sanctuary—"

"Where's Curatio?" J'anda asked, shifting in his chair and letting the wine slosh around in his goblet.

"Supremely busy," Cyrus said.

"It seems to me that Lady Vara would be a good choice for this sort of discussion," Mendicant said, speaking softly. "She is named for the Goddess of Life, after all, is she not?"

"Ahhh ..." Cyrus felt a grimace of his own appear. "I don't want to bother Lady Vara until we have something more ... uh ... substantial ... to share." He knew the eyes of the others were either upon him or averted politely, and he cleared his throat. "The question still remains—when a goddess goes missing, where does a mortal begin looking for her?"

"I don't know," J'anda said, rolling his eyes. "Why don't you ask an immortal?"

"I'll try and catch up with Curatio later tonight," Cyrus said, holding up a hand as though he could ward the enchanter off. "But before then, I'd like to at least have some ideas."

"You could try visiting her home," Martaina said from her place near the door. She maintained her icy demeanor as everyone turned to look at her. "It seems the logical place to start a search."

"The only problem being that apparently the guardians of her realm are a little touchy at the moment," Cyrus said. "But you're quite right, we should visit the Realm of Life, see if we can find out anything there." He paused. "Maybe bring a little army with us to be sure we don't get overwhelmed in case we have to stage a sudden retreat." He looked around the small group. "Any other ideas?"

There was a pause before Vaste broke the silence. "We're probably a little stalled in our thinking because none of us has ever had to find a god before. Usually they're quite good about staying where you leave them."

Cyrus saw a few smiles break around the room, taking special note of J'anda's. The dark elf, even in his illusionary state, maintained a distinctive air about him, his dark skin looking shadowed in the light of the torches that burned from sconces on the wall.

"Fair enough," Cyrus said. "If you come up with any other ideas, though—"

"Who would kidnap a god?" Mendicant asked, muttering under his breath.

Cyrus turned his head to focus on the goblin. "I'm sorry, Mendicant, what was that?"

"Oh," Mendicant said, suddenly flustered. "I didn't realize I was speaking aloud."

"Well, you were," Cyrus said, honing in on the green-skinned wizard, "and it sounded like a good thought. Say that again."

The goblin sat back, long fingers with the claws on the ends fingering his blue robe. "I was just speculating—pointlessly, really—about who would have the power to kidnap a god. Not a guild, or an army, in all probability—"

"Unless they beat her to within an inch of her life the way we did to Mortus," J'anda said. "He was begging for mercy by the end, after all."

"No, Mendicant has a point," Cyrus said. "Mortus was still trying to flee when he died. And for all the trouble it caused us, we were able to do what we did to him because his servants were dead first. Try and imagine fighting an army at the same time we were facing him."

"Scary thought," J'anda said.

"Whatever happened to her," Cyrus said, letting his fingers drum on the metal plate protecting his thigh, "she either went willingly, or it happened so quietly and quickly that her guardians didn't hear it. That would take … power."

"Unless her guardians were somehow complicit in it," J'anda said, raising the goblet to his mouth with a wide smile.

"Thank you for reminding me why I never became a constable in a city guard," Cyrus said with a sigh.

"You really don't have the disposition for it," Vaste said. "You'd ask three questions and then disembowel them right there for annoying you."

"I would not," Cyrus said, shaking his head. "I'm not Va ..." He let his voice trail off. "That's good enough for now. Keep thinking. I'll schedule an expedition to the Realm of Life to take a cursory look around. Until then, just keep trying to come up with other angles to think this thing through."

He nodded and smiled tightly as the meeting broke. Martaina was first out the door, without so much as a look back. Mendicant bowed to Cyrus, then J'anda, and finally Vaste, who waved him off with dismissive shake of his massive green hand. With only a nod to Odellan, the goblin skittered toward the door, claws clicking a fast pace until he was out in the hallway. Cyrus listened as the clicking slowed, the goblin's nerves presumably subsiding.

"It is quite the conundrum," Odellan said, pausing by the door. He carried his silver-winged helm from his days in the Termina Guard under his arm. "Having presided over more than a few investigations myself, I can honestly say I do not envy you this task."

"That's all right," Cyrus said, smiling at the elf. "I'm putting you in charge of the investigation anyway."

"I beg your pardon?" Odellan's question was spoken with the politest air, as though he'd simply misheard a conversation at a dinner party and was asking for clarification.

"You're running the investigation," Cyrus said. "You'll be asking the questions, should we find someone to ask them of." Cyrus sat back, letting his muscles relax against the wooden back of the chair. "You've done this before. I never have. I'll be right there with you, ready to ask anything that comes to my mind, but you'll be the lead investigator on this."

"Ah, I ... ah ..." Odellan's face flushed scarlet. "This is a bit ... larger than any previous investigation I might have undertaken."

"Nonsense," Cyrus said, clapping his gauntleted hands together. "You investigated on the occasion that the God of Death sent assassins after your citizens in Termina. This seems right up your alley."

"I failed in that investigation," Odellan said. "I believe you were the one who made all the determinations in that case. I merely ... uncovered perhaps a fact or two of note—"

"Which is exactly what I need now," Cyrus said, "an investigator with some experience in these matters." He stood, nodding firmly to signal that the topic was closed. "I know this is a little out of your purview. It's out of all of our purviews, but you're as qualified as anyone else to ask questions. Did you ever have to deal with missing persons in Termina?"

"On a few occasions, yes," Odellan said with greatest reluctance, as though Cyrus had taken a sharp implement out and prised the answer from his mouth by force. "But—"

"No buts," Cyrus said and waved him toward the door. "Do what you can. I'm not expecting miracles."

"An odd sentiment," J'anda said, following Odellan toward the door and resting a hand on his shoulder, "given that our victim is a goddess?" He smiled and stepped into the hall, taking care to shut the door behind him."

Cyrus watched them go and shook his head as though he could shrug off the strangeness of the task they were set upon. He turned his head and realized that one of the attendees was still very much with him, sitting on a chair and staring at him. "Vaste?" Cyrus asked. "Is there a reason you're leering at me?" He sniffed the air, caught a whiff of the distant smell of the cooking. "You've not become so overwhelmed by your hunger that you're considering eating me, I hope?"

"As disagreeable as you are outside my stomach, I can't imagine what damage you would do within it," Vaste replied, scowling. "No, I prefer to keep my diet strictly to things that don't give me indigestion, thank you."

"Very well," Cyrus said with a smile. "What, then?"

"How are you doing?" Vaste asked, standing. The troll towered over Cyrus by several feet, and for another, it might have been intimidating.

"I feel fine," Cyrus said, folding his arms. "Arydni said that the illness never took hold in my chest, that my breathing seems un ..." he searched for a word, "... deterred, I suppose. I'm fine, that's the gist."

"Are you?" Vaste said, staring down at him. "Are you truly?"

"Yes," Cyrus said, staring back. "Truly. I am not ill."

"Are you sure?" Vaste asked, tapping his tall staff against the ground. "Because it seems to me—and admittedly I am but a humble troll and outside observer—that in the last six months you've somehow foresworn the woman you've pined over for the last four years in favor of the one whose interest you've been spurning all this time." Vaste nodded, as if he were giving deep consideration to something. "That doesn't seem like the mark of a man who's got his wits about him."

"There's a little more complexity to the situation than that." Cyrus could feel the slow thrum of blood in his veins. *Oh, how I don't care to talk about this.*

"Is there?" Vaste asked. "Because, again, to my eyes, it looks daft. It makes those who have known you wonder if perhaps you simply need a good, solid thump to the head with a heavy stick." He tapped his staff against the ground again, the white crystal at the top catching Cyrus's eye. "Oh, look. I seem to be carrying a heavy stick."

"Vaste, she scorned me," Cyrus said, his voice low and quiet. "Before I left for Luukessia, she turned away my advances."

"Yes, and upon your return, she practically flung herself at you," Vaste said.

"She ... *talked* to me ... in the Council Chambers," Cyrus said. "I wouldn't say she 'flung herself' at me."

"Did she attempt to stab you in any way during the conversation?"

"What? No."

"Well, for Vara, that's practically like flinging herself at you."

"She didn't want me, okay?" Cyrus said, feeling the first flash of irritation. "She made it clear before I left. I'm sorry she changed her mind while I was gone. Things changed in the year and more I was in Luukessia. I got ... entangled."

"Yes," Vaste said, "that's a good way to put it. I noticed, though, that you didn't seem to have great difficulty disentangling yourself from the Baroness Cattrine when the time came for her to leave for the Emerald Fields."

Cyrus let his head slump. "There's more to that situation as well. It's not as simple as you're painting it—"

"Oh, yes," Vaste said, "I'm sure that fiery, energetic sexual escapades with a lithe, dexterous dark elven thief are incredibly nuanced and possessed of much depth. You probably have conversations in which you discuss the great elven literary masters of the day and the sordid details of dwarven politics." He focused his gaze on Cyrus. "No? It's just sex, then?"

Cyrus held up a hand, as though he could forestall the troll. "I ... look, I'm incredibly busy trying to be the General of this guild and steer our expeditions and incursions—"

"I'm having a hard time trying to figure out which of you is using the other more, you or Aisling," Vaste said, and Cyrus felt the silence draw in after the words were spoken.

"I'm not ..." he cleared his throat, which suddenly felt oppressively tight, like something within it was choking him, "I'm not *using* her."

"Are you in love with her?" Vaste asked, his piercing onyx eyes boring relentlessly into Cyrus's.

"I'm not ... not in love with her," Cyrus said. "I didn't know love was a requirement before—"

"Some civilized cultures think it helpful," Vaste replied. "Not the trolls, obviously. My people will gladly throw down with any random partner in any place, and feelings are not a concern at all. In fact, the more loathsome the partner, sometimes the better the—"

"I could stand to go without hearing the intricacies of troll sex, thanks," Cyrus said, squinting his eyes as though he could blot out the words.

"You're using the girl," Vaste said. "She's allowing it for her own reasons. Perhaps it's because you make her scream the way you do, or perhaps she feels something for the first time in years. I don't know. I don't care. Your furtive glances when we're in Council betray your actual feelings—the same way they have for the last four years."

"I screwed it up, Vaste," Cyrus said quietly, and the troll stayed silent as he watched Cyrus. "The night I came back from Luukessia, Aisling came to my quarters. I was tired and frustrated, and ... I grabbed hold of her as she passed, not even fully realizing who she was. I was just ... yearning for something. Alaric had ... I just wanted to feel *something*. And a knock came at my door later that woke me up, and when I went to get it, Vara was standing there. And she saw ..."

Cyrus gestured behind him, as though the scene were recreated there for the troll to see.

"Oh, dear," Vaste said, forming a perfect O with his lips from astonishment. "Yes. Okay. I see the problem now."

"Yes, I see the problem too," Cyrus said. "It doesn't matter if Aisling is using me—though I can't imagine what for. There is no chance with Vara now."

"You don't know that," the troll said quickly.

"I think I know it," Cyrus said.

"You won't know unless you try," Vaste said quietly.

"There's nothing to try," Cyrus said. "She won't even talk to me about anything other than guild matters. Won't even look at me except to acknowledge a direct statement or question. She's done with me, Vaste. Whatever was between us is now gone. Totally and irrevocably."

"I'm still holding this stick, you know," Vaste said, waving the staff slightly, "and I'm beginning to think you might still need an abrupt whack delivered to the back of your head. You've been so busy running these last few months—"

"I'm not running," Cyrus said, and this time it came out as a snarl. "I'm not running from anything or anybody, all right? I'm handling guild business. I'm scheduling and executing expeditions, incursions and battles to help us handle the responsibilities we have before us. It's a lot of work. I'm not running," he said again, more emphatically this time. "I learned my lesson about running last year. I have more than enough to face at present. It's that the fight …" he paused, letting his voice lower, "… is over."

Vaste raised his staff then lowered it and started toward the door. "I'm hungry."

"That's it?" Cyrus asked and looked around the empty chamber, torchlight flickering across the stone walls. "We're done?"

"Sure," Vaste said and paused at the door, looking back at Cyrus with that same piercing look. "If you want to spend all your time and energy convincing yourself that this battle is lost, and that you really do want to be spending your nights with Aisling, who am I to spend my time and energy trying to thump you solidly in the head until you realize the folly of your ways?" Vaste shrugged. "Supper is waiting, I'm one man, and my shoulders don't have enough strength in them to knock the idiocy out of your thick skull." With that, he swept out of the door, his robes trailing behind him, leaving Cyrus without a thing to say in his wake.

Chapter 9

Cyrus walked out of the hallway that ran along the side of the Great Hall and emerged into the foyer, the smell of dinner growing more potent. He could almost taste the fresh-baked pastry crust that accompanied the meat pies, his favorite meal. The scent was heavy in the air. The doors to the outside were open across the foyer, and Cyrus stared out into the fading sunlight as a slow-moving crowd passed in front of him, the staircase emptying the upper floors as the entirety of the guild filtered down for dinner.

One of the figures broke away from the staircase and took a right turn toward him, her gown a lovely piece of work. It revealed her shoulders, smooth, youthful skin at odds with the age of the woman who wore it. Cyrus smiled at Arydni, probably with a little more sadness than he intended. He had not seen her since presenting her offer to the Council.

"Did it go as you anticipated?" she asked, tentative.

"It did," Cyrus said. "We'll look into it."

"Do you have a plan?" she asked, her fingers clutching her gown to keep it from trailing on the stone floor.

"A basic one," Cyrus said, nodding at her. Her hair was up today, more formal, as if she were prepared for an event of some sort. "We'll need your assistance to reach the Realm of Life. We need to at least try and ask some questions of Vidara's servants if we're going to investigate her disappearance for you."

"Of course," Arydni said, bowing slightly from the waist. Her gown was tight-stitched around her sides in sharp contrast with what he'd seen her wear in the past. *Of course, in the past, her vestments showed off almost everything, so I suppose covering all that with tight-fitting cloth is something of an improvement ... or perhaps not, depending on how you look at it.* "Would it just be you and myself, or did you want to bring another person along?"

"I was thinking a small army might be best," Cyrus said. "For safety."

Arydni paled, her dark complexion giving way to a milky-white sheen. "I ... don't think that's terribly wise. The Life Mother's guardians are already on edge. To provoke them by bringing an army into their space could be incredibly counter-productive. They very nearly attacked us last time and only restrained themselves because we were unarmed pilgrims."

"Which is my concern," Cyrus said. "If they very nearly killed you and your party, who were known to them and plainly not a threat, I don't expect they're going to react well to utter strangers. I don't want to get pinned in a god's realm without any sort of assistance should things go ... undiplomatically."

Arydni's face fell, a tearing sort of embarrassment causing her to look away. "And I'm sure you won't do anything to provoke their ire."

"Well, I'll certainly try not to—Hey!" Cyrus said, catching the meaning of her tone. "What is that supposed to mean?"

Arydni sighed. "It means that you are a warrior of Bellarum, and as such, your first instinct is to lead with the sword and follow with diplomacy later. If at all."

"That a little insulting," Cyrus said.

"More than a little, I would hope," Arydni said, face bereft of amusement now, "but only because you must concede it is true."

"I'd concede it was true at one point," Cyrus said. "I'm no longer the leading edge of a blade, though. I can be diplomatic. Not every situation has to be a fight, and I know that."

"Then you're not a follower of Bellarum anymore," Arydni said, watching him carefully.

"Even though I'm the General of the largest guild in Arkaria," Cyrus said, keeping a thin tether on his patience, "I don't have the luxury of fighting every battle I think needs to be fought."

"Because you don't have the desire or because you don't have the resources for all those fights?"

"Both," Cyrus said. "I'm a busy man."

"So I've heard," Arydni said after a brief pause. "I will see what I can arrange. I would implore you to come with as few people as you feel you can if we are to engage in this endeavor, though."

"Can you guarantee our safety?" Cyrus asked.

Her hesitation before she answered told him all he needed to know. "No."

"Then we come with an army." Cyrus folded his arms, listening to the clink of the metal as he did so. "If Vidara's minions are spoiling for a fight, I will not be caught unready."

"I understand," Arydni said, seeming to age before his very eyes. "I must return to my people to put some things in order. I will meet you in Reikonos in seven days' time to venture to the Realm of Life."

"All right," Cyrus said. "Let me get a wizard to teleport you to—"

"I have already secured passage," Arydni said with a smile as she turned away from him to cross the foyer. "A wizard from my order awaits me outside your gates." She turned back to favor Cyrus with a weak smile. "Please do try to remember that I have hired you to aid the Lady of Life, not to leave her realm in utter wreckage while she is absent." Without waiting for a response from him, she turned and wove her way through the throng still crossing into the Great Hall for evening meal.

"Cyrus," a clear voice called out to him, causing him to turn. Curatio approached, his robes trailing the floor, his head cocked at an angle as he drew near to the warrior.

"Curatio," Cyrus said, bowing his head. "On your way to dinner?"

"In a moment," the healer replied. "I heard you had a meeting with some of the others regarding the Vidara investigation."

"I did," Cyrus said, "and our first step—"

"Why was I not invited?" Curatio asked, and Cyrus noted that his face seemed stiff, his eyes slightly narrowed.

"You're awfully busy," Cyrus said, shrugging. "I assumed you were—"

"You will inform me of any future meetings regarding this matter, and I will be in attendance," Curatio said, turning from Cyrus to move toward the Great Hall's massive entry doors.

"Curatio, your schedule is filled from sunup to well past sundown," Cyrus said, and the healer paused to look back at him.

"You're doing the work of a Guildmaster now. Let me handle the matters of the General—"

"You will keep me informed of any meetings related to this subject in the future," Curatio said, and there was not an inch of yield in his voice, like forged steel, hardened and folded over and over again. "This is not a matter that is up for discussion. I can be of assistance to you in this, and I am the most well-versed person in this guild in matters related to Vidara." He took a step back. "Or have you forgotten that I was the one who spread her gospel to the entire Elven Kingdom in my time?"

Cyrus froze. "I ... uh ... it was not uppermost on my mind, no."

"Did you think I would have undertaken that mission without reason?" Curatio stepped closer to him, and Cyrus saw a tightening of the skin around the healer's eyes as they narrowed. "Do you think I would take centuries to campaign across the entire Kingdom to bring her followers for no purpose? I know the woman, damn you." He snapped the words out. "I know her well, or did, and if she's gone missing, I will be involved in helping to find her. Do I make myself clear?"

"I will keep you informed," Cyrus said, feeling a slight tautness in his jaw from the burning in his face and gullet. *Let it go, Cyrus. He's raw and concerned that his goddess is missing. Put away your pride.*

"That is all I ask," Curatio said and turned, without a word more, and slipped away into the still-moving crowd as he disappeared behind the doors to the Great Hall.

"Cyrus," came another voice, softer this time, and he turned his head to look.

"Good gods," Cyrus said and sighed upon seeing who it was. "Oh, it's just you."

"I'll let that pass because I'm in a hurry," Erith said, "and because I need something from you."

"So does everyone lately, it seems," Cyrus replied. His eyes caught sight of a blond ponytail above a group of dwarves, and a shining silver breastplate that caught the rays of sunlight filtering in through the open foyer doors. "Well, almost everyone."

"I have a serious problem," Erith said.

"All right," Cyrus said, putting aside the jest he might have made. Erith's face was tight, her normally mirthful eyes weighed down with some emotion. "Go on, then."

"They've gone missing," she blurted out. "They were supposed to be on a routine patrol out of Reikonos, going west, but they left fourteen days ago and have yet to check in." Cyrus watched a droplet of water slide down Erith's blue cheek and tried to recall the last time he'd seen her actually shed a tear. *Probably never.* "The city guards have no idea where they've gone, and they can't even spare anyone to go looking for a lost patrol that's as small as they are—"

"Who?" Cyrus asked, wondering if he'd missed the answer somewhere in the healer's rush to unburden her mind to him.

Erith swallowed heavily. "My old guild, the Daring. They were called into service of the Confederation because of the war, because of their homestead clause—"

"Wait," Cyrus said. "You mean the whole guild?" He watched her nod. "Cass? Elisabeth?"

"All of them," Erith said, and another tear crept down her cheek. "They're seven days late returning. There's no sign of them, no hint ... nothing." She bowed her head. "They're just ... gone."

Chapter 10

"So," Andren said, "now you've got another problem to deal with." The elf stood next to Cyrus, tankard in hand. A fresh breeze blew around them as they stood out on the archery range along the side of Sanctuary's massive structure, the southwest tower casting its long shadow over them, the sun invisible behind it as it continued to set.

"Yes," Cyrus said, his left hand tautly squeezing the grip in his hand. It was a training weapon that he'd pulled it out of the nearby storage shed along with a dozen training arrows. He pulled it up and nocked an arrow, drawing it back to his cheek. There was a cool sensation as he held it there, the breeze blowing over him. His stomach rumbled at him for leaving the smells of dinner behind.

Cyrus released the arrow and it flew at the straw target at the end of the range, lodging firmly in the torso.

Andren let out a dry snicker. "What are you doing? Got delusions of being a ranger?"

"Warriors were required to learn every possible weapon at the Society of Arms," Cyrus said, drawing another arrow from the ground, nocking it and pulling it to his cheek. "I'm not as good with one of these as, say, Martaina Proelius, but I can use one in a pinch." He let the arrow sail and it stuck in the throat of the straw man. "And not terribly badly, if I might say."

"I'd be more impressed if the straw man were moving," Andren said, taking another slug. The smell of the booze washed over Cyrus. It was a thick, hearty stout that caused his stomach to rumble again. "I've seen Martaina on the hunt before, and it's quite a sight to behold."

"Oh?" Cyrus asked. "She does seem to do well with animals, doesn't she?"

"I was talking about killing people, but yeah, I'm sure she's good with them, too." Andren's beard twitched, his mustache frosted with the foam of his ale. "Although the way she looked doing it ..." He let his voice trail off in suggestion. "I might consider breaking my 'No elven women' rule for her. I bet she's a feisty one."

"Where did Arydni fit into that rule?" Cyrus mused, loosing another arrow. This one lodged in the groin of the straw man.

"She was the origin of it," Andren muttered and gestured at the straw man. "For about that reason, I might add."

"Didn't seem like you were too put off by her when she was here." Cyrus paused, pulling an arrow from where he'd stuck it in the earth and twirling it in his fingers. "Quite the opposite, in fact."

"Well, you know, I have some fond memories of her," Andren said, nodding. "Some things I wouldn't mind reliving, if you know what I mean—"

"I didn't drag you away from dinner to discuss your rampant libido," Cyrus said, turning back to the straw target. A cool breeze blew over them, cutting through the lingering heat from summer's end.

"Nor yours, apparently," Andren said. "Can we talk about Aisling's bedroom manner yet? I'm a mite curious—"

"No," Cyrus said and released the string. The arrow flew wide of its mark. "Dammit." Cyrus turned to Andren. "I brought you out here to talk about the Daring."

The elf nodded. "Right, yeah. You'll have to forgive me, though, as it's not quite as exciting of a topic as dark elven sex."

"A missing goddess and a missing guild," Cyrus said, drawing another arrow from the ground, "what are the odds of those two things happening at the same time?"

"What are the odds of you being pursued by a Baroness, a thief and a paladin all at the same time?" Andren asked. "I mean, up until now you've not exactly been a stud horse, if you catch my—"

Cyrus cut him off with a look. "What is wrong with you today? Can you possibly get your mind out of the rut you're in and listen to me?" He paused. "About something that isn't related to lusty bedroom activities?"

"I'm sorry, we're not all presently fending off every woman in Sanctuary with a blunt instrument, are we?" Andren said with a scowl. "Even the cook fancies you, always sending those tentative looks your way and fixing your favorite meals." He sighed. "A couple years ago, I was on top of the world with the women around here, and you couldn't find a scabbard for that sword in your breeches. Now, I'm sitting here competing with all these Luukessian men for a limited number of women, longing for a former wife I haven't touched in a century, and you've got—"

"The Daring," Cyrus said, utter exasperation infusing his tone. "Forget it, I can't talk to you about this now."

"Maybe you could find a sympathetic ear in Vara," Andren said with a chortle.

"Will you lay off?" Cyrus's tone went acid.

"Fine, fine," Andren said, waving a hand at Cyrus as though to lower his temper. "So the Daring went missing. So what? We haven't been allied with them for years."

"Not officially, no," Cyrus said, plucking an arrow from the ground and drawing back. "But on the day our alliance was dissolved …" he let his voice trail off, "… an offer of help was extended to them, if ever they should need it."

"By Alaric, you mean," Andren said.

"Yes," Cyrus said. "By Alaric. I can't help but feel that if they're missing, our assistance is needed." He looked down the shaft of the arrow. "And I owe Cass Ward a debt of my own."

"Lovely," Andren said, and Cyrus could hear him shuffling his feet. "What did he do, offer you advice on how to make your armor as bland as possible? I mean, you wear black, he wears grey—"

"Har har," Cyrus said, picking up the last arrow. "At least unlike the goddess conundrum, I actually know what to do about this one."

"Oh?" Andren asked, and Cyrus could see him out of the corner of his eye, tipping the tankard toward his mouth. A soft breeze whispered through the grass as the straw target rustled before him. "What's that?"

"Follow their path of patrol," Cyrus said, "with a hunting party." He let fly the arrow, and it struck the straw target squarely in the head. He looked at the skewered straw man, arrow jutting from where the forehead would be. "And fortunately, I know someone who can trace their path."

Chapter 11

They rode from the gates of Reikonos on the following day, crossing under the mighty wall that protected the city through the westernmost gate, called the Elf Gate because it guarded the roads leading to the Elven Kingdom. As they crossed under the wall, Cyrus stared up into the murder holes where soldiers looked down at him with little amusement through the slitted eyepieces of their helms. There was almost no traffic; trade had been severely diminished by the war.

They rode with the sun overhead, the clear plains around them buffeted by gusty winds. Cyrus could smell autumn in the air, even without the presence of trees anywhere nearby to give a hint of the turning of the leaves. He could almost taste apple cider on his tongue, a vaguely familiar sense from his days as a child when he remembered the apples flooding in from the Northlands to the markets in Reikonos.

He had a small army behind him, a thousand or so, roughly the size of the one he'd traveled to Luukessia with. The sun shone on his armor as he pondered that comparison briefly. *Hadn't thought of that when I made up the grouping.* At least half of them were Galbadien Dragoons, masters of horseback combat. Their horses stamped along the rutted, dried-out road as they made their way toward a gradually setting sun. They made camp an hour after midnight, set out a watch, and Cyrus bedded down early—alone.

In the morning they reassembled just after a breakfast of wizard-conjured bread and good hard cheese they carried in their packs. As Cyrus chewed on hard deer-meat jerky, he caught a sidelong look from J'anda, who was chewing on conjured bread and stroking his fingers through his greyed hair. He wore no illusion.

"What?" Cyrus asked the enchanter.

"Nothing," J'anda said with a shake of his head. He disappeared under an illusion, turning his lined face into that of a much younger human. "I was just thinking how much more pleasant it is to be back in the halls of Sanctuary nearly every night instead of sleeping in the wilds and the woods like we did in Luukessia."

Cyrus caught the aroma of campfire smoke in his nose. "We're never really going to outrun what happened there, are we?" He looked back at J'anda. "It left its mark on us all." Cyrus chewed on the jerky and looked at the illusory face that the dark elf wore to hide his real one, the one that looked so much older than when he had left Sanctuary for Luukessia. "Some of us more than others."

"I notice your gorget hides that ugly scar on your neck," J'anda said. His human visage wore a tight smile.

"And your illusion covers your wrinkles and the discoloration of your hair," Cyrus replied, suddenly no longer hungry.

"I don't think anyone who was with us in that land came away without some sort of mark to remember it by," J'anda said, tossing aside the conjured bread.

"No," Cyrus said, looking at the army around him, the Luukessian Dragoons already saddling up. "I don't think they did."

They rode west with the rising sun at their backs. Martaina was at the fore with Erith at her side, the healer following the ranger as though she might miss some critical clue at any moment. Cyrus watched it all with the eye of one who wanted little to get involved, but as the second day wore on and Erith's horse never moved far from Martaina's, he began to suspect that difficulty lay ahead.

"Erith," Cyrus said, pushing Windrider to close on the healer near the front of the formation, "may I speak with you for a moment?"

"But of course," Erith replied, her horse not removing itself from a direct path following Martaina's. The ranger glanced back at Cyrus with a cryptic look that Cyrus managed to decode from his long association with the ranger: *This woman is driving me nuts.*

"Over here, Erith," Cyrus said, gesturing to her to fall back. "In private."

The sun was high overhead. The healer's navy skin was darker than the blue of the skies, her lips pursed as she reined her horse back with greatest reluctance. Cyrus would have sworn he heard Martaina muttering a thanks in elvish under her breath.

"Erith, you can't keep following Martaina about," Cyrus said when the dark elf's horse was walking abeam his own. "It's torturous."

"What?" Erith's face twisted in outrage. "I'm trying to offer aid to her. I know these people, and I—"

"You are annoying Martaina, who is trying to do her job by finding them," Cyrus said as Windrider whickered.

"I can be useful in this," Erith said.

"How?" Cyrus asked. "Are you going to tell Martaina what Cass Ward smells like so she can sniff him out?"

Erith looked as though she were about to say something then stopped. "Well, he smells a fair sight better than you."

"There's no need to be hurtful," Cyrus said with a frown. "We're all here for the same reason. I know you're anxious about your friends—"

"I left them," Erith said, her face twitching with emotion as she said it. She turned to face forward, leaving her profile visible to Cyrus. "When things got unpleasant with the Alliance, when Goliath and our members were boxing you into a corner, I abandoned them because I thought Sanctuary needed my help more." She smiled almost ruefully, then sniffled as her face broke and her shoulders heaved once. "I left them to join you in the most horrible of times, and now I'm the only one who gives a damn that they're gone."

"You're not," Cyrus said, clutching Windrider's reins in tight hands. "Plainly."

"Which opens an interesting line of inquiry," Erith said as she sniffled. "Why are you so keen on this? You know there's no money in it."

"Not everything is about gold," Cyrus said tightly. "Sometimes it's about repaying those who have done you a kindness in the past. Paying your debts. Cass Ward was kind to me in a time when few were." He let the reins slip through his fingers, playing with the leather as he stared off into the blue skies in the distance, the occasional white cloud gleaming in the sunlight.

"Well, they were my family when no one else was," Erith said, looking sidelong at Cyrus. "Cass, Elisabeth, some of the others. They were my friends. They adopted me when I was poor and just starting out, after I'd left Saekaj Sovar. I owe them for that."

"If they're able to be found, we'll find them," Cyrus said with a nod.

"And if they're not?" Erith was chewing her bottom lip. "Able to be found, I mean?"

"Then we'll figure something out," Cyrus said. "I won't leave them forgotten if there's any lead left to be pursued."

"I believe you," Erith said, and Cyrus turned his head to look at her. She was staring back at him, and he could see the certainty in her eyes. "You and I are the only ones who would have gone looking, though."

"You and I are the only ones with a personal stake in seeing them found safely," Cyrus said. "Us and ..."

He saw her looking at him out of the corner of his eye. "You were going to say Alaric, weren't you?"

"Curatio too," Cyrus said, turning his face away from her. "But he's distracted at the moment."

"I'll stay back," Erith said, "from Martaina." She almost looked contrite as she said it. "I'll just keep my peace and ride along." She tried to smile but failed. "It's not easy, this feeling of roiling inside. It feels like I need to do something, anything, to quiet it."

"Aye," Cyrus said. "But there's nothing you can do. Just sit back and know that you're doing everything you can for now just by riding along and keeping your silence."

Erith began to steer her horse away from him, and he caught the faint smile upon her lips. "I don't think I've ever been any good at keeping my silence. I suppose this is as good a time as any to give it some effort." She slowed the pace of her horse and folded back into a group of spell casters to Cyrus's left without another word spoken.

Cyrus urged Windrider forward, bringing him alongside Martaina, who was keeping a steady pace on the path forward. "I trust if you'd seen anything of note, you'd have told me by now."

"Not a thing, sir," Martaina said with a quick glance at him. "Did you just remove a painful tick from my backside?"

Cyrus looked backward at Erith, who was barely visible in the throng of spell casters, slightly slumped over in her saddle, her long white hair catching the sunlight, but her complexion looking dim, her eyes downcast. "She's hurting, Martaina. Worried about her friends."

"And you?" Martaina asked, drawing his attention back to her. "What are you worried about?"

"Me?" Cyrus asked, saying it aloud while buying a moment to muse it over. "I'm worried about what would cause an entire guild to simply disappear this far into human territory. We're hundreds of miles from the front; this patrol they were sent on, it was bandit hunting, pure and simple." Cyrus looked ahead to the horizon, where he could see a few copses of trees to break the flat monotony of the plains ahead. "They were a hundred strong, with spell casters of their own." Cyrus shook his head. "I have no idea what they could have run into this far from the war that would make an entire guild disappear."

"Dark times," Martaina said. "Missing friends, missing gods. Why, hard to say what might take leave of us next—"

He caught the wry expression on her face and cut her off. "If you say my senses, be aware I'm fully expecting it and well aware that no one seems to believe me in full possession of my faculties any longer."

"I prefer to tread the paths that others do not," Martaina said, sniffing a little, as if in umbrage, "so I would have said your 'reason' had departed."

"Because that's dramatically different from what the others are saying." He turned his eyes forward, surveying the blank horizon. "What do these roads tell you?"

"Little," Martaina said with a frown. "The traffic on this route is but a fraction of what it was before even the battle of Termina. The King of the Elves has shut down the crossings. The most important traffic going between the Kingdom and Reikonos is now moved by wizards; otherwise it is done by large convoys protected by armies and inspected at the northern crossing. Whole armies move with them; mercenaries and regulars from the Kingdom or the Confederation."

"So they learned the lessons of the plains raids of years past," Cyrus mused.

"Some of them, anyway," Martaina said carefully. "You ask what the roads tell me? They tell me that local traffic dominates these paths; small wagons traversing from town to town, settlement to settlement, house to house. Individual horses and the occasional army pass through, though there is a month between them, if not more." She sniffed the air. "And perhaps something else, though it is too muddled to sift it out. Something baser than horses and men or elves, earthier than dwarves."

"Dark elves?" Cyrus suggested.

"Perhaps," Martaina said with a shrug. "Give me more time, perhaps I'll determine it. It could just be new goblin traders, or gnomes. The signs are hard to read from what I've seen, the scents are so scant and faded as to keep me from being certain."

"Fair enough," Cyrus said. "I have five more days before I have to return to Reikonos to keep an appointment with another of our armies. I'll meet you again after that at the far portal near the northern crossing."

"A busy general indeed," Martaina said with a little irony. "A conquering man who leads while his soldiers follow close behind him."

"All that would sound more impressive if you didn't dose it with a fair helping of your scorn," Cyrus said.

"It is fairly impressive when you consider how many men and women are at your command," Martaina said, and there was something grudging about the way she said it.

"I suppose," Cyrus said. "But I'm really just their General. I only lead them in battle."

"Quite right," she said, just a hint cryptically, and sent her horse to a gallop. He paused a moment and followed on as the army kicked into motion behind him. They rode on that way for a while, past the fall of evening, until it became dark and they had to stop for the night.

Chapter 12

The air crackled around Cyrus as he appeared in Reikonos in early morning. As the magic of the spell that carried him there began to disperse, he took a breath of the familiar autumn air, filled with the scents of the square. There was the sound of the fountain tinkling, of a blacksmith doing his work nearby, hammer clanging on anvil in jarring notes. The scent of horse was just as strong here as when he'd left the army he'd been with in the field. *They'll be fine with Longwell leading them,* he thought, looking over the square from atop Windrider. *He'll keep them going until I return.*

"Where are we going?" Nyad asked from next to him, her red robes draped over the sides of her horse, staff still clutched in her hand from casting the teleportation spell that had brought them here. He caught a whiff of some perfume as he turned to her, some sweet fragrance of rosewater that was just understated enough to catch his attention without smothering him.

"There's a portal in the tunnels under the city," Cyrus said. "It leads to the upper realms." He urged Windrider along the road toward the Citadel, the tallest building in Reikonos, and, in fact, Arkaria. It stretched far above them, bulbous upper floors at odds with the cylindrical lower ones.

They rode in silence, Nyad examining the sights. Cyrus watched the streets around them, too, streets he'd known for almost his entire life. They passed under the shadow of the Citadel, and Cyrus saw the city guards shuffling endlessly, tense and ridiculously stiff in their attentive posture. He almost felt bad for them in their gleaming armor, forced to endure it on hot summer days. As they veered to the left around the Citadel, they dipped into the periphery of the markets, and Cyrus could see the familiar stalls, remembered the hide and find exercises they'd done here when he was a child at the Society of Arms.

He'd tucked into the side of a stall when the Swift Swords had gone past. It had been a small squad, a group of boys no older than him and only a few younger. His peers. There was to be no violence in this exercise, one of the few where that was the case. It was at their peril, were there to be any bloodshed—the Guildmaster had been abundantly clear about that. No violence in the public eye, simple touch and capture only.

He'd watched them clumping past, Cass Ward at the fore. He was a tall boy, like Cyrus, strong and muscular even after only a few months in the guild. Cyrus knew that if it was down to individuals, it'd be him and Cass battling it out for top honors. It never came down to that, though; it was always a team effort. And Cyrus was on his own team.

"Remember," Cass had said to his fellows, loud enough that Cyrus could hear him from behind the stall, "We move as a group—and none of us is ever alone."

Cyrus could see that moment as clear as day as he steered Windrider back onto the main thoroughfare and out of the open square where the market stalls ended. He passed onto an avenue of shops as the ground sloped down toward the Torrid Sea ahead and the port. He could see the docks jutting out into the ocean, long fingers of wood lit by the early morning dawn. The first whiff of salt air came to him from the north wind. A chill wind.

The ground sloped down, a steep hill lined by cobblestones. He could hear the clop-clop of Windrider's shoes echoing over the quiet streets as the city of Reikonos began to wake around him. The hill took them down into an area of warehouses, and they turned west to follow a steep bluff that had buildings built right up against the edge.

"Is this where the wealthy have their mansions?" Nyad asked, breaking the quiet.

"No, they're on the east side of the city overlooking the Torrid Sea," Cyrus said. "Their cliffs directly overlook the ocean, no docks below to spoil the view. This is the port."

Nyad's nose was pinched, as though the salt air disagreed with her. "But it's only local traffic, right? From up the River Perda and the Emerald Coast and such, right?"

Cyrus shrugged. "I hear there are a few larger ships that come from lands beyond the Torrid Sea, but not many because of its damnable roughness and unpredictability. Most of their sea traffic came from the elves or from Aloakna before it was sacked by the dark elves."

They followed a line of wooden warehouses built up against the bluffs until they reached an open space in the cliff, like a vacant lot empty enough to build a small house on. A sheer, steep rock face gave way to a small wooden door that hung wide, its hinges squeaking as it slowly moved open and closed with the wind.

Cyrus dismounted Windrider and whispered in his ear, "Wait for me at the old guildhall. Make sure Nyad's horse goes with you." He received a whinny in reply, and the horse was off, shepherding Nyad's mount along.

"That really is impressive," Nyad said, watching the two horses make their way back to the bluff. "How does your horse do that?"

Cyrus shook his head. "Magic, for all I know." He turned toward the wooden door, the uneven boards looking like they would not bar the entry of even a small child. "Come on, let's go."

He stepped into the tunnel beyond. The hum of voices was audible, echoing off the stone walls. "Sounds like our army is already waiting."

"Oh, good," Nyad said, and Cyrus could hear just a hint of tentativeness in the way she spoke. "I would so hate to wait here in the dark, just the two of us."

"Scared of what fierce creatures might be lurking nearby?" Cyrus said with a slight smirk.

"Oh, no," Nyad said dryly, "I'm concerned about the frightening reputation of my traveling companion; he seems to have gone from being a mild-mannered, shy lad who hadn't felt the touch of a woman in many a year to some sort of crazed fiend that women can't resist." She batted her eyes slyly at him. "I wouldn't want to be in his proximity for too terribly long, lest I be overcome by his manly charms—"

"And they call me a smartass," Cyrus muttered.

"Please," Nyad snorted in amusement, "I was a smartass long before you were a randy little twinkle in your mother's eye." She cast a spell, hand glowing in light, and Cyrus's vision brightened the world around him.

He led the way into the dark stone tunnels carved into the hillside. They were exceptionally smooth, perfectly rectangular corridors hewn into the rock. They might have been conjured out of the ground itself. He ran a gauntlet along the wall as he went, his fingers screeching the metal across the flat surface.

"Do you know where you're going?" Nyad asked, a tentative whisper in the darkness behind him.

"Sure," Cyrus sad, taking his hand from the wall. "The Society of Arms used to train us down here in these catacombs. They run through the whole of the western city, for miles and miles. You get used to them after a while."

"What are they?" Nyad asked, and he could hear her breathing a little faster now that they were on foot. "I assume they pre-date the human settlement here, and they don't look like sewage tunnels." She sniffed. "Or smell like them."

"Good guess," Cyrus said with a small smile. "The sewers actually run above these tunnels for the most part. These tunnels are so well sealed there's no leakage. And you're quite right; they were not built by the Confederation or by Reikonos. Presumably the ancients left them behind, along with the portal ..." he turned a corner, and the tunnel opened into a massive, open space, more than large enough to hold the Sanctuary army that stood within it, "... here."

"Huh," Nyad said, staring down into the slight bowl formed out of the rock. "Kind of a funny place to put a portal."

"I suppose," Cyrus said with a shrug. He could see the faint glow of the portal in the center of the room, over the heads of the army surrounding it. "I have a feeling there are some things about the ancients that we just won't ever understand." He stepped over the threshold into the circular room and looked up to see stone buttresses holding up a sort of dome overhead. The air down here was stale, as though it hadn't moved in an age. *Just like I remember it from childhood.*

Cyrus moved through the gathered army, looking around him to confirm that what he had ordered had been carried out. It was roughly a thousand of Sanctuary's finest, with a bevy of spell casters at their command and more than enough rangers and warriors to hold off a line of offense if necessary.

He cut his way through the crowd toward the center and broke through to an open space near the portal. On the other side of the space he found Arydni waiting, her head in her hands, dark hair flowing over her fingers like falling water over a cliff face. She looked up to see him, and her pointed ears almost seemed to twitch at his presence. "I had hoped you would see reason and bring less."

"I'm not that reasonable where the safety of my people is concerned," Cyrus said with a breath of the dank air. "I prefer to be quite unreasonable by erring on the side of survival in those cases."

"Well, you've got the unreasonable part down," Arydni muttered, so low he nearly missed it.

"Your army awaits, General," Odellan said, emerging from the small cluster of officers standing just in front of the portal. Cyrus scanned them quickly to see Vaste and Curatio, with Vara standing coolly off to the side, her arms folded across her chest.

"All right," Cyrus said, "get them in formation, Odellan, lined up and ready to march in. You may have to snake the line somewhat to fit them in the room."

"I was already planning it," Odellan said with a nod, and he broke off, shouting orders at the army to form up. His strident voice echoed off the dome overhead, the rich baritone given additional resonance from the acoustics of the room.

"What can we expect on the other side of the portal?" Cyrus asked, taking Arydni gently by the arm and steering her toward where Curatio, Vaste and Vara stood.

"Furious guardians, mostly likely," Arydni said, completing the small circle as she stepped next to Cyrus.

"Excellent," Vaste said, "I do so enjoy a good fight in the morning, especially if it's against an evil goddess's guardians."

"Vidara is hardly evil, even to you, troll," Vara said with a quiet sort of reproach. "Stop trying to be ridiculous; this is not the moment for it." Cyrus watched her as she spoke; it was the most she had said in his presence for months.

"Is the other side of the portal still an open field laid before a thicket of hedgerows?" Curatio asked. Cyrus could hear a certain tension in his words.

"It is," Arydni said, locking onto the healer. "You ... have been there before?"

"More times than I can safely count," Curatio replied, hand upon his chin as though he were deep in thought. "And the guardians were creatures of her pure nature?"

"They were," Arydni said. "When last I was there, they had begun to fade somewhat, as though their essence had been darkened by something, I know not what. Perhaps the absence of their Godmother drains their vitality and spirit. In any case, they were much less pleasant than in previous encounters."

"Some of them were fairly humorless to begin with," Curatio said, removing his fingers from his chin, "so I imagine that this is not a change for the better." He looked sidelong at Cyrus. "Best have the army ready for a fight going in. Vidara feeds those creatures their life energy and controls the direction of the realm. Without her presence, it may become ... unruly."

"An unruly goddess's realm," Vaste said with all irony, "I can hardly contain my excitement. Why, last time I was in a ruly one, I was almost smashed to chunks. I can't wait to see what they come up with here."

"Whatever it is, I hope it hits your mouth first," Vara said, turning away from him. Her fair hair moved like a whip being cracked as she spun away.

"You say that now, but when you need a heal, it'll be a different song entirely," Vaste said. "You know, if you sang."

Cyrus looked back at the army already forming into a spiral around the portal, ready to march in a column ten wide. The spell casters were sprinkled in up front, Cyrus saw, dotting the first few rows here and there. *Good. That'll help if we get ambushed just inside the gate.*

"Officers," Cyrus said. Nyad formed the middle of a short line with Vaste and Curatio sandwiched between Vara and Cyrus, their swords drawn. He looked back to see Arydni next to Odellan. "You follow right behind, okay?"

"How do we get to the Realm of Life from here?" Nyad asked. "Doesn't this portal lead to other upper realms, as well?"

"Watch," Curatio said. "Eleni, iliara, eyalastar." The portal spun before them, the empty space around the longways stone ovoid crackling with energy and light of a sort Cyrus had never seen from one of them before. It glowed green, a verdant color like the grasses of Perdamun lit by a summer sun. The healer looked at Cyrus. "On your command."

Cyrus looked down the line at Vara and saw her give him a sidelong glance in return, subtle and cool, like everything else she did in his presence now. "All right," Cyrus said, "let's get this inquisition under way." He marched forward, the clank of his plate metal boots hard against the stone floor. The glowing green portal drew closer and closer, and Cyrus could see the runes etched on the outer stone surrounding it. He took one last breath of the stale catacomb air before he stepped into the glowing green energy and felt the world distort around him.

His sense of direction shifted as if he were underwater, as though his legs were pulled from beneath him and set right again. He looked next to him and saw Nyad distorted, her cheeks growing large as a chipmunk's, then her head shrinking to the size of a pin, as though he were looking at her through thick and uneven glass.

It was over in a moment, the distortion gone from his vision, and he stood on a moonlit field, the smell of something decaying filling his nostrils. He paused just for a moment to get his bearings. There was a dark shadow in the distance ahead, something that looked like a wild, overgrown hedge, with spiny sticks poking out over the top of it. The grass upon which he stood looked nearly dead, even under the moonlight. Cyrus looked back to issue a command to the army, but behind him stood an empty portal, the light gone out of the center, giving him a clear look through to the other side as though nothing had ever been in the middle of the frame.

"Uhh ..." Cyrus said, "our portal's gone out."

"Which means our army is stuck in Reikonos, yes?" Nyad was the first to answer him.

"Yes," said Vara succinctly.

"That leaves just the five of us," Curatio said, just down the line. "Two healers, a wizard, a paladin and a warrior." His head tilted toward the shadowed hedge in the distance. "And no exit close at hand."

There was a silence broken only by the sound of something like an owl hooting in the distance, until Vaste spoke, sounding much more jolly than Cyrus imagined he would have. "Well, gosh. No one said anything about an unruly portal."

Chapter 13

"You truly are a special sort of lackwit," Vara said. The atmosphere of the realm was bleak. Cyrus exhaled to see his breath mist in front of him from the cold.

"I do not lack for wit," Vaste said and thumped his staff against the ground. The crystal lit and began to shed light, confirming for Cyrus that it was indeed a hedge ahead. "Good taste from time to time, but who among us can't be accused of that?" He spoke even as Vara started to answer and cut her off. "Keeping in mind that not so long ago, your taste in men ran toward the affable and ignorant General who just led us into this mess."

Cyrus blinked. "Wha … why did you just insult *me*? As though I could have predicted that somehow a portal would shut off and trap just the five of us in a hostile realm?" He glanced down the line at Curatio. "Have you ever heard of anything like this happening before?"

"A woman going for a man with an overabundance of confidence and a sword? It's a tale as old as time," Curatio said, not taking his eyes off the hedgerow in front of them. Cyrus saw a ghost of a smile on the healer's lips as he surveyed the scene. "Oh, that's not what you were talking about?" He glanced back. "The portal has become corrupted with the loss of the Mistress of the Realm."

"Is that …" Nyad looked especially pale next to Cyrus. "Does that happen often?"

"No," Curatio said. "It happened often enough during the War of the Gods, of course. What seems to have happened here is that someone effected a spell upon it after we passed through, something similar to our own spell that can seal a portal shut for teleportation."

Curatio took a step back and placed his hand on the stone edge of the portal, tracing the line of one of the runes. "Perhaps we should simply teleport out." He looked over at Nyad and smiled once more, faintly. "If we are able."

Nyad perked up and began to cast a spell. Her hand glowed green, sparked with intensity, and then the light vanished, leaving only the spots in Cyrus's eyes, as though a fire had died in front of him. "It's not working," she said, shaking her head with emphasis. "I can't ... can't teleport us out." The barest edge of panic filled the elven woman's words.

"As I suspected," Curatio said with a nod. "Very well, in we go."

"Wait, what?" Cyrus asked.

"I see we've decided to abandon all sanity and hope of rescue and move straight to the part where we run willy-nilly through a dark and scary hedge, where I'm certain sunlight and warm days are waiting on the other side," Vaste deadpanned.

"Curatio, why would we—" Nyad began.

"There is another portal on the other side of the Realm," Curatio said calmly, certainly much calmer than Cyrus felt. "It is in Vidara's personal quarters, much like the one in Mortus's chambers."

"And does it lead to Luukessia?" Vaste asked. "Because if so, I think I'll just wait here for death to come and get me."

"It leads back to the portal in the Reikonos catacombs," Curatio said with a shake of the head. "Or a few other places, if you know how to use it. For our purposes, the Reikonos catacombs will do, I think."

"Ominous," Vara pronounced as Cyrus exchanged a look with her. *I'd have to agree*, he thought.

"Since you mentioned it," Cyrus said, "could that portal be the means through which Vidara was abducted?"

"Unlikely," Curatio said, seeming to ponder it, "but possible, I suppose."

"Who would be able to access her through it?" Cyrus asked, taking the lead as Curatio began to move forward.

"I do not know," Curatio replied.

They drew closer to the hedge, and Cyrus could see the bare branches jutting from the top like skeletal fingers. Cyrus sensed movement at his side and looked to find Vara there, sword in hand, walking alongside him. They exchanged a glance, but only that. She said nothing.

There was a gap in the hedge that Cyrus could see ahead, a small opening no more that half his width. The hedge ran off in either direction as far as his eye could discern. There was a heavy smell of rotting leaves, less pungent than rotting meat, but still unpleasant.

"I'll go first," Cyrus said as he reached arm's length of the hedge. Part of him expected it to swipe at him.

"I hope it eats you," Vaste said. Cyrus turned to favor him with a frown. "Better you than me," the troll added.

Cyrus shook his head and turned back to the hedge. The gap awaited, just a short space. Cyrus turned sideways and began to ease through. It was no more than a couple feet deep, and he could see open space on the other side.

He heard the scratch of thorns and branches breaking against his armor. His breastplate met resistance from a stubborn limb and he forced himself through. Cracking branches caused a rustle in the hedge, like a ripple across a pond that traversed the entire row.

Cyrus broke through to the other side and nearly stumbled, catching himself before he fell. Once he was back upright, he looked back. He could see the others through the gap. "Nyad, you're next," he said to the wizard. By the light of Vaste's staff, he saw her eyes go wide.

Still, she stepped up. He watched her gather her robes before he turned and began to slowly look left and right. There was another hedge just beyond, just as wild and brambly, extending off in either direction. He could see an end in both directions, a parallel sort of maze that wended into corners either way.

"I think this hedge is trying to expose me!" Nyad said. Cyrus turned to find her tugging at her robe, trying to pull it off of some wayward branch that had hold of it.

"Won't it be disappointed when it finds out how much easier that is with a simple bottle of Termina Cognac?" Vaste said. "All that effort for naught."

"Very funny," Nyad pronounced, finally tearing herself free with the sound of ripping cloth. She exhaled sharply and adjusted her robes as if she were gathering her dignity and then came to stand by Cyrus.

Cyrus said nothing, resuming his slow survey of the hedge path in both directions. He moved his head slowly but regularly, trying to keep watch on his left and right without being too obvious about it.

"Do you see anything?" Nyad asked as Vaste struggled through the gap in the hedge with exaggerated effort. His staff was through now, helping to light the area around them.

"I see thorny hedges," Cyrus said, continuing his watchful pattern. He took a step forward and heard the crunch of desiccated brown leaves that had fallen from the hedges. They crackled underfoot. The smell of them was more pervasive here, and they felt a little wet. The cold seared his lungs, and Cyrus listened carefully but could hear nothing save for the last struggles of the troll to get free of the hedge.

"Well, it would appear that you were not the only one that the hedge wished to see naked," Vaste said, stepping up to join Cyrus and Nyad. "Though I believe it tried harder with me, probably because of my powerful animal magnetism."

Nyad let out a sound of low disgust. "Who would want to see you naked?"

"I think the question you should be asking is, 'Who wouldn't?'" Vaste replied.

"Me," Cyrus said, and heard Vara chorus with him from somewhere through the hedge.

Curatio came through next, and his finger twirled, blazing with Nessalima's light, a spell that shed a pure, white luminescence in the dark. Cyrus watched the healer squeeze through the gap, robes barely touched by the stray thorns and branches.

When Vara's turn came, he saw Curatio dim the spell. The paladin harrumphed as the darkness rose again around them, broken only by Vaste's glowing staff. He pointed it toward the space where Vara was now clawing her way through, her sword out and actively slashing into the hedge, which seemed to be shrinking around her. Cyrus started to move forward to help her but stopped when Curatio's hand caught his arm. By the time he turned enough to see the healer's gentle shake of the head, Vara was through.

"Well, that seemed very difficult for you," Vaste said as Vara brushed broken twigs from her silver armor. "Based on the difficulty you had squeezing through, it would seem that I'm thinner than you."

Cyrus looked from the wide-bodied troll to the thin elven woman in the gleaming armor; a greater contrast between them there could not be. Vara was not only nearly half of Vaste's height, but she was easily half his width.

"More likely the hedge found me to be a tastier and more appealing morsel than you," she said stiffly. "But as I do not allow my private parts to dangle freely beneath a simple robe, it found me a more difficult seduction."

"I don't think I was seduced by it, exactly," Vaste said, feigning pensiveness, "although that would explain the twigs it pushed up my robe when my back was turned—"

"Ahem." Curatio cleared his throat. "If I may suggest we be on about our business?" His tone of voice made it clear he was not suggesting.

Cyrus turned to look left, then right. He'd gotten distracted while the last three had come through the gap in the hedge and had forgotten to check. There was nothing moving to either side, but he would have sworn something was different, that there was a subtle shift in the hedges somehow.

"Oh, look, our path of retreat has disappeared," Nyad said without even a hint of surprise.

"That's all right, I didn't want to go back there anyway," Vaste said. "Damned cold place to stay, and the vegetation was much too grabby for my taste. I like it to take me out for a night on the town before it gets too forward, you know, allow me some time to talk and get to know it—"

"Must you babble ceaselessly?" Vara's voice whipcracked through the darkness, and Cyrus turned to realize that things had moved again. The hedges still seemed roughly the same, but something had shifted. Vara stood in front of him, her back turned. Vaste, Curatio and Nyad stood opposite them, almost ten feet away, facing Cyrus and Vara like game pieces on a board. *Weren't we all standing together a moment ago?*

"Vara, Vaste," Curatio said, "please do stop your quarrel for now." The healer, too, seemed to be watching the hedgerows, and Cyrus had a vague feeling they were closing in on them.

"Does anyone else feel like—" Cyrus began.

"Yes," Curatio interrupted him, and his voice was one of infinite calm. "When we become separated, work your way forward. Always forward, never back. Do not even spare a glance back, save for to look at your comrades." He shifted his piercing gaze to each of them in turn. "Do you understand?"

"Do you think you'll be abandoning us soon, then?" Vaste asked, and Cyrus could hear a change in pitch in the troll's voice.

"We'll be pulled apart soon enough," Curatio said, supremely calm—something Cyrus wished desperately he felt. "Keep your wits about you, fight with everything you have at your disposal, and you'll come out the other side."

"When all else fails, I'll raise my robe and start whacking them with my—" Vaste started.

"SHUT UP!" Vara said. "Do you find this funny? To be trapped in the realm of a goddess gone missing? To be surrounded by ill things and shadows that move when your back is turned? To be faced with very real separation from your comrades so whatever evil lurks here can slowly carve the heart and spirit out of you until it breaks apart the empty shell for its own amusement?"

"No," Vaste said, and there was a very real quiver in his voice. "I don't find it funny. But if I don't at least try to make light of the situation, I'll weep at the thought of potentially losing you all—my friends."

A silence fell over them, and Cyrus exchanged a look with Vara, whose cheeks were flushed red. She averted her eyes after a moment, turning to look toward the hedge.

There was a rustling as the wind kicked up, a powerful gust that shook the walls, blowing branches into the air around Cyrus. The ground shuddered beneath their feet, and Cyrus was nearly knocked to the ground by the force of it. The walls moved, the rows of hedge marching while Cyrus tried to regain his balance. He felt something anchor to his arm and realized it was Vara's gauntlet. He met her gaze as he fell to his knees and she fell beside him.

The realm stopped shaking a moment later. The wind died down. The long, thin corridor that Cyrus had been looking down only moments earlier was now truncated in front of them, an impassable hedge standing where Vaste, Curatio and Nyad had been.

"Curatio!" Vara shouted, dropping her grip on Cyrus's arm and scrambling to her feet. "Nyad! Vaste!" she called into the depths of the bleak hedge, not even a rustle within the thing to indicate that there was anything behind it.

Silence answered her call, silence ... and a sickening feeling that permeated Cyrus's heart.

Chapter 14

She only took a moment to compose herself, Cyrus noted. The smell of rotting greenery was still heavy in the air, and Cyrus wished he could block it by thrusting his gauntlet to his nose. Instead he took a breath through his mouth, and nearly gagged as the smell of rot seemed to become more potent, dancing upon his tongue.

"What now?" she asked, and Cyrus did no more than glance back to see her standing with her head bowed, staring at the hedge.

"Come on," Cyrus said, and he grabbed her by the arm and pulled her forward with his free hand while he drew Praelior with the other. She came without resistance, and he heard her draw her sword with her other hand. "You heard Curatio—we need to move forward and not look back."

"Where do you suppose they went?" Vara asked after they had walked through the hedge for a few minutes. The twists and turns became less obvious, and the hedge began to dissolve into individual trees and patches of brush. The first tree Cyrus was able to distinguish was gnarled, with a trunk twisted as though a windstorm had spun it about at the base, sculpting an upward spiral into the branches as it rose. The bark was hardened as if it had become fossilized, reminding Cyrus of a valley of stone trees he'd seen once in the Northlands.

"I think they're being pushed along, like we are," Cyrus said, and he maintained his grip on her arm. She didn't protest, so he didn't let it go. She was walking along with him, leading as much as he was, and he did not fight her when she turned to adjust their course, nor she him when he did likewise. "Whatever's pulling the strings in this place is trying to separate us. Divide and conquer, I think."

"It's doing a fine job with the first half of that," Vara said. Her tone was only a little brusque.

"Indeed," Cyrus said, and they moved into a wood, the path dissolving before them in a thicket.

They were now in a brambly forest, all the trees as twisted and ugly as the first they'd encountered. It seemed like the woods had crept in around them, marching to encircle them in a moment when they had paid little heed. Cyrus knew they had been walking, had come into it on their own, but it felt different, like it was gradually drawing them in.

Deeper into the dark. Into the depths of it.

"This feels utterly wrong," Vara murmured.

"Without doubt," Cyrus said, feeling her arm stiffen even through the armor.

"I have heard tales of this realm for as long as I can remember," Vara said. "Tales of the great trees that speak to the weary traveler, that love the Mother of Life and her ways, that would answer questions and tell you of the days when they were young and barely more than saplings. This is supposed to be a place of magic, of life, of holiness." Her voice took a harder edge. "To see it perverted into this darkness and gloom is an insult to all who worship the Life Giver."

They walked in silence, the dark, brambly woods quiet around them. The place was shrouded in an eerie calm, and Cyrus tightened his grip on Vara's arm as a fog began to seep in. The air around them became hazy and he stepped closer to Vara, allowed his pauldrons to clink against hers. She, for her part, did not seem to mind.

"So …" Cyrus said after a few more moments of silence. It was beginning to grow unbearable.

"Not now," Vara said as they passed a tree with bark gnarled in such a way that it almost looked like it had a face.

Cyrus looked at her with a frown. "Not now what?"

"Not now for any conversation of depth or emotionalism you might wish to have," she said, not looking at him. Their pace was even, and he had to walk faster than he might have otherwise in order to keep up with her long strides. "I doubt whatever foul evil runs rampant in this realm will allow us the time for a leisurely conversation about the mountain of unresolved emotions we might have built over these last months and years."

"So you do have unresolved emotions for me," Cyrus said with a slight smile.

"If you would be so kind," Vara said searingly, barely turning to look at him, "try not to be an arse."

"That could be difficult," he said, looking into the fog enshrouding the trees ahead. She did not reply.

They walked on, Cyrus uncertain of the direction they were taking. Gnarled, ugly trees continued to seemingly spring up in the middle of the heading he had taken. There was no point of reference in the distance—no light, nothing to break the monotony of the glade.

"This plane is not unruly," Vara said as they steered around the massive trunk of a tree that reminded him of the King's garden in the palace in Pharesia, "it is full-out evil, and darkness drenches every surface of this realm."

"What about the servants?" Cyrus asked and paused. Something just beyond his sight was moving, and he heard it in the brush, rustling.

"I cannot imagine they would escape the touch of whatever is claiming this place for its own," Vara said, her voice full of caution. She stood next to him, eyes fixed in the same direction as his, and he would have sworn he saw her pointed ear twitch.

"What kind of servants would the Goddess of Life employ?" Cyrus asked, feeling his hand tense on the hilt of Praelior. He could see the grass moving now, something shuffling just beyond his sight.

"What you might expect to see in a glen, according to legend," Vara said, every word strained. She watched with him, the anticipation growing taut. "Her land was to be a natural and pure haven for life."

"So—" Cyrus did not get another word out before something burst from the brush in front of him.

Chapter 15

It was a deer—or perhaps had been at one point. Where smooth, brown and white fur might once have been, now was a raven-colored pelt, matted down. It charged at Cyrus, massive pronged antlers pointed directly at him. He did not react in time and one of them caught him in the shoulder and spun him about.

Vara went tilting in the other direction, and Cyrus lost track of her as he hit the ground. He kept his grip on Praelior, wondering how it was possible that some hart bursting from the bushes had been faster than he.

I have my sword in hand. He shook his head, trying to clear it. *That thing is fast.*

Cyrus started to his feet and something hit him squarely in the back, ramming him hard to the ground. Hooves stomped at him, pummeling his backplate and racking him with pain.

He thrust his sword blindly up and hit something. A harsh snort filled his ears, and the dark forest was still. Cyrus rolled and the deer fell from his blade, dead. The black evil that covered it melted with its fall, disappearing like black water draining off onto the ground. It vanished into the earth as Cyrus watched, still down on one knee, leaving the deer's corpse behind.

"Are you all right?" he asked Vara, who stood, a little crooked, just on the other side of the deer.

"I've just been run over by a four-legged animal," she said, and he noticed she was leaning heavily on her sword. "I believe it's broken my shoulder."

Cyrus took a breath and felt a pain in his chest. His exhalation came out as a visible mist in front of him. "Can you fix it?"

He could see her glare from where he stood. "Possibly," she said with a great deal of sarcasm, "if you might find it in your cold and unrelenting taskmaster heart to give me a moment to catch my breath."

He nodded, trying to shift his body to see if he could make the pain subside. "I don't think I'm the one you're going to have to worry about rushing you along. The master of this realm is much harsher than I."

"Bloody hell," she whispered, and a light appeared at the tips of her middle and forefinger on her right hand. It sparkled in reflection on her breastplate, and then she stood straight again. "Yes, well, good enough."

"Okay," Cyrus said, trying to find his bearings. The thicket that the deer had burst from was straight ahead of him, and a slightly less thorny path ran just to the left of that. "This way." She fell in beside him and they went on.

Every step he took was agony, a fire traveling down his side as though someone were jabbing a knife in his back every time his boots hit the ground. After a moment he saw a light in Vara's hand again, and the pain subsided. He gave her a look.

"You should have said something." She glared at him.

"I didn't want to be a bother," he said.

"You're several years too late for that," she muttered, and they went on, into the deepening cold of the woods.

They came to a clearing, and Cyrus emerged from the cover of the trees slowly. It still bore all the signs of the darkness that crept about in the rest of the realm, but a path seemed to cut right through the center of it, worn ground bereft of grass. "Are we fools to follow the path here?" Cyrus asked.

"We were fools to come here at all," Vara said at his side. "Following a path seems to be the least of our sins at this point."

"I was just trying to—" Cyrus began.

"I know," she said, quietly. "You were trying to help. Arydni, this expanded version of Sanctuary you've created, you were trying to help them all." There was something in the way she said it that provoked his interest, made him think there was something she was holding back.

"But?" he asked. He stopped and watched her as she took a couple steps forward without him.

She stopped and her head bowed, the blond hair drooping with her mood. She turned back to him, and when she spoke he could see the reticence melt away. "But ... what we have done of late ... the new men we've adopted from Luukessia? The mercenary way we've pursued payment for service? It's not exactly the Sanctuary of old, is it?" She tilted her head to look at him. "With Alaric gone, we've not really stopped to ask ourselves how far off the path we've strayed. He would not even recognize Sanctuary as it is now."

"We were expanding before he died—" Cyrus said.

"We were roughly five thousand strong on the day he left us," Vara said. She spoke with cool detachment, bereft of the heat of passion he might have expected of her. "We are now more than fifteen thousand strong and have branched out into being an army for hire." She kept her head down, not even meeting his eyes. "I have not protested any of the actions undertaken, because I understand the motives for all of them. However, we are rapidly becoming something other than the Sanctuary of old and are quickly leaving behind the days when we steered the course of our own destinies and were masters of our own fates."

Cyrus listened until he was sure she was finished. "I agree with everything you've said. But I don't know what we could do any differently, other than surrender on upholding our obligations," he lowered his voice, "*My* obligations—to the people of Luukessia."

"We are in an untenable situation," Vara said, even more quietly. "I remain uncertain what can be done to preserve us as we were, other than shirking all these new responsibilities, and that is not the Sanctuary way, either." She shrugged. "But I feel as though we have lost our way, and it pains me." She looked around the clearing, and a leaf blew past her face. "In more ways than one."

"Yeah, well—" Cyrus turned his head at the sound of movement behind him. There was motion again in the darkness, a rustle of grass, and he saw red eyes staring at him from out of the dark. "Aw, hells."

"Yes, more of them," Vara said. Her sword was in her hand. She closed the distance between them and stood at his elbow. Red eyes were appearing all around them, little glowing orbs in the dark. "It would appear that Vidara's servants were plentiful."

"Well, she did run the Realm of Life," Cyrus said, pushing closer to her and placing his back against hers. He heard the clink of his backplate lightly against Vara's and stopped, adopting a fighting stance. "I would have expected she'd know a thing or two about how life is made, and made plentiful."

There was a pause as the red eyes began to grow larger, approaching.

"Was that some crass joke about the Mother of Life being a harlot of some sort?" Vara asked.

"What?" Cyrus whipped his head around. "No. More like an acknowledgment that she held dominion over making these creatures reproduce as quickly as—say, rabbits." He caught a glimpse of her frown. "It's an expression—'breeding like rabbits.' It's what we say when we mean someone is having offspring rapidly." He saw her frown dissipate. "You don't have that expression?"

"Not exactly," Vara said, and her reply was laced with amusement. "In the Elven Kingdom, the closest approximation is, 'breeding like humans.'"

Cyrus gave a dry chuckle and was surprised to hear it echoed lightly by her. "I've rather missed this."

"Indeed," she said, near a whisper. The figures were emerging from the darkness, almost beyond number. They had the same wide bodies, the same pronged antlers, and were covered by the same darkness as the ones that had come before.

"Back to back," Cyrus said. "Like on the bridge in Termina."

"Yes," she agreed, "save there is no friendly line to work our way back to here."

Cyrus looked at the red eyes, the dark creatures emerging from the woods of night. "Then I suppose we'll have to kill them all, won't we?"

"If anyone could do it, I suppose it's us," Vara said, and he could feel her behind him, feel her for the first time in months. Not a cold shadow, but her, truly her. "Why is it always us?"

"I assume we're simply the best there is," Cyrus said. The red eyes were unblinking, and he could feel them readying, preparing to charge.

"And there's the ego," Vara said.

"It could be that we just go looking for more trouble than most," Cyrus conceded.

"We should make a pact to stop that," Vara said, and a furious stomping of hooves nearly blotted out what she said next. "If we survive this."

Cyrus felt a rough anger fill him, a fighting spirit that he'd found again on the Endless Bridge. "I wouldn't worry about that. I'm much too frustrating to die."

"At last, a point upon which we can both agree," Vara said. "But … I am glad it is you here with me."

"Because there's no one else you'd rather have at your side for a fight like this?" Cyrus asked.

She made a *pfft* sound with her lips. "Because I'd rather not have anyone else in Arkaria die in such a damned fool manner."

Cyrus nodded, still smiling, as the line of enemies around him broke into a charge. He backed tight against Vara and readied himself as the beasts came, heads down, at the two of them.

Chapter 16

"We haven't laughed like that in a while," Cyrus said as they walked on. Both of them were caked in blood, and Cyrus was covered in dirt. Vara's shining silver breastplate had a streak of grass staining it where she'd hit the ground during the fight.

The fight with the deer had been long and brutal, but their lives remained in little doubt. The deer failed to penetrate the tight circle held by the two of them, and they had rebuffed every attack until every last one of the creatures had been slaughtered. Cyrus ran a hand up to wipe a cold spot on his forehead, and found a bit of frozen gore stuck to his helm. It was growing progressively colder as they walked.

"You were gone for over a year," Vara said, walking at his side. Her sword was still drawn and tight in her hand. Black blood caked her gauntlet where Cyrus had seen her punch through the chest of a still-living deer, killing it. "And since, you've been—" There was a flash of darkness across her face as she crossed under the branch of a tree.

"Otherwise engaged," Cyrus said quietly.

"I was going to say, 'busy fornicating with a dark elven slattern,' but then I never was good at speaking to your more delicate sensibilities." Her voice didn't carry as hard an edge to it now as he had become accustomed to in council, but it still contained bite aplenty.

"A year is a long time," Cyrus said. "Especially when—"

"You need not explain yourself," Vara said abruptly. "Your time across the bridge was quite a metamorphosis." She seemed to bristle slightly as she said it, her posture changing to bring her more upright and stiff.

"I think some of that change might have happened before I left," Cyrus said, and he hazarded only a slight look across at her as he said it. They walked on in silence.

When they came to another clearing, Cyrus paused on the edge and Vara held position with him. "Do you think the paths are changing to respond to whoever is pulling the strings here?" he asked. The field before them was covered in a dusting of snow, pristine and lacking in any sign of the path, which had disappeared under the layer of snowfall.

"Possibly," she said. "I wouldn't know, having not been here before and being bloody uncertain of exactly what we're dealing with."

"Let's hope there's not an army of deer waiting to ambush us this time," Cyrus said.

"Why? Are you growing weary in your old age?" Vara wore a smirk.

"You're older than me," Cyrus reminded her.

"Yes, but I age with considerably more grace than you," Vara said, still smirking. "I think it's beginning to show."

"I'm not sure how you could tell under all this icy blood I'm apparently wearing on my face," Cyrus said with a slight frown. His fingers brushed his forehead and found dried ichor frozen to his brow. He found more on his cheeks, splattered on in the heat of battle. "Exactly how drenched in entrails am I?"

Vara rolled her eyes and let out a small, amused noise. "Don't let your ego run away from you by presuming anyone is present who cares how you look."

"Well, that's lovely," Cyrus said and started across the field before him. His boots crunched in the snow. The cold was becoming bitter, an aching chill that seeped into him through his plate mail. He reflexively clutched at his armor, clinking his gauntlet against his vambrace. His hot breath came out in a mist in front of him.

He could hear Vara's steps following behind him, the same sound of snow crunching. A flake went past his nose, surprising him. "Oh, great," he muttered, and took his next step.

Something gave out beneath him with a sickening crack, and he thought for a moment he'd fallen down by accident. Then his boot filled with an icy shock of water, and the rest of his armor followed.

Cyrus plunged into the dark water. His vision cut out like he had placed the darkest curtains over his face and the brutally cold water rushed over him. He almost exhaled but couldn't, the frigid water paralyzing any attempt.

Cyrus lost track of which direction was up, and there was no light to guide him. Blackness seeped in all around, and the weight of the water held him down. The cold stole the air from his lungs, and he did not even feel it go. His whole body felt like icy fingers had run over it, crawled over every inch and started to squeeze.

The water rushed into his nose and he had a brief flash of the Temple of Ashea only days earlier. This was different, though, worse somehow. He had Praelior tight in his hand, slowing down the world. *If only I knew which way to go ...*

A light flared somewhere above him, a faint glow, like a lamp someone had set out to show him the way home in the dark of night. He thrust his arms and swam toward it. As he got closer, his vision sharpened in the brutally cold water. A hand was reaching down toward him, reaching for him, sunlit day shining behind them—

He grasped it and felt it pull, yanking him up. His head broke the surface and he found Vara there, prone across the ice. She started to crawl back, clutching his hand in her own, their gauntlets freezing together in the frigid air.

She pulled him onto the flat ice shelf. As the water rushed from his ears he could hear voices, shouts, urgent, coming closer to them from somewhere in the distance. She stared at him as he dripped, and he felt the ice beginning to form on his armor and within it, freezing from exposure to the frigid air. "Well," she said after a moment, "at least you got rid of all that blood on your face that you were whinging about."

He chuckled and stayed prone, as did Vara, and he followed her as she crawled back across the snow-covered ice toward the forest's edge. His armor scraped across the surface, and he heard crackling as it strained under his weight. By unspoken agreement, neither of them stood until they were almost back to the treeline. Vaste, Nyad and Curatio were there waiting for them.

"Fancy meeting you here," Vaste said, almost nonchalant.

"Do you mean freezing to death after this lunkhead nearly drowned himself in a lake?" Vara asked, shivering in the cold, "or do you mean here, as in the Realm of Life in general? Actually, never mind, I don't fancy any of it."

"Looks like you found your way through the hedge maze," Cyrus said, trying to keep his teeth from chattering.

"No," Vaste said, "we're actually all dead and possessed by that same black ichor that's taking over the animal life around here, you just didn't notice because Nyad and Curatio are always so quiet."

"You ran into those too, huh?" Cyrus asked, shuddering from the cold and the memory of the deer. "Nasty bit of local wildlife, those deer."

"Oh, you got deer?" Vaste seemed almost amused. "You lucky devil. We were attacked by an army of squirrels, chipmunks and hedgehogs."

Cyrus exchanged a look with Vara. "That doesn't sound so bad."

"That's because you didn't have to pick a hundred blackened quills out of a troll's arse," Nyad said without amusement.

"I did so appreciate that," Vaste said. "It's not like I could easily reach them myself."

"Here," Nyad said and her staff belched a line of flame at him after a moment, burning through the snow on a nearby shrub and lighting its withered branches on fire.

Cyrus huddled closer to the bush and Vara followed behind. She gave him a reproachful glare. "What?" he asked. "You didn't know it was a pond either. It could easily have been you falling through that ice if you hadn't been so tentative."

"Tentative?" Vara asked, nearly at a screech. "This from the man who epitomizes the old adage about fools rushing in where gods fear to tread."

"Can't blame the gods for avoiding treading around here," Vaste said, "what with the evil hedgehogs and all."

"We shouldn't tarry here too much longer," Curatio said calmly, cutting across any further discussion. "If I recall correctly, our destination is just on the other side of this lake."

"And what awaits at our destination, I wonder?" Vara mused. "Ten thousand badgers possessed by evil? A nest of dark hornets?"

"Bears," Vaste said. When everyone had turned to him, he said, "Well, you have to admit, as far as scary animals go, they're right at the top."

"Hm," Curatio said, and he started to turn to walk around the shore, his hands kept close to his body beneath his robes, "I would have gone with dragons, personally."

There was silence for a moment as the healer began to walk away, and then Nyad spoke. "Dragons? Dark dragons? Oh gods."

They followed along behind Curatio, skirting the edge of the frozen lake. A parting of the trees highlighted a path, and Cyrus watched Curatio follow it wordlessly, leaving footprints behind in the snow with each step.

Soon they came upon two stone pillars; dark grey towers warding either side of the path. Curatio led on, Cyrus and Vara only steps behind him, trying to keep up with the healer. Cyrus cast a look back every few moments to assure himself that both Nyad and Vaste were still behind him. After the sixth time, Vaste began to wave coyly and wink at him each time.

"Still here," Vaste said the next time just before he turned around.

"Of course you are," Vara muttered, "it's not as though you could vanish for very long."

"Did you want me to be gone for longer than last time?" Vaste asked.

There was a supremely long pause, and then Vara quietly said, "No."

Cyrus waited, but Vaste did not say any more on the subject, his large feet leaving wide tracks in the snow.

The forest opened up before them, the snowy ground becoming uneven. It rose up in mounds here and there, then swept forward to a bridge ahead of them. Cyrus walked between the mounds toward the bridge, following Curatio, the cold still chilling his skin, his fingers numb in his gauntlets.

"Not much farther now," Curatio said.

"This looks awfully familiar for some reason," Vaste said, "and I'm fairly certain it's not because I've been to the Realm of Life before."

Curatio halted, stopping in the middle of the path, his head bowed and shadowed. Cyrus could not see the expression on the healer's face but he could see his gloved hand balled into a fist. "Because it looks like the garden behind Sanctuary."

Cyrus blinked, the frosty air in his eyes affecting his ability to see. He surveyed the ground again and realized that Curatio was right. The bridge led over a low spot that might have been water, like the pond on the Sanctuary grounds. The mounds, frozen, bereft of the sweet-smelling petals that dotted the Sanctuary landscape in spring and summer, he now recognized as flower beds.

"It's exact," Cyrus whispered. "Like someone pulled the garden off the Sanctuary grounds and plopped it into the Realm of Life." He looked to Curatio, still turned away. "Is whoever is behind this mucking with the realm? Changing it on us to—"

"No," Curatio said with a shake of his head, then turned to look at the four of them. His eyes were lined, and slightly swollen. "It was always like this here. Other than the snow and darkness, obviously." He looked back toward the bridge as though he were surveying it. "Our garden has always matched this one."

There was a pause before Vaste spoke. "And why exactly would that be?"

Curatio didn't answer at first, taking a few steps forward before a low mutter made itself heard. "Because Alaric made it so."

"Alaric lives on in mysterious spirit if not in fact," Vaste said under his breath, "not only leaving tantalizing mysteries behind, but teaching his successor to half-answer with vagaries that keep us all scratching our heads in wonder."

"Shut up," Vara said.

There was the silence of a fresh snow falling even as the temperature grew colder as they crossed the bridge. Cyrus ran a hand over the railing of the bridge and stared down into the fresh white powder below. He suspected it was as deep as the pond in the Sanctuary garden—only a few feet at most—but it was covered over with snow so thick he could not tell.

"So," Vaste said, creeping up next to Cyrus, "a walk in the woods alone with Vara."

Cyrus felt a strain inside and gave him a sidelong look to match it. "What of it?"

"Was it everything you hoped for?"

Cyrus looked past Vaste to Vara, who, he was sure, was pretending to take no notice of their conversation. She had not worn her helm on the excursion, and he could see her ears were red from the frigid temperatures. "It was cold, frightening at points, and ended with me being soaked in freezing water."

"So ..." Vaste said, "... about like you would expect?"

The snow streamed down now, illuminated by the light from Vaste's staff. Curatio, too, held a hand out and light flared from it as though he held a white fire in his palm. Just beyond where the boundary of the garden would be in Sanctuary stood a circle of tall stones, something strange and out of place about it. They stood at oblong lengths, some pointed and others flat, holding a center of smooth snow that was trampled by only a single set of footprints that Cyrus saw as he and the others crossed into the circle.

"This is it," Curatio said, stopping in the middle next to a footprint that was already becoming covered over by the falling snow. He brushed his shoulder, dislodging the flakes falling there as though it were of no concern to him, and looked up. "This is where Vidara held her court, and it would be where anyone looking to usurp her power would be."

"You will find no usurpers here, Curatio," came a voice from behind a distant stone. It sounded oddly familiar, and a man-shaped figure emerged from behind one of the oblong spires of rock, the one with the set of snowy footprints leading up to it. His steps crunched faintly in the new-fallen snow, and he began to walk toward them.

"Who are you?" Vaste asked, squinting into the dark. He lifted his staff to try and cast illumination at the figure making its way toward them, but it revealed only a dark cloak with a cowl over it.

"One who knows your heart and mind all too well, troll," came the reply.

Cyrus chanced a look at Vara and saw her usually pale face flushed blood red, her sword hand shaking with the rage that she could barely contain. "Are you responsible for the disappearance of the Goddess, you loathsome—"

"I am not, Shelas'akur," came the voice in reply again, and Cyrus recognized it now. The figure crept closer and closer. "I am but a humble intermediary—a messenger if you will—here but to ward those who might step into this wayward realm and send them on their ways." He stopped, and Cyrus could see the outline of the face beneath the cowl now, but the expression was masked in shadow. "I am a sentinel, here to warn—"

"Why don't you just cut out the protestations of your innocence," Curatio said, annoyance cutting through his voice, "as it is doubtful we'll believe them in any case, and get down to delivering whatever message you are here to give ... Gatekeeper?"

Chapter 17

"You have no idea what you have stepped into," the Gatekeeper said in a low drawl. He swept the cowl back off his face and he was obvious now, the same figure that Cyrus had been dealing with for over two years in the Realm of Purgatory.

"I am going to guess we've stepped into an overly dramatic and self-righteous monologue," Vaste said.

"I would have said dung," Vara added, her eyes never leaving the Gatekeeper and her sword still clenched in her hand.

"The fate of gods and men hang in the balance from the events that have transpired in this place—" the Gatekeeper went on.

"I hate it when I'm right," Vaste said then shot Vara an apologetic look. "Well, I suppose we both were."

The Gatekeeper continued, acting as if he hadn't heard either of them, snow falling around him but not seeming to touch him at all, "—this very realm falls into turmoil with the loss of its mistress." He turned to look at Cyrus. "I believe you have seen the results of a realm in turmoil before?"

Cyrus felt a chill beyond the cold, beyond the ice that had formed in his undergarments from his fall in the water. "Will something like what happened in the Realm of Death happen here?" He took a step closer to the smiling Gatekeeper. "Will we see something like the scourge afflict Arkaria because of Vidara's disappearance?"

Quiet hung in the air as the Gatekeeper smiled and looked at each of them one by one. "No witty repartee to that? No banal comments, petty insults? No references to stepping in excrement at the thought of another monstrous tide turned loose—"

"The scourge was kind of like Mortus's excrement, in a way," Vaste said, his voice quiet, almost pensive. "So I could go that route—"

"You insufferable trollish prick," the Gatekeeper said, his cheeks now flushed. He made a motion and Curatio held up a hand as if to stay him. He looked through slitted eyes from Vaste to Curatio, and his smile returned, though only faintly. "Fine, then. We'll just keep things pleasant."

"If so, then you'll need to leave—" Vaste started, but Curatio held a hand out to him as well. The healer did not even turn to look at the troll, merely made a gesture, and Vaste fell silent, though he made his displeasure clear by sticking his tongue out at the Gatekeeper.

"Go on," Curatio said. "Say your piece."

"The Goddess is gone," the Gatekeeper said, his smile now thin. "This brings consequences to the Realm of Life." He waved a hand around the circle of stones that surrounded them. "Some of them are already apparent. The warmth of life is fading, and this land is experiencing a winter that will leave it a wasteland more frigid than your paladin's heart and nethers," he made a slight gesture at Vara. "More empty and inhospitable than the space betwixt your troll's ears," he said, and pointed to Vaste, "and more lifeless than your own kingdom will be in a thousand years," he said, turning to Nyad. With each insult, his smile grew broader. He turned to Cyrus and said nothing, merely stared.

After a moment, Cyrus spoke. "No insult for me?"

"I need not insult you, Lord Davidon of Perdamun," the Gatekeeper said without expression, his face reduced to an enigma once more, "as your own running of your life is insult enough. Your own choices insult you, make you a trollop among men, unsuitable for the attentions of the woman who you would have had if you'd shown just a little more restraint." He shook his head slowly. "No, I need not insult you, for the purpose of insult is to cause pain, and your own decisions continue to reap more agony into your life than ever I could sow with my humble words."

"Is there anything else you would have us know about the disappearance of Vidara?" Curatio asked, squelching Cyrus's reply before he could think of one to make.

The Gatekeeper paused, and his face showed a hint of discomfort, pursed lips puckered. "I am the Hand of the Gods," he said. "I am their servant, their steward and their herald." He looked from Curatio to Cyrus. "I am possessed of more power than any adventurer, given a fraction of the godhood myself, power enough to kill an entire guild eighteen times over."

"Liar," Vaste coughed.

A searing look shot from the Gatekeeper to Vaste, but he spoke without acknowledging the insult. "With all my power, I still cannot rein in what has been done to this realm." He stepped closer to Curatio. "What has been *done* ... to this realm. This is no accident. Seeds have been sown here in the absence of the Goddess, seeds of ... something." He looked to Cyrus, and his expression quivered with a slight smirk turning up a corner of his mouth. "The thing about planting seeds is that eventually, someone will be along to harvest them."

"So someone did do this to the realm," Curatio said, taking in the darkness and snow that surrounded them. "Someone took her. And someone is steering the course of this place, the portals—"

"I am steering the course of the portals," the Gatekeeper said, his eyes wide and a slight anger evident. "It was I who locked your guild out so that you could brave this wilding realm on your own. So that you could test your mettle against the things that are starting to grow here, see if you were worthy of even the little knowledge I had to offer." His sneer smoldered. "You are, for now."

"You really haven't told us anything, of course," Vaste said, and Curatio did not bother to even try to quiet him. "Just made vague allusions to something corrupting this realm while Vidara is gone and then told us you were using us as your personal playthings to deal with them." Vaste took a step forward. "What's wrong, Gatekeeper? Didn't want to face the squirrels on your own? I mean, I can understand, I suppose, as they did leap up my robes and attempt to bite me on the—"

"I have no difficulty with the squirrels," the Gatekeeper said coldly.

"I would say not, being as you are probably hung like they are and thus they'd have to jump very high indeed to inflict any pain on you—"

"Enough," the Gatekeeper said and turned back in the direction he had come from. A faint glow appeared, something ovoid and orange, barely visible through the growing blizzard. "This portal will lead you back to the tunnels under Reikonos. Begone with your frivolity." The Gatekeeper lifted his cowl and covered his head once more, beginning a trek through the snow toward one of the stone pillars surrounding them.

"Gatekeeper!" Curatio called and waited for the Hand of the Gods to turn around. "Why not just dissolve the barrier that prevents us from teleporting out of the Realm of Life?"

The Gatekeeper's face was almost unreadable as the storm around them worsened, the winds picking up into a howl louder than any druid's spell. "Alas," he said at last, "I cannot do this thing. It is beyond my power." He adjusted his cowl, letting it fall lower over his eyes. "But you already knew that, did you not … Curatio?"

"I suspected," Curatio said, and Cyrus could see a glimmer in his eye. "Thank you for confirming it."

The Gatekeeper said no more, merely turned away from them again and resumed his course, trudging through the rising snow. He waved them away, toward the faint glow in the distance.

"Is that the portal?" Vaste asked, starting toward it. "Should we actually head in the direction he's suggesting? Because I have my doubts about trusting—"

"It is the portal," Curatio said, turning toward it and beginning to walk. He shouted back over his shoulder to be heard over the rising fury of the blizzard that had swept down upon them. "And we should by all means go through it, unless you wish to spend the rest of your days as a frozen statue here in this inhospitable hell!" Cyrus could tell he was shouting, but his words were all but lost to the winds.

They moved forward at a steady, hurried pace. The snow was deepening, and Nyad was buried up to her thighs with every step as they passed beyond the border of the stones. The frigid chill was taking its toll on Cyrus, and he could feel the ice crystals forming in his nose hairs and on the days of stubble he carried on his upper lip.

Vaste was leading the way now, his long strides unhampered by the snows ensnaring the rest of them. Vara leapt high into the air and landed just in front of the portal. Cyrus could see her outline against the orange glow, her silhouette reminding him of the first time they'd met, in fire caves with a similar cast.

"Come on!" Curatio shouted as he cut through the snow a few dozen paces behind Vaste. The troll reached the portal next and waited beside Vara, holding position.

"I ... I can't ..." Nyad whispered, her teeth chattering. They were still twenty feet from the portal at least, and the joints of Cyrus's armor were beginning to freeze.

"Come on," Cyrus said. He picked her up in his arms, maintaining his grip on Praelior. He felt her slump in his grasp, go limp under her thin robes, and he took care to make certain her staff did not fall from her hand as he tried to cross the last few feet to the portal.

I don't think I've ever been colder. What is happening to this place? Cyrus could feel ice creeping up in chunks around the joints of his armor, breaking apart with every movement. His skin burned from where the water had frozen solid to it under his metal plating, as well as in his boots. He had little feeling in his hands, and the rushing of the wind around him blotted out any other noise that might be made by the others as he took long, lurching steps to follow Curatio up to the portal.

Vara, Vaste and Curatio were just black shadows against the orange of the portal's glow, nearly blotted out by the furious snowfall. It was coming down sideways, and Cyrus's eyes ached as he forced them to stay open. He chanced a glance at Nyad. Her skin was white as the snow, her lips blue like the seas when he had been on the ship only days earlier. *Or was it weeks? A lifetime ago, perhaps, when I felt that warm?*

Cyrus stumbled up to the portal and saw Curatio blur and disappear within its bounds, his figure distorting as he vanished. He felt strong arms at his back—Vara's gauntlet landed on one of his shoulders and Vaste's on the other. They pushed and he fell through. He could feel their touch as he watched Nyad's face twist with the energy of the portal. The freezing, aching sensation held to his skin, though, as the world spiraled around him and finally flashed white.

Chapter 18

Cyrus fell upon the hard ground, the scent of musty air surrounded him. There was a sudden pressure as Vara's armor hit his then rolled off, and then Vaste landed on him and failed to move. There was a loud clink of metal boots and other footsteps around him, and shouting began to fill the air.

"Get off!" Cyrus grunted.

"Oh, simmer down," Vaste said, his voice weak but audible over the sound of the Army of Sanctuary. Cyrus looked up to see them all there, in formation, watching. The cold still permeated Cyrus, though the air was lovely and warm compared to what he'd just come out of. "I'm a little frozen here. Give me a moment to thaw."

Cyrus strained and pushed himself up, throwing Vaste off his back. "You're crushing Nyad!" He stared down at the wizard, whose lips were still blue, her hair and eyebrows crusted with ice. "Is everyone all right?" Cyrus looked around.

"Let me take a look at her." Arydni was in front of him, kneeling next to Nyad, her dark hair cascading over her shoulders. She wore her full robes, and he saw them collect dust from the chamber floor as she knelt. "Goddess, she's frozen!" Arydni ran a hand over Nyad's face then looked up at Cyrus. "And you—what happened!"

"The Gatekeeper," Vara said, drawing Cyrus's gaze to where she now stood behind him. Her armor was dripping, the ice that had accumulated upon it beginning to melt. Cyrus watched as droplets of water traced their way down her breastplate to drip off the hard edges of her armor. "He happened."

"It was not his fault," Curatio said, and Cyrus realized suddenly that the healer was standing in front of him but off a little ways, his white robes sodden with melting snow. "He is quite correct, that realm is being affected by other forces."

"Yes, the hedgehogs and chipmunks convinced me of that," Vaste said, and Cyrus looked back to see the troll get to his feet. His green face was a lighter shade, the usually dark green skin tone closer to a yellow. "The question is, what is causing it?"

Curatio shook his head. "Honestly, any one of the gods possesses the power to do what has been done there."

Arydni looked around at the healer, and her eyes narrowed. "But would any of the gods in particular do this?"

Curatio stared back at her, pondering, and then looked away. "I do not know. Mortus would have been the most likely candidate, but ... keep in mind that a god abducting a god is not a common thing. Vidara is hardly helpless girl. The Goddess is a fierce fighter when provoked, more than able to defend herself." Curatio shook his head. "I have a hard time imagining any of the gods removing her from her realm forcibly, even if they were of a mind to."

"Yet she is gone," Arydni said, and she turned her focus back on Nyad. "How would you explain that?"

"I cannot," Curatio said and turned away, his robes leaving streaked water trails on the dusty ground.

"General," Odellan said, stepping forth and jarring Cyrus out of his focus on the conversation, his sword and shield in hand. "Are we going into the portal, sir?"

Cyrus thought about it for a second. "No, our excursion is done."

Odellan nodded and pulled the winged helm of the Termina Guard off his head. His expression was tentative, mouth a thin line. "Permission to send the army back to Sanctuary? I hate to have us linger here if there's no action to be had."

Cyrus nodded. "So ordered." He glanced at Arydni. "Would you mind seeing to her care?" He gestured to Nyad.

"She'll be fine," Arydni said, looking up from the wizard's side. "She needs the warmth of a hearth for a time, to have the ice and water dried from her, and some good hot tea, I think."

Cyrus looked back to Vaste then Vara. "Are you both all right?"

"My genitals have retracted inside me from the cold," Vaste said. "They're so far up there I think I probably look like you at this point."

Cyrus raised an eyebrow. "Oh, right," Vaste said, "forgot who I was talking to. Yours are always deployed nowadays."

Cyrus felt the slight burn on his cheeks as he looked to Vara. Her eyes were fixed in a thousand-yard gaze. "Are you all right?" he asked.

Her eyelids fluttered and she seemed to come back to herself. "I shall be fine."

Cyrus turned around to look at Curatio. "And you—"

"I'm fine," Curatio said, waving him off. "Though I must return to Sanctuary. I have a considerable number of matters to attend to, as well as some research to undertake when time permits."

"Research?" Vaste asked, and Cyrus could see the troll's mouth curve down, his enormous teeth still sticking out of his lips. "What sort of research could you possibly be doing about this?"

Curatio sighed, and the healer's face slackened. "I'm going to read some of my old journals, if you must know." His neck straightened, and he cast an annoyed look at Vaste. "When you get to be seven or eight thousand years old, you realize that you can't remember everything and start to write down as much as possible so you'll have it available when necessary."

Vaste's mouth became a thin line, punctuated only by his two largest teeth. "Somehow, I don't think I'll live long enough to have that problem."

Curatio's eyebrows raised and his shoulders rose with them. "No, at the rate you go around insulting powerful beings, I expect you'll be dead within the year."

Vaste sighed. "I just can't help it. My mother always said that my mouth would be the death of me."

"She was probably referring to your diet," Vara muttered. "Eating an entire pig at a sitting cannot be healthy."

"But it tastes so good," Vaste said, a hand rubbing his ample belly.

"Odellan, have a wizard teleport the army back to Sanctuary," Cyrus said, shaking his head. "I'll need another wizard to teleport me to the Wardemos portal near the River Perda."

"Right," Odellan said with a crisp nod. "I need a volunteer—a wizard to accompany the general," he called out over the front rank of spell casters."

"I'll go," came a calm voice. A woman pushed her way to the front, wearing grey robes with a white vestment around her neck bearing the runes of a wizard. She also wore a pointed hat that was unlike anything Cyrus had seen on a wizard—or anyone else, for that matter.

"All right, Verity," Odellan said. "I'll need someone to teleport the rest of us to—"

"Hang on," Verity said, adjusting her hat. Her fingers glowed and there was a flash as blue light filled the tunnel dome. Glowing blue orbs appeared in front of every person in the room, like circular balls of cerulean flame. They hovered in place, roughly a foot from Cyrus's mouth, and he stared at it as members of his army began to disappear in flashes of light.

Cyrus felt a rough hand on his shoulder, felt water fall on his neck as he turned. Vaste stood looking down on him. "Be careful."

Cyrus frowned at him. "That seems an odd thing for you to say."

"Well," Vaste said, straightening up, the yellow flecks in his irises seeming a bit warmer than usual to Cyrus, "you know how I worry."

"I'll be gone a few more days," Cyrus said with a perfunctory nod. "Hopefully Martaina will have found some sign of the Daring by now."

"Just keep in mind," Vaste said, drawing up to his full height, "that anything that can cause one guild army to disappear," his hand came up to clutch at the glowing orb hanging in the air in front of him, "could cause another to disappear as well." The troll's massive green hand disappeared in a burst of blue energy that caused Cyrus to squint his eyes. As the light from Vaste's passage faded, he turned to catch a glimpse of Vara, still standing in front of the portal, which was now dark.

She stood, her armor's gleam faded now that it was wet and dripping. Her ponytail was limp with dampness, and her pale face was drawn, almost tired-looking.

"Are you going to tell me to be safe as well?" Cyrus asked. There were flashes around him as the last of the army vanished in the magical ether that would carry them home.

"I don't think I will be so trite as that," Vara said, and her voice dragged like she had a great weight on her. "And you would not heed such advice in any case."

"True enough," Cyrus said, and tried to force a smile. He knew by the feel of it that it came out wan at best. Feelings crawled through him, and he tried to push them down. A black coldness settled in on his heart as if he had brought something back with him from the Realm of Life, and his stomach churned as he looked at her.

"Fare well," Vara said, and she looked away abruptly. Her hand reached out and took hold of the orb, disappearing into a burst of spell energy. The chamber around him was silent, all others gone, and Cyrus turned to find the wizard, Verity, standing at his back, her arms folded under her grey cloak.

"That was painfully awkward," Verity said. She raised her hand, a smooth, polished blackwood staff with a dark crystal affixed to the top of it clutched in her fingers. "Come along, then. Teleport to the portal of Wardemos, coming up—"

"Hold," Cyrus said, lifting a hand. "I need to retrieve my horse—and Nyad's—from my old guildhall in the slums. He turned toward the arched entry in the far wall and started toward it, his boots sloshing with every step.

"No, you hold it," Verity said, and Cyrus felt a strong hand grasp his gauntlet. He looked back to see the wizard staring up at him from beneath her hat's brim. "Why walk when you can fly?" She wore a slight smile, and her fingers were sparkling already. "Reikonos Square, coming right up."

The light of magic burned around Cyrus's eyes, and he felt the world shift around him, sparkling and exploding, blinding him as the spell carried him onward.

Chapter 19

The world began to come into focus around Cyrus, bright sky hanging in the air above him. The blue of the heavens above was nearly blinding. A moment earlier he had been standing with Verity in the slums, holding Windrider's reins while the wizard held those of Nyad's horse, the dark, shadowed canyon slums blotting out most of the light. *I could get used to having a wizard teleport me around*, Cyrus had thought. *Much easier than walking back to the old Kings' guildhall to retrieve the horses.*

As the world resolved into focus around him, Cyrus saw the great, open sky above, replacing the tall shanties and woodwork buildings that blotted out any view of the sun above.

He took note of something else as well—he was utterly surrounded by men with swords and spears, all of which were pointed at him.

"This is a lovely thing to wander into," Verity said disapprovingly from behind him.

"Well, if it is not the General of Sanctuary, Cyrus Davidon," came a voice from Cyrus's right. He turned his head to look and saw a man in the uniform of the Reikonos Militia, a black tabard with a horse's head on it denoting his unit. Cyrus recognized it as the Lyrus Guards, a horsed cavalry regiment that he'd come across once before. The man who spoke was also familiar to Cyrus, though his helm revealed only the center of his face. A new scar on the man's upper lip left a pale line through the black stubble of his beard's growth and made his sneer look especially puckered.

"If it isn't the resident jackass of Reikonos, Rhane Ermoc," Cyrus returned. "I see you've acquired a new scar since last we met; you should take care to be less aggressive with your fork at mealtimes. The food isn't going to run away if you take your time eating it, after all." Cyrus kept his hand on the grip of Praelior but relaxed. He could feel the power of it coursing through him as he surveyed the small army that kept their weapons aimed at him and Verity.

"Most people would perhaps not insult the man in charge of those pointing sharp objects at us," Verity said in a low mutter.

"This is why I'm the General," Cyrus replied.

"You're going to get me killed," Verity breathed.

"I've got this under control," Cyrus said under his breath. "Rhane Ermoc," he said, raising his voice, "is there some reason your army is pointing their weapons at my wizard friend and I?" He caught a dirty look from Verity. "Companion." The look did not soften. "This poor, unfortunate, random wizard whom I paid to bring me here."

"We handle all threats to the Confederation in such a manner." The smugness oozed off of Ermoc, just as it had when last Cyrus had met him.

"I'm a threat to the Confederation, am I?" Cyrus said with a nod. "I'm flattered, I think. I hadn't received word from the Council of Twelve that they considered me such." He smirked and looked back at Verity, who was shaking her head like a mother chastising her child. "Again," Cyrus conceded. "Because we proved our way out of the last one that you delivered, you know."

"You may fool the Council of Twelve," Ermoc said with that same smugness, but the smile vanished from his lips, "but you don't fool me. You continue to grow an army down in the Plains of Perdamun—"

"Which was rather useful in repelling a large and aggressive dark elven host a few months ago," Cyrus said dryly.

"—unwatched and unchecked," Ermoc said, his dark eyes narrowed. "Now I hear you've made inroads into elven territory, establishing a village in the south of their Kingdom."

"It's not mine," Cyrus said with a light shrug. "But some of my people do live there."

"Indeed," Ermoc said, and his face twisted into a sneer that made his stubbly face look even crueler. "If one didn't know better, one would think you were building an empire."

"And since you don't know anything, let alone anything that could be classified as 'better,'" Cyrus said with a slow, weary exhalation, "you of course are one of those ones that think I'm building an empire." He raised a mailed finger. "Leave aside the fact that I'm not the Guildmaster of Sanctuary—"

"A trifling detail," Ermoc said, "for you are the General and control the army."

"—and I don't have any control over the town of Emerald Fields of which you speak," Cyrus said, going on.

"A blatant land grab," Ermoc pronounced. Cyrus listened but heard nothing from any of the soldiers in Ermoc's army.

"Yes," Cyrus said, "a blatant land grab—of territory given to us by the King of the Elves." He slowly nodded, layering on the sarcasm. "Indeed, we were too clever for him by half, prying those acres out of his reluctant fingers." Cyrus clinked his thumb and forefinger together in as close to an approximation of a snap as he could with his gauntlet on. "Oh, wait, he gave that land to our people freely and without us asking. We must be truly impressive enchanters to pull that feat off."

Ermoc stared at him as a cloud, the bottom shadowed and grey, rolled overhead. "Indeed. You do have enchanters aplenty."

Cyrus restrained his eyeroll. "Are you going to sit here and bluster at me all day, Ermoc, or am I free to go?"

Ermoc shifted his gaze left, then right, to the men that surrounded Cyrus. Cyrus's eyes followed and saw humans with stubble and beards that told him they had been here on the edges for some time. Their eyes were clear and filled to brimming with anger. He saw squinting, narrowing, mouths twisted.

They're looking for an excuse to fight, something they haven't seen here on the far end of the Confederation. They wish for a part of the war. He held tight to Praelior. *If I have to, I can give it to them—all of them—in more volume than an army of dark elves.* He estimated their number at less than a hundred and wondered if there were more in Wardemos, garrisoned in the town.

"You may pass," Ermoc finally said, his voice low and filled with loathing. "I shall be keeping watch on you, in case any convoys go missing."

"No, that was the goblins," Cyrus said, urging Windrider forward. "I'm not surprised that you missed that detail, though, busy as you were hurling a helpless, armless one off the Citadel at the time." He kept an eye fixed on Ermoc as he went by. "I did hear a guild went missing out here, though."

Ermoc stared back at him as though he'd just made a bland pronouncement about the weather. "Is that so?"

"It's so," Cyrus said, steering through the small corridor of men on horseback that were moving aside for him and Verity to pass. "Since this area is presumably your responsibility, shouldn't you know if Confederation forces are going missing within its bounds?"

"I know naught of what you speak," Ermoc said and threw a hand out to dismiss him. "I am charged with this portal, not the disposition of forces in the western Confederation. Leave me to my assigned duty and annoy someone else with your troublesome inquiries."

"Yeah," Cyrus said as Windrider carried him past the edge of the ring of soldiers surrounding the portal, "I think I'll go find someone who has some answers. Maybe I could try the local whorehouse; they're bound to be better informed than you, Ermoc." He kept on, listening to the silence behind him as Windrider's hooves thumped against the dusty ground. "Better disposition, too, though that much is obvious."

Verity waited until they'd ridden east for almost five minutes before she said anything. "That was reckless. They could have killed us."

"They could have tried," Cyrus said with a grunt. "And they wouldn't be the first today, either, or the strongest." The sun was shining overhead, beating down on him. It was a marked contrast to what he'd felt in the Realm of Life. He could feel the ire rattling through his bones as Windrider bore him along.

"They could have done it," Verity said, shaking her head. Her pointed grey hat shook with her. "Your arrogance was rumored, and now I've seen it. Humans." She said the last bit with more than a little umbrage.

"What?" Cyrus said then traced the brim of her hat to peer at her ears. "Ohhh." He saw the point now, the top of her ear arching up. "You're an elf."

"Quick study, you are," Verity said. "No last name, pointed ears. Took you nearly an hour to suss that out."

"If I'd gone by attitude, I'm sure I'd have gotten it quicker," Cyrus said airily, "but my mind was on other things."

"You have problems with elves, General Davidon?" Verity asked. Cyrus saw her eyebrow stretch up under the hat brim.

"I have had *some* problems with *some* elves," Cyrus said. "I don't have problems with all elves."

"You know why you have problems with some elves?" The wizard asked, turning to face the road again.

"No, but I'd bet five hundred gold pieces you're about to tell me."

"You're impetuous, like humans are," Verity said, "and we older elves are wise enough to call bullshit on it."

Cyrus chuckled. "I've met a few humans willing to do that, too, and more than a few elves who don't call me on it." He thought about it for a second. "Also, the elf most likely to call me on it is only a year older than I am, so it's probably not much to do with age."

Verity remained silent for a moment. "You speak of the shelas'akur."

"The very one." Cyrus almost sighed from weariness, not longing.

"You have a strange relationship with her," Verity said after a moment. She still did not look over at Cyrus.

"You don't say."

"Always the sarcasm," Verity said, "as though you don't want to have a civilized conversation. Do you have a problem with people criticizing your decisions?"

"I don't love it," Cyrus said and looked sideways at her. "I don't know anyone who enjoys having their decisions criticized, do you?"

"Having your actions examined is a part of life," Verity said. "Expecting no one to ever question you is a very dim view for a leader to take. Especially one who has some fifteen thousand people following him."

"I'm not a l ..." Cyrus caught himself before finishing the statement, and he looked to Verity to find her in the midst of a very small smile, filled with utter self-satisfaction.

"You were about to say you're not a leader," she said, still smiling in that self-satisfied way.

"I'm not *the* leader," Cyrus said. "The guild is not in my charge except in a raid."

"Hem!" she said, and it sounded like a grunt to his ears. "If you can find another person that Sanctuary looks to in greater number—"

"Curatio," Cyrus said, not even bothering to let her finish. He steered Windrider along the rutted road, the ground made hard by days of sun and little rain. Dust followed from every step the horses made, and Cyrus's eyes swept the flat land of the horizon as they headed east.

"In name, he is leader," Verity said, her lips twisted at the end. "But leadership is more than a title."

"That's nice," Cyrus said. *This is a pointless conversation.*

She held her tongue for almost an hour before speaking again. During that time Cyrus felt oddly at peace with himself.

"You and the shelas'akur," Verity began, speaking slowly.

Cyrus braced himself, felt his muscles tense. "Yes?"

"You have known each other for some time," Verity said. Cyrus looked at her, but she did not return his gaze.

"A few years." He sniffed the air, caught the scent of horse, and the faint smell of the plains air with its mixture of dust and drying fields.

"Only a few?" Verity asked.

"Four years, I think," Cyrus said. "Of course I was gone for over a year in there."

Verity took a long moment before she next spoke. "Curious."

Cyrus thought about snorting, about losing his patience with the wizard and her odd and nosy manner. "What is curious?" he asked instead, being as patient as he could.

"I have seen the two of you exchange more in a look than most can in a life," Verity said, and her every word came slow like rich cream poured over dried oat cereal. She glanced over at him and her face was open for once, regarding him with clear interest. "I say it is curious because it is close to a phenomenon we elves call 'covekan.' It is—"

"I know what covekan is," Cyrus said quickly.

"Do you?" Verity said. "Do you, truly?"

"I know it takes something along the lines of a century to form that sort of bond," Cyrus said, letting his eyes fall along the flat horizon, taking in the occasional tree far in the distance. He could see some woods, but they were far off; it was miserable ground for any sort of ambush. "I know it's a closeness that elves share with each other that a human could never ..." He let his words trail off, felt the emotion well within him and suppressed it. "... never experience. Not at that depth."

"Indeed," Verity said with a nod. "That is a passable explanation, given by one who has clearly never experienced it himself." She sat up straighter in the saddle, and Cyrus suddenly felt as though he were being lectured by a teacher in one of the classrooms at the Society of Arms once more. "Being covekan is not as much about time as bond. It is about reactions. It is about communication—not the verbal but the instinctive, the subtextual. Body language and movement, the encapsulation of one person's thoughts and being able to read them as though they were a volume you picked up off the shelf. No difficulty in understanding them."

"Well," Cyrus said, "I don't quite know what you're getting at, because it's abundantly clear to me that I never know exactly what Vara is thinking."

"That is the curious thing, isn't it?" Verity said, nodding sagely. "I think it strange because the only time when I see the two of you share such a bond ... is when marching into some fight or another." She nodded again and pursed her lips. "Isn't that odd?"

"Yes," Cyrus said and licked his dry lips. "Most odd, indeed." And it was, he had to concede, as he rode east on his horse, thinking of little else but that for the rest of the day.

Chapter 20

It was after sundown when Cyrus heard them approaching. He and Verity had stopped in a small glade a half-day's ride from the portal at Wardemos. The scent of the trees was in the air, and there was no need for fire in the early autumn night, so they did not build one. Verity conjured them a simple feast of bread and water, and Cyrus ate it quietly while listening to the sounds of the forest in between bites.

"Hear that?" Verity asked him, her grey pointed hat laid aside along with her staff.

"No," Cyrus said, pausing to listen. After a moment he caught a faint whisper of something in the distance.

"I believe that's your army," she said. Her hair was long and light brown like dark straw and just as brittle looking.

"As you're a member of Sanctuary, it would be your army as well," Cyrus said, taking another piece of the soft bread out of the middle of the loaf. The yeasty flavor was blander than the fresh offerings made by Larana in the Sanctuary ovens, but it was hardly the worst thing he'd eaten. By comparison to some of the conjured breads other wizards had made, Verity's was considerably better in his opinion, and he told her so.

"Age and experience," she replied crisply, but with a hint—he thought—of pride.

The approach of the horses took some time, and in that interval Cyrus waited silently with Verity, chewing his bread with as little noise as possible. He suspected it would not take long, and he was not disappointed.

"There you are." Martaina's voice came from out of the shrubs to his right, and Cyrus turned his head in mild surprise. All the noise had come from the opposite direction.

"You really are quite a wonder, aren't you?" Cyrus said, lounging on his bedroll.

"Nice of you to finally take notice," Martaina said, striding into the campsite. Verity acknowledged her with a tip of the hat. Martaina nodded her head quickly to the wizard with—if Cyrus was not mistaken—just a hint of unease.

"I've always noticed," Cyrus said with a shrug as he moved. His armor groaned as he shifted his weight. "I just so rarely say anything because I assume you've heard it all before."

"A compliment withheld is like meat stored away for later; it sours before you get any use out of it," Verity said sagely.

"Much like over-opinionated wizards, in my experience," Cyrus said dryly.

"We've found signs of an ambush," Martaina said, cutting off any further repartee. Cyrus sat upright in his bedroll, all his levity gone. "A few miles east, off a side road."

"Any signs of life?" Cyrus asked, watching her attentively.

"No," Martaina said, shaking her head, her hair carefully bound in a long ponytail behind her, "but neither is there sign of death."

"And the perpetrator?" Cyrus asked, trying to study her face. It gave away little.

"I decline to say," Martaina replied, and Cyrus could see she was holding something back by the tentative way she answered. "You should see for yourself."

"Let's go," Cyrus said, dragging himself to standing and quickly rolling up his bedroll. He pushed the bread into his mouth before he did so, biting on the heel of it to keep it from dropping as he began to roll up the soft cloth.

They saddled up and were ready to ride in minutes, Verity grumbling all the way about the disruption to her supper. They headed east into the crisp night air, no breeze but the one that came in their wake to stir the leaves of the trees. The sky was black without a hint of a moon, and Cyrus followed Martaina closely, a spell that Verity had cast upon him the only thing that allowed him to see.

Only the hint of flat plains was visible to him as he rode on, clouds above shrouding the stars but for small points of light here and there. He was surrounded by nearly a hundred men and women of the army; the rest waited somewhere ahead. A tingle ran over him as he cinched his traveling cloak tighter around him. *Shouldn't have left this with Windrider when I went into the Realm of Life.*

"You're shivering," Verity said from next to him.

"Still recovering from my icicle experience earlier today," Cyrus replied.

"Icicle experience?" Martaina said, looking back at him as she spoke. "I thought you were going to the Realm of Life? You know, lush green fields and forests teeming with happy squirrels."

"According to Vaste," Cyrus said, "the squirrels are just not that happy anymore. And the realm has taken a chill." He tugged at the cloak, making sure it was still tight around him. "Quite a chill."

They rode for nearly an hour before Cyrus saw torches burning in the distance. They came upon a host, a portion of the search party holding fast at a muddy crossroad. A faded path went north and disappeared out of Cyrus's sight.

"This way," Martaina said, and they rode north, the horses' hoofbeats against the wet ground still echoing in the night.

There was less of an interval this time, and soon enough they entered a moonlit glade, a small wood where the road bent its way through thick old oaks and maples that had grown for centuries on the soils of the northern plains. Martaina held up a hand to stay them as they drew closer to countless torches, the remainder of the army.

"Do you know what we'll find here?" Martaina asked, turning back to look at him, her green cloak and brown hair both almost black with the lack of light. Her eyes were moving in the darkness, but he could scarcely see them, and they looked like pools of shadow.

"Are you playing a game of riddles with me, woman?" Cyrus asked. "How would I know what we're going to find? You told me you'd found a site of an ambush and little else."

"You didn't ask for anything else," Martaina said, her eyes still in shadow.

"I assumed we'd find some suggestion of who might be responsible," Cyrus said with a hint of impatience.

"What made you think that?" Martaina asked. Her face did not move from its stony facade.

"Your expressive personality," Cyrus said, and dismounted. "Show me what you would have me see."

She shook her head from the back of her horse. "What I would have you see is so obvious that even your eyes could not fail to miss it here in the dark." She nodded her head. "Go and look for yourself."

Cyrus let out a muttered sound of irritation and did as he was bidden. He felt the ground give with each step. It was not quite mud, but nor was it dry, packed soil. It had seen rain enough to be loose, and sun enough not to be sodden. He squinted his eyes and looked at the road. There were ruts from the passage of wagons visible to his eyes, a thousand dimples where feet or hooves had trod, small enough he could place a hand within them if he knelt down to do so. Sprinkled throughout, though, were larger craters.

Cyrus frowned, his brow drawing down as he took a step forward. Here was another crater, and another, large enough to swallow his own footprints whole with some room to spare. He looked down, staring into the dark, sunken impression, trying to see what mystery he could untangle from a place where something—someone—had stepped.

He knelt, furrowing his brow as he studied it. The spell upon his eyes helped illuminate the indentation as he grew closer to the ground. It was large indeed, larger than his foot, larger than a horse hoof. It was elongated, not like the pad of an animal but more like the heel-to-toe arrangement of a being that walked upright. Like a dark elf.

"This is too large to be a dark elf's footprint," Cyrus muttered to himself.

"Tell me something I don't know," he heard Erith say in the darkness. "Honestly. Go blaming my kind for everything ..."

Cyrus leaned closer, and the shadows receded from the bottom of the small crater. There were obvious details now—a massive heel, the forward pads of a foot and individual toes, each punctuated by—

"Claws," Cyrus said, staring into the footprint before him. "They have claws."

"Well, you're not the world's worst tracker," Martaina said, still on horseback, "but I wouldn't want you searching after me if I'd been taken." He glanced up at her and she looked back at him. "So, they have claws. Claws and great, mighty feet. What conclusion would you draw from that?"

Cyrus stood, the joints of his armor scraping against each other, making a little cry in the night. He looked east, feeling the burning in his blood that raged against the cool night air. *Somewhere out there*, he thought. *Out of the swamps and—*

"Well?" Martaina asked, breaking his thought cleanly off. "Out with it. What do you think?"

"You know what I think," Cyrus said, in a voice so low that he knew only her being an elf would allow her to hear. "You know damned well what we're dealing with. What ... got them.

"Trolls."

Chapter 21

"Troll ... slavers?" J'anda's polite, cultured voice was only lightly salted with disbelief. *No*, Cyrus thought, *not disbelief. More like skepticism.* "Trolls slavers have not operated in the Human Confederations since—"

"Since the war," Cyrus said. The Council Chambers were roaring with fire once more, the hearths burning and giving off a pleasant warmth and sweet smell. Cyrus cracked his knuckles loudly. Next to him, Erith hissed at him in irritation. He ran his tongue along his teeth and tasted the last residue of the conjured bread he'd finished hours ago. He was famished but had had no time to stop in the kitchens on his way to the Council.

"What makes you automatically jump to the conclusion they're slavers?" Vaste said, and Cyrus could hear a note of outrage. "Why, they could have been some fine, upstanding citizens, merely out to help passing humans with—" He stopped and sighed. "All right, yes, they were almost certainly slavers. Sad that they're at work in the Confederation again, as I thought that the last war had taken it right out of them. Apparently the gnomish and dwarven acquisitions they've been picking up secondhand from the dark elves are not enough to satiate their grotesque appetites for labor."

"I'm afraid I'm not terribly familiar with this matter of slavery to which you're all referring," Longwell said, his head tilted slightly to the side and one eye narrowed almost to the point of closing. He peered around the table. "Surely you don't mean to suggest that these trolls are—"

"Seizing people all willy-nilly and forcing them into servitude doing backbreaking labor and menial chores?" Vaste asked. He sounded more aggravated than Cyrus could recall ever hearing him before. "I don't suggest it; I state it flatly. I've seen the slave markets outside Gren, seen the wickedness, the coercion, the torture, the beatings and whippings." The healer's massive frame shook. "It is a disgusting practice, and yes, it continues to this day in spite of every accord signed to end the war with the humans." Vaste slumped back in his seat, his oversized body flowing over the side of the chair.

"Many a paladin has made it their lifelong crusade to free the slaves," Vara said quietly across the table. Cyrus looked over at her, and she back at him. Her indifference had faded somewhat. Now she looked merely tired. "It is a problem of Gren and of Saekaj Sovar, though I have only heard anecdotes about it myself."

"I have seen the slaves of Saekaj Sovar," J'anda said with his hands out expressively, long fingers dangling. He wore his true face now, with his platinum-tinged hair and wrinkles in full appearance. "Humans, elves, dwarves and gnomes forced into grueling labor in the surface farms." His long fingers came up to cup his face. "I did not know that the trolls were still slaving, though. I had assumed it ended with the war."

"Barbaric," Longwell pronounced, shaking his head.

"Yes, well," Nyad said, sending him a glare, "how were the women treated in your lands?"

"Better than that," Longwell said with a little fire.

"Irrelevant," Curatio snapped, drawing the attention of everyone around the table. His breath hissed out. "Now we have two disappearances with little to go on—a missing goddess and a missing guild. At least the guild, we suspect, is enslaved."

"The footprints were definitely troll," Cyrus said, looking to Curatio, "and there were so many of them and of enough variation that Martaina says it was not simply one troll passing through and … walking in circles or somesuch." He shook his head. "It was an attack party. In human territory, in defiance of all treaties on the matter."

"Another excellent to question to ask," Vaste said, "is how they managed to transport the Daring back to troll territory."

"Overland, one would assume," Ryin said with a blank look.

"And one would be an idiot to assume that," Vaste said with a sneer.

"I miss the days of civility in this Council," Ryin said with a sigh.

"You cannot travel in the Confederation as a troll without being stopped and interrogated," Vaste said. "I cannot imagine that traveling as a pack with prisoners would allow for much more freedom in the matter."

"What would you suggest?" Cyrus asked. "They teleport in and out?"

"Yes," Vaste said with a nod. "Exactly."

"Except that they'd still have to travel overland," Cyrus said, "in order to get to the point of ambush. Because the portals are guarded by massive numbers of men with swords and spears."

Vaste let his hand come to his face, claws scratching lightly at his green skin. "Yes. I had forgotten that."

"So we know it is trolls," Erith said, speaking for the first time since they had come to Council. She, too, wore a weary look, but that was to be expected. It had been long days of riding for her, Cyrus supposed. "What we lack is how they invaded the Confederation to do so and where they went afterward."

"Gren," Vaste said without pause.

Erith turned to look at him. "Are you certain?"

Vaste gave a slight nod. "There is nothing else in troll lands but Gren and swamps. Few of my people live in the outlands, and there is nothing even close to a town in that area." His face tightened. "Anymore. There was once, obviously. But not anymore."

"Can I submit an alternate theory?" Ryin said, and though he did not sound tentative, his posture was upright and his nerves showed.

"Sure," Vaste said, "we could use more idiocy around here."

"Vaste!" Curatio said with another snap. "Curb your tongue lest you find yourself ejected from Council." A quiet pervaded the chamber in the wake of that which lasted near half a minute. Curatio's eyebrows were arched, his face cracking with fury, lips pressed in a harsh line. "Ryin, you may proceed."

"Ah ... thank you?" Ryin said. He tore his eyes from Curatio, though Cyrus noted many of the other Council members kept watching the healer, waiting to see if the Elder's uncharacteristic outburst was to be followed by another. "Last year, when we were under siege by the dark elves, they sent a division of trolls against us." Ryin's words came faster as he went, as though he were gaining confidence by the mere act of speaking. "It would not be out of the question to assume that perhaps the dark elves were behind this in some way. That they were using a troll brigade of some sort to fill their own slaving needs." Ryin looked tentatively at Vaste. "Now, you may resume your diatribe by calling me an idiot once more."

Vaste stared at the druid. "That is ... possible."

"From you, that's almost like a compliment," Ryin said with a half-smile.

"From you, it almost sounded like reason," Vaste replied. "Trolls don't have wizards. At best, I know of one shaman remaining in the swamps around Gren. Even assuming there were more, shamans do not possess the ability to teleport. There are no portals near Gren, not anymore. Therefore, a wizard of outside origin would have to be involved in some way."

"And the lack of portals around Gren blows a hole in your theory that the trolls would have teleported home," Ryin said.

"Yes, I see that now," Vaste said with more than a little chagrin. His complexion darkened.

"A question," Cyrus said, frowning. "The Daring was possessed of several spell casters, presumably at least one or more wizards. Yet they were defeated by this band of trolls."

"Did Martaina ever put a count to their number?" Vara asked, looking directly at Cyrus.

"No," Cyrus said, "but I would have to assume at least one hundred in order to overcome the Daring as they did. My point, though, is that they would need a wizard to keep the Daring's wizards from teleporting out."

"A cessation spell," Ryin said with a nod.

"It tilts the playing field dramatically," Vaste said, tapping his fingernails upon the table. "Trolls can overmatch nearly anyone in strength given the opportunity to fight without magic. With all due respect to Cass and the Daring," he made an apologetic bow of the head to Erith, "they would have been overwhelmed."

"So, a dark elven wizard," J'anda said with slitted eyes.

"Presumably," Ryin said.

"Possibly," Vaste corrected.

"And trolls," J'anda went on. "For the Sovereignty." He nodded slowly, eyes wide. "Well, that is quite a lot of conjecture wrapped into a nice ball and thrown against the wall."

"You have a better theory?" Vaste asked.

"I do not," J'anda said, folding his hands and putting them on the table before him as he leaned forward. "Far be it from me to suggest that the Sovereignty is anything but greatly evil. They are fully capable of such a thing. But it seems an odd waste of their resources at a time when they are falling back on all fronts—" J'anda stopped, his face changed in a moment, scanning the table around him.

Cyrus felt it too, a change in the atmosphere of the room, a subtle movement among a few of their members. He honed in on Vara, whose face had returned to a stony countenance. "What?" he asked, waiting to see who would speak first. "Something has happened," he said, glancing over to Vaste, who was slumped once more, head down. "What is it?"

"The news was waiting when we returned to Sanctuary earlier today," Curatio said, the strain evident on his face. The dark circles under his eyes were even more shadowed now, and his mouth was a thin line when it came to rest as he paused. "The dark elves have begun a new offensive." He pursed his lips for just a beat before he went on. "They have struck out into the Human Confederation in a lightning assault and taken massive territorial gains in the Riverlands and the Northlands."

Chapter 22

"Why the Riverlands and Northlands?" J'anda asked, his weathered face torn by surprise.

"Food," Cyrus said dully. The sweet aroma of the hearth smoke filled his nostrils as his thoughts swirled in his head, the stone block that comprised the Council Chambers glinting here and there in small sparkles of light from the odd reflective grain on the surface. Cyrus knew every head in the chamber was now turned to him. "If they had struck west, into the Plains of Perdamun, it would gain them nothing at present." He lifted his head and surveyed the table as he answered, the taste in his mouth sudden and acidic. "The plains are engulfed in shortages and famine from the last efforts of the dark elves."

"But the Elven Kingdom?" J'anda asked. "Surely it would be a rich prize—"

"If there were some beachhead for the dark elves, it surely would be," Vara spoke, stiff and upright in her chair. "But there is none. To take the Kingdom would be to fight their way over the bridges in Termina—and could only be accomplished after cutting a safe supply line across the Plains of Perdamun, which leaves them vulnerable along a line in the north from the Confederation—"

"And with a knife against their belly in the south from us," Curatio said. "More troubling yet for the Sovereign, because we have shown little reluctance to stab at him in such a manner after we dislodged his army from Prehorta."

"As you say," Cyrus agreed with a nod to Vara and Curatio in turn. He turned his gaze back to J'anda, who waited patiently, listening. "Rather than have to re-establish the lines of supply to wage such a battle against the elves, the Sovereign turns toward greener pastures, sending his armies marching around Lake Magnus to the north and south, hitting the breadbasket of the Confederation. They're far enough from Reikonos that help will not be swift in coming. They face no threat from the gnomes or goblins in the south, presumably, and the humans are unlikely to receive the help of the dwarves from the north, so …"

"The real question," Longwell said, "is where did the Sovereign get the troops to stage such a massive incursion?"

"The line around Reikonos, surely," Cyrus said. "They've had the city bottled up for a long time now without pressing any sort of attack there. He probably called his dogs off there and—"

"No," Curatio said, shaking his head. "There have been repeated battles along that line of late, assaults staged by the Sovereignty, and there is no weakness in that front."

"If anything," Vara said, shifting her gaze to Cyrus, "Isabelle reports that the fighting around Reikonos has grown more fervent. The dark elves throw troops into the battle in numbers that they have not previously been willing to commit."

"How fares your sister?" Cyrus asked, while his mind whirled and worked on the problem at hand.

"She is well enough," Vara said, though her jaw tightened. "Weary, but well enough. The assault on Reikonos proceeds along a line fifty miles south of the city, but in her last correspondence she mentioned that they were losing ground. That was a week ago, though. I have no idea how things might have changed in the interim."

"Whatever the case," Curatio said with an air of finality, "and no matter how our interests might run, this is not our problem at present. And may I remind you all that we have quite enough of our own concerns to deal with."

"Curatio," Vara said gently—for her, in Cyrus's estimation, "are you quite all right?"

Curatio held steady for a moment, and then his countenance darkened. He sat in the chair next to Alaric's old one—largest of all of them in the room, with its great sweeping back. Yet in the moments that followed, Cyrus would have sworn that Curatio grew taller than the chair of the Guildmaster.

"We stand in the middle of crisis," Curatio said, words beginning low in his throat, almost a growl. "Disappearances that we have taken the responsibility of solving. All fine and good. Mysteries to unravel, even as the world unravels around us. I, however, can only weather so much unraveling." Curatio stood, and his chair scraped forcefully across the uneven stones of the floor. "We grow at present, we face the strains of it, and it falls on one head—*and one head alone!*" His face darkened still further, then lightened for but a moment. "I did not ask for this responsibility. I did not want it." He closed his eyes and bowed his head, but the scowl remained. "And I only wish Alaric would come back and take it."

With that he reached into the neck of his robes and pulled out a pendant upon a chain. Cyrus could see it in the dim light of the torches and hearth, and it looked familiar. It was circular, almost like a perfectly round stone, but flatter and small enough to fit in the palm if absent the chain. He could see etchings swirling around it, but they were illegible in the dark. It took him but a moment to realize that it was the pendant that Alaric had handed Cyrus before destroying the Endless Bridge.

"I carry this unwanted thing," Curatio said, and his eyes were open now, searching each and every one of them. "I carry this burden unasked. I was never to be the leader!" He was shouting now. "It was always to be him, never me! I did not desire it, did not seek it—" he let the heavy pendant drop on the table and it landed with a thump, "—and I no longer want it. The healer's face grew into a mask of disgust. "I am the Elder of this guild and no more. Decide among yourselves who wants the responsibility of being the Guildmaster."

There was a pause longer than a breath. "Curatio," Vara said first, "electing a new Guildmaster now would be—"

"Entirely appropriate," Curatio said, his words strong, like beaten iron. "And inevitable."

"It is not time yet," Vara said, and Cyrus could see her hand shaking where it was clenched on the table, her gauntlet rattling against the wooden edge. "He has not been gone but for—"

"Six months," Curatio spat and leaned toward her across Alaric's old seat. "Do you not see what the rest of us find blindingly obvious? He is gone, child. Gone, and not to return. The rest of us are left holding what remains, but none lead."

"You could," J'anda said, looking to Curatio. "You have."

"I cannot," Curatio said, and his hands came up to cover his face. "I cannot any longer. I have troubles on my mind, worries of my own." His hands came away, but the face remained the same—weary and tired, though the anger was gone. "It is not for me to fall into this role unelected. The charter forbids it. I am no longer capable of bearing the burdens that this puts upon me, and no longer willing to accept the strain. Not now." He spoke quietly, and to Cyrus's ears his words were nearly a plea. "Find someone else."

After brief seconds looking around the Council's table, he moved to Alaric's chair, holding his hand against it, then stepped toward Vara and clasped her on the shoulder. He leaned down to whisper something in her ear that caused her to close her eyes. When finished, he straightened and began to thread a steady path around the table edge toward the door. He did not stop until he had reached it, and then only long enough to open and shut it quietly.

Cyrus looked across the table to Vara, where she sat next to Alaric's old chair, still empty. Her eyes were closed, and a single tear was working its way down her pale cheek.

Chapter 23

When it was obvious that the Council meeting was ended, Cyrus was one of the first to leave. He did not care to sit and stare at Vara, who still sat in her chair, unmoving.

He left the door to the Council Chambers open behind him, passing torches burning on the wall. Darkness was visible outside the windows, and he could feel the pull of fatigue as he approached the stone stairwell. Somewhere below he could hear talking, laughing—as though there were no cares of any sort in Arkaria.

"Walk with me," Vaste said, putting a strong hand upon his shoulder and steering toward the stairs going down, rather than the passage leading up. Cyrus found himself dragged along for a step until he caught his footing and fell in beside the troll. Someone else appeared at his right side but with a much gentler touch. It took him a moment to realize it was J'anda, hurrying along to keep up with Vaste's long steps.

"What the hells is this about?" Cyrus asked as they descended.

"Your future," Vaste said.

"My future involves a long wrestling match with my pillow," Cyrus said with more than a little annoyance. It had been a day that he'd begun waking under the stars, that had continued with a journey into the frigid, fearsome Realm of Life and ended with him picking over the site of a slaver ambush before entering another dispiriting, revelation-filled meeting of the Sanctuary Council.

"And a feisty dark elven thief, I'm sure," Vaste said.

"I am not so sure," Cyrus replied. "I don't think I have the energy for that at present."

"Whatever the case," Vaste went on, his heavy arm still draped across Cyrus's shoulders, "we're not talking about your immediate future. I need you to look a little longer-term than that."

"I can imagine my breakfast tomorrow," Cyrus said, "which, by the way, is only about three hours from now."

Vaste let out an airy sigh. "You're a dense one." He turned and looked down at Cyrus. "We want you to run for Guildmaster."

Cyrus heard himself groan. "I have a lot on my plate right now."

"I don't see a plate," Vaste said. "All I see is a long drop in front of you, which, by the way, is sort of a threat."

Cyrus looked at the long, central shaft of the circular stairwell. It was quite a ways down. "You're not exactly motivating me, here."

"I was mostly kidding," Vaste said, his irises glittering yellow in the torchlight. "Mostly."

"You are the natural candidate," J'anda said from Cyrus's left. "You are the General of Sanctuary. We already follow where you lead, and your record as a commander in military situations is impeccable."

Cyrus let that one hang in the air a moment before responding. "You do remember that under my leadership we lost the entire land of Luukessia, right?"

Vaste waved a hand at him. "A trifling concern. Nobody cares about that."

Cyrus felt a frown crease his face. "I think the ten thousand Luukessians we have in our ranks might care at least a little."

"You have been leading since the day you got here," J'anda said, shooting a glare at Vaste. "You have led us on many successful campaigns, and whenever you have made an error, trifling or no, you go out of your way to try and make it right."

"You were the chosen of Alaric," Vaste said. "His right hand."

"I think you're thinking of Curatio," Cyrus said. "Alaric was quite displeased with me the last time I had a full conversation with him."

J'anda smiled. "Oh, he was angry with you on the bridge?"

"Not on the bridge," Cyrus said. "The last time I had a full conversation with him was the night before we left for Luukessia."

"That was over a year and a half ago," Vaste said. "I suspect he found time to consider you his favorite again after that. He did come to save your ass on the bridge, after all."

Cyrus found himself begin to respond, then stopped. He never could think of the phrase 'save your ass' without remembering Niamh. *Another death*. "He did. But this is irrelevant. Curatio was his chosen second, he was the Elder."

"And now Curatio is out of the way," Vaste said, lifting his hand off of Cyrus's shoulder and into the sky as if mimicking a bird taking off, "so who is left?"

"I don't know," Cyrus said with a shake of the head. "You—"

"I'm not running," Vaste said. "I don't have the disposition for it."

"J'anda—"

"No. I have another task," J'anda said, quelling Cyrus with a raised hand, "which we will discuss soon.

"Fine," Cyrus said. "Pick one: Vara, Longwell, Erith—"

"No, no, no," Vaste said.

"—Ryin or Nyad—"

"Basically the same person, and no," Vaste went on.

"—all right, enough!" Cyrus said. "Why none of them?"

"Because you are the General," J'anda said quietly.

"We are not a mercenary guild," Cyrus said, feeling a deep sense of shame. "Well, we were never supposed to be one. That, in my mind, is argument enough why I shouldn't be Guildmaster."

"It is easy to talk about what you should or shouldn't do," J'anda said with a slow nod. "For example, there is a subset of the wealthy in Pharesia which only eats vegetation. No meats, only vegetables. They do this because it is supposed to be a healthier diet and obviously kinder to animals."

"I find that unconscionable," Vaste said, deadpan. "My day is incomplete without a helping of the flank torn off some suffering beast."

"My point is this," J'anda went on. "Were they starving, they would be forced to eat anything that came their way, meat included, or else they would die. Those in a position of peace and splendor are allowed different choices than those in war and famine. It is fine to pontificate on the morality of Sanctuary's recent decisions, but when you have tens of thousands of mouths to feed and a land in upheaval, the time to pontificate is over. In the time of war, choices are a luxury we no longer have."

"That doesn't really sway me," Cyrus said. He could tell they were reaching the bottom of the stairwell. "If you don't hold to what you believe in times of difficulty, then you don't truly believe in it. It's easy to say you believe in something when it's untested. It's only when you're put through the fire that the truth of the blade comes out." He lowered his voice. "And we failed the test. *I* failed the test. Alaric believed in a guild that was to serve the greater good and not be mercenaries, and however we want to honey-coat it, on the purest level, we failed. We took a job for money."

"That we might have taken anyway," Vaste said. "This is not some lily-white pure league, Cyrus. We kill beasts, armies, enemies. We fight for a living."

"We're supposed to adventure," Cyrus said dryly.

"And if the world were a perfect place filled with no danger, we might not have to do those things," Vaste replied as they drew near to the end of the steps. There were voices echoing through the foyer, the guards on duty still raucous in the night. "But it is not. We live in a world where powers are at war, where nature itself would turn on you and send chipmunks after your genitalia."

Cyrus stared up at Vaste with his mouth slightly open. "I don't think that was nature."

"Who says that today is the first time angry chipmunks have attacked me in such a manner?" Vaste replied. "You cannot tell me that a lion of the Gradsden Savanna would pass on eating you if given a choice."

"I have been told they do eat people if given a chance," Cyrus conceded. "Your point is taken. We live in an unsafe world. But we were to be an example, to stand above the rest."

"It's really hard to help the people who are down on their knees," J'anda said quietly, "when you're busy standing above them in example."

"I'm not a leader," Cyrus said. He took the last few steps, boots clinking all the way. "Not for this guild, not for—"

They entered the foyer, and the raucousness ceased. There were men and women standing around the center crest, warriors and rangers. Farther back he could see a few spell casters clad in robes. They went silent when they saw him, a hush that spread over the room quickly as every face turned to look at him. The warriors in their plate and leather armors straightened, snapping almost to attention. The rangers, woodsmen and women, usually a rabble at best, stood stiff with their bows at their sides. Cyrus could see the spell casters in their robes in the corners, fewer than their counterparts that battled with steel and wood but still in some approximation of military attention.

"As you were," Cyrus said, and he could feel the tension in the room release, though it did not become as loud as before he had entered.

"I can see why you think you're not a leader," Vaste said, nodding his head subtly and slowly. "Obviously no one respects or listens to you."

"I don't—" Cyrus stopped as he heard the clank of plate boots on the stairs behind him. Vara emerged from the stairwell, a navy cloak wrapped around her shoulders. "Vara?"

"I'm going out for a bit," she said, shouldering her way past Vaste.

"The gates are closed for the night," Cyrus said.

"They will open for me," Vara replied without looking back. She walked across the crest, through the partition and down the middle of the guard force as she made for the front doors.

"Will they open for her?" Vaste asked.

"Probably," Cyrus said, watching her go. "I hear tales of her wrath and wroth among the newer members. I doubt any of them are true, but they spread like fireboils among troll whores in any case—"

"Hey," Vaste said, "I'll have you know that fireboils don't just spread among troll whores. They're perfectly happy to foist themselves upon normal folk, too."

"You would know," J'anda said.

"I don't want to be Guildmaster," Cyrus said, spinning to look at the two of them, now standing between him and the stairwell.

"No one who actually wants to run for the office should by any means ever be elected to it," Vaste said. "We want you because you don't want to run."

"Is this that famed troll logic I've heard about?" Cyrus asked. "Because it is not exactly winning me over."

"Bear with me," Vaste said. "Whether you want to admit it or not, the Guildmaster of Sanctuary is a powerful role. They would hold immense sway over the single largest guild in Arkaria, and one of the most powerful armies in the land. Whoever sits at the chair at the head of our table has the power to help decide the outcome of wars, assist lands in grip of famine, and help make wealthy the members of this guild. It is an awesome responsibility."

"I keep waiting for you to stop sounding serious," Cyrus said.

"You'll be waiting a while," Vaste said. "This is the single most important event in our guild's recent history, because whoever sits in that chair will help steer our course. Anyone who desires the power inherent in that role is immediately suspect in my mind. The officers we have now are largely the same ones we have had since before the days when we had that much power. They remain—for the most part—uncorrupted by the influence at hand.

"Anyone who steps forward to claim that role will have a motive," Vaste said. "And the motive stated by them to go after the Guildmaster's seat may not be the one that sits within their heart. That scares me. I dwell on it and have for months now, since the day I realized we would have to elect a new Guildmaster. Much as I might want to postpone it, we cannot wait any longer. So now we need a leader uncorrupted by the power at hand, someone who will make the right decisions, someone for whom the job is an unwelcome task rather than an opportunity to expand their reach."

"We need someone like you," J'anda said. "Someone who would do it for the right reasons—even if they didn't want to be in the chair."

Cyrus let out a slow breath, felt it drain out of him. "I don't want to. Truly, I don't."

"Then ask yourself," Vaste said. "Who do you trust with the most powerful independent army in the land?"

"I already said—"

"Nyad could deploy Sanctuary's armies to aid her father in unpleasant and dangerous battles," Vaste said. "Ryin is a contrarian who would intervene in nothing, even when sorely needed. Erith is a self-indulgent and somewhat spoiled woman whose personal vanity occasionally eclipses her better judgment. Longwell is a man in the clutches of a depression over the loss of his land, which is still fresh in his heart—and which he might do anything to reclaim. J'anda is—"

"J'anda is ... unavailable," the enchanter said. "For reasons of health—and other duties."

Cyrus stared flatly at him. "How much longer do you have left?"

J'anda smiled at him. "I am not entirely sure. A few years, I think. Less if I push myself too much. Which is why I pass on this opportunity to put more strain on my body."

Cyrus looked to Vaste. "And you?"

Vaste stared back at him, but Cyrus could see the troll's eyes cloud. "Even if I were to win—which is not certain, because I am a troll among you people who rightly fear my kind," he held up a hand as though he could ward away Cyrus's protests to the contrary, "I cannot trust myself with this power, either." His face darkened. "My first instinct after what we've seen and heard today would be to deploy our army into the heart of Gren, to sack and burn the town and slaughter every slaver we came across. And as satisfying as that would be, the cost would be … great." He seemed to come back to himself, his face going slack in the torchlight, shadows covering his eyes. "I am something of a self-hating troll, I think. It would be best if I were to not be in command of an army, especially if my own people continue to do … what I think they're doing. The day we deal with them, it will require a more judicious approach than I am capable of."

Cyrus nodded, watching Vaste's face, and then he turned to stare at the doors of the foyer. "There's one name left."

"Ah, yes," Vaste said. "Vara is not able to lead at present. The burden on her heart is far too great for her to manage it and still handle the duties a Guildmaster role would require." He paused. "Plus, let's face it—she's horrible with people. Half the guild would leave within a fortnight."

"Be serious," Cyrus said, staring at the doors. The dark wood had shadows of the guards playing across it, lit by the light of the hearth.

"A moment ago you told me you were waiting for me not to be," Vaste said. "Make up your mind."

"She's stronger than you think," Cyrus said, looking back at Vaste. "She mourns Alaric, but she's strong enough to handle more. To handle whatever may come her way. Duty is first to her, it always has been. If she had the responsibility, she could take it. Better than me." He sighed. "It might even help her get over his death—unburden her heart, as it were."

"It might," Vaste said, and he looked to J'anda, "if in fact Alaric were the burden on her heart that I was referring to." He paused. "But *Alaric* is not."

Cyrus watched the troll carefully, then J'anda. "You meant me." He glanced back at the foyer door. "You meant me—I'm on her heart."

"Somewhere," Vaste said. "For a while longer, anyway."

"I'll think about it," Cyrus said, and turned away from them. He found himself walking faster as he cut through the center of the foyer, his guardsmen on either side saluting as he made for the grand doors.

"You do that," Vaste shouted at him. "Try not to be a burden, will you?"

Cyrus shot the troll a grin as he pushed his way through the heavy wooden door and burst out into the night on his way to the stables—and hopefully, to her.

Chapter 24

Cyrus ran toward the stables, his boots crunching the grass underfoot. He could see faint lights between the wooden seams of the building's planks. It was a massive, squared building with room to house more horses than any other stables he had ever seen. As he ran toward it, he stared. Everything around the grounds was so familiar that he barely even looked any more. *Were the stables really that big when I arrived at Sanctuary?* He knew full well they had to be; they'd never been reconstructed or added onto.

He could hear the sound of guards atop the walls. The watch fires burned on the towers that linked the segments of the stone wall together. They appeared to him in the distance as little spots of light atop the black emptiness where he knew the curtain wall stretched around Sanctuary's grounds.

There was noise from in front of him, and the stable door creaked open. Cyrus slowed as he approached, the smell of hay and horses something he was used to and barely noted now. Someone was opening the wide door to the barn, and another figure atop a horse was coming out.

"Lord Davidon!" called the figure opening the door. Cyrus squinted and recognized the outline of the lad; his name was Dieron Buchau.

"Dieron," Cyrus said. "I need—"

"Windrider is already saddled and coming to you, m'lord," Dieron Buchau said, bowing to Cyrus. "He made a frightful fuss to be let out, and I've learned by now that his moods tell me when you're coming for him."

"Clever lad," Cyrus said with a smile.

"Clever horse," Dieron replied, dipping low again. His red hair was highlighted in the lamplight. The sight of Dieron still made Cyrus feel a great discomfort; the lad had once been the stableboy at Enrant Monge, the keep in the center of Luukessia.

"Both of them cleverer than the rider," Vara said from atop her horse, which cantered out of the stables. "I suppose you're here to follow me or some such foolishness?" He could barely see her expression in the darkness, her face shadowed with the barn alight behind her, but it did not look amused.

"I'm going with you, yes," Cyrus said. "We need to talk."

"And here I thought we'd had such a marvelous conversation in the Realm of Life that it'd be a year or more before we'd need to speak again." She let out a long sigh as she brought her horse to a stop in front of him. "Yes, well, I am on my way out, obviously—"

Windrider trotted out of the open door behind Vara, making his way directly to Cyrus and stopping only a foot from him before letting out a loud—and rather theatrical, in Cyrus's opinion—whinny. "I'll come with you," he said, stroking Windrider's mane.

"Fine," Vara said, a little tightly. "But if you slow me in any way—"

"I would think you'd know my horse well enough by this point to know that if one of us slowed the other, it'd be—"

"I was not referring to your horse," Vara said. "I was speaking about you, dawdler." She pulled the reins and steered her horse around toward the gates. Cyrus mounted Windrider in a rush and followed her. With a signal from him, the portcullis was raised and the gates opened. He followed Vara through and watched as she steered a course northwest. Cyrus looked up at the bright starry sky as the horses broke into a gallop, following the road toward the Waking Woods.

"Anything in particular you're out to do tonight?" Cyrus asked, bringing Windrider alongside her.

"Yes," she said.

Cyrus waited for a moment, and when she did not speak further, he broke the silence again. "Care to share your plans with me?"

She looked at him as they gained speed, now at a full gallop across the plains, a dust trail kicked up behind them and her cloak in full flight, flapping as it trailed her. "You'll just have to wait and see, interloper."

"Interloper?" Cyrus asked. "I haven't been called that by anyone since that time the God of Death nearly smacked me into pieces."

"I am pondering doing much the same," Vara said tightly, "if you do not shut up and allow me the time to think which I came on this ride for in the first place."

Their horses thundered across the plains, hooves beating against the firm dirt as they ran. Cyrus kept quiet, staring up at the stars gleaming above him absent the lights of Sanctuary's watchfires and torches. There was enough light to see a dark aspect rising above the flat plains ahead. The top of it was wavy, uneven with the varying heights of the trees, and he knew it on sight.

The Waking Woods.

They reached the entry, and Cyrus watched the stars disappear into the darkness above him, faint outlines of branches visible only barely through the occasional break in the solid canopy of boughs. The trees were massive, in Cyrus's estimation eclipsed in size only by the enormous Iliarad'ouran woods. He followed Vara as her horse slowed to a trot and the path began to wend through the forest.

"I can't see very well," Cyrus said.

"Then you should have remained behind."

"And let you ride into the darkness unescorted? What kind of gentleman would that make me?"

"You are not, in fact, a gentleman of any sort," Vara replied. He could barely see her silhouette ahead of him. "Thus whether you escort me on this endeavor or not is rather a moot point."

"I am not a gentleman," Cyrus repeated, hearing the words come out evenly. "What would you say I am, then?"

"A pain in my arse," she said without a moment's pause.

"Other than that."

"When you're experiencing pain in your arse, there's really nothing other than that, unless there's a greater pain you are feeling elsewhere," Vara said.

"You don't make this easy, you know?" Cyrus said.

"I did not ask for your assistance in this," Vara said with a sharp exhalation.

"I came because I wanted to talk to you."

"I made clear that I was in no mood for talking, but you came anyhow," Vara said. "If you want to talk so damned much, then understand that part of talking is conversation—which includes listening to the other party. Unless you wanted to give me some form of lecture, in which case I would have told you I am in no mood for anything informative, nor do I have the disposition to listen to a diatribe at this moment without disemboweling someone."

Cyrus sensed her motion halt and felt Windrider match her horse's movement, unasked. His hand fell to the grip of Praelior by sheer instinct.

"You hear it, don't you?" Her voice cut through the quiet of the night. It was followed by a howl in the near distance and a horrible rattling.

"I can feel them, too," Cyrus said and realized his skin was prickling. There was a noise behind them. Cyrus turned to look but realized he could not see in the darkness. He drew Praelior and let the soft azure glow of the blade shed its light. He saw little, but more than he had been able to a moment earlier.

"Allow me to assist you," Vara said, and Cyrus heard her draw her blade. Her voice lowered to an indecipherable mutter, and a moment later the woods were lit by fire light as Vara's sword burst into flames from the quillons to the tip. It blazed with an orange, crackling fire that forced the shadows around them to retreat behind the nearby trees and revealed faces in the dark.

Cyrus could see them now. Ghouls. Undead.

He rolled out of the saddle and heard Vara do the same ahead of him. He found his back against hers, and realized that they had moved toward each other instinctively.

"Have you ever fought them before?" she asked.

"Once," Cyrus said, "with Terian." He lowered his voice. "A long time ago."

"Ah," she said. He could hear her feet crackling against fallen twigs.

Cyrus could see they were surrounded now, bones and half-rotted faces staring back at them in the dark. There was a glow in their undead eyes. And there were so very many eyes.

"It was here that I learned how to truly cast the spell that has my blade aflame," Vara said, and from her voice he could hear the recollection. "Have you seen it before?"

"Once," Cyrus said. "I saw Alaric do it as he faced an undead beast when we took a trip into a crypt." Cyrus glanced back at her, the flames rippling over her blade. The ghouls had yet to attack them, and Cyrus suspected that was the reason. "It's sort of the paladin equivalent of the resurrection spell, isn't it?"

"Yes," Vara said. "Only a true paladin, one with a noble heart and a holy fury can manage it."

"Well, you've certainly got the 'fury' part down."

She ignored him. "Alaric taught me how to do it shortly after I first came to Sanctuary. I am not supposed to know it; a League would require two further years of instruction to allow me to do this. He showed me how in mere hours." She stared out at the ghouls, lingering uncertainly at the edge of her fire's light, bones clacking together in the night.

Cyrus felt his lips purse as he tried to decide what to say. "He was—"

There was a howl of fury from behind him and he heard Vara leap. The sound of bones shattering and an unearthly scream followed a moment later. Cyrus fell into shadow as the light followed with Vara in her attack, and he forced himself back as the ghouls came forward. He struck and struck again as they attacked, Praelior shattering bones into dust when he hit them.

"You could have let me know you were moving," Cyrus said as he caught back up to her, placing his back against hers again.

"What's wrong?" she asked. He heard her breathing hard with exertion as the sound of her blade cutting through the air and striking bone rang out. "Afraid of the dark?"

"I can fight anything you put in front of me," Cyrus said with a grunt of displeasure as he slashed another ghoul to pieces. "But I have to be able to see it."

"That is your great weakness," she said, and he heard her leap again and again the light faded.

"Sonofa—" The shadows grew long around Cyrus, and he used the faint glow of Praelior to strike down the red eyes in front of him one by one. He heard a rattle behind him and struck in a backward arc that cut a ghoul in half at its spine.

About twenty feet away he could see Vara, blazing sword cutting through ghouls and lighting them aflame for a brief moment before they died. He could hear screams that ceased as her blade passed through each of them, the sound of undead souls fleeing bodies torn asunder by her magic.

Cyrus started to scramble to catch up but turned to deal with another ghoul behind him. His blade cut through the last, tearing rotted flesh with a sound like ripping cloth, and he sprinted toward Vara and fell in behind her once more. "It's not that I can't fight in the dark," he said. "It's that I see better with a little light."

"Learn to fight in the dark or you'll forever be at the disadvantage of the dark elves in a battle," she said.

"There's magic to overcome it in a battle," Cyrus said.

"Yes," she replied, sounding a little snooty, "but *you* can't use magic. So what do you do when you're facing a dark elf in the deep of night with no spell at your disposal? Lay down and die?"

"I can still fight," Cyrus said and smashed a ghoul's head in with the side of his blade. The cracking of bone didn't sound as sickening without the wet rending of flesh.

"But could you win?" she asked. "That's the question."

"I can hold my own," Cyrus said.

"Yes, but you'd prefer a dark elf hold it for you," she said dryly.

He paused, not sure he'd heard what he thought he had. "Uh—"

"Ready yourself," she said, and a moment later the fire vanished, and all that remained was the clacking of the ghouls around them.

Cyrus stood in the dark and listened as the wind rattled trees like bones. The howling had ceased and he could hear the muted whisper of things moving in the woods around them. The faint light shed by his blade was not enough to do much more than illuminate inches in front of his face and give him a vague idea of shapes in front of him. "This is not funny," he said, listening for a response.

None came.

Chapter 25

"Vara?" Cyrus heard the nerves in his own voice. His skin crawled with bumps as the cool night air prickled at it. A rattling behind him forced him to turn. Praelior's soft glow lit the face of a ghoul.

Cyrus slashed and felt the blade make easy contact with the creature. Bones clacked as it broke apart. He could hear the pieces of the ghoul hit the dirt with a thump as something came at him from behind.

Cyrus slashed backward but missed as something clattered to his right. He felt a hand thump against his back and spun again, his blade already in motion. A face appeared out of the darkness, inches from his, and he stopped his blade at the flesh of a neck that was, under the soft glow of Praelior, bluer than it should have been were it that of a human.

"Aisling?" Cyrus whispered.

"Yes," she said and then pushed past him. He heard the whirling of blades as she struck at a ghoul, which moaned as she cut it to pieces. "I saw you leave and followed you."

"Why?" he asked and then spun about to bring his sword across a ghoul's chest in time to bisect it.

"Because I'm jealous and possessive," she said with a distinct lack of amusement.

He paused, a moment of dead silence falling around him. "Really?"

"No, not really," she said and he could hear her moving again in the dark. "Well, maybe a little. But I followed you because I was curious where you were going with the frost witch. I didn't exactly expect her to leave you in the dark to die."

"I am still here." Cyrus heard Vara's voice to his left, and suddenly the woods came alight again as her sword burst into flames again.

"And oh so very helpful, turning out the lights and leaving him practically blind against an army of ghouls." Aisling's blades were in motion as she spoke, disassembling the bony ghouls that were moving in around them. They rustled against the underbrush, the rotted flesh sprinkled around their skeletons catching the flame's light as they moved toward Cyrus.

"I was trying to help him," Vara said as she moved closer to them, casually hacking a ghoul's head off as she came.

"Help him what? Die?" Aisling shot back.

"I was helping him to learn what to do when swallowed by the darkness," Vara said coolly. "Something I'd wager he needs since I suspect he's swallowed by you on a regular basis."

Cyrus's head whipped around at the repartee between the two of them and caught Aisling's malicious grin. "I bet that just eats you up, doesn't it?"

"No," Vara said, "I was implying that you eat him up, or are you so dull of wit that you missed it?"

"Does it make you jealous, thinking of me warming his nights?" Aisling said, slicing another ghoul. Her daggers cut through a rotted face and sent the skull shattering against a nearby tree. "To think of me in his bed, where perhaps you wish you were?"

Vara had her back turned, dispensing with two ghouls that staggered at her with a measured scream. "I'm quite all right, thank you," she said with a surprising evenness considering her exertion. Cyrus paused to diagonally slash a ghoul through the ribcage. "I think I'm worthy of more than the strumpet he's become."

"Hey!" Cyrus said. "I am not a strumpet. I have a …" He glanced at Aisling, who looked back at him. "I have a … relationship with Aisling—"

"You have a fiery need to grind your groin against something in the night," Vara said, still not turning to look at either of them, "and apparently little else since I never see the two of you together in the light. I do not think that makes for a 'relationship,' exactly."

"And you would know how?" Aisling spat at her. "I doubt you even remember what the touch of a man feels like—if you've ever felt one at all."

Cyrus paused, watching two mindless ghouls shuffling away from them, moaning in the dark, and wished he could retreat with them. There was a soft breeze rushing through the woods, shaking the leaves overhead. "I don't think this is—" he started to say.

Vara turned to them, her face a mask. "You are quite right, of course," she said to Aisling. "It's been some time since I have done much more than kiss a man. Of course, that might have something do with—"

"Oh, shit," Cyrus whispered under his breath.

Vara's head snapped toward him. "Do you know what I'm about to say?"

Cyrus let out his breath slowly. "Yes ... Archenous."

"Of course you know," she said, and he saw the reflection of her blade in her eyes. "Perhaps she does not, so I will say this plain: I have known the touch of a man, and I have felt love, long ago. I have heard the promises whispered and broken, have heard all the trite sayings that follow in love's departure. 'Love conquers all.' 'Love is the great salve.' 'Love will find a way.'" Her face quivered and her lips moved slightly downward. "All lies. 'Love will find a way'?" She laughed, loudly and humorlessly. "More like love will find a slave. Well, I can tell you this much—I intend to be my own master. Always."

With a flourish, Vara spun her blade upright and blew it out like a candle, the fire disappearing as if snuffed by a strong wind. "You are more than welcome to him. Worry not that I'll ever be in any sort of competition for him, for he is yours." There came the sound of the underbrush stirring as Cyrus suspected she turned, and then her voice came back to them once more, but quieter. "And I wish you all the best of luck with everything that entails."

Aisling was silent for a minute. "She's gone now." He felt her arms slip around his neck, felt her press herself against his front. "Slave?"

Cyrus tried to look in the direction he thought Vara had gone, but the disappearance of her blade's light had left him once again in a darkness more complete than before she'd lit the sword. "Windrider?" He heard a whinny a short distance away and then motion as the horse trotted toward him. "I don't know. I think maybe the slave thing was just the first thought to float to her mind."

Aisling ran a hand along his face, down to his neck, her nails scratching lightly against his skin. "Maybe she needs some chains in her life."

Cyrus held his quiet for a moment. "I doubt that." He felt the thump of Windrider's nose against his back. "A fine help you were in the fight," he muttered.

A whinny came back at him as he used a lone hand to guide his way around to the horse's side. "Where's your horse?" he asked Aisling.

"I turned her loose to run back to Sanctuary," she said as she put a foot in the stirrup. "I figured you'd need me to guide you home anyway."

"Yeah, all right," Cyrus said as he hoisted himself up and situated himself behind her. He waited quietly and nothing was said for a long moment. "Any time now."

"Aren't you going to thank me?" Aisling asked. He could feel her turning in the dark to face him, twisting around at the waist to look at him. He felt her fingers on his lips, softly. "For helping you?"

"Thank you," he said, a little numbly.

"You're welcome," she said and leaned in to kiss him. He could taste the cinnamon on her breath, could smell the nearness of her. But though he kept his eyes open the entire time, he could have sworn the face in front of him was that of someone else—of the one he wished were with him.

Chapter 26

Cyrus stirred, waking from a drowsy sleep. Sunlight was streaming in the window of his quarters, the drapery doing an impossibly bad job of blocking it out. He rolled to see the bed empty next to him. Aisling had accompanied him to sleep last night after she'd exacted a toll from him for the incident in the Waking Woods. She had not spoken the entire time, but her eyes had been dark and narrowed even in the torchlight.

The smell of their night's lovemaking still lingered in the warm, stuffy air. Cyrus wondered at the hour, wondered when she had left. His tongue was dry and carried the lingering taste of bile. He felt the hunger rumble inside and suspected that the hour was late indeed. *Must have slept half the day away.*

He washed off and dressed, putting his armor on as quickly as he could manage. He reached the foyer minutes later where the smell of baking bread filled his nose and gave his stomach more cause for complaint. There was a small crowd in the foyer mixed with the guard force on duty, but he paid them no mind until someone called his name.

"Cyrus!" He turned to see Erith Frostmoor standing with another woman in the middle of the room, atop the Sanctuary seal. He tried to dismiss them with an idle wave of greeting, but Erith called out again. "Cyrus, over here!"

He turned, the sunlight streaming through the window above the doors, lighting the room and casting the woman next to Erith in silhouette. She wore a traveling cloak and had her hair bound up in braids of some kind. He could not tell the color from where he stood.

He cast a look at the Great Hall, toward the smell of the bread his stomach cried out for as he altered direction to detour to Erith.

As he got closer, the woman with Erith became clearer in his eyes. Her hair was brown, her skin bronzed from days spent in the sun. She hadn't looked like that when he'd first met her; she had been a noblewoman, after all.

"Cattrine," he said with a forced smile as he stepped closer to the Grand Duchess Cattrine Tiernan, who stood next to Erith with a muted smile of her own.

"I had worried that I would be late for our meeting this morning," Cattrine said with a bow of her head in greeting, "but it would appear that I was forgotten entirely."

"I didn't forget—" Cyrus stopped himself as an impish smile made its way onto Cattrine's lips and he realized the futility of lying to her. *She can read me like a parchment.* "I apologize. I've been embroiled in a search for a missing guild and a missing goddess as well as a few other ... issues ... and I'm afraid it's clouded my thoughts. I did forget our biweekly meeting, but ... uhm ..." He looked around the foyer quickly. "We need three officers for this—"

"As set down by your Council when we began this formality, yes," she said with a nod. "I'm quite content to discuss it with just the two of you, though—"

"We should follow the rules," Cyrus said, still scanning the crowd. No other officer was in immediate proximity. "Perhaps we should reschedule—"

"I see Vara," Erith said, causing Cyrus to jerk his head around. Erith was smiling, nearly grinning, in fact.

"I'm sure she's busy," Cyrus said abruptly.

"I'll go check," Erith said and slipped away toward the entry doors.

"Get me a loaf of bread while you're at it?" Cyrus called out to her retreating back. Erith's hair did not so much as stir to give any sign that she had heard him. He turned to face Cattrine, his steps somewhat stiff and measured. "So ..."

She smiled politely, but there was some warmth to it. "How have you been?"

"Busy," he said, feeling a little tense. "Yourself?"

"Much the same," she said. "Building a town for the refugees has been a gargantuan task. I was trained to administrate a kingdom for my brother, but I never learned how to build one, town and all, from the ground up." She smiled faintly. "I suppose it was assumed that Actaluere would always stand and that starting over again would be unnecessary."

"She's not busy," Erith said. Cyrus turned back to see her approaching, Vara in tow with a look much the same as Cyrus suspected a lioness being dragged against her will might wear. Vara's ears were flushed red at the tips and her cheeks were slightly mottled. "So, I guess we can still do this meeting." Cyrus looked at Erith, and she bore a wide smile—wider than he'd seen on her in some time. "Vara, this is Cattrine Tiernan. Lady Cattrine, this is Vara." She bowed before each of them with a flourish in an introduction worthy of a court somewhere, Cyrus suspected.

"So very nice to meet you," Cattrine said, stepping forward to extend her hand to Vara. "I've heard so much about you."

"Indeed?" Vara said, gripping Cattrine's hand somewhat woodenly. "I hope it was all of it unpleasant, else you've been told only lies."

Cattrine's smile faded slightly, as though unsure of what to make of the paladin's statement. "No, much of it was quite the opposite."

"You've been talking to fools, then," Vara said abruptly, and that quelled the conversation for a beat.

"Well, this is a little awkward," Erith said with that same broad grin.

Cyrus stared at her and she smiled back at him. "I hate you for this," he said flatly.

"That's all right," Erith replied, still smiling, "it's so worth it."

"Right this way," Cyrus said, gesturing toward the door next to the stairwell opening. He let Vara lead the way as she stormed past, her armor clinking as she moved. He thought it odd for a moment, as she rarely made noise in her movements, then decided she was doing it on purpose. She moved at full speed down the hall in front of them. Cyrus knew there was a conference room toward the back of Sanctuary.

He listened to their footsteps echo down the stone hall, resonating in the confined space. The sound of souls at breakfast could be heard through the wall. The clink of plates and cutlery, the laughter and noise of fellowship caused Cyrus's stomach to rumble once more. He reached the bend in the hallway as it turned left and paused, extending his arm to indicate Cattrine should go before him. He smiled at her as he did so. Once she passed, he sent a nasty look at Erith, who just kept smiling.

They settled in the conference room, the three officers of Sanctuary across from Cattrine, whose navy traveling cloak was pulled back off her shoulders to envelop the back of her chair. She wore a white blouse and tan breeches; Cyrus tried to recall seeing her in a dress since they had left the shores of Luukessia and had to concede he did not recall any such extravagance from her in recent memory.

"I appreciate you taking the time in your busy schedules to make this accommodation," Cattrine said with a bow of her head. She smiled pleasantly all the while, and Cyrus suspected she meant it. "Especially you, Vara, as I know you would rather be elsewhere." Vara nodded somewhat stiffly, as though she had been caught off guard by the acknowledgment.

"We are glad to be able to be of assistance," Cyrus said, clearing his throat sharply. "I expect there are a few matters you wanted to talk about …?"

"We did have a few concerns," Cattrine said, folding her hands across each other. "The detachment of troops you've left for us, for instance …"

Cyrus frowned. "Do you require more?"

"Ah, less, actually," Cattrine said with a small smile. "The area we are in appears quite peaceful, and we feel very comfortable with decreasing the numbers should you feel it necessary to deploy them somewhere else, somewhere they might prove more lucrative to Sanctuary's efforts …" She let her voice trail off, surveying each of them in turn.

Cyrus felt a sudden rush of discomfort. "We have no particular use for them at the moment, m'lady. However, I will keep that in mind should matters change. Our concern is that word is getting out about your town's tie to the guild, and the last thing any of us would wish is to see your people massacred or held hostage in some attempt to make us suffer or extort cooperation from Sanctuary—"

"I understand completely," Cattrine said with a nod, "but I have been assured by your man Belkan that a thousand warriors and rangers combined with the numbers of wizards, healers, druids and enchanters you have left us would be plenty enough to defend the Emerald Fields from a portal-based invasion. And that's to say nothing of the rock giant."

Cyrus blanched slightly at the thought of Fortin. After the fall of Alaric, the rock giant had packed a fairly minimal bag and retired to his land holding bordering the Emerald Fields. Cyrus could still see his rocky face staring as he made a last proclamation before leaving. *"Until you find someone who can defeat me in single combat, I'll be in Rockridge."* He had leaned toward Cyrus. *"I will keep an eye on your villagers—as a neighbor would help his own—but do not call on me for aid to Sanctuary unless you can find someone willing to challenge and defeat me."*

Cyrus's hand came up and ran metal-clad fingers over his face, rubbing the bridge of his nose before he removed his helm and set it upon the table with a clink. "I worry about Fortin's reliability in a fight, honestly. He's somewhat unencumbered by great concern for lesser beings."

"He's been very decent to all of us," Cattrine said with a smile. "He comes down from his mountain and plays with the children in the square."

Cyrus froze and cast a look toward Erith, who appeared similarly stricken. "And he doesn't … uh … eat them?"

Cattrine's expression went to shocked in a second. "I should say not!"

Cyrus held up a hand. "Just checking."

"He shops in our markets, laughs with our people. He has friends among us, and many of our own would count him as theirs." Cattrine leaned forward, her cloak billowing over the back of the wooden chair. "He is in every way a citizen of our tiny nation and welcome in our homeland. I trust him to aid our defense if need be."

"Ah," Cyrus said, looking down. "I had only a brief exchange with him before he left; I had not had much of an impression that he would do more than look down the mountain and perhaps throw himself into a battle if it amused him to do so."

"He is one of us," Cattrine said and leaned back. "And we count ourselves fortunate indeed to have him."

"Fair enough," Cyrus said. "We were fortunate when we had his aid as well. May you never suffer the loss of it."

"There are other things I wished to discuss with you, only briefly," Cattrine said and seemed to take two breaths before she spoke again. "Gold and crops."

Cyrus looked to his right to see Vara sitting there, her flesh almost back to its usual paleness. The traces of angry red so obvious earlier were now settled and almost gone. She turned her head slightly to look at him, impassive once more. He turned back to Cattrine. "Go on."

"We could use more coin," she said, and in spite of her pause it came breathlessly. "In spite of our best efforts, we have stored away enough grain only to last through one season. Our livestock have not grown to sufficient levels to sustain our people yet, and the price of every crop we try to buy seems inadequate to what we have—"

"Yes," Cyrus said and bowed his head. "In many ways, our timing for this could not have been worse. Your people come to Arkaria in the days of the first famine we have experienced in a hundred years. The price of food has soared commensurate with that—"

"We just need a little more," Cattrine said, and she sounded like she was pleading. "I hate to come to you with this, but—"

"It's fine," Cyrus said stiffly. "It can't be easy to run a burgeoning land of—" He paused. "How many do you have now?"

"Counting the soldiers that remain housed here, one hundred and six thousand, seven hundred and fifty two." She flushed. "We had three babies born yesterday, one of them to a young couple who met on the long retreat from Luukessia."

"That makes yours one of the largest settlements in Arkaria," Cyrus said with a sigh. "I'm afraid we're going to have to send spell casters to conjure bread to make it through the winter."

"There is no more, then?" Cattrine asked, looking at each of them in turn.

Cyrus caught the look of discomfort from Erith. Vara remained unsurprisingly aloof, though she showed a hint of uncertainty for an eyeblink that Cyrus caught. "I'm afraid our guild bank is exhausted," he said. "We're at the end of our reserves. We're working on a few things to replenish it, but ... it's all gone." He held up his hands. "Money comes in, it goes right back out." He sighed deeply. "As soon as we have more gold, I assure you that we'll be sending more your way, but for now we have nothing. I'm sorry. We'll send another expedition to Purgatory in the next week or so, but prices for those goods are fallen to depths so low ..." He could feel the contrition run through him, almost a sense of shame at not being able to send her on her way with sacks of gold to aid her efforts.

"We'll make it, though," Cattrine said with a faint smile. "Which is more than our brethren can say. You have given us what you could, allowed us to use your wizards to transport us to the distant portal nearest the bridge where our carpenters still gather lumber to build our settlement at no cost. You have allocated soldiers to defend our lands against all encroachments we might imagine, and you've given us all you have to feed our people." Her smile was not quite glowing, but it held the light of encouragement. "We'll make it, and that is what is important."

"I wish that we could do more," Cyrus said, leaning his elbows upon the table. "That there was something else we could give to ease your people's troubles."

"You have done more than anyone else would do, I believe," Cattrine said, acknowledging each of them in turn. "We could scarcely have asked for more faithful friends than Sanctuary."

"We are to be a refuge in times of trouble," Vara said stiffly, "and a haven for those who need it most. We could not have done anything other than what we have." Her face was paler now, the last hint of rosiness gone from her cheeks.

"It is incredibly important to us that your people know that they are not alone," Cyrus said, gripping the table. "That they never feel they are in this by themselves, without aid or friend in all Arkaria."

"I don't think they have ever felt that way," Cattrine said. "Not once since arriving on these shores." She pushed her seat back from the table, carefully pulled her cloak over the back of the chair to keep it from snagging, and let its hem fall back to the ground. "You have never given us cause to feel that way. And we are grateful. I can see a day when the Emerald Fields will be prosperous in our own right; the seeds are planted, and now we must simply continue to sow until that day of bountiful harvest comes."

"May it come soon, m'lady," Cyrus said, standing and then bowing at the waist.

"It's not 'm'lady' anymore," Cattrine said. "I don't think it has been since the day we rowed the sea with Caenalys burning at our backs. My old titles all burned with the city." There was a tightness at the edge of her eyes. "It is merely 'Administrator' now."

"Not anything grander?" Erith asked with a note of surprise.

"The King of the Elves confers titles in the lands we inhabit," Cattrine said. "He gives us a great deal of autonomy, but not so much as for us to overthrow his authority. No, it is only Administrator now; we may have been Barons, Duchesses and Kings in the old world, but now we are in a new one, and fortunate to have what we have." She smiled. "A humble title reminds me of my place in this new land and reminds me to keep my humility about me. We are not now what we once were, and to forget it would be to let seep in the old entitlements. No, I'll take the new titles, and with them the new equality that has come between men and women in this land." She straightened. "For I am a pragmatist and live in the now."

"Administrator," Cyrus said, and bowed his head.

She smiled faintly. "Only you could say it in a way that still makes it sound like 'M'lady,' Cyrus Davidon."

He returned her smile. "I try. If there's nothing else, I can escort you out—"

"No," she said, holding out a hand to stay him. "If it's all the same to you, I'd like to be escorted out by Lady Vara." She smiled. "Since I've had the ears of you and Lady Erith for quite some time already."

"Certainly," Vara said with a curt nod. It was impossible to tell from her expression what she was thinking, but she moved quickly enough, stepping from behind the table toward the door. "If you'll come with me …" She held the door for Cattrine, and Cyrus watched them both go.

"Trying to decide if that bodes ill for you?" Erith's voice reached his ears and Cyrus glanced at her with a frown. She wore a grin. "They seem to get along well." Cyrus said nothing for a moment, and Erith's tone changed. "That thing you said, about none of us being alone … Cass used to say something like it all the time to the Daring."

"He used to say it long before that, too," Cyrus said, watching the door that had closed only moments earlier. The sound of it still echoed in his mind, like a reflection of other doors that had been closed to him as well.

Chapter 27

"We are none of us alone."

The words echoed in Cyrus's ears as he made his way back down the long hall toward the foyer. He could hear it in Cass Ward's own intonation. It lingered in his mind as he shuffled along, taking his time. Erith had gone on before him as Cyrus sat alone in the conference room for a time after her departure, the words of Cass—his friend—echoing in his ears.

Finally the smell of the bread baking in the kitchen off the Great Hall had gotten to him, and he could wait no longer. As he entered the foyer once more, the smell grew stronger, mingled with something else—cooking eggs, Cyrus thought. It had been a long time since they'd had those.

"Cyrus," came the soft voice from near the stairs. J'anda Aimant stood resplendent in his blue robes, his true face unhidden, wrinkles, platinum hair and all. "I must speak with you."

"Can we do it while I eat?" Cyrus asked, gesturing toward the open doors of the Great Hall. The smell wafting out was getting to him, his leg twitching with desire to carry him toward the smell of food. A peal of laughter followed the sounds of revelry within, and they called out to him.

"Absolutely," J'anda said and gestured him on. He clasped a hand onto Cyrus's shoulder as they walked through the entry doors.

The Great Hall still held a reasonable crowd, even at this hour. Cyrus scanned the room, which stretched far back into the distance. He wended his way between the tables, J'anda following close behind. The noise was loud enough that Cyrus did not attempt to speak as they made their way through. J'anda broke off and began his trek toward the officer table at the front of the room as Cyrus continued toward the open pass-through into the kitchen.

"Larana," Cyrus said with as much joviality as he could muster with his stomach rumbling. The timid druid was at the window in a moment, face downcast but glancing up every now and again at him. "I know breakfast is over, but I had some ... ah ... guild matters to attend to." He smiled. *No need to mention that I slept late with Aisling.* "Is there anything left?"

Larana's tan face was nearly hidden by ringlets of tangled brown hair. He did not see any expression from her, and she turned wordlessly away to reach over to a table sitting in the center of the kitchen. She took hold of a plate with shaking hands and turned back to him, setting it upon the pass-through between them, then stepped back and lowered her head so her locks could cover her face again. He still saw her eyes peering out at him.

There was a crusty pie waiting before him, smelling of pastry and egg. Cyrus reached out and took it, feeling the warmth through his gauntlets. "Thank you," he said with a bowed head of his own. "I can always count on you to make sure I don't starve." He started away from her, thought he heard her say something and turned back. She was already gone, vanished out of sight. He frowned and shrugged, moving on toward the officers' table.

J'anda waited for him around the massive round table at the edge of the room. Cyrus sat and heard the hearty thunk of both the plate and his armor against wood. J'anda sat close by, only a chair away from him instead of in his usual place across the table. "So," Cyrus said, pulling the fork off the table and breaking into the top of the pie. Heavenly smells of egg and melted cheese wafted up at him, causing his mouth to water.

"We have a problem," J'anda said, and there was a great tentativeness hanging about the enchanter. Cyrus watched him as he shoveled the first spoonful of the pie into his mouth.

"We have many problems," Cyrus said. "Of which are you speaking?" The egg was laced with cheese and ham, as well as hints of smoky bacon. Cyrus closed his eyes and savored.

"Saekaj Sovar," J'anda said, and Cyrus's eyes snapped open once more.

"Yes," Cyrus said after a moment. "They are indeed a problem."

"They are probably aiding the trolls in slaving," J'anda said. He was being coy, Cyrus was certain, as the enchanter seemed ... reserved. "Their resurgence in the war is ... troubling."

"That's two problems," Cyrus said, taking another bite of the pie. *This is damned distracting. Can't we have a serious conversation some other time?*

"We are at a great disadvantage," J'anda said, holding up one of his hands. "The dark elves are our enemy. To see them win this war against the humans would mean them turning their attention to us, with ill results."

"It would mean our destruction," Cyrus said carefully. The bite of the pie, which had seemed so satisfying only a minute earlier, was now somehow unappealing. "And likely an eventual hegemony wherein the dark elves rule all Arkaria."

"No one wants to see that," J'anda said quickly, and Cyrus watched him carefully. He seldom saw the enchanter without his illusions firmly in place, and the depth of feeling that had just shone in the dark elf's eyes was not at all like J'anda's usual calm, cool demeanor.

"I think the dark elves do," Cyrus amended.

"Not even all of them do," J'anda said, and looked Cyrus directly in the eyes. "Saekaj Sovar is a keg of Dragon's breath waiting to be lit. They are kept in line by the fear of the Sovereign."

"Ah, the mysterious Sovereign," Cyrus said and took an experimental bite of the pie. It still tasted fantastic, but he chewed slowly, his appetite suddenly suppressed. "The one whom no one will name."

"No one *can* name him," J'anda said with a quick shake of the head. "All who have known him fear him more than anything."

Cyrus watched the enchanter intently. He placed his silverware upon the table with a light clatter and leaned forward. "Why? Why do you—so far outside his reach, one of the strongest enchanters in Arkaria—why do you fear him?"

"There is no place outside his reach," J'anda said quietly, in a voice that reminded Cyrus of dry dust blowing in a desert wind. "No place he cannot reach you, no place he cannot harm you if he is of a mind to."

"You had a death mark against you two years ago," Cyrus said. "By his order. If he's as powerful as you say, why didn't he kill you then?"

"He could have, I am convinced," J'anda said. He held up a wrinkled hand. "At any moment. As for why he did not …" J'anda sighed, eyes looking about at the tables nearest them. They were empty, chairs pulled out and abandoned, nothing remaining upon them but dirty plates and half-filled cups. "I do not think you know how old I am."

"I don't—"

"I am one hundred and thirty eight years of age," J'anda said with an absolute calm. "I was a little over thirty when the last great war between my people and the elves came upon us. I fought in the Sovereign's service during that time, with great distinction. I was a middle-class child, one of the few, and I came up from the mids of Sovar to become the single most acclaimed enchanter in the Sovereign's army."

Cyrus watched J'anda, unblinking. "I've always known you were good, but—"

"I am without peer," J'anda said quietly. "Believe me. I have traveled the world—Reikonos, Pharesia. With the exception of some of the elves who have practiced their craft for thousands of years, I am the single greatest enchanter under the age of three thousand in Arkaria. In the entirety of the Elven Kingdom, there are perhaps ten enchanters who could best me in all the facets of our art. Such is my skill that I was offered a teaching position at the Gathering of Coercers in Reikonos—which as you may know is the only enchanter league still open outside of Saekaj. It is run by seven of the elves whom I would consider my betters."

Cyrus waited for him to say anything that could be disagreed with. He heard nothing, so he merely nodded. "You'll get no argument from me that you're the best."

"I do not wish to brag, but I wanted to establish something," J'anda said, and a flash of discomfort made itself plain on his face. "I was a hero of Saekaj. My abilities won many battles in the last war. The Sovereign praised me personally, bestowing every possible medal of the dark elven army upon me. His eye settled upon me, and his ministers held me up as an example of the new wave of leadership and heroism coming up in the army. I was toasted, praised, put up as someone to aspire to. A great enchanter from a good family, with the right skills, whose belief in the Sovereign," his expression turned pained, "was absolute.

"Within a year, I left and never returned until I was summoned back to account for my crimes during the time when we were accused of raiding convoys." J'anda's shoulders had settled as though there were a great weight upon them. "The Sovereign ... he drove me out."

Cyrus gave that a moment's thought. "He exiled you?"

"It is ... difficult to explain," J'anda said with a sigh. "He did things to me, to someone who was dear to me ..." the enchanter's face fell, "... unspeakable things. Things that frightened and horrified me enough to leave without ever looking back. I went from the noble hero to unmentioned in an instant, a stinging blow to the Sovereign's propaganda machinery, I am certain."

Cyrus leaned forward just a little more. "Why are you telling me this?"

"Because I fear him," J'anda said, looking up. "*Everyone* fears him." There was a hardness in the enchanter's eyes. "And I don't want to fear him anymore. I want to stop him. I want to end his reign, to find the way to beat him again the way the elves did a hundred years ago. I am sick of people suffering on his account, on every side of this war. Some child is being drafted into his army and handed a spear right now, thrown to the front lines at Reikonos so that he can die for the Sovereign's purposes." J'anda straightened. "I must return to Saekaj Sovar."

"What?" Cyrus blinked. "Why?"

"We need to know what he is up to," J'anda said, calmly. "We need someone on the inside."

"They'll know you're an enchanter," Cyrus said, letting the urgency of his words carry them out of his mouth. "They have cessation spells, they'll annul your illusions and expose you—"

"He will take me back into his army," J'anda said, his Adam's apple moving up and down in his throat. "He will accept my return without question."

"You've fought in Sanctuary *against* his army," Cyrus said. "You're a traitor to him, and he will execute you."

"No, he won't," J'anda said with a shake of his head. "All I need do to return is come into his presence, beg forgiveness, tell him I am cured of my ..." a look of disgust crossed the enchanter's face, "... deviance, and that I have come back to the fold, and he will allow me back in."

"This is ridiculous," Cyrus said. "It gets us nothing."

"You are wrong," J'anda said with a shake of the head. "I will be in the heart of the enemy. I can spy upon them—"

"You'll be caught," Cyrus said. "Their first instinct will be to assume you're a traitor—"

"Some will believe that," J'anda said. "Not the Sovereign, though. He is ..." J'anda made a face of deepest disgust, "... attached to me. He will find some use for me outside of sensitive areas until I can prove myself to him once more."

Cyrus paused, letting the noise of the Great Hall take up the silence between them. "What will you have to do to prove yourself to him?"

J'anda sighed. "Things I do not care to do."

"Kill people?" Cyrus asked. "Kill humans?"

"Doubtless," J'anda said. "Humans that would die anyway, but yes."

"Worse than that?" Cyrus asked.

"There is nothing worse than killing," J'anda said, "but I will have to prove myself reformed in other ways, yes."

"Such as?"

"None you need worry about, my friend," J'anda said with a reluctant smile. "The Sovereign is getting troops from somewhere. We need to know where from. He has an alliance with the trolls to some benefit—we need answers on that as well. I can get us this information—at some cost to myself, yes," J'anda said, "but I see no other way to it but through this."

"J'anda, we'd be sending you into the heart of the enemy capital with no assurance you'd come back alive," Cyrus said, his pie entirely forgotten. "It's not worth it."

"I have great regrets from my youth," J'anda said, using a hand to push the hair out of his eyes and looking up at Cyrus with a straightened form. "I helped crush a rebellion within the depths of Sovar that might have driven the Sovereign out of Saekaj once and for all. I aided the Sovereign's war against the elves and the humans, helped kill countless people. I hid who I was behind an illusion designed to protect me from the scorn and reprisal of my own government. Because of my actions in Luukessia, I am now an old man." He leaned toward Cyrus, and his voice became hushed. "I do not know how much time I have left, but I do not wish to die filled with all these regrets. Give me your blessing to go to Saekaj. Let me learn his secrets so that we can break him—together."

Cyrus leaned back in his chair, let his fingers caress the stubble on his cheeks and upper lip. "Let's say I believe you could do all these things—gain the Sovereign's confidence, find out his secrets, avoid getting killed, and erase some of these regrets. You're talking about mastering your fear of someone who's held a chain around your thoughts since before you left his service." He waited a moment as J'anda nodded. "How am I supposed to believe you can do all this—confront all this, play this role—when you can't even say his name?"

J'anda smiled faintly. "You are clever indeed, my friend. You twist my own words around and point them back at me to get me to tell you what you have longed to know." He leaned back, and his eyes drifted up contemplatively. "You are right, of course. Fear keeps his name hidden from the outside world; I have not dared to speak to any other the identity of the Sovereign, even a century removed from his rule." He blinked and focused once more on Cyrus. "Very well, then. If I tell you the name of the Sovereign, will you give me your blessing to carry out this mission?"

Cyrus stared at J'anda, pondering it for just a second. "You have my word."

J'anda nodded slowly, looking down. "Then you shall have your name." He seemed to steel himself, like he was summoning it up from deep within. "And that name is ...

"Yartraak. The God of Darkness is the Sovereign of Saekaj Sovar."

Chapter 28

"So you let him go?"

It was Vaste who had asked the question as they all sat arrayed around the Council Chambers, occupying their usual chairs. Cyrus sat with his hands folded over his mouth, surveying the remainder of them. *The chambers seem to grow in size, but in reality, it is we who shrink in number.* "It was not my place to hold him here against his will," Cyrus answered.

A quiet hung in the Council, every one of them watching him, lost in their own thoughts after his revelations.

"I have to admit, I'm more than a little surprised that the Sovereign is Yartraak," Ryin said after a pause. "How is that not a widely known fact?"

"Yartraak is an intimidating beast," Curatio said quietly. "The fact that he directly runs Saekaj is what I would consider a closely-hidden open secret. It is known by many yet spoken by few outside the caves of Saekaj. Or within it," he added.

"Why do they fear his reprisal?" Ryin asked. "Have they some cause to fear?"

"Fear the hand of the Sovereign?" Curatio said, looking over his hands at the druid. "Why, yes, in fact. Aloakna was the last affront to him, I believe."

"Aloakna?" Nyad said, more than a little disturbed. "What do you mean?"

"He had his troops sack and burn the city recently, if you will recall," Curatio said. "A largely neutral place, but one filled with a dark elven populace that had rejected his darkness and traded with everyone in equal measure. His troops destroyed it while we were in

Luukessia, salting the earth, pulling down every edifice stone by stone, and annihilating the populace. It was a place where his name was spoken as a jest, as a curse and in defiance of his edicts." The healer wore a grim look, still seated next to the high backed chair of the Guildmaster that remained empty. "So, yes, there is cause to fear the Sovereign. He is vengeful, and that is perhaps one of the lighter of his heavy-handed strikes over the last ten thousand years that he has ruled Saekaj."

"He is frightful," Erith said, and Cyrus watched her bow her head to hide her face as she spoke. "He was gone before I was born and did not return until after I had left, but the sense of what he'd done to the people of Saekaj Sovar was so pervasive, so dispiriting that even the children who had never known his rule feared to speak his name aloud in any context that connected him to command of the city."

"But why?" Ryin asked, and he slumped back in his chair. "There are gods, and they walk among some of us. Why fear to speak of that? Why would not Saekaj embrace that and trumpet it from their rooftops, that they are guided by the fingers of their divine?"

"There has long been an understanding," Curatio said, "since the days of the War of the Gods, that there is only so much interference in the affairs of mortals that they will brook from one another."

"Now this is interesting," Vaste said, suddenly sitting more upright in his seat. "Exactly how much is too much?"

Curatio sighed. "I am not prepared to speak on this at length because there is much about the events of that war that is simply ... not wise to indulge in thinking about. However, for an example, every ruler of the major powers has some method of contact for each of their matron and patron gods, and can receive some assistance from them as needed."

Something clicked in Cyrus's head. "A few years ago, Isabelle told me that in the wake of the Big Three's destruction of Retrion's Honor, Pretnam Urides and the Council of Twelve threatened to remove them from the city. She seemed to genuinely fear whatever they had threatened her with."

"It was gods," Vara said quietly, meeting Cyrus's gaze only briefly. "She mentioned to me last year that thanks to recent events, they were less beholden to the Council of Twelve's edicts. She was likely speaking of the death of Mortus."

"It would not surprise me if Urides pulled something of that sort," Curatio said. "He was never reluctant to exercise his power over others when need be, and having a god or multiple gods confront the heads of the most powerful guilds in the land is precisely the sort of power play that would put an overweening guild in its place."

"We're back on gods again," Longwell said with a deep sigh from across the table. "We just can't seem to get away from them for whatever reason."

"Their marks are stitched into this world," Curatio said quietly, "their fingerprints indelibly upon all that they touch, including mortal lives and affairs. Their currents of magic eddy about us still, and all they have done is still intertwined with the powers of our days."

"That's great," Vaste said, "but much like Longwell, I just wish they'd all bugger off and let us be."

"I hate to bring this back to business since we're having such a lovely anti-theistic conversation," Cyrus said, "but we are being paid to look for one of these deities, and we've made little in the way of progress thus far. I hate to send Arydni a missive telling her we're going to have to duck out on the job she's paying us to do, but I don't see any paths forward, only dead ends."

"Do not dare send any such message," Curatio said, looking grim. "I am doing a rather exhaustive amount of research at present, trying to find notations about any similar phenomenon to what we saw in the Realm of Life that I might have observed during the War of the Gods when deities were killed."

"I take it by your response that you've had no luck thus far?" Cyrus asked.

"Little to none, yes," Curatio said, frustration apparent in his scowl. "I have a rather exhaustive list of journal entries from those days, but the problem is that none of the ones I keenly remember seem to match what is happening in the Realm of Life at the moment."

Vaste spoke. "Did I miss something, or did you just admit to penning a firsthand account of what happened when some of the gods died?"

Curatio stared at the troll, unblinking. "Mortus was not the first god I witnessed die, if that's what you are asking."

The silence persisted at the table until Vaste spoke again. "How many of them did you watch die?"

Curatio's answer felt like it was an age in coming. "More than I care to count."

Cyrus started to ask a follow-up question to that, but a knock sounded at the door. "Go away," Vaste said loudly, "we're in the middle of a rather important line of inquiry here!"

The door cracked and Thad Proelius's head peeked in. "I apologize for the disturbance, but you have an urgent emissary from the ... uh ... the Human Confederation."

"Tell them we'll be with them in a bit," Vaste said, waving his hand in dismissal at the Castellan of Sanctuary. "We're busy at the moment."

"I'm afraid this can't wait," Thad said, and Cyrus turned around in his seat to look at the warrior. His face was red as a cabbage leaf from the reaches of Greeuwton, and his breaths came in gasps, as though he'd just run up the stairs. "The envoy is—"

"Some prim, prissy little officer of the human army, I'm sure," Vaste said, waving a hand again at Thad. "Look, we're in the midst of an important discussion which—"

"Which can wait, I presume?" The high voice came from behind Thad as the door to the Council Chambers squeaked open, revealing a figure behind the red-armored warrior.

Thad moved aside as though the man had poured scalding water upon him, leaving the new arrival framed in the door. He was portly, though much of his bulk was hidden under brown robes. The staff he had used to push open the door was resting in his grasp now, crowned by a crystal at the top that indicated it was not just a walking staff. *He carries power with him*, Cyrus thought, recognizing the figure for who he was.

"Pretnam Urides," Curatio said, rising to his feet and bowing his head. "Welcome to Sanctuary."

Chapter 29

"May I enter?" Pretnam Urides asked with a little flourish, a wave of his staff.

"By all means," Curatio said with but a moment of hesitation.

The head of the Human Confederation's ruling council entered the chambers, trailing behind him a smell that reminded Cyrus of gold. It overtook the sweet smell of the hearth as he walked behind Cyrus, staff hitting the ground with each step. His cloak rustled, and when he reached the head of the table, he stood next to Alaric's old chair. He stared at it, though he seemed to hesitate in its presence and made no move to sit.

Vara, in the seat next to where he stood, fidgeted slightly, easing herself subtly away from the head of the Council of Twelve. She noticed Cyrus looking and blanched, as though she had been caught doing something embarrassing.

"What brings you down to the Plains of Perdamun?" Curatio asked without preamble. The healer was still standing, facing Urides with only Alaric's old seat between them. "I trust this is not a social visit."

"Hardly," Urides said with a stern look around the table. His eyes lingered on Cyrus for a moment longer than any of the others before traversing onward. "I have a purpose in hand, and it is the hiring of Sanctuary's army for immediate deployment."

There was a quiet silence. Vaste spoke first. "You think you can just walk in here and throw gold at us to get us to do your will?" He paused. "It's like you know us or something."

"What task did you have in mind?" Cyrus asked as Urides stared at Vaste with a half-scowl, as though not sure what to make of the troll. With greatest reluctance, he turned back to Cyrus.

"The keep of Livlosdald in the Northlands," Urides said. He waited to see if any of them would react. "Have any of you heard of it?"

"I've passed it," Cyrus said. "A few years ago, in a trek through the North."

"It guards the town of Etriehndell," Urides said and adjusted his wire-rimmed spectacles. "The dark elves are moving upon it now, and we have little in the way of defense in the area. We would have your army interdict the dark elven force moving up to take the keep. Without aid, it will fall by the morrow."

"How much would you be offering us to guard this keep for you?" Longwell asked.

Urides stared at the dragoon. "I'm not offering you a single piece of gold for merely guarding the town. You could form a little line around it, weather a charge or perhaps two, declare yourselves outmatched and withdraw with my money. No, I'm not offering you anything to merely guard the town. I will pay you fifteen million gold pieces should you hold the dark elven armies off the keep until we can get our reinforcements in place."

"First of all," Cyrus said, "thirty million. Second of all, you'll need to set a time and day when your reinforcements will be relieving us, or else I'm not committing to the battle."

Urides watched him shrewdly. "And why is that, may I ask?"

Cyrus sat back in his chair. "Because you could delay reinforcements until we broke and were killed and declare our obligation unfulfilled, then sweep in afterward with your reinforcements and win the battle hands down after we had weakened your opposition."

Urides nearly smiled. "Quite right. Twenty two million gold pieces, and you shall hold until noon on the day after tomorrow."

"Wait," Vaste said. "How many dark elves would we be facing?"

"Some fifty thousand," Urides said as though it were naught but a pesky detail. "Do we have a deal?"

"Yes," Cyrus said.

"That was a quick vote of the Council," Vaste said sourly. "Why, I've never seen us come to an accord so swiftly."

"All opposed?" Cyrus asked, not taking his eyes off Urides. He waited for a count of five. "The ayes have it."

"Excellent," Urides said, with a quick bow of his head. "As I think we understand each other, I will have half the gold transferred to you immediately, with the other half held back in case you should fail." He leaned forward. "And if you should fail, I don't think I need to warn you that we'll be wanting—"

"Your gold back, yes," Cyrus said. "It was implied."

"I mean not to leave any room for misunderstanding," Urides said, narrowing his eyes. "I will have it sent as a sign of good faith. Do not disappoint me." He straightened and gave the chair to his left one last perfunctory look. It stood taller than he by several heads. "Garish." He looked around the table once more. "Now, if you'll excuse me—" He tapped his staff once against the ground, and it began to glow with the light of a return spell. With a flash he disappeared.

There was a long pause, and then several voices began to speak at once.

"I think we should have talked that over before agreeing—" Vaste said.

"Fifty thousand against our fifteen?" Ryin asked.

"Long odds," Nyad said, a hint of nervous flutter in her voice.

"I hope you know what you're doing," Erith said, sotto voce.

"My men are ready for a fight," Longwell said with a hard edge to his voice. "More than ready if it means helping our people in the Emerald Fields with the proceeds from this."

"What is your plan, General?" Curatio asked, his voice coming last and overpowering them all.

"I'm going by memory," Cyrus said, ignoring all that had been said save for Curatio's question, "but if I recall correctly, Livlosdald is at the mouth of a forested valley, with the town of Etriehndell about a mile or two north down the valley. We won't need to worry about getting flanked because the valley will make army movements around us impossible—unless they were to have sent an advance force to the next nearest portal north. That's unlikely because it's several days ride from Livlosdald, but I'll send a scout anyway—Nyad, if you could, please. Check on that for us."

"Now?" The wizard stood, looking a little dazed.

"No time like the present," Cyrus said. "You should be able to teleport to … I think it's called Verklomrade."

"It is," Curatio said, staring at him.

"Check with the guard contingent around the portal to make sure they're still there, no dark elves passed through recently, then come back," Cyrus said. He waited a beat, and when Nyad did not move—"Haste is rather important."

"Oh." She held up a hand, and it shook as she cast a spell that teleported her away with a flash of green magic.

"We'll move the army directly to the Etriehndell portal," Cyrus said, tapping a finger on the table as he thought out loud. "Everything we have, save for a contingent of five hundred to keep the Emerald Fields under guard and another five hundred for the wall here. Before we leave, we seal the foyer portal and close the gates."

"Gods, your mind moves fast to war and all the possibilities," Vaste said.

"This is what a General does," Longwell said, voice radiating a kind of quiet awe.

"The force they'll meet us with is going to be predominantly foot soldiers of some kind or another," Cyrus said, pushing back his chair and causing it to screech against the stone floor as he stood. "There will be spell casters, though, and cavalry. We have the advantage in that department, but they'll—"

"I think I've heard enough," Vaste said and stood. "I trust you'll be blathering like this for some time yet?"

Cyrus blinked at him. "There are strategic and tactical concerns to work through—"

"You'll handle those just fine whether I'm present or not," Vaste said, and started toward the door. "I'll tell your squire Odellan to get ready for a volley of orders while I start haranguing the healers into getting ready."

"I'll go organize the druids and wizards," Ryin said as he stood slowly, almost reluctantly. "Since it would seem we're once again locked into a course that will carry us into battle for the sake of gold." He held up his hands, palm out. "Not that I am complaining or suggesting we do otherwise, merely giving voice to that which all of us are thinking."

"Yes, well, you could have let the rest of us think it for ourselves," Vaste said as he opened the door. "Presumptive bastard."

"I'll marshal the dragoons," Longwell said, standing with a little more spring in his step than Cyrus had seen when he'd entered the chamber. "Should I assume you'll need us on horseback?"

"Definitely," Cyrus said. "The mobility of your cavalry is one of our greatest advantages. Also, Samwen?" He waited for the dragoon to look back at him before speaking again. "Track down our man Forrestant. We'll need his division to start preparing immediately. Have them find a wizard and get to the battlefield with a scouting party to start making preparations."

"Can do. I'll get to work, then," Longwell said and thumped the table with a jolt of enthusiasm before he exited behind Ryin.

"I'll get out of the way, too," Erith said, standing slowly.

"Matters to attend to?" Curatio said with a wan smile.

"No." Erith paused at the door. "All this talk of strategy and tactics bores me." She shut the door behind her.

"I should like to do a bit more research before we leave," Curatio said from his place at the table. "I trust you have all this well in hand?"

"Sure," Cyrus said, half in thought and half watching who was left in the room with him.

"Very good," Curatio said, and walked toward the door. "I'll leave you to it, then." He disappeared through the door with nary a sound.

Cyrus stared, thoughts of the impending battle gone from his mind momentarily. Vara sat across the table from him, staring down at the pitted surface of the wood. "And you?" Cyrus asked. "Do you need to ... rally the knights or engage in some preparation?"

She shook her head slowly, still staring down at the table. "It's going to be like this from now on, isn't it?" She looked up at him, her eyes full and tired. "Going from fight to fight, taking gold in exchange, for as long as we've got the Luukessians to support."

"They won't need our help forever," Cyrus said. "We just need to get them up and running, self-sufficient—"

"And until the day they are, we'll be whoring ourselves out for gold." Vara shook her head slowly. "This was not how it was supposed to be."

"You said yourself there was no other way."

"There must be some other way," Vara said. "Some other way than casually falling into line with the plans of Pretnam Urides within minutes of his arrival. He throws shiny metals in our direction and we instantly debase ourselves before him? Without even a hint of discussion before deciding?"

"The purse was rich," Cyrus said. "More than we'd get from Purgatory in these days."

"Purgatory," Vara said. "There was a time when it was paying us sixty million gold pieces per trip. You cannot tell me that even in current conditions we cannot get—"

"Two hundred and fifty thousand gold pieces," Cyrus said, and his gauntleted fingers rubbed at his brow. "Last trip. We offered the spoils to our contacts in Fertiss, Huern, Reikonos, Pharesia—even Enterra, for the love of the gods! There are no buyers. Other guilds have begun to regularly best the trials, and the market is flooded. Soon we'll be fortunate indeed to get a hundred thousand gold for a trip." He raised his hands. "This is it. Mercenary work pays in this time of war."

"And we are mercenaries." Her voice dripped with reproach.

"We have consequences to pay for," Cyrus said, and he could feel a pain in his chest. "I am sorry for them, but they are there. We owe these people for what we unleashed. They grow closer to self-sufficiency by the day. Another year, perhaps two, and I think we'll be free of—"

"Then what?" Vara said. "Our guildmates get a piece of the spoils, and they've become accustomed to the proceeds of these mercenary jobs. Do you think they'll settle back into a routine of idle treasure—like the bauble we gained from the Mler—hunting for possible rewards when definite ones are waiting? Do you know what the word in Reikonos is right now?" Her face flushed red. "If you're looking to join a guild, go to Sanctuary. Because we're getting wealthy while everyone else is being bled dry by their homestead clauses." She had no humor in her expression, which was somewhere between sorrow and fury. "Except we're not, are we? Perhaps our members are, but the guild is poorer than we were at the start of this bloody war."

"We have no control over the war," Cyrus said, speaking cautiously. "We have no control over the price of goods for our endeavors in Purgatory. We have no ability to take back the actions that led us to this place—killing Mortus, losing Luukessia—all we have left is the choice to move forward the best way we know how. That's by taking care of the people we are obligated to, however we have to do it." He paused and licked his lips. "Defending Livlosdald is not a bad thing. They would surely be overrun by the dark elven army if not for us—"

"Don't," she said, snapping as she stood. "Don't justify our mercenary actions by saying we would do these things anyway because they are righteous. If they were truly righteous, we should not have to take payment to do them, and we would not set a date of withdrawal, we would stay until the defense was done!" She lowered her head again, her gaze on the table. "This is not how he would have wanted it to be."

"If I could figure out what Alaric would have done in these circumstances," Cyrus said, "I would do it."

She looked up at him, face cold. "You are not him."

Cyrus stood slowly and felt the distance of the table between them. "I'm fully aware of that."

"I heard them talking to you," she said, staring at him. "I know what Vaste would have you do—what he would have you be. Guildmaster."

"I don't want it," Cyrus said, looking away. "I don't want to be in charge."

"It isn't always about what you want," she said, drawing his attention back to her. "You won't run unopposed."

"I don't know that I'll run at all," Cyrus said, and he felt himself redden. "I didn't ask for the position."

"Then don't take it," she said. "Because if I win, my intention is to hold the role of Guildmaster until the day Alaric returns—"

"He's not coming back," Cyrus said and punched his fist at quarter strength onto the table top for emphasis. "And every time you talk about it, you sound like a delusional madwoman, like one of the washers who wander the streets of Reikonos and wring their garments out after laundering them in the fountain. Spewing your daft ideas across anyone who will listen—"

"He is not dead," she said, her face flushed red as fire. "I know it sounds mad, but I can feel it. He is not dead."

Cyrus placed his other knuckle on the table and leaned forward, lowering his head and shoulders so that most of his weight rested on his hands. "Yes. It sounds mad."

"Well, you know what sounds mad to me?" Vara said, and she moved from her place at the table around toward him, only a few feet away. "The idea that a man who can go insubstantial on a whim would drown without leaving so much as a hint of his body behind. Nothing. Not a sign but his helm to indicate he is actually dead."

"He would not leave Sanctuary," Cyrus said, still resting his weight on his knuckles but looking sideways now at Vara. "He would not abandon us."

"You didn't see him at the end." Her body was frozen, stiff and unmoving. "He was slipping. In the last days of the siege he was not himself, he conversed with me in ways that he had never before spoken to me, and about things that felt … simply odd. He snapped and killed Partus in a fit of pique, he acted as though he were drunk and taken to deep ponderings—"

"I don't need to know this," Cyrus said, and turned his head back to the table. "I have a battle to plan."

"Do you think me mad?" she asked, and he could feel the stiffness of her posture as he stood there. "Truly mad?"

"I don't know."

She did not say anything else, and he heard her slow, dignified steps as they carried her out the doors of the Council Chamber. It was only after she left and the door shut softly behind her, that words came back to him, ones he had heard nearly a year and a half earlier—the night before he had left for Luukessia.

"Goodbye," Cyrus had said to Alaric, *"We'll see you then."*

"No," the Ghost had said, *"you won't."*

Chapter 30

Night had nearly fallen upon the Livlosdald keep by the time their preparations were completed. Cyrus stood in the last rays of the sun, shining on him from where it rested on the horizon ahead. Forests flanked either side of the road, a rutted dirt path of the sort found in the more provincial parts of the Confederation. A breeze kicked up and blew cool air with traces of wildflower scent from the open meadow that stretched before the Army of Sanctuary, leading up to the trees in the distance.

A steady hum of conversation went on behind Cyrus, the dull roar of an army over twenty thousand strong in formation. He stood out front with the other officers, ahead of the massive lines of Sanctuary's force sorted neatly into divisions as he'd laid them out on the map. He took slow, steady breaths as he stared into the fading sun, knowing from the scouting parties he'd sent ahead that their foes were nearly here.

And that thought brought only a grim smile to his face.

"Ryin?" Cyrus called up to the druid, who floated thirty feet in the air above him, the Falcon's Essence spell allowing him to levitate.

"I can see them," the druid said, his voice drifting down to Cyrus. "Less than a mile away and about to come through the trees. They're perfectly on the road, so it would seem they've discovered our preparations."

"Good," Cyrus said. The afternoon had been spent pitting the road through the forest on either side to keep the dark elven army in a long, narrow line. The pits were about three feet deep and concealed well enough that they would be a wicked surprise for anyone who took a wayward step onto them.

"Their front lines are trolls," Ryin said, and his voice was higher, alarmed. "Three dark elf knights lead them on horseback."

"Oh, good," Cyrus said under his breath. "I hope they're not Unter'adons."

"Those are children of the Sovereign, yes?" Vaste asked. "Can't pretend I'm not a bit curious how that works."

"Perhaps someone will educate the troll on the art of conjugal relations later," Vara said with a half-smile. "So long as it's not me."

"That was actually funny," Vaste said. "But the question remains—immortals fathering children with mortals?"

"As though that has never happened before," Curatio said, somewhat amused. "It will happen again, I expect."

"Planning ahead, eh, Curatio?" Vaste said. "You old dog."

Curatio sighed. "One does not get so old as to lose appreciation for the good things in life."

"The first rank is approaching the edge of the forest," Ryin said. "The three dark knights are still leading the way. They're getting a bit far out in front of the trolls now."

Cyrus looked toward the horizon. The sun was set, a faint purple glow lighting the sky. He could see shadows and silhouettes in the gap between the trees. "I need an Eagle Eye spell, please." His vision lit a few seconds later and he could see the trolls snap into focus as the whole world became lighter around him. "Thank you, whoever did that."

"It was me," Vaste said. "I wouldn't want you to have to fight by the light of Vara's blade alone."

Cyrus shot Vaste a look. "How did you hear about that?"

Vaste shrugged. "As a creepy necromancer once said, 'dead men tell tales.'"

"Ugh," Vara said. "Malpravus. I could have gone the rest of my considerable life span happy without being reminded of his bony arse ever again."

"Why do you immediately think of his arse?" Vaste asked.

Before Vara could reply, Cyrus's attention was diverted to the three horsemen riding ahead of the troll legions. They were halfway across the clearing toward the Sanctuary army, hundreds of feet from the front rank of trolls and galloping faster toward Cyrus and the officers.

"Looks like somebody's keen for a fight," Erith said.

"They want to kill Cyrus," Curatio said shrewdly. "They presume that if they kill him before the battle, it will go badly for us."

There was a pause, and the sound of the hoofbeats drew ever closer.

"Nyad," Cyrus said, making a split decision, "I need a cessation spell."

"Wait, what?" Nyad asked, edge of panic in her voice. "You mean to fight them? You won't be able to be healed if I've got a cessation spell up!"

"Just do it," Cyrus said, drawing Praelior. He could smell the leather of the hilt as he drew the blade, the sound of it pulling free like a song to his ears. He took a step forward, then another, the world slowing down around him. The chatter of his army faded. "The rest of you hold position here."

"And now we come to the point in the battle where our general goes out and gets himself killed in the name of stubborn pride," Vaste said.

"This is foolish," Curatio said. "You have nothing to prove to them."

"It's not them I'm proving something to," Cyrus said and broke into a run. His feet thundered against the ground. The three black knights were only a hundred paces ahead, their armor shadowed as he would have expected from their kind. It was smooth, blued steel that looked navy, near black, and his eyes almost slid off it. They rode dark horses as well, big destriers that were as bred for war as the men atop them. Plate mail was even draped across the horses, designed to protect them in a battle.

The first of the knights dismounted, and the second followed him a moment later. The third remained ahorse, hanging back.

"Your head will make a fine trophy for my master," the first dark knight said with a grunt as he approached, slowing to a walk, "and I shall carry your sword into battle as my own."

"This old thing?" Cyrus waved Praelior at the dark knight, now only a half dozen paces from him. "You sure you want it? Let me give you a closer look."

Cyrus leapt at the dark knight, blade extended before him. The dark knight had no time to react, and Cyrus buried the blade under the dark elf's chin and thrust it up. He ripped it down, hard, and the blade pulled free, knocking the dark knight's helm from his head. As the man hit the ground, Cyrus saw that half his face was hanging off. He twitched against the dirt path, well on his way to death, dark blue blood spilling onto the dark ground.

"Anyone else want my head for a trophy?" Cyrus asked, wheeling to face the other two. The one on the ground came at him, but he was too slow. *They're all too slow*, Cyrus thought. He whipped a leg out as the dark knight came at him and kicked the dark elf in the knee. He heard bones break and ligaments tear as the dark elf lost his balance and hit the ground.

Cyrus plunged his sword through the dark elf's gorget as though it weren't there, severing the head in one smooth motion. He stooped to pick it up with one hand and pointed his sword at the last dark knight, the one still on his horse. "Come on, let's get this over with."

If the dark knight feared him, he did not show it by his action. He spurred his horse into a charge directly at Cyrus. Cyrus, for his part, hurled the head at the third dark knight and hit him squarely in the helm. The clanging of the head against the helm rocked the dark knight's head back as Cyrus leapt into the air.

By the time the dark knight was focused back on Cyrus again, it was too late. Cyrus led with Praelior and found the center of the dark knight's chest plate. His sword slid to the nearest crease in the dark knight's armor at the shoulder. There was a tearing noise as Cyrus pulled the dark elf from his horse and something gave way.

A dismembered arm fell before Cyrus, hitting the ground with a thud that was followed a second later by the dark knight himself. Grunts of pain filled the twilight as Cyrus turned from the approaching troll army, still a quarter of a mile away, back to the dark elf with one arm only a few feet from him.

Cyrus passed over the dark elf's body and dipped his sword down just long enough to stab the dark knight in the back of the neck. His struggling ceased instantly, body going slack. "Looks like I'll keep my head for at least a little longer," Cyrus said as he broke into a jog back toward the Sanctuary line.

"Best not to tempt fate with that whole 'keep my head' thing," Vaste said as Cyrus closed the distance back to the line of officers. His boots thudded against the packed dirt of the road with heavy footfalls.

"You heard that?" Cyrus asked, frowning. "The dead came over and had a talk with you?"

"Yes, they're rather displeased with you at the moment," Vaste said. "For some reason I can't fathom, they think you cheated, beating them three on one like that in mere seconds. Something about how they're all good soldiers, from good families, and it's just not fair—" Vaste's face changed to a frown. "They're really quite the group of whiners. I'm glad you killed them."

Cyrus fell back into the line and exchanged a look with Vara, who made a harrumphing noise as he turned to face the coming trolls. "What?"

"You were toying with them for entirely too long," she said, glancing at him out of the corner of her eye.

"Maybe I'm just not as good as you," Cyrus said with a faint smile.

"You were showing off," Vara said.

"I had something to prove," Cyrus said, and looked to Curatio. "Not to me, not to them, but to our army. You can't ask our people to face overwhelming odds without at least showing them that victory is possible in that sort of battle. It's a morale thing."

"I bow to your august wisdom in leading an army," Curatio said. "But the trolls—"

"Ah, yes," Cyrus said. "Ryin?" He looked up. "Signal Forrestant to begin."

"Aye," Ryin said. "Forrestant—BOMBARD!" The druid's call echoed over the Sanctuary lines.

Somewhere in the back of the Sanctuary army, in the sudden silence that followed Ryin's call, Cyrus could hear faint shouting. A moment later, the creak of wood straining, of machinery moving, came loud over the army. In mere seconds, balls of flame overflew Cyrus's position, trailing fire behind them on their way to the forward line of the trolls.

The first impacts came with thunderous explosions. Blasts of fire hit the front rank of the trolls and enshrouded them in orange. Cyrus could feel the heat even at that distance, and the noise that followed was like the loudest thunder he had ever heard.

The front troll line disintegrated under the bombardment, disappearing beneath the flame as surely as if a wizard had sent a spell against them.

"I have to admit," Vaste said into the quiet awe as another wave of flaming spheres filled the air above them in a lazy arc toward the troll legions, "when Mr. Forrestant came to our doors with his proposal, I was somewhat skeptical. I mean, who has even heard of a ... a ..."

"Combat engineer," Cyrus said.

"Yes, who has even heard of one of those?" Vaste said. Another wave of explosions detonated a little farther back, lighting the black smoke left by the first wave's landing. "And when he started talking about building catapults with bombs of Dragon's Breath, and ballistas, and trebuchets—I mean, I honestly tuned him out. But this—" Another explosion filled the air with fire up to the height of a three-story building. "This is impressive. I'm almost awed into silence. In fact, I think I'll just shut up now."

"Finally," Vara said.

Trolls began to stagger forward through the smoke in ones and twos, their green, armored forms appearing out of the dark and shadow. "Archers!" Cyrus called out. "Fire!"

Rangers with bows were stationed on both sides of the formations, out in front of the left and right flank of the Sanctuary army. They looked curious in their cloaks and light leather armor, but when their bows came aloft in perfect synchronization, Cyrus almost felt like he should blanch and duck away. When they loosed their volley of arrows it was not the aimed shots that he was so used to from Martaina. This was a black cloud of arrows, the shafts darkening the twilight sky as they flew in a lazy arc toward the trolls advancing on the Sanctuary army.

Trolls were thick-skinned creatures, Cyrus knew, but as they advanced it was clear that they had lighter leather armor rather than hard steel or mystically enchanted plate mail. The arrows landed among the first wave, a half dozen of which were still advancing, and brought them all to the ground.

"They're certainly not as well equipped as the ones that invaded us last year," Erith said. "Those had hardened armor."

"That stuff is expensive," Cyrus said. "I'm guessing the Sovereign saves it for his elite troops." He looked back at the trolls falling upon the earth before them. "Not the chaff."

The catapults fired again behind Cyrus, and the sky was once more filled with burning projectiles, like shooting stars of incredible intensity propelled through the twilight. They made a screaming noise as they passed overhead, and Cyrus wondered idly where from sprang the noise.

From the fire and storm of flame, dark shadows marched forth. Few here and few enough there, but they gathered on the closer side of the blazing maelstrom, backlit by the light of the inferno. Cyrus saw the arrows descend in volley after volley, a steady downpour of fletchings, wood, and steel, but still the shadows gathered. They formed, a trickle coming onward through the scorching heat, and they marched for the front rank of Sanctuary's army.

"A determined lot, these," Ryin said.

"I don't think determination was missing from the last few groups," Vaste said, "it was their skin, their limbs, and their lives being burnt away that kept them from coming at us the way these are."

And on they came, as Cyrus watched. They closed the distance, more trolls filling in behind them, survivors of the blistering heat of the Dragon's Breath that fell in continuous explosions on the road.

"Up there!" A voice cried, and Cyrus looked. Above the falling projectiles was the outline of a figure, running across the air.

"Druid?" Cyrus asked. They were only a hundred feet away from the front line of the Sanctuary army and partially obscured by smoke. "Martaina—!"

The figure cast a spell that shot from an aimed hand toward the back of the line. There came a great cry from somewhere at the rear of the army, and an explosion roared behind Cyrus, knocking him forward a step. He looked up, and saw an arrow catch the running figure through the head. It fell like a lifeless doll as the explosions in the road in front of him ceased, and the sound of the one behind him faded in his ears.

"Well, damn," Vaste said, casting a look back. "I can't say for certain, but I think that was our catapults."

"It was," Ryin said from above them. His face was as ashen as the falling powder that came to rest on Cyrus's cheek. It was nothing compared to that which he had seen in Termina, but this product of the Sanctuary bombardment was much closer. "It was an ice spell, freezing a lit bomb to a catapult—"

"Yes, well, next time perhaps mind the skies while you're up there so someone doesn't blow up our artillery," Cyrus said, more than a little crossly. The trolls were advancing unhindered now; a trickle at the front, still harried by the falling arrows of the rangers, but bulkier, heavier lines followed not far behind. "Remember!" Cyrus called out to the army behind him. "The bigger your foe is—"

"The harder he'll pound you into stuffing when he hits you," Vaste said under his breath.

"—the bigger the target," Cyrus said, sending Vaste a searing, sidelong glare as he lost the thread of his thought. "And also, if you can see the whites of their eyes—"

"Quickly relocate to somewhere less dangerous," Vaste said. "Such as the Sovereign's throne room."

"Shut up!" Cyrus and Vara hissed in chorus. They exchanged a look, and Vara blushed before turning back to the advancing troll army. The earth shook beneath them, and Cyrus could feel the shocks in his legs. Acrid smoke drifted toward them on the wind.

"Oh, to the hells with it," Cyrus muttered, trying to remember what he'd been thinking of saying before Vaste's jibes had distracted him. "Just follow me!" he shouted, loud enough for it to echo over his army.

The nearest trolls were advancing, only forty feet away now. The front line of Sanctuary officers was holding their ground and waiting. "Follow," Cyrus said and began his advance. He started to run, gripping Praelior tight and turning his gaze toward the troll at the front of the line ahead of him.

Cyrus felt his legs shake with each step, the combination of the trolls' immense weight shaking the ground coupled with his own momentum. The world had slowed around him.

The nearest troll was in front of him, jaws wide, eyes fixed. The blood lust was visible in his eyes, the yell of a war cry on his lips. Cyrus matched it with one of his own, and he saw the subtle blanch from the troll, the moment's hesitation. The fear.

You are mine, Cyrus thought. The smoky air reverberated with the voices of a thousand angry men and women rushing into war. *This army is mine, my weapon, my instrument, and I will use it like I use my sword to strike you down.* He kept his gaze fixed on that first troll. *The frontrunner. First to fall.* He had marked him as such.

The ground between them drew to nothing, and they were nearly upon each other. Cyrus could still smell the hesitation, as obvious as the smoke on the wind. It was the stink of fear, and it permeated the battlefield. *I would have expected more of a troll army.*

They were nearly face-to-face now, though Cyrus was only as tall as the troll's chest. He stared at the eyes, though—those yellow eyes, wide to the whites. *I am the master of fear, the master of death in this place,* Cyrus thought. *And you will bow to me—willingly or not.*

With the last cry of appeal to the God of War, Cyrus brought Praelior down in a strike that severed his trollish foe's leg, sending him to the ground on his remaining knee. The scream of fear, of pain, of terror, echoed in his ears—and it was only the first of many.

Chapter 31

"General!" The shout reached Cyrus's ears from the thick of the battle. He sliced Praelior through the thick leg of another troll, sending the beast toppling to the ground. He was surrounded by piles of green bodies taller even than he was. *I'm used to looking down on my foes in battle; this is a dramatic change for me.*

"What?" Cyrus impaled another and quickly swung his blade around through the thickest part of the troll's body to catch another on a diagonal slash that cut its massive body in half from waist to shoulder. He spared only a glance to see that Odellan was trying to catch his attention, fighting alongside three other warriors to bring down a troll that had gotten past him.

"They are sending a flanking column on our right side, sir!" Odellan called as a massive troll fist came crashing down on one of his compatriots. Odellan landed a spearing blow with his fine blade, stabbing into the troll's chest. A roar was followed by a massive green fist that Odellan blocked with his shield. Cyrus heard the joint-rattling impact even over the chaos of the battle. "It is a schiltron of shielded dark elves, sir!"

"Martaina!" Cyrus called as he swept to the left. He moved almost five feet, cutting the leg from underneath another troll before he realized that it made little difference if he moved; she could surely hear him.

"Sir?" The elf appeared just behind him as he fended off another troll, dodging a heavy-bladed attack and cleaving the troll's wrist as a price for the audacity of striking at him. The sun was now down, the battlefield shrouded in twilight's coming darkness, the orange skies behind the advancing trolls shedding the only light save for the lamps of the army still mostly lined up behind him and the keep that lay far back behind the moat in the rear of their lines.

"The dark elves are trying to send a schiltron up my arse," Cyrus said, gritting his teeth as he hooked Praelior around and leapt, taking the head of the troll whose hand he had just severed. He landed and avoided the falling body. The ground was thick with green corpses, the stacks of them growing in size as the Sanctuary army felled them by the hundreds.

"I'd think they'd pick a target less ripe," Martaina said, and it took Cyrus a moment to catch her sly tone. "By ripe, I mean in terms of smell, not opportunity—"

"Yes, I got that," Cyrus said, pausing to watch Longwell impale a troll so hard the beast was thrown back on its haunches. The dragoon barely held onto his lance as the troll fell, clutching its chest and making a grunting, wailing noise. Their foes were so enormous that Cyrus could not see over the first two ranks of them; for all he knew, they stretched clear back to the horizon. "Would you mind?"

"So you want me to cross the battle," Martaina said, "and break open the shiltron by firing arrows into the gaps in their formation's shields so that our other, less skilled rangers can help pick them apart before they hit our right flank, which," she paused, and he knew she was using her sharp eyes to survey the situation, "have yet to make contact with any enemy forces?"

"That's it exactly," Cyrus said, and he blocked a troll blade with Praelior before throwing it back in his attacker's face so hard that the beast cleaved his own skull. "You've got it."

"Uh huh," Martaina said, near-tonelessly. "Do you realize how well-nigh-impossible it is for an archer to break a schiltron? They have shields all around their formation. It's like a turtle crawling its way across the battlefield. A steel turtle."

"Yes, I realize how nearly impossible it is for an archer to do it," Cyrus said, gritting his teeth as two more trolls came at him. He dodged low and spun to cut both of their knees from beneath them. "Which is why I'm asking you to do it and not some new ranger who just picked up a bow three weeks ago. Are you not capable of this?" Cyrus asked, feeling a note of uncertainty.

"Of course I can do it," Martaina said, and he spared a glance to see her knowing look. "I just wanted to make certain you knew how difficult it was." Without another word, she dashed off, disappearing behind the formation of rangers on the right flank that had retreated closer to the lines of warriors on the right.

"The schiltron, sir," Odellan called to him.

"It's handled," Cyrus said, turning his attention back to the trolls coming at him. They seemed thinner now, their ranks lessened. He felled another, then another, and realized that there were dark elves behind them, peeking from behind the trolls' trunk-like legs. "Is it my imagination or are we coming to the end of the trolls?"

"It's just your imagination!" Vaste called from somewhere behind him. "You'll never see the end of all the trolls, for I will be there to torment you until your dying day!"

"For some reason, I don't doubt that," Cyrus said beneath his breath.

"Imagine how boring your life would be without Vaste to offer retort and commentary on all the questionable choices you make," Vara said, and Cyrus looked to his right to see her there.

"I'm sure you'd take up his slack with greatest glee," Cyrus said.

"I am uncertain that I have time for such an endeavor," she replied, raking her sword across an uncovered green throat. Pea-green blood showered down and she narrowly dodged it. "For there are so very, very many."

"Says the madwoman." Cyrus spoke under his breath, but he caught her gaze for a moment in the midst of the fight and held it. "All right, I'll admit it—you're not mad. Perhaps, anyway. But I don't think he's coming back."

"Are you still on about that?" Vara's voice took a tightness as she answered him back. "I thought you weren't running for Guildmaster."

"I remain undecided," Cyrus said. "But I don't believe he's coming back. He said something to me before he left—that he wouldn't be here when I got back from Luukessia."

"Do you believe he is dead?" Vara said, and she unleashed a blast of force from her palm that sent three trolls toppling into a line of dark elves that had been squeezing their way forward.

Cyrus thought about it long and hard. "Yes. I think he's dead." He paused for just a second, and when she did not answer, he buried Praelior in the neck of a dark elf in leather armor and continued. "Whatever he experienced toward the end—dark thoughts, fits of rage, mysterious ramblings—he knew what he was doing, walking onto that bridge. He knew he was leaving us, which is why he handed me the amulet and destroyed the bridge under himself. He could have done it farther down the line; he chose to destroy it from underneath us because—for whatever reason—he wanted to die." Cyrus lowered his voice. "He wanted to die, Vara. He had reached his end."

A thunderous blast of force rocked the battlefield and swept a path thirty feet wide down the remains of the muddied road that had once led to their lines. Vara's spell swept the dirt from the path and sprayed it over the remaining forces on either side. Bodies were flung limp through the air and came raining down on their compatriots. There was a pause as silence fell over the battle for almost a second in the wake of the spell.

Vara stood with her hand extended, a cone of empty, shredded ground covering the three hundred feet in front of her. Cyrus could see her chest rise and fall under the silver armor with each breath as she stood there, sword in one hand and palm extended from the other.

"Remind me not to get on your bad side," Cyrus said, eyeing her as the roar of battle surged again around them, and dark elven soldiers in boiled leather began to flood back into the empty space left by her spell.

Vara swept her blade back up, both hands on the hilt, and held it in position next to her face. "You are perpetually on my bad side, Cyrus Davidon. You have made camp there, you live there, and I think you exalt in doing so, all the while innocently protesting that you want to be anywhere else."

"Sir, the enemy schiltron is folding!" Odellan's voice reached Cyrus before he could reply to Vara.

There were dark elves swarming them now, and Cyrus dealt a deathblow to four with a long sword swipe that toppled heads from bodies. There was a rank odor in the air, something heavy and rotten that lingered like death blown on a hard wind. "What the hell is that?" Cyrus asked.

"A schiltron is a formation of shielded dark elves," Vaste said from a few paces behind him. Cyrus shot him another annoyed look before realizing it would have little effect. "You should know, you just ordered its destruction not five minutes ago."

"I was talking about that awful smell," Cyrus said, "but I didn't realize you were haunting my steps with such vigor. Clearly it's just you."

Vaste sniffed. "Wow, I hadn't noticed that until you said something. Is it my imagination or is it worse than—"

"Than the trolls?" Vara asked, slicing her way through a charging rank of dark elves clad in full armor. "It is. I always knew corpses emitted a smell following death, but whatever these trolls are doing after they die is possibly the most repugnant thing I have caught scent of since a certain unwashed warrior of Bellarum breezed through the doors of Sanctuary several years ago."

"What the hell was that for?" Cyrus asked, fending off a hacking attack from a bulky dark elf wearing a full suit of plate mail.

"For calling me a madwoman," Vara replied. "Did you think I would merely forget that insult?"

"I think you hurt Vara's feelings," Vaste said.

"Don't be ridiculous," Cyrus said, blanching away from the smell as he plunged Praelior through the flimsy chestpiece of the dark elf, "she doesn't have feelings."

"I actually do," Vara said primly as she fired another blast from her hand, less forceful this time. Twelve dark elves were flung into the rank of soldiers behind them. "There are three distinct emotions—annoyance, blinding rage and 'stab you in the face.'" She buried a sword in the open center slot in the middle of a dark elf's helm, penetrating through the back of his head and the steel beyond. "I suppose it would be obvious even to a dullard such as yourself which state I am presently in."

Cyrus was about to answer when an arrow lodged itself in the face of the next dark elf he was turning his attention to. He paused as the dark elf fell to his feet, then shrugged.

"Oh, no, don't bother turning to see who saved you the trouble of killing that one," came Martaina's voice from behind him.

"You may have killed him, but I still have fifty thousand of his fellows to worry about," Cyrus said, not turning back as another dark elf came at him. "Excellent work on that schiltron, Martaina."

"How would you know?" she asked. "It's not like you could see it from here."

"Rumors reached even my ears," Cyrus said, Praelior cutting through a dark elf's blade as he blocked a strike.

"Well, I have another rumor for your ears," Martaina said, sounding more than a little put out. The stink of the battlefield seemed to be growing stronger, wafting into his nostrils enough that Cyrus felt an involuntary cough come upon him.

"I hope it involves a certain someone's slutty behavior," Vaste said. "And by a 'certain someone,' I mean Cyrus."

"Gods, I could do without your constant monologue on my life, troll," Cyrus said. "What have I done to deserve this?"

"You want a list?" Vaste asked. "Let me get a long parchment."

"Excuse me," Martaina said with faux politeness, "I have news you'll want to hear."

"I am all ears," Vara said from behind a solid line of three dark elves that she was fending off with quick sword work. The clanging of blades was loud enough that Cyrus could hear it from ten feet away over the cacophony of battle.

"A peculiar thing for an elf to say." Vaste's tone was filled with amusement.

"While eliminating that schiltron, I caught sight of the enemy General at the back of the line with the reserves," Martaina said. "We're about to have a problem."

Cyrus waited then glanced at Vaste. "What? No quip for that?"

"I wouldn't want to lighten the mood before she delivers the calamitous news," Vaste said. "Then you might be smiling in amusement as the axe descends. I'd rather cheer you up after you lose your head."

"That doesn't make any sense!" Cyrus said as he caught a dark elf without a helmet in the temple, shearing the top of the soldier's head off. A thick knot of black hair spun in the air, slinging blood that peppered Cyrus's armor as it fell.

"I suspect that fellow would get it," Vaste said.

"If this news doesn't get delivered soon," Vara said, and Cyrus could hear the tension bleeding through her voice, "I am going to turn this blade around and begin hacking my way through our own lines, starting with the troll and going next to the woman whose sole purpose in life seems to be to fling thin pieces of wood through the air at our foes while being vague about important information in the midst of a battle."

"We know the General of the dark elven forces," Martaina said, face twisting with loathing. "And his army. It's Malpravus. And Goliath. They're sitting in reserve waiting to sweep in on the next wave."

Chapter 32

"Spell casters?" Cyrus asked as he grabbed a dark elf and ran his blade across his enemy's throat, blocking a sword strike with his vambrace. The clanging sound of the metal clashing echoed in his ears and he felt the sharp pressure of the hit reverberate up his arm.

"Aplenty," Martaina replied. "They've got them on a line protected by the forward advance of their infantry. Bowmen, too, led by a helmeted ranger that I believe you've made the acquaintance of." Cyrus felt his hand clench harder around Praelior. "All told, looks like about five thousand in number."

"That's surely not their whole army," Vaste said. "They were more numerous than that when last we encountered them."

"They were also being exiled from most of the civilized world when last we encountered them," Vara said. "I can't imagine that's been good for their recruiting."

"I don't know, I would think it would open all manner of possibilities if they sold it right," Vaste said. "'Join Goliath, and become the violent, pillaging brigand you've always wanted to be!'"

Cyrus felt his mind ticking away as he brought his sword down against another dark elf. The smell was rancid, like death had walked among them. He tried to filter it out of his mind.

"Cyrus," Vara said warningly, "do not choose this moment to go empty of skull upon us."

Cyrus shot her a frown. "I am not going empty of skull." He dodged a sword blow and hacked off the arm that had attacked him, leaving a dark elf screaming with blood geysering from the stump. Cyrus punched the dark elf in the face and the screaming ceased.

"Although I am surprised you would say that, given at any normal time you'd say that was my natural state."

"We are about to face off with a guild replete with spell casters," Vara said as the clangor of swords and axes, screams and cries rang over the once-verdant field. It had been pretty once, Cyrus supposed, though he'd been too busy with preparations before the battle to notice and too busy with the battle to spend much time thinking about it since. He stepped into a puddle of blood that splashed upon his black boot. "This is not a common battle with an army like we faced in Termina," Vara said, drawing his attention back to her as she finished beheading a dark elf.

"I suppose you'll be surprised to learn I'm aware of that," he snapped at her, "and I have a solution already prepared."

"Tell me it does not involve our two sides grinding each other up in some facsimile of the process of making sausage," she said.

"What?" Cyrus asked, genuinely agape at her. "No, it does not resemble the process of making sausage." He paused and gave it a moment's thought before a sword blade coming at him forced him to dodge. "At least not any more than any battle does, I suppose."

"Sounds like a winner to me, then," Vaste said. "What do we need to do? Because it looks as though this wave of dark elves is thinning rapidly."

Cyrus looked across the battle and had to concede Vaste was right. The end of this rank of soldiers was visible, and there was a space between them and the next. Cyrus could see a more mixed force over the heads of the dark elves; the lighter skins of humans and elves were visible in the lines of the army, as was the garb of spell casters and even some bows to indicate the rangers in their lines. "Martaina, signal all the wizards to cast a cessation spell over the field of battle and maintain it continuously."

There was an immediate ceasing of the conversation, a long pause in which the sounds of battle filled the air. "Oh," Vaste said, "this old chestnut again."

"And you call me mad?" Vara asked. "Not all of us carry the sword of a god to give us advantage in combat without magic to support us."

Cyrus cut through the last three dark elves in his field of vision and stood, chest heaving with the effort thus far. "Martaina, deliver my orders."

"Yes, sir," the elf said, practically leaking sarcasm. "I can't wait to see how this turns out." When he turned to say something else to her, she was already gone.

"This does seem on the face of it to be a rather odd order," Vaste said, and Cyrus gave him a cocked eyebrow. "See how I said that without any noticeable trace of mockery or derision?"

"I was looking for it," Cyrus said.

"I'm not using it because I'm concerned," Vaste said, face deep with expression. Someone screamed loudly nearby, but Cyrus ignored them as the troll went on. "Concerned that you might think that facing an army of superior numbers without magic to heal our front rank is somehow a valid strategy."

"Relax," Cyrus said, waving him off. Vara lingered nearby, watching, and his eyes met hers. Her irises blazed blue even in the last dying light of the day, and they assessed him, looking straight through him. "We're only going to hold them in place here while they get hit by forces used to fighting without magic."

"You mean to deploy the Luukessia dragoons against them," Vara said. Her icy eyes were still suspicious. "Hit their delicate flank?"

"I do," Cyrus said with a nod. He turned to look toward the Goliath legions, but they were halted in place. "It should be a rather interesting experiment."

"They could die, Cyrus," Vara said. He could see in her eyes the seriousness.

"It's a battle," Cyrus said. "We all could die, though the odds against us go up rather a lot if we choose to waste our numerically inferior forces against spell casters. We can't win a slugging match. Brute force in this fight is pointless. The name of our game is to face them in manageable numbers and with all the advantages in our favor." He paused and looked to his left, where he could see the lines of dragoons on horseback in the distance, just waiting to be turned loose. "Besides, I'll get them a round of resurrection spells after we've won."

"Wow," Vaste said, "is it my imagination or have you become a lot more cavalier about dying?"

"Indeed," Vara said. "I can recall a moment during our first battle in Purgatory in which you told me you wished for none of your troops to die for fear of what they would lose."

"I've died a lot since then," Cyrus said, keeping his eyes fixed on the Goliath army. "It's allowed me a new perspective on life and death."

"I had just assumed you'd forgotten your good sense," Vaste said. "You know, after one resurrection spell too many."

"He—" Vara started.

"Never had any," Cyrus cut her off. "I'm growing tired of that one. Too predictable. If either of you have any better ideas, I'm open to them." He waited, letting the cool twilight air filter in through the cracks of his armor. He moved his neck to the side, willing the heat building up within to escape. "No? Okay, we'll go with my idea, then. Vaste," Cyrus said. "I need you to get back behind the lines with the other healers. I can't take a chance that Goliath might break through and kill any of you, so get your people—"

"*My* people?" Vaste asked, sounding insulted. "I'm not dragging any of those corpses, have you seen the size of them? Plus there's the smell …"

"—get your healers situated in the middle of the lines," Cyrus finished. "Now would be a good time to do that." He made a waving gesture toward the troll.

"You're just sick of me, I can tell," Vaste said, turning away with what looked to Cyrus like reluctance. "I'll be back to annoy you later. Unless they kill you, in which case I suppose I'll have to cast a resurrection spell. If you forget that I'm going to annoy you, though, I'll be most cross with you."

"That very thought will haunt me into staying alive, I assure you," Cyrus said. He watched the troll wave and push his way back through the lines, parting warriors of Sanctuary by nearly knocking them aside.

"You failed to mention the real reason you're doing this," Vara said, as Cyrus turned back to him. "The cessation spell?" She watched him, and he could see her waiting for his reaction. "You lied to him about why you're employing it."

"It would have just upset him," Cyrus said, and the uneasiness within. "And you know how he gets. Best he's forgotten, or else I'd never have gotten him off the front line and back to safety."

"But you didn't forget," she said, almost accusation.

Cyrus shook his head. "No, I didn't forget." He looked back at the Goliath lines, at the massing formation of soldiers, rangers, and spell casters. They waited in the distance, an army of dark elves behind them in lines as far as Cyrus could see. "I'm not sure Vaste did, either, really." He sighed, and looked at Vara, who stared back at him. "After all, it's hard to forget we're facing a foe who can use his magic to raise the corpses of the dead to fight for him."

Finally, Cyrus turned to look across the empty gulf between the lines. The Goliath army still stood well back, prepared for a charge but as yet unmoving. They were line after line of foes, and even to his eye, the mix of spell casters with the warriors and rangers signaled a new sort of challenge. His eyes wandered, the spell that Vaste had cast upon him giving his sight additional clarity with which to hone in on the figures in the distance.

Far to the back of the Goliath line, almost fading into the next rank of dark elves from the Sovereign's army, Cyrus saw him at last. He wore his black cloak and cowl for this occasion, but the cowl was down and his skeletally thin face was visible to Cyrus's aided eyes. He could just make out the smile as Malpravus stood staring across the battlefield. *He smiles, as though he can see me looking at looking at him.*

He probably can, Cyrus thought, staring at the necromancer. He didn't look any different than he had when Cyrus had last seen the Guildmaster of Goliath; just as ungainly, just as bony. And the smile—it was ever the same as it had been. The whole appearance of the dark elf sent a warm rage through Cyrus. He fixated on the enemy general, staring, waiting for him to order his army to move.

It took almost a minute of staring for Cyrus to realize that Malpravus was deep in consultation with the man on his left. He was speaking, mouth moving, thin and satisfied, occasionally opening to grin in a manner more fitting for a deeply satisfying conversation than a battlefield where his army was losing.

"Do you see him?" Vara asked, interrupting Cyrus's reverie.

"Malpravus?" Cyrus asked. "Of course. He'd be hard to miss."

"No," Vara said, and her voice held a mournful tone. "Not Malpravus. Who he's talking to."

Cyrus blinked and refocused his eyes. The spell gave him great clarity of detail, but it took some getting used to. He squinted his eyes, opening and closing them, at first unsure of what he was seeing. *That is not possible.* He blinked again, trying to clear his vision, but when he opened his eyes, what he saw remained exactly the same.

To Malpravus's left stood a man in armor of a dark hue. Spikes on his pauldrons made it look as though an accidental turn would impale the necromancer through the head. His face was hidden under a helm that bore protrusions of its own, spiked like a crown. "It can't be," Cyrus said, scarcely believing it. "He wouldn't …"

"He would," Vara said. "He has."

Cyrus shook his head, never taking his eyes off the dark elf until the man lifted his helm. As the spiked helmet came up, a shock of blackest hair fell from beneath it, and the face became too obvious for even Cyrus to deny any longer.

Terian.

Chapter 33

The army of Goliath came charging only moments later, finally diverting Cyrus's attention from Malpravus and Terian. The two of them stood at the back of the lines as the first warriors of Goliath began their charge. Cyrus met the eyes of a yellow-armored troll in the front rank and knew that the beast would be coming for him.

"Yei," Vara said.

"Verily," Cyrus said with a smile.

"Are you making a joke?" Vara asked, clearly perturbed.

"Sure, why not?" Cyrus kept his eyes on the troll that was charging directly for him. There were others of his kind down the lines, a handful of troll warriors speckled in among the humans, elves and dark elves of the Goliath charge. Their lines were large, an imbalance obvious in the size differential. Cyrus looked down the Sanctuary line and saw much shorter, smaller figures.

"Because we're about to engage a front rank that puts us at a disadvantage," Vara said. "This gallows humor—"

"Is all I have right now," Cyrus said, taking a deep breath of the rank battlefield air. "Well, that and a godly weapon, a plan, and a few prayers I should throw to the God of War."

"And quickly," Odellan said from down the line.

"Vara, Odellan, take a troll each," Cyrus said. "I'll get Yei. Pass the word down the line that anyone with a mystical weapon is to take on a troll and have the rangers try and assist them as the Goliath charge gets close.

The first volley of arrows fired from the rangers now on either side of Cyrus's main line. The warriors at the front had reformed in battle order after the clash with the last dark elven charge. He noticed few gaps, those that had died having been dragged back toward the rear of the lines where they waited to be resurrected by Sanctuary's corps of healers. The swishing sound of the arrows taking flight made little impact on the furious cries of the Goliath army's charge.

"I imagine their spell casters will discover that their spells aren't working right about now," Cyrus said, settling into a ready stance. "And won't that be a lovely surprise for them. Ready the counter-charge!" He waited and heard his call taken up down the line, the rattling of metal weapons against armor and scabbards a fearsome sound that drowned out the Goliath battle cry, if only temporarily. "CHARGE!"

He sprang forward, only a hair faster than others down the line. Cyrus felt a note of surprise; by this point in the battle he expected his forces would be wearying, but there seemed to be a fresh enthusiasm driving them forward. Arrows whistled overhead and he saw Goliath's front line begin to bend, the smaller humans and elves falling from the bombardment of the arrows. No Goliath arrows reached the Sanctuary army; they were simply too far forward of the Goliath line at this point for accuracy.

The clanking of his armor and the pounding of his feet formed a steady drumbeat that pushed him forward. Cyrus took care not to out-advance his army, as Praelior would have given him license to do. He moderated his pace and kept with them, eyeing Vara and realizing she was doing the same. *United in a firm line we pose a much greater threat. Though this doesn't feel as much like leading from the front.*

He angled toward the troll in yellow even as the troll swerved toward him. Cyrus had known Yei back in the days in which Sanctuary and Goliath had been allies. *He's no pushover, but neither is he one of the great tacticians of our time. He's a brawler, and he knows how to use his strength to his advantage.* Cyrus felt the smile come on. *Let's see what he does against someone with more speed, strength and dexterity than him.*

The troll warrior's steps thundered against the ground, rattling Cyrus's teeth. Yei was easily three heads taller than he was, wider than most of the other trolls they had faced, and armored from top to bottom in a way that the trollish soldiers had not been. The yellow paint on the metal plate mail was smeared and cracked from battle, and Cyrus's eyes scoured the surface for the weakest points as he closed the last ten feet to the troll.

A bellow from Yei split the air, a deafening roar that reminded Cyrus of the time he'd heard an elephant from the south make a trumpeting noise while in the square at Reikonos, but louder. Cyrus focused in on the troll's eyes, saw a flaring red iris through the slit in the helm, and shot back an icy stare of his own. Then he smiled as he closed the gap between them.

Yei's sword was massive, taller almost than Cyrus himself, with a blade as wide as Cyrus's thigh. The troll brought it down in a sloppy, overhand diagonal motion as they approached each other. Cyrus guessed if he stayed on his present trajectory, the blade would cleave him in half the way he'd done to countless enemies over the years. The attack was quicker than Cyrus expected.

But not quick enough.

Cyrus slid into the dirt, back armor skidding as he went low. His strength carried him into the slide, momentum pushing him forward under the troll's massive slash. The blade missed the top of Cyrus's helm by less than an inch as he slid between the troll's legs and jabbed up. He plunged Praelior into the gap at Yei's knee.

The blade slid into the chainmail beneath the plate armor, and the sound of links breaking reached Cyrus's ears. Something between a grunt and a scream made its way from between Yei's lips, and Cyrus saw a mighty leg begin to buckle. Cyrus slashed hard, and dark green blood squirted from the wound he'd made, sliding down Praelior's slightly glowing edge.

Yei began to fall, tilting to the side as Cyrus watched the lines of Goliath warriors following behind closing in on him. He could see them moving slowly, as though trapped in the slide of tree sap down a trunk. They were moving at normal speed, though, he knew that much from experience. It was only his perception in which they were slowed.

Cyrus tore his blade free from Yei's knee joint as the troll began to fall. Cyrus had felt his sword cut through the tendons, shredding the troll's limb. He rolled to his right as Yei fell to his left, and the echoing power of the warrior's heavy landing reverberated through the ground and into Cyrus's armor.

Cyrus fended off three warriors in mismatched armor as he saw motion down the line. The Goliath trolls were moving toward him in a stream, eddying the currents of battle like boulders immune to the tide. They swept through the lines of the fight scarcely deigning to notice their own warriors as they pushed through, nor those of their Sanctuary foes as mailed fists and blades of steel were thrown to cast all opposition aside.

They're coming for me, Cyrus thought with a little smile. *They must have been told to charge me if Yei failed.* Cyrus thrust his blade into one of the long eyeholes of Yei's helm, then twisted as a geyser of green blood fountained up for only a second before it fell back down. He stabbed down again into the gap between gorget and helm in the troll's armor and was rewarded with a lesser spurt this time, blood so dark that Cyrus could tell it was green only thanks to the spell augmenting his vision.

Cyrus pulled free his blade and drew back. Goliath warriors swarmed at him, lesser creatures that stood heads and shoulders shorter than the trolls charging at his position. He quickly counted five of the mammoth beings, their size the only thing that told him what they were. Every square inch of their flesh was covered by the hardened metal that protected them from most—most!—of even Praelior's blows. He studied them all with a glancing eye as they came. They would arrive one by one, and he would have to face them as such to avoid being overwhelmed by their sheer numbers.

Cyrus raked his sword across the neck of a Goliath warrior charging at him and watched with satisfaction as the head flew from the neck. *Strength of numbers indeed.* The lesser were still coming, warriors numbering more than his ability to count them, and all of them seeming to flow toward him like a flood across a dry riverbed.

His sword moved out of habit, severing limbs and heads as quickly as he could move it. The next troll came at him within seconds by his measure. It felt to him like ten minutes. This one carried an axe and swung low at him in a roar that even Cyrus had to concede was a worthy war cry.

It did not even make him hesitate, however.

Cyrus brought Praelior up with furious strength, catching the axe mid-blade. He had seen the dullness of the thing, the lack of glint in the light, and knew it was mere steel and overwhelming strength that this troll carried into battle. *Probably splits his foes' skulls and bodies well enough just with the force of his muscle and ability.*

Cyrus smiled. In the contest between steel and quartal, there was always a clear winner and a clear loser. And it was never a contest.

The axe blade was split jaggedly down the middle with a sound of tearing metal as loud as the most fearsome scream that had ever reached Cyrus's ears. Even before he shredded through the last of the axe's blade, he had used his own strength to push it back. The opposite side of the blade skipped off the troll's breastplate and up, burying itself just below the troll's gorget.

There was a gurgling noise and the green, viscous liquid poured down like dark ale spilled over a washboard. The troll hit his knees and his hands fell from the axe's handle. Cyrus mounted a hard kick, using his superior, Praelior-supplied strength to slam his boot into the edge of the blade that was still bared to him. It caught on the bottom of his foot, his armor held, and all his strength rushed through it and into the axe.

The axe flew free, pushing through the trifling bone and tissue that had kept it lodged in the troll's neck. Cyrus watched it fly into the rank behind the troll, blade-first, and it wiped out some several poor bastards all in a line before it became lodged in two of them and stopped fast, causing them to keel over. There were screams and more screams. Cyrus could not differentiate the voices of those in whom the axe was stuck from those of every other voice on the battlefield.

Cyrus recovered his fighting stance as a long, faint shadow fell over him from his right. He looked up and saw a darkened face, a darkened body, stretching up and blotting out the bare twilight purple above him. He began to whip his blade around to defend but felt other motion behind him.

Long years of training had taught him to face the threat he knew was there rather than the phantasm of one that only might be. He threw up a blocking motion against the troll only feet from landing a blow on him, and he saw the shadow grow longer and taller, something stretching above it, lengthening the silhouette.

A glint of metal above the top of its head gave him pause and he realized what he was looking at. Vara landed her blow against the back of the troll's neck a moment later, and another green head tumbled free in a slow, vertical spin. It landed at Cyrus's feet, and Vara clanked to the ground a moment later, missing him by only inches.

He stared into her blue eyes, visible on either side around the nosepiece of her helm. Her eyes were wide, drops of dark blood spattering her pale cheeks as her lips were right there, only inches from his—

"Duck, you fool!" she said, and he felt her hard elbow reach up to knock him aside. He was already moving when her elbow hit him. His reflexes allowed him to roll with it, and he moved as she directed, sliding to the side.

He caught a vision of her blade arcing through the empty space that had been occupied by his body only seconds earlier. Her sword sparked in contact with the weapon of troll, driving it back even as her feet skidded backward from the impact. It was a contest of strength against strength; the only advantage for the troll was the lack of grip Vara's boots provided.

The troll was smaller than Yei. *As though that says anything.* He was still larger than the majority of the trollish troops had been in the start of the battle, and Cyrus watched as Vara held firm, her stance tightening as they were both pushed back. She recovered in inches, the troll in a foot or two. He brought his weapon up again, and the stink of filthy troll breath flared to where even Cyrus could smell it a few feet away from their clash.

Cyrus saw the lines of Goliath closing on Vara from the other side. There were at least five warriors all in a row, on a charge, their weapons at the ready. Her hands were occupied keeping the troll from bisecting her with his weapon, and Cyrus could still see the heads of the other trolls moving toward them through the fight, only seconds away. *Those ... I might be able to stop. Even as many as they are.* The thought was futile, though, and nearly died as he pondered the second threat.

The greater threat.

Because for the Goliath warriors coming for her—now only a blade's breadth from her side—the seconds he had left would not be nearly enough to save her.

Chapter 34

A bevy of arrows peppered the faces of the Goliath line, so fast that even with his senses enhanced by Praelior, each arrow appeared to Cyrus to land mere heartbeats after the last. They were perfectly aimed, perfectly timed, and took down all five Goliath warriors on the charge a second before they could strike down Vara.

For her part, the blond elf pushed hard against the troll that she was locked against, knocking him off balance to duck under his weapon and bury her blade in his guts. Her hand moved with lightning quickness, repeated stabs that caused the troll to shudder before he fell to his knees. Vara dodged out of the way just before his upper body keeled forward. He lay on the ground for a moment before a low flood of dark green blood began to pool out from underneath him.

"I suppose my purpose of sending shafts of wood through the air doesn't seem quite so frivolous now, does it?" Martaina spoke from behind them, and Cyrus turned to see her with her bow in hand, green cloak billowing behind her.

Vara glanced at her, nodded, and said nothing. *Which, for Vara, is roughly the equivalent of a sloppy kiss of thanks. Well, almost.*

"Martaina," Cyrus said as he alighted his eyes back to the trolls coming toward them. "Signal the cavalry."

He heard her sigh audibly behind him as he stepped up to stand next to Vara. The blond elf glanced at him then turned her eyes back to the trolls coming at them, only seconds away now—

A flaming arrow sailed overhead in a low arc, clearly not meant to do any harm to anyone. It landed in the chest of an elven warrior of Goliath, putting the lie to Cyrus's passing thought about that.

"Yeesh," he said. "You see a flaming arrow coming, you'd think you'd move."

"You would move," Vara said, "and I would move, but the vast majority of these poor soldiers lack the speed to avoid such a thing."

"Perhaps a shield," Cyrus said as the trolls closed on them. There were few enough of them now, just three, and they had surged into the gap in the wake left by the Goliath warriors that Martaina had killed. "You could carry one of those and hold it aloft—"

"That sounds exhausting," Vara said, as though they had no other concerns but their conversation.

"Yeah, I was never much for a shield either," Cyrus said, and the nearest troll was finally close enough for him to see the missing teeth, the jutting lower jaw, the yellow eyes. He sniffed a hint of the foul breath, like dead things inhabited the places where his missing teeth had once stood. *And he's not even close enough to really breathe on me yet.*

Vara broke right as Cyrus took the troll on the left. He saw her move out of the corner of his eye, saw her lift her hand and smite the troll with her sword, cleaving a leg off at the knee. She struck it while it was down, twisting her blade to rip the limb free.

The troll lashed out with an uncontrolled kick that she barely dodged, but it also flailed its arms and knocked over the third troll coming at them. "Nice move," he said to her as he tilted toward his foe to strike with a low slash to the gap in the hip armor.

"Mind your own battle, dimwit," she said.

There was a clear circle around them now, the Goliath army giving them wide berth and funneling around Cyrus and Vara's battle as though there were some invisible curtain wall routing them left and right. Cyrus knew it was merely smart movement on the part of the Goliath attackers—after all, who wanted to be hit by a flailing troll?

The troll Cyrus was facing brought a hand down hard and Cyrus blocked it with his blade, forcing the troll's arm back. He struck for the hip again and was rewarded with another grunt from the troll. The gap-toothed grimace and yellow eyes were pointed toward him and a bellow filled the air, followed by curdled breath that nearly caused Cyrus to blanch. *Worse than being stabbed, almost.*

He kept from gagging only barely and drove Praelior home to the hip one more time, this time opening up the already nasty slash fully and driving the blade all the way through. He felt the tip of Praelior exit the troll's buttock and he brought it down with all his force. The troll staggered and Cyrus tugged his weapon free. The troll wobbled for just a beat before the leg tore loose completely and the beast hit the ground with a scream. Blood squirted from the green monster's exposed pelvis, and Cyrus shook his head and grimaced. *Not a fun way to go down.*

"You lollygagger," Vara said, and he turned his head to see her shaking hers at him. She stood waiting, eyes thinly slitted, watching him. Her shining silver armor was completely green from the waist down, and he saw the trolls she'd faced lying finished on the ground. The rest of the Goliath army was still surging around them, though now Cyrus suspected it had more to do with the fact that the two of them had massacred every troll thrown their way.

In his ears hung a near-silence. Certainly, there was still the buzz of the battlefield and the cries of war and clashes of metal that came with it. But near to them there was a pocket of quiet, as even the Goliath warriors that charged round their small, peaceful space on the field kept their voices subdued. They made no war cry, just ran into the Sanctuary lines with eyes darting toward Cyrus and Vara. They ran headlong into spears and swords waiting for them, awestruck and frightened.

He saw this all in seconds, saw more than one of the Goliath warriors continue on in spite of the obvious reservations on their faces. *What horror would await them if they failed to charge?* he wondered.

This thought was interrupted by the long, low, blowing of a horn. It was followed again by another, then another. Cyrus felt the smile creep across his lips as it echoed through the air, and the area around him remained peaceful, free of any Goliath warriors.

The thundering of hooves was the next sound to break over the battle. Even knowing it was coming, he was not prepared. It started low and grew louder, coming to a crescendo as the horses drew in sight to Cyrus's left. They swept along like the tide running up on the beach. The army of Goliath was driven before them like the grains of sand under the waves, hit sidelong and utterly unprepared. Few of them had spears; even fewer of them managed to turn them to make use of them.

The line of Goliath's assault broke, their charge began to crumble. Warriors ran away from the coming cavalry, away from the heart of the battle, trying to find some escape.

The Luukessian cavalry had reached the area in front of Cyrus. Their swords and spears and axes rose and fell as they galloped across the field of battle. Blood filled the air in a haze, clouds of red and angry splashes of violence running along the length of the entire Luukessian column. The charge went on for long minutes, and Cyrus watched the whole time, Vara at his side.

Malpravus was visible, here and there, through the horses. He and Terian both were, though the dark knight less so. The dark elven army behind them—the last of the Sovereign's force to throw into the battle—was already folding and running, their retreat obvious even through the charging line of horsemen that was even now snaking back around to pursue. This Cyrus knew because it had been his orders.

"Think they'll catch him?" Cyrus asked, still watching Malpravus through the line of battle.

"Not a chance," Vara said, oddly still. "He'll run. Terian, too." As if to emphasize her point, Cyrus saw a sparkle of light through the cavalry, and Malpravus was gone. "It would appear the day is won, General."

Cyrus glanced at her—just out of the corner of his eye, almost afraid to look at her straight on. Her cheeks were flushed from battle and possibly more. "Indeed," he said. "Looks like we're almost done here."

He watched the retreating columns of dark elves, falling back down the road into the forest, and saw the first sign of the cavalry's long, charging column snaking its way onto the path to pursue the fleeing dark elves. *A whole army. They just threw away a whole army here. I wouldn't have thought the Sovereign had any of those left to waste like this.*

"But we're not done with the war, are we?" Vara asked. Her voice was cold and clear and lingered in the night—and he knew that she did not need him to answer.

Chapter 35

"That took the piss right out of them." Longwell was jubilant, and to Cyrus's ears he sounded more alive than he had in roughly forever. "Nothing like a cavalry charge to put a damper on a dark elf's day."

"They do seem particularly susceptible to being run over by men on horseback," Vaste said. "Though I suppose this time it wasn't just dark elves, but the whole mixture of overlarge brutes that Goliath employs for their warrior corps."

"The reason they're particularly susceptible to men on horseback," Vara said, sounding to Cyrus like she was explaining something very basic to a child, "is because they don't carry spears among their warrior class. It's hard to break the charge of a galloping army by holding out a sword and hoping for the best."

"That was a very technically proficient explanation," Vaste said, "but I think you left out the part where it's difficult to maintain a formation when everyone in front of you is screaming, crying and dying from getting trampled by hooves."

The battlefield already smelled of rotten, stinking death. Cyrus watched the Council members bicker with little interest. The black of night had settled in over them, and only a few hundred of the Luukessian dragoons were still riding scouting parties down the trail. A thousand campfires were spread across the meadow where the battle had been fought, and there were guards posted all through the woods and along the road to insure that the army was not taken by surprise. Cyrus had ordered a quiet vigil and suspected that his order was not received very popularly. Still, there had been minimal grumbling that he'd heard—not that many would have had the courage to complain to him.

"Do you think they'll come back?" Vaste asked, and Cyrus glanced over to see the troll looking directly at him.

"Probably not," Cyrus said, feeling the heat of the nearest fire cut through the cold night air. He looked back at Livlosdald keep and saw the light of the torches and watch fires up on the high walls. *Looks like they'll see the dawn. And they wouldn't have if we weren't here.* "I would have to guess we killed greater than half their number. Goliath alone probably lost some four thousand."

"Along with a goodly portion of the spell casters," Vara said. "Too bad Malpravus escaped with their officers."

Cyrus lapsed into a silence with the rest of them at that point, and the crackle of the fire filled his ears. He had checked carefully among the corpses, but there was no sign of Orion, nor of Selene. There were a few spell casters he recognized from the days before Goliath had broken from Alliance with Sanctuary, but very few. They were all much like Yei—he knew their faces, might have remembered their names, but they were little more than acquaintances. "You know who I didn't see?" Cyrus asked, still contemplating. "Tolada. I wonder if he's still in Goliath."

"Hard to believe he could find a place elsewhere," Vaste said. "Most guilds have basic competency requirements, after all."

"We don't, apparently," Vara muttered.

"General." Odellan's voice caused Cyrus to tilt his head to look. The elf was making his way toward the officers' fire from where the front line was still standing guard. "The dark elves have sent an envoy under flag of truce to discuss retrieving their dead."

Cyrus stared at Odellan blankly. "Their dead? Since when do the dark elves care enough to retrieve their dead?"

Odellan shrugged, removing his winged helm. "Since now, apparently. They've sent unarmed men in empty wagons to do it."

Cyrus blinked. Repatriating the dead was a long-held practice—for the humans and the elves, at least. *I've never heard of the dark elves giving so much as a blue fig for their dead.* He turned his head to face Erith. "What the hells?"

She shrugged, at least as confused as he was. "I don't know. Unless the dead are highly esteemed, they're used for compost in a place called the Depths."

"You compost your dead?" Vaste asked, and the troll had one shining yellow eye larger than the other in the darkness. "And grow what with them?"

"Mushrooms," Erith said with a shrug. "Wildroot. Staples of the diet of the poor."

"You essentially feed your dead to the poor, then," Vaste said, nodding. "Suddenly, so much makes sense about Saekaj Sovar."

"This is more of a Sovar thing," Erith said, though not very loudly.

Cyrus felt a desire to chew his lip, but resisted. "Fine, go ahead and allow the dark elves to come and get their dead. It's not like they're going to be able to resurrect them." He paused. "Wait, can Malpravus bring them back to life to fight for him now?"

"No," Vaste said, shaking his head. "His magic can only bring back the recently dead that way, and—" He froze. "You son of a bitch!"

Cyrus eyed him warily. "Just got it, didn't you?"

"You knew he'd bring them back to life," Vaste said, voice rising, "if you didn't cast the cessation spells over the battlefield—"

"Go ahead, Odellan," Cyrus said, feeling all the energy bleed out of him with a sigh. "Might as well be decent to our enemies. Keep a close watch on them, though, and have archers standing by with bows drawn, spell casters with hands at the ready. If this is some sneak attack, kill them first and resurrect later. I won't have us get annihilated by some treacherous trick Malpravus schemed."

"Understood," Odellan said, and with a sharp salute, he retreated into the darkness.

Cyrus could feel the fatigue settling in on him like nightfall. The day's battles had taken their toll, and his eyes fought to stay open.

"You should get some sleep," Erith said with—to Cyrus's surprise—sympathy.

"Yes, sleep, you devious bastard," Vaste said, still eyeing him. "Sleep, and enjoy this triumph of outwitting me, because it shan't happen again."

"Perhaps you should set a more aggressive goal for him next time," Vara said, "such as being more swift-witted than a gnome."

"You know," Nyad said, "there are some truly clever gnomes out there ..."

Shuffling off into the dark, Cyrus did not catch the rest of the wizard's statement. He looked again to the towers of Livlosdald keep, wondering what was going on within them now. He sniffed the air; the same aroma of dead things hung heavy. Campfires were burning closer to the keep as well, now, and Cyrus knew from the reports of the division he'd tasked to guard the portal that even now Pretnam Urides's army was massing nearby. *A scant few more hours and we'll be relieved. For some reason, I doubt Malpravus will rally in time to give us another headache before he leaves.*

There was a tent set only a hundred paces away, and he could see a half dozen warriors standing in a perimeter around it with a wizard and a druid in close attendance. The warriors saluted as he approached, and in the shadows just behind it he caught a hint of movement. He peered closer, almost certain what he would find. Martaina stepped out just far enough for him to see her, a distant fire's light catching the curve of her bow, and then she melted back into the shadows. *Always watched, now.* He pushed through the tent flap after returning his salute to the warriors and found a lamp already lit inside for him.

A small cot lay in the middle of the room, and a trestle table with a map of the battlefield and surrounding area stood just to his right. There was a scent of the lamp burning to help blot out of the stench of war and death, but only just. The lingering scent hung with him, as though it was somehow seared into his flesh.

"You should be more careful." He turned to see Aisling lurking just behind him to the left, sitting in a wooden chair that had cloth stretched over it and was hinged to fold. She was on it only lightly, poised to strike to his eyes, though she sheathed the dagger she had in her hands as soon as he turned to see her. "Your guards do not make you invincible."

"No, they make me guarded," Cyrus said, and took a step toward the desk. He lingered there, staring across the tent at her, feeling the gulf of distance between them. "But not from you, apparently. Did they let you in or did you steal in all on your own?"

"'Steal' is a funny choice of words," she said, nearly impassive.

"An appropriate one," Cyrus said. "And not one I think you would take offense to."

"No," she said. "No offense taken." She stood, her hardened leather armor making not even a whisper as she did so. She had faint hints of blood here and there, a little dark blue clumping together at the ends of strands of hair on her left side. "You won a great victory today."

"I won a victory today," he agreed. "Minimal losses for us, maximum losses for the Sovereignty. I guess you could consider it a good victory."

"I think it would be considered great, as I said before." She stirred, and he felt again an odd distance between them, both literal and emotional. "You led us to success against the most formidable army in the land. To beat the Sovereign at this point—"

"You knew he was Yartraak all along, didn't you?" Cyrus watched her stiffen, watched her mouth shift in a subtle way. He wasn't used to seeing her like that, not even when he'd first begun to figure out how to corner her years before. She was a curious creature to him still, mercurial in her temperament, strange in many ways, and unpredictable in her responses.

"Of course," was all she said.

"I suppose you couldn't tell me any more than any of the other dark elves could," he said.

"Not really."

"Why not?" Cyrus asked, turning back on her. "We're lovers, aren't we? We're—"

"Are we?" She stepped closer to him. "Are we lovers? I think if you would open the flap to your tent and let everyone see us right now, they might come away with a far different idea about what we are. Strangers, perhaps."

"Well, we do things together that I wouldn't exactly do to a stranger—"

"But those are all physical," she said. "To call us lovers is laughable. You keep your distance from me, never letting me get truly close. You'll bury your head in my breast in the night but you wish for morning so I'll be gone."

Cyrus felt the sting of her accusations, felt the sting of the truth in them. "I don't ..." He cringed, unsure what to say.

"Don't hold back and practice a lie," she said. "Tell me the truth that is on your mind."

"You told me once that you wanted only what I could give you," Cyrus said. "I think you know by now that love is not one of the things I can give. Nor is closeness, nor true intimacy, nor any of the things you might wish of me. The only thing I have given you since we got back from Luukessia is the physical, because I think it's all I have left to give you. I made a mistake—"

She eased closer to him, and he could feel her begin to change in that moment. "You didn't make a mistake. You made a choice. You wanted, on some level, to be with me—"

"I wanted to—" He cut himself off again. "What I want is—"

She leaned in and kissed him fiercely, cutting across the distance between them. Her hand came up and found his side, reaching for the straps that secured his breastplate and backplate together, and he turned them aside. She broke from him, the surprise in her eyes obvious even to him in his dulled state. It faded quickly, though, whether because it didn't disappoint her or because she hid it, he did not know. "What do you want?" she asked.

"I don't know," Cyrus said. "I want to not wonder for a while. Not wonder how many things I'm doing wrong. How many things I'm screwing up." He removed his helm and set it upon the desk, watching the sharp edges on the bottom crinkle the map's parchment with its weight. "I want to walk through my life not feeling like I've made monumentally stupid choices that continue to haunt me every day." He smiled faintly. "I want—"

"It's not always about what you want, you know," she said quietly.

He turned in slight surprise. "Didn't you just ask me, though? Change your mind?" *Afraid the truth might be something incompatible with what you want?* A thought of Vara flashed through his head.

"You're a leader," she said and brushed against him, leaning on his back as he turned away from her. "You don't always get to choose what you want. You have ... obligations."

"I have obligations," he agreed. "But I'm only the General of Sanctuary. The rest is—"

"Soon to be your responsibility as well," she said.

"I don't want it."

"Doesn't matter. You make a difference to these people." Her words were low and breathy, warming his ear in a way he didn't really want to feel right now, as satisfying as they were to his ego. "You're a man of influence—the most influence in Sanctuary. You lead them whether you want to or not." She hesitated, and he heard it in the way her voice broke. "You can be like Alaric—"

"I'm nothing like Alaric," Cyrus said, not turning to face her. He felt a slight smirk emerge with a thought that bubbled out. "You want to sleep with the Guildmaster of Sanctuary?"

She kissed his neck and he did not stop her. He closed his eyes and felt the gentle, teasing touch of her tongue against his skin and it gave him a little thrill. "I want to sleep with you," she said. She kissed his neck again, standing on her tiptoes to do so, tugging him down just enough to reach. He let her do her work, did not fight it. *It doesn't matter what I want*, he thought. *Not really. Everyone needs something from me. And I need—*

I need—

He felt the urge and heeded it, keeping his eyes shut tightly as he leaned down to kiss her full on the mouth. He ignored the cinnamon, pretending it was something else, and unfastened her leather armor by hand, from memory—pretending all the while that it was shining and silver instead.

Chapter 36

When Cyrus awoke, sunlight was streaming in from the gaps in the tent's cloth. He flinched, blinking from the brightness. He wondered only for a moment at what time it might be, then shifted on his cot to find he was, unsurprisingly, alone. *She never stays, and it's probably just as well.* He let a low sigh. *She might have been right about that one thing, though. They all hang on my every word around here, they set up guard on my tent without me asking. Even the damned dark knights of the Sovereign come at me first thing in a battle in order to get me out of the way.*

The thought came with great reluctance, like a donkey being dragged along against its will by a troll. *I'm a leader. They expect me to lead, and not just in battle.*

But I'm not Alaric.

I could never be Alaric.

He shifted the light furs that covered his cot and sat upright, feeling his naked flesh against the softness of his covers. His underclothes were all spread across the ground, along with his armor. Eyeing the tent in the cold light of day, he realized that someone had gone to a great deal of trouble to bring the maps and desks and cot out here. *Or perhaps they conjured them*, Cyrus thought. For some reason he found that easier to tolerate somehow, as though it absolved him from having to concern himself with the idea that someone had gone to the trouble of bringing all this for him.

He dressed and had nearly finished strapping on his breastplate when there was a rustling at the flap of the tent. He could already hear the sounds of the army outside—raucous, filled with laughter and yelling and good cheer. When the flap moved, his eyes went to it immediately, dropping the last strap of his breastplate, hand falling to the hilt of Praelior.

One of the warriors stuck his head in. "Visitor for you, General."

"Thank you," Cyrus said, nodding at the man. He didn't know his name. How did he not know his name? The fellow had a square jaw and looked to be more human in appearance than elven. They always had smoother faces, somehow. "I'll be out in a moment."

He finished with the last strap, listening to the satisfying sound of the leather stretching as he pulled it tight, and hastened toward the exit. He pushed back the flap of the tent and squinted against the daylight. A gleaming silver breastplate topped by shining golden hair awaited him.

"Vara," he said, acknowledging her with a nod as he let the tent flap fall shut behind him. Guards flanked the tent, different ones than he had seen when he had entered it the night before.

"Gnome groin," she replied, almost indifferent.

Cyrus frowned. "What the hell is that supposed to mean?"

"They reproduce even more swiftly than your kind," she said, and he caught a strong hint of disapproval from her. "They're constantly rubbing up against something."

"Why do you hate gnomes so much?" Cyrus looked at her. "They're not all like Brevis, you know."

"He was plenty enough to make me wary of the rest," she said. "I have come to inform you of our current status."

Cyrus stared up into the sky above and saw the sun high, nearly overhead. "Is it noon yet?"

"Very nearly," she said, stiff and unyielding as she turned. He followed alongside. "Much to my amazement, Pretnam Urides has kept his word and has his forces massed along a defensive line nearer to the keep. Our scouts have returned and reported that the dark elves have entirely fled the region. Any reinforcement from them is days away, assuming they were to decide to try to hammer this particular anvil again." She walked with her hands clasped behind her, strolling as though she were on a military inspection rather than leading him through a battlefield. "The Confederation forces stand ready to relieve us, and they have the remainder of our payment for services rendered." She angled her head just slightly to look at him. "I hope this pleases you."

Cyrus felt a long sigh coming on. "It pleases me we won." He paused, trying to decide how to phrase what he had to say next. "I've decided to run for Guildmaster, Vara."

She halted, entire body straightening stiffly. He paused a step before she did, allowing her the courtesy of hiding her face from him if she so chose. She did not turn at first. "Was this decided before or after your wild, flailing, awkward round of rutting with the dark elven thief last night?"

"You heard that?" Cyrus asked.

"I doubt there is anyone on this side of Arkaria who failed to hear it," Vara said, turning just slightly to look at him. "What prompted this decision?"

"You knew I was considering it," he said.

"I knew you were undecided," she said. "What decided it for you? The whisper of a cinnamon-breathed little night skulker—"

"That's not fair," Cyrus said, his muscles become tenser with each word. "You know very well that the people of Sanctuary look to me for at least some leadership—"

"Leadership?" she scoffed. "Oh, yes, you lead us—for example you just led us into battle in your own homeland."

He felt his own countenance darken. "I didn't hear you complain when I led us into battle in yours."

She favored him with a cold glare. "You are quite the servant of Bellarum, aren't you? Spreading war everywhere you go."

"I didn't start this war," Cyrus said, and every word tasted like ash to him, as bitter as anything he could imagine. *I don't want to be having this conversation with her. Not this way. Not like this.* "Nor do I truly care to profit from it. We have obligations, and I have to take a pragmatic approach to meeting those obligations—"

"Oh, is that what a leader is?" she almost spat at him. "A compromiser? Someone who believes in high-minded principles until the difficult times arrive, and then they forsake them as easily as if they left behind a—" She flushed red. "Never mind."

He narrowed his eyes at her, sensing the hint of what she had perhaps meant but not said. "Do you mean to say—"

"If I had something to say, I would say it," she cut him off. "But I have nothing more to say in this matter; you and I appear to be quite resigned to charging at each other on the field of this election, and we will be forced to see whose vision of Sanctuary will reign supreme when it is all done and counted." She straightened, returning to the stiff, nearly full-at-attention soldierly bearing. "The General of the Confederation forces awaits you at your leisure. Now, if you'll excuse me—"

She kept that straight-backed bearing as she almost marched away from him. He thought about watching her go, but instead he stared at the rough, beaten ground in front of him and saw streaks of blood puddled in ruts—the sign of a battle still fresh in his mind.

Chapter 37

The Council Chamber was lit by the crackling torches and fires, flickering in the silence and filling the air with the sweet, smoky smell that once more reminded Cyrus of home. It was different now, though, than it had been before. The last taste of dinner remained upon his tongue, along with the hints of the brew he had had in its aftermath. It had been a peaceful afternoon once they'd returned to Sanctuary, peaceful up until he'd received the summons to Council. It had been anticipated, yet still—*I could have used another day before we did this.*

"Cyrus and Vara," Curatio said calmly, letting his eyes wander over the Council members. Cyrus did not look at Vara; he could see out of the corner of his eye that she did much the same. "Does anyone else wish to put forth their name for Guildmaster?"

"At the risk of inserting myself into what is obviously a most personal quarrel," Ryin said, with a slight smile, "I'd like to put my name forward."

Vaste made a loud sigh. "Why do you hate yourself?"

"I don't hate myself," Ryin said, now serious. "I love this guild. I love what it stands for. And I think it could use a breath of fresh leadership."

"Yes, well I think—" Vaste began.

"You're treading ever closer to the line," Curatio said, giving Vaste a stern look. "Respect, Vaste."

"I'll try and muster some," Vaste said without an ounce of audible contrition.

"This will take a couple weeks to arrange," Curatio said, scratching Ryin's name onto the parchment in front of him. "We should consider running some officer candidates at the same time to make our lives easier."

"Diluting our power," Ryin warned.

"Allowing our guildmates to exercise their right to help control the destiny of the guild," Vaste said.

"I think we should allow the guild to settle this question for us," Curatio said, still looking at the parchment. "More officers—at least a few—would not be unwelcome. If by chance they don't vote them in, which is always an option, then we can look at approaching things from a more military standpoint. Appointing subordinates or something." He looked up. "For now, though, we should take some nominations later this week and put them to a vote with the Guildmaster election." He waited, and it took Cyrus a moment to realize he was looking for dissent. When he found none, he merely nodded once and looked back down to the thick, yellowed parchment in front of him.

A knock sounded at the door, ending the seconds of silence that followed. "Come," Curatio called and waited for the door to swing open.

A hooded figure entered and swept his cowl back to reveal his white hair. "J'anda," Cyrus said, looking over the enchanter's lined face and feeling a rush of affection for the dark elf.

"Hello, my friends," J'anda said. He looked even more tired to Cyrus's eyes than he had when he left, a deep-seated weariness hanging upon him that went beyond the aging he'd suffered in Luukessia. "I am afraid I missed the summons for this meeting, so I hope you will forgive me for my tardiness."

"What are you doing here?" Cyrus asked, sitting up in his chair. "I thought you were trying to re-enter the Sovereign's service."

"I have re-entered the Sovereign's service," J'anda said, and the lines of his face grew deeper. "I am here to spy for him in my capacity as his double-agent."

"Why, how dare you betray us in such a way," Vaste said mildly. "And to have the gumption to tell us to our faces that you're going to do it! Cheeky. Very cheeky."

J'anda bowed his head slightly. "I am nothing if not possessed of a sense of wit, I think you'll all agree. The irony of spying on the Sovereign while he thinks I'm spying for him is not lost on me."

"How do you know that he believes you when your loyalties are so clearly flexible?" Vara asked, breaking the silence that had hung over her since she had announced her candidacy with only a syllable.

"Because I have betrayed Sanctuary to him," J'anda said with a raised hand. He waited, just a moment, and Cyrus felt a flicker of uncertainty. "Oh, I wouldn't worry about it. I haven't told him anything but personal details and minor accounts of things going on within the walls. I had to give a rather exhaustive retelling of our adventures over the last few years." J'anda turned to Cyrus. "He has some interest in you, in particular, that I have no explanation for."

Cyrus blinked in surprise. "Me?"

"Him?" Erith echoed. "Why would the Sovereign give two vek'tag silks about Cyrus Davidon?"

"Hey," Cyrus said, feeling a hint of umbrage. "I'm an interesting person, you know. The story of my rise is a fascinating tale that should be studied in military academies all across Arkaria—"

"And humble, too," Curatio said with a faint smirk. "Still, the fact that our esteemed General is an object of curiosity to the Sovereign should not come as any surprise. He has been responsible for several extremely painful defeats to Yartraak's army now, probably more than any other person still walking Arkaria."

"Does he mean to kill me?" Cyrus asked. He noticed Vara move awkwardly in her seat out of the corner of his eye.

"I don't think so," J'anda said. "I believe he would have you killed if he were presented with an opportunity, but he has not targeted you as yet—which is something that is well within his power to do. I remain uncertain as to why."

"Because Cyrus is the favored of Bellarum," Curatio said quietly. His eyes were heavily lidded, almost slits, and they hid much of his emotion. "To do so—to target him—would cause some discord between the God of War and the God of Darkness, I believe. With his forces fully embroiled in fighting this war, I doubt Yartraak desires that particular boil be opened."

There was a silence in the Council Chambers for a few seconds following that. Cyrus saw Vara glance at him, saw the flash of resentment in her eyes, but she said nothing.

"Must be nice to have the God of War as your patron," Vaste said. "I suppose it makes sense, though, since he did give you that lovely sword."

"I ..." Cyrus's discomfort swelled within him. "It's not like that."

"It matters little at the moment," J'anda said, steepling his hands. "I have news."

"What news?" Ryin asked. Cyrus saw the druid lean in. *He's trying to take the lead—to act like a leader.*

J'anda raised an eyebrow at Ryin then turned to look at Curatio. "Something is going on in Gren."

"Slavery," Vaste said. "Mostly slavery, I would say. And perhaps just a little buggery with goats."

"Almost all the troll men have left the city—" J'anda said.

"Perhaps the famine has caused them to run low on goats," Vaste said.

J'anda paused, looking around the Council table. His dark blue features were lit in the flickering illumination. "I did not come by this information from the Sovereign, so you may freely use it without fear that it will get me into trouble, but Vaste is correct." He hesitated. "About the slavery, in any case. I have heard nothing about the goats and would be forever grateful if none of you were to mention it should you find out the other is true as well."

There was a moment's silence before Curatio spoke. "So ... the trolls *are* returning to their slaving ways."

"Slavery is happening in Gren," J'anda said. "The Daring are likely there. Slaving parties—aided by dark elven wizards—have been dispatched into the Human Confederation, the Dwarven Alliance, the Elven Kingdom, even the Gnomish Dominions. They are trying to make up for the loss of labor caused by the troll men being away at war for the Sovereign."

"Hardly a surprise that the trolls are fully involved in the Sovereign's war," Cyrus said, shaking his head. "We've seen so damned many of them in dark elven company lately."

"They are all in now," J'anda said. "Completely committed. Which is why there is a rise in slave raids. To run the troll economy with the men gone to war requires workers. One overseer to watch over ten or twenty slaves frees up their men to strap on armor and help the

Sovereign reshape Arkaria in a way that will be more pleasing to the people of Gren."

"One in which they aren't confined in a swamp and kept from conquering and pillaging their way across the land, surely," Vaste said. "It figures my people would do this. But I find it hard to believe that the men could all leave. There are no portals and the river Perda is blocked at every crossing by the elves—"

"Ahhh," J'anda said, and he smiled the tight smile of a man about to deliver uncomfortable news. "Gren does have a portal now. It has been provided by the Sovereign."

Vaste did not blink, and Cyrus watched him for a reaction. There wasn't much of one. "That's impossible."

"No more impossible than Sanctuary having a portal," Curatio said. "With a certain amount of strength at your disposal, they are movable."

"Trolls are strong," Cyrus said. *With a portal in Gren ... Gods, what a disaster! They're not held back by the river Perda.* "They could land an entire dark elven army up in the Dismal Swamp and march down into the Elven Kingdom without anything to stop them."

"And they most assuredly will," J'anda said with a nod. "Once they have concluded the war with the Confederation, the elves are surely next on the Sovereign's—Yartraak's—list of revenge targets."

"That son of a bastard whore," Vara said, shocking the table into silence.

"Does the God of Darkness have a mother?" Vaste asked.

"This is grim news indeed," Curatio said, "both in the short and in the long term."

Cyrus moved his tongue within his mouth, ran it over his sharpest teeth. "We have business with the trolls anyway, I suppose."

Curatio looked at him with a subtle, narrow-eyed look. "Do you mean what I think you mean?"

"They have no magic to speak of," Vaste said. "And if their men are away, they'll be an easy conquest." He paused. "Or ... relatively. I mean, the women are still trolls, after all, and possessed of the disposition of an enraged elven paladin at the best of times."

"They're slaving," Erith said, and Cyrus looked over to find her watching him as well. "They're in violation of the treaty they signed after the last war." Her face hardened. "And they may have the

Daring even now. Any one of those reasons would be good enough for me. Add them all together, and my scales tip over."

Longwell spoke up for the first time since the Council had begun. "I suspect it won't be much trouble convincing the Luukessians to march into the swamp if there are personal scores to settle. They've already developed a mad-on for the Sovereign and his armies; convincing them that doing this will bloody his nose makes it an easy sell."

Curatio looked across the table to the Princess of Pharesia. "Nyad, need I even ask?"

The wizard was pale. *I'd be pale too, if I'd just found out my ancient enemy had a means of invading my homeland.* "We'll need cursory permission from my father to enter the Kingdom at Nalikh'akur—the closest portal to the swamps." She looked quite faint. "He'll need to obtain—again, cursory—permission from the Lord of the town—"

"It's Lady," Vara said, more than a little pale herself, "not Lord. And the permission is granted, obviously." *I forgot that Vara was Lady of Nalikh'akur.*

Nyad stumbled over her words for a moment before continuing. "Once I tell him what J'anda just told us, I cannot imagine he would find any reason to deny it. Every one of his troops is tied up in Termina and watching the Perda. If trolls and dark elves came south out of Dismal Swamp right now—" She halted, and the last vestige of color drained out of her face. "Please." She nodded her head so quickly Cyrus feared it would fall off. "Please, let us do this, I will do anything—"

"I suppose I'll be the voice of dissent in this," Ryin said, drawing a look of fierce anger from Nyad and Vara. "Not a strong voice of dissent, as I understand where every last one of you are coming from, but I should point out that we're once more interfering in matters outside our concern and tying ourselves more deeply to this war."

"We are tying ourselves to one side of this war," Vara said, watching the table coldly. "The side which does not believe in slavery and conquest. While I am the last to believe we should sell ourselves for monetary gain, this is a pure good. Slavery is evil. The Sovereign is evil. Taking a hammer to his left hand while his right is busy wreaking havoc is a cause I can get behind with greatest gusto." She shifted her gaze to Curatio. "I think you know how I vote."

"Oh, good," J'anda said, nodding. "And I was worried this would be difficult to convince you of, especially after you just got back from another fight."

"You should have known better," Ryin said sourly, "after all, didn't you hear? The General of our Armies is the favored of Bellarum."

"This war will go on whether Cyrus wants it to or not," J'anda said, cocking his head to look at Ryin. "He did not start it, and at every turn he has done what he could to protect people—innocent people—from its course." The dark elf turned to look at Cyrus, and he had an almost plaintive look in his eyes. "There are more things I know. Things I cannot tell you for fear of word escaping and getting back to the Sovereign. He has ... dreadful secrets." The last part echoed in hollow words in the Council Chamber. "Things he is doing—things he has done—that are dark beyond description." The enchanter straightened in his chair and waved a hand in front of his face. For a moment, his youthful appearance returned and then fell away again as though he had lost the concentration to keep it there. "The only thing I can tell you is that this war will roll on for years—or forever—until he wins. Unless *you* stop him." J'anda pointed at Cyrus and then turned to point at each of the Sanctuary officers in turn. "It will be a long road, but it begins here. If you want to end this war, go to Gren. Destroy the portal, put the fear in them once more and get their men to return home." J'anda slumped back in his seat. "For believe me ... as long as the Sovereign has them as allies by his side ... there is no hope that this fight will ever end."

Chapter 38

Cyrus could see the cloudy skies hanging low above the trees as the light of teleportation faded. He was looking up as he appeared, just as he'd been staring at the ceiling of the Sanctuary foyer before the spell had been cast. He was anticipating the skies, almost looking forward to seeing them, and when they appeared and were not blue, he felt a whisper of disappointment.

A breeze blew through, rattling the branches around the clearing that surrounded the portal outside Nalikh'akur. A circle of elven soldiers stood in a formation that ringed them, and Cyrus stood, waiting for one of them to say something. Anything, really.

"Army of Sanctuary, I greet you in the name of King Danay, the first of his name." This came from a soldier with a helm that had vague hints of shaping like a tree trunk. He bowed his head to Cyrus, singling him out. The man carried a spear—all of them did—the better to strike down teleporting foes quickly and at a distance should an army try to invade through their portal. He also made a deep bow to Vara, who stood at Cyrus's right.

"In the name of the Army of Sanctuary, I accept your greetings and suggest you make way," Cyrus said. He made no attempt not to be terse. There was no easy way to bring an army of nearly ten thousand into a foreign land, and trying to be excessively polite was simply not something he had the inclination for at the moment. "My aide Odellan will inform you as to the specifics, but suffice it to say we'll be teleporting our forces in for some time yet to come." He made a rough motion with his hand, all that was necessary to compel his soldiers into motion. This first wave was only a few hundred, to be followed every thirty seconds by more until the entire army was here.

"Of course," the soldier said. Cyrus suspected he bowed again but he did not bother to look back to check. He was too busy moving at the rough head of the formation toward the road he remembered vaguely being just ahead of them. It was a rough path, similar to numerous trails between cities he'd seen in his time. This one was perhaps rougher than most because it was on the very edge of the Kingdom, far from the most-traversed trade routes.

They walked, not a horse among them. Cyrus stayed at the fore, and a few of the officers lingered behind him. Vara, for one, remained close by, as did Nyad. He had asked them to stay close to ease their passage through the Kingdom, figuring that between the shelas'akur and the heiress to the throne, they shouldn't have much resistance.

They walked mostly in silence, the military discipline of the Sanctuary army keeping them in time and formation. Cyrus glanced back every now and again and watched the formations leave the clearing and enter the road, forming as they went. The strong tang of the late-blooming melett trees was sweet in the air, and a gentle, slightly chill breeze blew out of the north.

Cyrus heard a rustle just behind him and turned to see Aisling with her cowl up. He raised an eyebrow at her, but that was all the attention he spared her before he turned back to keep his eyes on the path ahead.

"So, Guildmaster," she said, "when is the formal election to tell us what we already know?"

"I find it surprising that an election could tell you anything you already know," Vara's voice crackled from behind Cyrus. He glanced back to see her cheeks slightly red. "As it does not seem to relate to anything involving sexual positions or maneuvers."

"Is this the only line of attack you can find for me?" Aisling's voice came from beneath the cowl and was all smiles, even though her face was largely hidden. "Call me a harlot over and over again until it washes away the pain of knowing that I took something that you wanted?"

"I am not a thing," Cyrus said with a hint of annoyance.

"I'm not surprised you have your cowl up to hide your face," Vara said. "I doubt a thief like you would be welcome here."

Aisling's reply was cool and assured. "In case you forgot, I'm a Lady of the Elven Kingdom."

"And a whore in the bedroom, by all accounts," Vara said with a snap.

"Okay, that's enough," Cyrus said, lowering his voice and letting it cut over the responses both of them were starting. "Aisling, would you be so kind as to keep an eye on the back of the formation?"

"So that you can get me away from this jealous elven bitch before she tries to call me a slut again?" Aisling asked, her words as thin and sharp as any blade's edge.

"Jealous?" Vara said mockingly. "Of you?"

"Yes, of me," Aisling said. "You flaxen-haired ice bitch. It's fortunate he didn't choose you, because any child of yours would die from frostbite while nursing."

There was a sound of a shocked silence, and then Andren's voice came from a row back. "All this talk of nipples is getting me thirsty."

"Exactly how many bottles of Pharesian brandy did your mother go through while she was nursing you?" Vara tossed back.

"Enough!" Cyrus said. "Aisling, go!" He sent a searing look at Vara, but she turned away. "Just ... enough of this. We have a mission." A rattling breeze ran through them, and Cyrus felt the cold find the cracks in his armor. *Where's Curatio when I need him?*

A silence settled over them for a few minutes, and then Cyrus heard heavier footfalls behind him, falling into roughly the same place Aisling had occupied only moments earlier. He turned to see Vaste pushing his way through as the lines reformed behind him. Cyrus felt himself annoyed at the troll but somewhat proud at his army's adaptation as they maintained their formation.

"Hihi," Vaste said. "I heard I was missing a catfight, so of course I came straightaway."

"Gods, Vaste," Cyrus said, keeping his eyes on the town of Nalikh'akur, which was just ahead on the horizon. "Not now."

"I missed it, didn't I?" Vaste said. "I knew I should have run faster. This would be so much simpler if you didn't have everyone in these stiff lines. Can't we just sort of walk in a clump? I could run to points of possible drama much quicker if we did things that way."

Cyrus gave a long sigh. "You didn't miss anything worth talking about."

"Apparently I did, because they were talking about it two divisions back," Vaste said. "I heard Vara and Aisling were near to drawing swords on each other." He glanced back at Vara, who stared back at him sullenly then turned her irritated look upon Cyrus. "I'd put my gold on Vara, of course," Vaste said with exaggerated loudness. When Cyrus did not reply after a moment, he leaned in closer. "It would seem you've aimed to make your entire life a ribald joke."

Cyrus maintained the lid on the boiling pot of aggravation he felt bubbling inside. "I wouldn't say I aimed for it."

"Well, you hit it nonetheless, as unerringly as an arrow launched from Martaina's bow." Vaste straightened. "Your relationship problems may be a sticking point come election time." He glanced again at Vara, who was still glaring at them both. "Not for you," he said to her, "for him."

"This concerns me little," she replied, "as I have no relationship with him."

"You have some relationship with him," Vaste said as they entered the town. "Peculiar and twisty as it may be."

"I agree with Vara," Cyrus said, more than a little irritation bleeding out of him, "if she and I had a relationship, the high point was probably when she tried to drown me." He made a vague gesture toward a pond in the distance. "Coincidentally, it happened just over there."

"That's not very cheery," Vaste said.

"But it's accurate," Cyrus said and sunk into silence.

"I was trying to keep your feverish brain from melting within that oversized gourd you call a head," Vara said quietly. "Though you were so addled I doubt you would remember."

Cyrus glanced at the pond, a brownish puddle of water scarcely bigger than his quarters. "I remember."

"Right, well then," Vaste said after a few moments of silence, faux-marching and swinging his arms with a little too much enthusiasm to be genuine, "this has become uncomfortable. And not the fun kind of uncomfortable, where I can make witticisms in order to lighten things up. No, this has become the dark kind of uncomfortable, the kind that you find when you make a few too many jests at a funeral."

"What do you think happened to Vidara?" Cyrus asked, changing the subject.

"I haven't the faintest idea," Vaste said, his arms losing their exaggerated swing. "Either she left her realm to the God of Winter or she got dragged out by someone, I suppose."

"But why?" Cyrus asked.

"No idea," Vaste said.

"Really?" Cyrus asked, and he heard the sound of his boots making every step along the road. "Hm."

There was a pause that lasted another moment, and then it was Vara who spoke. "Your mind is moving."

"Finally, you concede that it does that," Cyrus said, managing a weak smile of triumph. "Do you remember when the Hand of Fear was trying to kill y—" He did not even finish the sentence before she sent him a scalding look, even by her standards. "Of course you do," he said.

"I rescind my comment about your mind moving," she said, her eyes so narrow he doubted he could have fit an elvish coin in the space between her lids.

"Right, well," Cyrus said, turning to look at the road ahead where it wended off into the distance. Trees rose high above either side, leaves covering every bough on the nearest. In the distance, the greenery diminished the closer the road grew to the swamp. "Something about this whole Vidara endeavor reminds me of the time we spent trying to chase our tails back then. We stumbled about in the dark trying to figure out who the Hand of Fear was, why they would want to kill Vara, and—"

"It's probably just the association with the business of the gods in your mind," Vaste said with a shrug of his ample frame. "What with the Hand of Fear turning out to work for Mortus and all."

"Maybe," Cyrus said. "Or maybe it's just the general mystery of the whole thing. Forces at work behind the curtain, making moves in service of plans that we don't even see until they're too late." He shook his head. "I don't know. Maybe this whole thing is beyond us. Maybe Longwell was right and we should keep our noses out of the business of the gods."

"It would almost certainly result in all of us living longer," Vaste agreed. With that, he slowed, falling back into the line behind Cyrus.

Cyrus glanced to his side and saw Vara still keeping pace with him, near at hand. "And what do you think?"

She did not speak for a long moment. "I think ... that the goddess has gone missing. And that if you don't continue your search for her ..." She blinked her eyes and turned away from him, her golden hair blocking any view of her face, "... it is unlikely she will ever be returned to her realm."

He started to say something but stopped himself mid-thought. His pace slowed, though it took a moment for him to realize it had. She kept on, though, leading the column, and after a moment he picked up speed again and returned to the fore, marching into the swamp ahead with a strangely renewed sense of purpose.

Chapter 39

The weather was cool, carrying a promise of the first strains of winter, though fall had only just come upon them. They traveled for the rest of the day and stopped in a flat-topped hummock that spanned the swamp road with more than a little exposed ground besides. It was the highest point they had seen since entering the swamp, Cyrus reflected. The road had been pitted and long, with dark water stinking of death in ditches on both sides and even running over the road in some low points.

There was little in the way of high, flat ground. There was plenty of bog, though, and until they found that first large hummock, Cyrus wondered if they might not be forced to sleep on the road to keep from being submerged. Dinner that night was conjured bread, and there were no fires for warmth, just masses of people huddled together beneath cloaks. The occasional moan of lovers at their evening labors echoed in the night. To Cyrus it sounded lonely, as he laid his head upon the ground by himself, cloak covering him. He had seen naught of Aisling since her spat with Vara that morning, and he suspected he would see little of her for the rest of the journey. Some things were predictable in that regard, and her behavior after being scorned was one of them.

The day dawned dingy and grey, and Cyrus felt his bones settle, cracking and popping as he stood in the early morning dim. The cool air had seeped into his armor through the myriad gaps and caused the sheen of sweat that he'd worked up over the course of the day before to turn into a stiff, sticky solution that kept his underclothes bound to him. He sighed before moving in an attempt to peel them free of the most uncomfortable places.

They set out an hour after dawn, a company grumbling and irritable at the provisions available. *They've grown accustomed to the feasts that Larana can provide; even the ones who were with us in Luukessia don't care for the taste of conjured bread and water now. Once upon a time, it was life itself to them.*

Most of them carried packs on their backs, Cyrus knew, and within those packs were wheels of cheese and apples and dried meats. Still, there were few enough of those things that Cyrus watched at lunch as the bread was apportioned out once more, and nearly everyone took a helping. He watched Nyad make her way between small groups of soldiers and wondered how much magical energy she was expending. *Could be a concern; after all, what better time to attack an army than when their spell casters are unable to help repel an attack?*

He chewed the hard jerky he had brought with him, supplemented with small bites of a wheel of cheese, which helped make the conjured bread more palatable. He took a sip of water from the dried bladder he carried on his belt. The water he'd brought with him from Sanctuary had been gone within hours the day before; this was conjured by Nyad, who filled the skins and cups as she went about feeding the army.

The afternoon turned warmer. The clouds that had blanketed the sky had disappeared, replaced with a blue and unbroken vista. The sun shone down, and the chill of fall Cyrus had felt in the morning was gone with the clouds. They walked in a rough formation through the day, and the grumbling was now audible in between the gaps of silence.

The road narrowed during the day until it had become barely wide enough for four men to walk abreast. They walked into the night, failing to find a campsite until just before the last light had disappeared. Once more there were no fires. Over the sounds of camp and the insects, Cyrus heard a deeper call of coyotes or wolves in the distance, and the sound reminded him of the ghouls of the Waking Woods.

On the third day, Cyrus awoke before dawn to someone shaking his shoulder. He blinked his eyes once, then twice, seeing lines in the face that was nearly down upon his own. It took a moment to shake off the sleep enough to recognize it. "Belkan?" he asked, his gauntleted hand rubbing at his eyes.

"None other," the crusty old armorer said. He made a sucking sound with his mouth, and it took Cyrus a moment to realize he was trying to get something from between his teeth. He opened his lips and Cyrus saw a tongue moving around within the armorer's gaping maw. "Ahh," he said, presumably knocking loose whatever bit had been vexing him. "Come on."

"Come on where?" Cyrus asked, listening to the pop of his back as he sat up.

"Come with me, lad," Belkan said, now standing. He made no noise as he stood, which to Cyrus sounded odd in the wake of his own bones making such a racket.

"Belkan, it's the middle of the night," Cyrus said, looking up in the sky to realize it was literally true. There was no sign at all of illumination in the sky in any direction, just the soft glow of the stars overhead in the gaps where there were no clouds. "I have an army to march forward on the morrow, an invasion to oversee—"

"And you'll do all those things just fine and admirably with a mite less sleep," Belkan said, his low, grinding voice taking on a gruffer quality. "I have something I wish to show you. Come with me."

I must be mad. This is surely what madness feels like. He stifled a yawn. "Can you give me any indication of why I'd wander into the swamp with you?"

"Certainly," Belkan said, his leg armor clinking quietly as he shifted his weight. "I once promised you that I would take you here."

"Here?" Cyrus said, looking around. "I don't seem to recall you ever saying you'd take me to the swamp—" He blinked and felt a chill. "Here. This is it, isn't it? This is where—"

"Yes," Belkan said, nodding. He turned his craggy head just a little to the left. "Or more precisely, about three miles through the swamp in that direction." He pointed west, off the road. "There's a trail not far from here. We go now, we can be back just before the army moves."

"All right," Cyrus said, getting up off the ground. He had no bedroll because he had no horse to carry it, and its absence was sorely felt. "Let's go."

He followed the old man to the edge of the encampment where he was challenged by the guards manning the perimeter. A few quick words and they passed, and it was only then that Cyrus realized that Larana had fallen in quietly behind him.

They stole out of camp in silence, the sounds of snoring and quiet murmuring disappearing down the trail behind them. After a mile, they turned onto a barely marked side path that Cyrus would never have noticed. Belkan seemed keenly aware of it, giving no hint he'd even been looking.

The path was scraggly, twisted trees jutting out into the middle of it. It led through mire and mud more than a few times. Their progress slowed, and when Cyrus lost his footing once, he swore loudly. He looked back to see Larana watching him, her face indecipherable. "Sorry," he said. She gave him the barest hint of a nod, as though she accepted his contrition. With a wave of her hand, he felt his vision lighten, and he could see far more easily. *Sometimes, I forget she's a druid with real spells and everything. She's just too good at cooking and serving and blending in to the background.*

The sky gave no hint of light, but he had the spell to guide his feet. He followed the steps of Belkan in front of him, making his way through the lowlands and the hummocks, trees scattered amongst the lesser vegetation and high grass. He felt the brush of a thousand leaves and blades against his armor and heard the swish that heralded their passing. Through it all he kept on, following the old armorer. He could hear Larana just behind him, keeping close.

They walked for some time, past Cyrus's ability to calculate it. No hint of light pervaded the sky when they came upon another hummock, this one higher than the rest. It rolled out of the water in front of him, the smooth slope of the rounded hill raising it out of the murk. Cyrus felt the slosh of water that had accidentally run over the tops of his boots and sighed at the feel of it chilling his skin.

He stepped up onto the hummock and felt the aura of the place change around him. There was a darkness here, a palpable sense of something heavy, like a pressure on his mind, against his chest. "You feel that, do you?" Belkan asked, looking back at him then glancing behind him.

"Yeah," Cyrus said, and followed Belkan's eyes to Larana, who stood quietly just behind him. "It's like … like a gloom that goes beyond the night."

"The shaman that died here cast a curse darker than almost anything I've ever seen, save one," Belkan said. He straightened, adjusting his plate armor, pulling at his belt. "Left a gruesome mess, and then that business a few years later took place here as well, gave the entire area a sense of utter desperation." He let out a noise that was somewhere between a grunt and a sigh. "Here we are, though."

"Where?" Cyrus asked and cast his gaze around the clearing.

Belkan stepped aside and gestured to reveal a simple rock cairn. Time and weather had worn it to the point that it looked like nothing more than a mound of stones. Cyrus took a step closer and stared as though he could see something in the gaps between the rocks. There were many, and they varied from the size of a melon to no bigger than his fist.

"We built it in haste, of course," Belkan said. "After a battle. Didn't have time to dig into the dirt for a proper grave, and by the time we got back here a few years later, after the war was done and Gren had fallen, the swamps had done their worst and there wasn't anything left to bury."

Cyrus stood over the stone monument, trying to see into its depths, wondering if there was anything left of his father down there—

"Nothing remains," Belkan said quietly, reading the question in Cyrus's thoughts. Cyrus tilted his head to look at the armorer. "You're wearing all that he left behind." He paused. "Well, you're wearing it, and you *are* it."

Cyrus cleared his throat, felt it scratch as he tried to compel speech from it. "I guess I expected … I don't know. Something." There was a curious pressure down there, a lump that had settled around his Adam's apple. "A grand headstone, maybe? A giant sign to mark his passing here?" He laughed, but it was a rueful and mirthless sound. "I don't know what I expected. Something that showed that he was even here."

"He was here, lad," Belkan said. "Be assured of that. The trolls certainly knew he was, when he fought them."

"I don't really remember him," Cyrus said, staring at the mound. "I guess I just figured he'd leave more behind than an empty grave." He shook his head. "Stupid to expect, I suppose, when all I remember of what he left me before was an empty house."

"That's not fair to him," Belkan said darkly.

"Life isn't fair," Cyrus said and turned away, giving the crumbled grave one last glance. "Let's be on our way back. I have an army to move."

"All right," Belkan said, and Cyrus could hear the hints of some defiant reply itching to burst out, but the old soldier kept whatever it was to himself. "This way, then." He surged past Cyrus with a will, his legs carrying him with strength and fury that was obvious in his movement.

"Don't think ill of him," Larana said, voice near a whisper. "You know as well as anyone else that this is what warriors do—go to war for years at a time." She lifted a thin finger and pointed at Belkan's back, almost as an afterthought. "It's what he did as well. And it's what you did last year." She turned, wordlessly, and followed her father back down the trail, the sound of branches moving before them carrying off down the slope of the hummock.

Cyrus stood there a moment longer, then knelt, for just a moment, at the foot of the stones. He stared into them in the darkness one final time, and this time he would have sworn he saw something—just a hint of substance, really—in the cracks between them.

Chapter 40

Cyrus followed behind Belkan and Larana at a distance, a dark mood swirling around him. The gravesite had been unexpected, a surprise when he'd sussed out what Belkan had woken him for. He'd felt a thrill of something in the dark of the night when he'd realized where they were, and it had been unexpectedly dashed by the reality of the grave.

What were you expecting? he asked himself as he kept walking. He could hear the faint crunch of Larana's steps less than a hundred feet ahead of him, heard Belkan splash into a low channel of swamp water just in front of her. *Him to jump out of the grave to greet you with a great bear hug and an "I'm proud of you, son"?* He gritted his teeth together as he missed a step and felt his ankle give slightly in pain. He held it in, though, and kept from cursing out loud or making any sound to indicate the slight trough in the path he was following.

He's dead. He's been dead for as long as you can remember. Like Belkan said, you're wearing his only legacy. You just don't want to feel like you're alone—

We are none of us alone.

Cyrus froze as the sound of a soft curse hit his ears from directly behind along with the sound of a missed step and the clank of armor. He whirled and saw a hint of gleaming in the darkness. His heart raced and his hand fell to Praelior's grip, then he felt himself relax as he realized who was following him.

"I always thought you were a creature of extreme grace," he said, calling into the darkness. "But I guess even you make missteps like the rest of us."

"Yes," Vara said, emerging from the brush whisper-quiet. "Even I have been known to set my foot in a dip in the path unexpectedly, especially when the clomping bear I'm following behind gives no indication that there is a rut the size of a mountain pass in the trail."

Cyrus smiled. "I hit it myself, but I used it as an exercise in self-discipline to keep myself from crying out or giving a hint of the pain."

"I suppose that comes in handy in the Society of Arms, where they give you nothing but a sword and wish you the best of luck in your endeavors of war."

"It doesn't beat having a healing spell at hand," Cyrus agreed, still feeling that faint smile upon his lips, "but it's what I've got." He stood there for a moment as she drew up to within arm's reach. "You were following me?"

"Yes, well," she said, and he caught the slight hint of blush on her cheeks, "forgive me for being more than a little inquisitive about where the General of Sanctuary, leader of our assault, was sneaking off to in the middle of the night." She let her face fall into a more prim expression. "You should be more circumspect about your personal security."

"Surprised you didn't just assume I was sneaking off to a rendezvous with my dark elven harlot," Cyrus said.

She blinked. "I'm a little surprised you would refer to her in such terms."

"I was mimicking you," Cyrus said, turning away. "I don't hold the low opinion of her that you do."

"Clearly," Vara said, falling into step behind him. He could hear the footfalls now that she made no effort to hide them. "Or at least one would hope."

"You're acting a bit strange lately," Cyrus said, pushing aside a branch with his gauntlet.

"Just lately?" she asked with a hint of levity.

"You've been mercurial," Cyrus said, listening to the soft whistle of a bird in the distance.

"That is no great stretch."

"Even for you, I mean," Cyrus said. There was only the faintest hint of light on the horizon as they broke into an open space. Cyrus stared onto the long body of water that stretched to his east and looked at the sky. With the aid of the spell upon his eyes, he could see the faint hints of coloration that marked the place where—eventually—the sun would rise.

"I don't care for your course of action of late," she said simply. "As well you know. I see no reason to retread this ground."

"Do you have feelings for me still?" Cyrus asked, carefully measuring her response.

"Other than annoyance?" Vara asked, cocking a thin, blond eyebrow at him.

"Do you still care for me?" he asked.

He heard her gait miss a step, and it was a long moment before she answered. "I care for you as a friend, a guildmate and a pigheaded nuisance who has occasionally done me a good turn."

"Any more than that?" Cyrus asked.

"There is no more than that to be had," she said simply. "Seeing as you are attached at the crotch with the thief." She paused, let out an abrupt exhale, and turned to face him. "You have a … a … hells, a dark elven concubine, let us say. All else is beside the point."

"What if I didn't?" Cyrus asked.

"Then you would be exhibiting considerably better judgment in that area than I have previously assumed you capable of." Her footsteps crunched in the path behind her, but it was a delicate sound compared to that made by his heavy metal boots.

"I made a mistake," Cyrus said. "In the dark of the night on the eve of my return to Sanctuary—"

"I need hear no more of this," Vara said, cutting him off. "Whatever might have happened in the past, you have made your choice. I need not know of how you slipped your blade into some unwitting subject to—bloody hell, that's a terrible metaphor. The harm is done," she said. "Whatever you might have meant to happen, it doesn't take away from what you did, from the choice you made—"

"But it was the wrong choice," Cyrus said, stopping in the path to turn and face her. "Haven't you ever made one you wished you could take back?"

She stopped, flushing as he blocked her way. "More than a few, but once they were made, they were made. You cannot simply take back a choice once it is done. And furthermore, as a leader you should know that decisiveness in action is crucial to your ability to stand before an army or a guild and carry them to victory."

"I'm a man," Cyrus said.

"I am dimly aware of that fact."

"I make mistakes," he said. "And one of them—"

"Stop, just stop," she said, holding up a hand. "I will not have this conversation with you."

"I made a mistake—"

She snorted. "You made a sequence of mistakes, if you wish to claim them as such, and that sequence has yet to reach its end by my reckoning." She sniffed. "Even over the swamp I can smell your most recent liaison upon you."

"You can smell that? Gods, it's not just the ears with you, then—"

She rolled her eyes. "Not literally. It was a metaphor to indicate that whatever your protestations about 'making a mistake,' you continue to engage in evening frolics with the thief. I can jab you with my sword once or twice, General, and call it a mistake, but if I do it repeatedly, you know what they call that?"

"Murder?"

She made a noise of frustration that originated deep in her throat and blossomed forth from her mouth to fill the air around them. "Not a *mistake*, that's for certain. Even the greatest idiot cannot willingly err as much as you have, if indeed you consider your continuing evening horizontal rendezvous with her to be, indeed, a 'mistake.'" She paused. "And I would not use that wording with her, were I you, at least not if you wish to keep the thing with which you err connected to your body."

Cyrus blinked at her. "You think that's really a danger?"

She did not deign to look at him, casting her gaze out into the swamp instead. "Can we continue back to camp now?"

"I want to know the truth," Cyrus said. "You and I, we're the only ones here—"

"Save for Belkan and Larana, who lurk and listen even now."

"—is there any possibility for you and I?" Cyrus asked. "Is there a chance for you to put aside your anger and—"

"No," she said abruptly, and stared at him for a long moment. "Our decisions have carried us in different enough directions, I think. Mine let you slip away once, and the man who returned from Luukessia is quite a different one than the one I lo—" She stopped. "… than the one I knew before he left."

Cyrus stared at her, at her unblinking facade. She had always been hard to read, but now she was as stone-faced as ever she had been.

"Very well, then," he said, and stepped to the side of the path. "Why don't you go first and I'll follow?"

She hesitated, opening her mouth only a hint as if she wished to say something more but held it back instead. She took a step forward, even and strong, and then another, her usual gait unaffected by their conversation in any visible way.

Chapter 41

The road to Gren was long and arduous. By the time the last day dawned, Cyrus was sick to death of conjured bread and even more sick of rain. He had been drawn and irritable after the visit to his father's grave. The weather turned worse in subsequent days, slowing the army's advance to a crawl as a chill, torrential rain came down around them for a full day and a half.

The road began to wash away after the first day, and the night had been filled with a torrential downpour that had forced them to move camp in the middle of the night. It had been a mess, and a disorganized one at that, as they tried to form ranks standing in an inch and rising of water.

It had scarcely gotten better the next day, fording high water in the swamps that reached halfway to the waist of most of the members of the army. Cyrus had it slightly easier, but every crossing that high required the removal of plated boots among the warriors as well as the rolling of pants among the rangers.

"Just be grateful it's still and not moving water," Andren said as they took another ford. "That much water in a river would sweep away half the army." Cyrus had managed a grunt of acknowledgment as he slipped his wet feet back into his boots.

Affliction with leeches became a common occurrence, and a half-dozen people caught some form of swamp malady and were teleported out. When the last morning dawned and Cyrus took his conjured bread, he had well and truly had enough.

"The army is in a mood," Curatio observed as the Council stood in a rough circle.

"Morale is low?" Nyad asked.

"It is better described as 'annoyed,'" Vara said.

"You would know, being somewhat of an expert in annoyance," Vaste said.

"They have been feasting on conjured bread for several days, they have been rained upon, and this swamp is damnably unpleasant," Vara said. "The army is irritable." She straightened, her silver breastplate not bearing a single smudge from the crossings. "I should think that would make them better at fighting when the moment comes."

"It might make them better at pillaging, were that our goal," Cyrus said from his place in the circle. "Vaste, what can we expect here?"

"I already told you, goat buggery," Vaste said, looking a little sullen. "And slavery."

"What do they have to fight us with?" Cyrus asked, holding his patience. "We're less than two hours march from Gren, and I need to start considering how we're going to do this."

"I have no idea," Vaste said. "You won't need to worry about magic unless there are dark elves, so my recommendation would be to put your eagle-eyed elf out front and have her fill to the brimming any non-troll she sees that's not one of ours. Use your wizards to drive my people back, because they're afraid of magic here in the homeland. Some nice fire would likely send them to running." He shrugged. "Anyone who fights, cut them into sausage meat. Anyone who runs, let them live in fear. There, now you have a plan."

"Not quite what I was looking for," Cyrus said. "But it's a start."

"I don't know much more than that," Vaste said. "It's been a long time since I've been here, and I was only in town for a few hours last time before I was beaten to death. Suffice to say, my knowledge of Gren is rather limited at this point."

"Fine," Cyrus said, shaking his head. "We'll … plan as we go, I guess."

"There's a place near the city," Vaste said. "An overlook. There's a watch post. It only had three guards manning it when last I was here, and there are probably fewer now. If we can kill them, we'll have a fine view to plan your assault." The troll sounded strangely detached, the usual sense of irony gone from everything he said.

"Okay," Cyrus said. "We'll find this watch post and use it as our rally point." He nodded once at the officers. "We move."

They marched deeper into the swamp, the flies thick as the sun came out once more. It was the slow buzzing that began to drive Cyrus mad, his irritation rising to anger, and the anger giving way to rage as the day and the march dragged on. He found himself consciously avoiding giving orders where possible, letting others take the responsibility upon themselves so as to avoid snapping at those who spoke to him.

He slapped a fly that had landed in his matted hair, and when he withdrew his gauntlet, the sensation of the metallic impact on his skull remained, making his ears ring slightly. He hissed air out slowly in a ragged breath then glanced at the palm of his hand. The remains of the fly were stunningly large, almost the size of the tip of his smallest finger.

"Everything is grossly large out here," Vaste said, appearing next to him. "It's almost as bad as the Gradsden Savanna in that regard, except here it's largely restricted to the insects."

He looked over at the massive troll, who ambled along with a little more starch in his step than usual. "You're antsy," Cyrus said, and to his own ears he sounded like he was accusing the healer of something.

"You should talk," Vaste said, not looking at him. His head jerked slightly as he tracked a black fly orbiting his own head. "I hate this place. I want to destroy it and be done, and go back to my nice comfortable bed in Sanctuary and my lovely running water that I can cool or warm myself with, however I need it. I don't care for this swamp, I don't care for its occupants, and I truly despise the acts that they commit which sully the name of my entire race."

"That much is obvious," Cyrus said and let a silence lapse briefly. "Are you certain there's nothing else you can tell me before we attack?"

"They will fight you tooth and nail," Vaste said, and he flashed something that crossed between a grin and a grimace that bared his teeth, then brought his fingers up to show the hardened yellow nails that protruded from each of his digits. They were solid and long, each as big as two of Cyrus's fingers held close together. "And with trolls, that means something."

"How are their weapons?" Cyrus asked, the uneven road causing him to adjust his gait accordingly. The ruts here were spectacular, he had to admit, and he wondered only briefly how the trolls got wagons through before remembering that, indeed, they almost certainly did not.

"Piss poor when last I was here," Vaste said. "Almost certainly better if the dark elves are in alliance with them."

Cyrus felt his eyes squint. "I wish I knew what kind of fight we were in for. What sort of resistance your people truly have to offer, outside of vague suggestion. What I want to know is how many fighters there are in the city, whether they'll run when we knock them back—"

"I doubt it," Vaste said darkly. "Trolls don't typically run. It's why we lost the last war. It takes a mighty fear to drive us back."

They settled back into silence, and Cyrus did not press the issue any further, though a thought tickled the back of his mind: *Quinneria made them run.* The swamp began to lighten as the road gradually wove its way to higher ground.

They came to a break in the twisted trees, and Cyrus held up a hand to halt the army's advance. There was a sulfuric smell in the air, that swampy aroma that had lingered for days. It seemed fainter here, mixed with other strong, earthy aromas of moss and peat that hung from the branches of the trees. Cyrus made his advance along the road slowly, boots making quiet noises against the loose-packed sand.

He squinted his eyes over the slight rise ahead as Vaste hunched next to him, slinking closer. "Watch post," the troll murmured.

"How many guards?" Cyrus asked.

"Two or three," Vaste replied. "Ill-disciplined. Possibly sleeping."

Cyrus felt his eyebrows rise. "Sleeping?"

Vaste's mighty shoulders rolled in a shrug. "Who would be mad enough to attack Gren?"

Cyrus nodded sagely and noticed Vara at his side. He had not even heard her approach. "Pass the word to the army that we're nearly here. In case our newer guests are unaware, pillaging is not the Sanctuary way, and any of our people found to be taking advantage of the locals through plundering or other bestial acts will be cut loose from the guild—and their life."

She raised an eyebrow at him. "You think any of our guildmates would try to press a troll into the service of their fleshly desires?"

"You think any of the trolls would willingly let them?" Vaste replied. "They'd die first, and probably take a dozen of our own with them. They're a feisty people."

"Plainly," Cyrus said. "I want the word passed nonetheless. I will not have a stain on our honor because some new recruit hasn't received the message that we don't operate like the dark elves in this army."

"I will make your wishes known," Vara said simply. "What is your plan?"

"Kill the guards," Cyrus said. "Dance on their corpses." He shot a sidelong glance at Vaste, who frowned at him. "I was answering that like I thought you would."

"I wouldn't suggest dancing on their corpses," Vaste said. "Trolls are not big believers in baths, and when they do bathe, well … let's face it, this is a swamp."

"I'll go deliver your orders and leave the both of you to your corpse dancing," Vara said. "Though that does sound just a bit like what you're prohibiting your troops from doing."

"I think I'll stick to dark elves for now," Cyrus muttered.

Vara made an exasperated sound and disappeared behind him.

"Right then," Vaste said. "These first ones. If they sound the alarm—"

"Yeah, I know," Cyrus said. "Let's make sure they don't." He looked back at the army and saw Martaina waiting in the front ranks, staring at him in anticipation. He beckoned her forward and she came to his side in moments, picking her way across the dusty road as though she had not a care. "Martaina—"

"I know," she said, and her bow was unslung. "As ever, I am your only plan. Have you considered finding other people of skill to carry out your will in moments such as these?"

"It's easier to just use you." Cyrus nudged her. She fired him a gaze of pure malice, lips flattened in a dull line.

There was a whisper of breeze through the trees at that moment, and Cyrus watched the ranger nock her arrow as she ascended the last few steps to take her to the top of the hill. Cyrus could see the watch house from where he stood, but only barely. It was a shack at best, a wooden building that looked as though it might have been built by the most unskilled carpenter in all of Reikonos. The boards that composed it were spaced erratically, giving the shack gaping holes. The roof was poorly thatched and looked as though it had merely had dried fronds thrown atop it. Cyrus saw them shift in the wind.

The first arrow found a target in the eye socket of the troll standing nearest them. It plunged into him with but a whisper. The troll exhaled and made a guttural noise, something that made it sound as though he did not even perceive the harm that had just come to him. Another arrow plunged into his throat, and that made a slightly louder sucking noise.

The troll fell at that, dropping to his knees, staring at the blood that ran nearly black down his fingers. He had a vacant expression in his remaining eye, hands shaking as he stared at them. Cyrus wondered if he had time to perceive what had happened before the last arrow took his other eye and he flopped face-first to the ground.

Cyrus moved up the incline. The guard post was occupied by another troll, but this one had its back turned. It wore chainmail of some sort, but the links were large enough to slide a dagger through, and it reached only as far as his midsection, revealing a paunch of fat extending beneath the mail. The troll wore little in the way of pants, a thong of leather tied neatly around its waist in some sort of loincloth.

"Gods," Vaste said under his breath, "why even armor your upper body if you mean to leave your lowers exposed like that?"

"Yeah," Cyrus said, "seems like you'd be open to attack by all manner of hedgehogs and chipmunks."

The next arrow fell on the troll's unarmored neck, lodging itself in the vertebra of the back of his head. Cyrus admired the mastery of the shot, perfectly centered, and watched the troll fall without so much as a chance to call out. He fell right into the wall of the flimsy shack.

Wood cracked under the weight of the troll's impact, boards splintering not from force but sheer lack of strength. The shack collapsed, falling around the corpse of the troll. Splintered slats fell across the back of the beast and covered him neatly as he landed on his face, backside up in the air. The remains of the guard post came down around him, covering his back and head, leaving only his massive green rump exposed and sticking up in the air.

Cyrus stood there, staring in slow disbelief, unable to remove his eyes from the ridiculous spectacle. "Is he ... showing us his arse?"

"An unintentional final insult, I suppose," Vaste said, shaking his head. "The loincloth does little to preserve his dignity, doesn't it? I can't say you're seeing the best side of my people here."

"He did fall in the most peculiar way," Martaina said, her bow still clutched in her hand but now at rest. "I doubt you could have orchestrated things to go exactly in that manner if you gave me a hundred shots just the same."

"At least he didn't—" Vaste began and stopped as a burst of flatulence as loud as a thunderclap filled the air, followed by a rancid smell. "Oh, wait, yes he did."

Cyrus nearly choked at the smell of it. "Gods! I know bodies do that after their death, but that is particularly foul."

"We need to move quickly," Vaste said, holding his nose. "We need to get the army down into the city before they have a chance to mobilize—"

"Yeah, yeah," Cyrus said, waving a hand in front of his face. He signaled in the air with a quick motion, and the Army of Sanctuary started forward with a thousand simultaneously taken steps. Their uniform movement reassured him even as he tried to clear his nose of the vile stink. "Form up!" he called, falling into a front rank.

"I see you've once again led us into a terrible situation," Vara said, falling into step beside him as they reached the apex of the hill.

"A terrible-smelling one, at least," Cyrus agreed as they crested the rise. The troll corpse and the remains of the shack it rested in passed on their right as they moved to avoid it. Below them stretched a flat plain, absent the lowland marshes that they had traversed the past few days. The ground looked slightly rough but easily passable, none of the rocky hummocks or heavy trees surrounding the city.

Gren stood at the edge of the short plain, a city encircled by a wooden wall of pikes. They were only about the height of a troll and a half, and Cyrus realized he could climb it in a pinch, if necessary. It was a rough fortress designed more to obstruct the passage of natural predators than stop an army. There were gates built into the front of the wall, and the road upon which they stood wended its way across the short-grassed plain to end at those very gates. They stood wide open, without any hint of guard or watch, as if opened for the Sanctuary army to enter.

"This looks easy enough," Vara said as they began their descent. The other side of the hill was a slow descent to the plain, and Cyrus estimated the city of Gren was no more than ten minutes walk from where he stood.

"You'll regret saying that." Vaste's voice called from behind them.

Cyrus did not bother to turn his head to look at the troll. "I hope she's right. We could use an easy battle here."

"They're trolls," Vaste said. "'Easy' and 'battle' do not go along with their name, much the same as 'good' and 'smell.'"

Cyrus walked over the hill, watching the passage of the short grasses to either side of him as he finally caught a glimpse of the base of the hill—

And saw a troll running down it at full speed.

"Damn," Cyrus said, throwing up a hand to shield his eyes from the sun's light. "A guard got away."

"Must have run when he heard his companion trumpet the alarm," Vaste said with a healthy dose of irony.

"I do not think a burst of post-mortem flatulence counts as an alarm," Vara said archly.

"You heard that?" Cyrus asked.

"It would be impossible to miss, even with your ears," Vara replied. "He will warn them in the city."

"Right you are," Cyrus said, shaking his head. The cool breeze blew from the east, chilling the sheen of perspiration on his forehead. "Army, double time!" He stepped up his pace.

"This will not be any good for the gnomes and dwarves!" he heard Nyad shout from several rows back. The sound of boots against the road was loud, but she made herself heard even over it.

"They shouldn't be in the thick of a troll battle anyway," Vaste said.

"I shouldn't be in the thick of a troll battle, either," Andren said from a couple rows back, his distinctive accent allowing Cyrus to pick him out of the sound of the army on the move. "I'm delicate, you know."

"Just drink until you're numb," Vara said, "if you're not already; it will help to mitigate the pain when they start to rip you apart."

"I don't appreciate your suggestion that they'll be ripping me apart," Andren said. "Why, they might take one look at my handsome face and decide to keep me as a slave for their baser needs."

"That's possible," Vaste said. "Your hindquarters do look a bit like a goat's."

"Quiet down," Cyrus said, keeping to his trot. *Oh, how I miss Windrider.* He could feel the aches of the days of travel, and a rumble sounded within his belly from the pitiful sustenance that the preserved cheeses, dried jerky and conjured bread had provided. *I suppose they were right; I am ornery and quite ready for this battle.* He adjusted his helm, moving a lock of his long hair back behind his ear.

"Why don't you," Vara said, and he could feel her gaze burning on him, "use that sword of yours to run that guard down?" She gestured into the distance, where the troll was still hurrying toward the gates, running with a most peculiar gait, as though he were clenching something between his buttcheeks. *Probably holding in what that last fellow let loose.*

"And abandon the army?" Cyrus asked. "I don't think the warning is going to do them much good. We're a force of ten thousand; they're a bunch of civilians. They can't stop us."

"But they can bloody us," Vaste said. "And they can—"

"If the next words out of your mouth involve the phrase 'goat buggery,' I'm going to bugger you with a sword," Vara said.

"Fine," Vaste said archly. "Did I mention they like to eat elven meat? They do. It's a delicacy. Human, too, though it's a little tougher, obviously—"

"Have you eaten human meat before?" Cyrus asked Vaste with a dawning sense of horror.

"I didn't care for the taste," Vaste said, completely nonchalant. "Elves, though—they're quite tender."

Vara turned her head slowly to look at him, eyes burning in fury, even as she continued her steady run down the hill. "Is there any part of me that you would describe as 'tender'? Choose your answer carefully."

"Well," Vaste said, "I can't fairly answer that. Perhaps if you'd warmed up to our randy and potent General just a bit longer before turning on him, he might be able to tell me—"

"Die, troll," Vara said, abruptly turning away from him.

"Knowing what we're marching into, I just might."

"They'll probably close the gates once they're alerted," Cyrus said, and he quickened his pace slightly. The troll was still running wildly across the plain. *I could catch him. I could. Am I truly holding back because I want to stay with the army? Or am I holding back because I'm about to march ten thousand people into a city of civilians?*

Either sounds reasonable to my mind.

"He's in," Vara said, sounding the moment when the guard crossed under the gate. Cyrus watched him go with curious emotions.

There was a time when I would gladly have slain every troll in that city, with a song in my heart and a swing of my sword. When did that go away? After I got to know Vaste? He blinked. *After Enterra? I've never been reticent about killing when needs be; and they've got our allies, so needs would seem to be …*

"There's no movement at the gates," Vara said. The steady sound of the army's advance over the flat, dusty plains road filled Cyrus's ears. "It's almost as if there's no one to guard them."

"That would go hand in hand with what J'anda was telling us about their men all leaving to fight for the dark elves," Cyrus said. *Leaving their women and children alone.*

We are none of us alone. Cass Ward's words rang through his mind again.

The gates grew larger, the individual splinters showing on the worn pikes surrounding the city of Gren. And pikes they were, Cyrus realized as he got closer. They stood tall, but were ultimately trees that had been shaved to a hard point. Bones rested atop them, worn ones that had seen many years of sun to bleach them and winters to smooth them over.

"Those are human bones," Vara said.

"Or elven ones," Cyrus added. He saw her jaw tighten, but she took no issue with his pronouncement. "They've been there for a long time, I think."

"Since the war," Vaste agreed. "Or at least that's when I remember them placing skeletons atop each, after they'd been picked clean for dinners and—"

"I think I've heard about enough of that savagery," Vara said.

The smell of swamp was fading, replaced by the smell of something else. It was the stink of city, but fouler and heavier than that of even Reikonos. The aromas were nauseating to Cyrus, causing his stomach to quiver. He drew his blade, even though he saw no immediate threat, and he heard his action repeated in the ranks of the Army behind him.

He was the first under the gate, Vara at his elbow less than a pace behind; and this gap he knew she only allowed because he had taken a long stride just before they reached the entrance. Guard towers on either side lay empty, the streets quiet before him.

"I heard shouting before we came in," Vara said quietly, low enough for him to barely hear her. "If they are here, they know we are coming."

"Ambush," Cyrus said, eyeing the rough hovels that lined either side of the muddy street.

There was no other word for them but hovels. They were mud-packed huts, built with shoddy, dried dirt that had been fired for strength and laced with straw or something to give it hold. The quality of the brick was pitiful, and clear signs of the ravages of weather were upon every single dwelling within their sight.

Cyrus could taste the strong tang of acid on his tongue, the flavor of his insubstantial meals come back to visit him. He swallowed it down and ignored the prickling sensation running across the flesh of his back. He gripped Praelior tighter in his hand while his eyes swept over the houses lining the street. He could see a square in the far distance, but the detail was too faint to make out.

"Looks like Termina after the evacuation," Cyrus said, this time low enough that only Vara could hear him.

"But much better kept," she sniffed.

"Termina or Gren?" he asked with a smile, not bothering to look back.

She made a harrumphing sound but did not reply with the acidic retort he had expected. *That in and of itself is probably a sign*, Cyrus thought.

He kept walking, slowing his advance as he made his way down the avenue. He looked to the door of a hut to his right; the only thing blocking the dark, shadowy interior was a hanging, tattered cloth. He glanced left and saw the same.

"Shall we search the houses?" This came from Vara, but she sounded terribly uncertain to Cyrus.

"Not just yet," Cyrus said. "If this is a trap, I suspect they'll spring it soon."

"And you wish to walk deeper into it?" Vara asked. "What sort of daft strategy is that?"

"Deft strategy," Cyrus said. "We're an army. They're a civilian populace."

"Hubris is quite unbecoming on you," Vara said to him after a moment's pause. "Much like that black armor."

Cyrus frowned. "You don't like my armor?" She rolled her eyes but did not reply, letting his words sink into the silence.

The wind gusted through the town gates and swept between his legs. He half expected to hear the sound of an animal, anything, but there was naught.

I stand in the city of Gren. He looked over the mud houses and suppressed a shudder. *Here, in a place that sent out armies that menaced half the lands, in a place that my father died trying to reach, and I walk in at the head of an army less than half the size of the one he came with.*

Hubris? Perhaps. Perhaps Vara is right.

He glanced at her and felt the hint of a smile. He did not turn away quickly enough to escape her notice. "What was that about?" she asked.

"Nothing," he said, suppressing the smile.

"Oh, you are aggravating," she shot back.

"Always," Cyrus said. "In fact—"

There was a hiss from a doorway, and Cyrus cut himself off. It was followed by another, and then another, the sound of flimsy cloth being ripped from its hangings as bodies rushed out of every doorway on the avenue, and green, mountainous trolls poured into the ranks of the Army of Sanctuary in furious assault.

Chapter 42

They came from every direction at once, a true fury of claw and tooth, the way that Vaste had described. They moved quickly for being so large—but not quickly enough. Cyrus had split three of them into pieces before he realized just how surrounded they were.

"Fire spell!" someone called. It sounded like Andren's voice, cutting loud above the chaos.

"Hold!" Cyrus shouted. "No flames!" He made himself heard in a bellow that scratched his throat, giving it a rough feel, like he had taken a long drink of hard sand and rock. "Short ranged spells only! Do not set those houses afire!"

"You're so restrained," Vaste said from behind him, staff whirling as he delivered a crushing blow to the side of the head of a female troll. "I assure you they won't be."

"They already aren't," Cyrus said. He brought Praelior down on the brow of a female troll that was charging him, bisecting her furious face and casting her aside. Mammoth trolls were cascading from between the houses in lines of roaring, frothing fury, their faces torn with anger and bellowing into the fray. "I don't think burning the whole city to the ground and killing children and women will change their minds."

"They're already throwing the women and children at you, fool," Vara said, and Cyrus looked back to see her blond hair stained with green blood. "They are the sole defenders of this city."

Cyrus turned back to the fight and brought his sword across three trolls that came at him in sequence. They were each of them only a hair taller than himself; short, relative to trolls he had dealt with in the past. He saw the patches of loose hair and realized that every one of them was female as well, the shape unmistakable even to his war-filled eyes. "Son of a bitch," he pronounced.

"They will throw everything they have at us," Vaste said. "They will come and keep coming unless you kill them all. This is their home."

Cyrus felt the fury crease his forehead even as the sweat of exertion began to roll down from within his helm. He could feel it soaking the top of his head, running down through his hair as he swung his sword over and over. This swing killed a woman. The next a teenage boy, his green face mottled with spots.

"FLAME!" Cyrus called, his anger rushing out along with a fury and bile he felt deep within. *They truly are savages. Vaste was the exception. They will offer no quarter and accept none. They will overrun a battlefield with corpses until something—anything—makes them break with fear.* "Cast flames before us and send them to running!"

"Yes, sir," Nyad said, and Cyrus caught a kernel of eagerness couched in her reply. A thin line of fire stretched past Cyrus, a gushing geyser of flame that looked no bigger around than his leg as it pushed forth like breath blown forward.

"Out of the way, girl." Cyrus looked back to see Verity knock Nyad aside, adjusting her grey hat upon her head as she did so. "Let me show you how to cast fire."

Verity's staff emitted a belch of flame that became a gout. A bonfire-sized burst shot forth in a line that forced Cyrus to step aside to allow its passage. It grew into a wall that stretched twenty feet into the air, solid and wide, and then it proceeded to walk forward into the approaching trolls, catching them in its sweep like a broom pushing forth nothing more troublesome than dirt.

"This rabble shall prove no problem," Verity said, stepping forward in time with the movement of her spell. It spread before her like nothing so much as a great shield of flame, one that stretched the span of the entire avenue.

"This looks familiar," Cyrus said, jostling into someone next to him clad in armor. The battle had paused, the trolls coming out of the side alleys halted in fear of the spectacle of flame unleashed.

"That's because my mother did something very similar in Termina," Vara said, shoving him back from where he'd encroached on her space. He caught a look of annoyance. "Powerful spell, more than the princess of Pharesia could muster on her best day."

"Hey!" Nyad said, her blond head emerging from behind Vaste's bulk to send them a reproachful look.

Cyrus raised his voice again, shouting over the roaring of the flames. "Run for your lives, swine! We come to you now with the strength of sorcery, with the power of forces you have not seen since the days that Quinneria sent you scrambling back into your swamps!"

"That's dramatic," Vaste said.

"He's always a bit dramatic," Vara said.

"Always has been," Andren said, taking a sip from a flask. "Plays to the crowd with the best of them."

"Stand before us and your village will burn!" Cyrus said, ignoring them all. "You have felt the wrath of our kind before, and it broke you. Stand in our path again, and there will be nothing left but ashes. Flee this city now, while you have the chance, or your lives will be forfeit, and we will burn the flesh from your bones, leaving nothing blackened ash of marrow in the ruins of this place!"

"See?" Vaste said. "Dramatic."

"Think he'd do it?" Andren asked.

"Don't push me," Cyrus said, casting a dirty look in the direction of the healer. He looked back to the side streets, the gaps between alleyways. He could see the uncertainty in the eyes of the trolls that waited there, the fear. They took uncertain, shuffling steps back toward the safety of the darkness, away from the light of the street, lit by the midday sun and the Verity's glorious flames.

"My name is Cyrus Davidon, son of Rusyl Davidon," Cyrus said, raising his voice. "I am the slayer of dragons. I am the destroyer of the goblins. I am the fear of the dark elves. And this is my army."

He delivered the last with a rush of heat, with the satisfaction of emotion, with a grinding sense of long-festering anger let loose. He saw the eyes, the tentative eyes, and they faded. The fear took over, moving among the trolls like a pox, and they ran, full flight back into the alleys and the huts. Cloth was torn and adjusted as they hid, wide eyes staring out at him, tremor-stricken hands visible against the mud bricks.

"Let's go," Cyrus said, surveying the street around them. It was quiet, and as Verity pulled down the wall of her flame, the path before them was clear. He took up the lead, striding down the street of Gren, a conqueror here in a land that his father had died trying to reach.

Chapter 43

The square was a depressing place, a center for a city caked in the grime and dirt of the swamps and ovens, unclean and still possessed of that same stink. Cyrus walked along steadily, waiting for no one but not outpacing his army. He could feel them at his back, waiting, following, and it carried with it a reassurance even in the silence.

The sky above held an odd tinge of yellow, the sun refracting through a large cloud. Plants sprouted in the cracks between the dusty dirt roads, making the city look half-abandoned even though he knew by what had happened only moments earlier that this was not the case.

"There are slaves in some of the houses," Vaste said from behind him, and Cyrus halted at the edge of the square. He turned around to look upon his army even as he shot a glance at Vaste; the army seemed to be in fine condition. Bodies of their foes, on the other hand, lay strewn in the street on either side, giant green-skinned mounds pushed out of the thoroughfare and abandoned.

Cyrus felt a sigh build behind his lips. "Assign groups to go house to house. Do trolls understand the human language?"

"Well enough to get the job done, as you just witnessed by your speech," Vaste said. "Still, I can handle this; there are only a few words of troll necessary to convey the meaning we're looking for, and I think I can make myself understood." He paused, and then let loose a sonorous voice that seemed to reach up to the yellowed sky above. "Unchundah, for-unadhn, Cyrus Davidon! Charenay, ghruntal yas jhraunsah, erti chraumastie!" He adjusted his robes as he stopped speaking, and Cyrus could hear nothing but bare silence over the army and the city.

"What did you say?" Cyrus asked.

Vaste stared at him, unblinking. "'Now comes the master of your city, Cyrus Davidon of Sanctuary; make way for him and cast out your slaves, or he will become the master of you through spell and sword.'"

"How poetic," Vara said, and try as he might Cyrus could not discern whether she was being sarcastic or not.

"I'm not making myself master of anyone right now," Cyrus said as he caught motion in the doorways behind them. He stared, and bodies began to appear from behind the cloth curtains, haggard figures with bowed backs, ranging in size from gnomes to men of a height with Cyrus himself.

Cyrus stared; fewer than half the homes had cast out slaves. He pondered it for a moment and cast the gaze over his army. "Find out from each of the slaves just cast out if any of the neighboring houses are harboring unfreed slaves." He made a motion with his hands, which was matched by immediate movement in the army.

"And if they are harboring unreleased slaves?" Vara asked, sidling closer to him so that she could lower her voice. "What then, oh master of Gren? Spell and sword?"

"If need be," Cyrus said, coldly watching the street. He turned his head slowly to take in the abandoned square. There were carts set all about like some half-prepared circle one might find in the Reikonos markets. Not one of the shopkeepers remained, though. "We need to start spreading out if we're going to do this in a reasonable time. Vaste?" Cyrus turned back to the troll, who was staring straight ahead with his jaw slightly to one side in contemplation.

He stirred and looked back at Cyrus. "Yes?"

"How long will it take us to clear the city?" Cyrus asked.

"There are only three avenues like this where you might find slaves," Vaste said. "This one," he pointed to their right, "that one, and then the last," he pointed to the left, "which leads to the slave markets themselves. You can expect perhaps some resistance in the markets themselves; I doubt you'll get much of anything from the wealthy down that way." He gestured to the right again.

"There are thousands of side streets and alleys in this city," Vara said, glaring at him. "You are telling me that none of them contain slaves?"

"Slavery is a privilege of those with status," Vaste said with a shrug. "As is having your home on a main avenue. People in alleyways are the poorer strata of troll society. They aren't allowed to own property as valuable as a slave."

"What a charming society your people have built," Vara observed.

"I take it by your sarcasm that you missed the part about goat buggery?" Vaste quipped. "We're not exactly the most civilized people."

"Where else will we find slaves?" Cyrus asked. "As many as they're apparently taking, you can't tell me it's all going to service less than a thousand households."

Vaste pursed his lips, turning them an even deeper green. "If my people have returned to the old ways—and obviously they have—most of the slaves are working the fields or harbor, or they've been sold to Saekaj. The fields are past the slave market, and it'll be fairly obvious to see once we're done there. The harbor is straight ahead, but unless something has changed you'll find only a handful on the wharfs because not many ships come this way. So …" He blinked. "Saekaj. There's good money in sending workers to Saekaj, and my people need money. That and favors from the Sovereign."

"Saekaj will have to wait for another day," Cyrus said with a swift hand motion he intended to indicate his closure of the debate.

"What the hell was that supposed to mean?" Vaste asked, mimicking his motion. "We're supposed to lop off their heads?"

"I think it's a gesture to suggest we fling swords at their faces?" Vara's nose was wrinkled as she stared at him, befuddled.

"No, dolts," Andren said from slightly behind them, "it's plainly to indicate he's about to draw his sword, so take a step back."

"I doubt his sword is so large that anyone need take a step back," Vara said a little sourly.

"Wouldn't you like to know," Cyrus said, frowning. "I was trying to close the topic of conversation about Saekaj; plainly next time I just need to say, 'Let's focus on Gren right now instead of daydreaming about some day freeing all the slaves of Arkaria.'" He shook his head. "My life is not so much a ribald joke as a comic farce. I never imagined commanding an army and invading lands would so easily lend itself to the utterly ridiculous—"

"Conquer now, gripe later," Vara said as she started past him. She smacked her pauldron against his vambraces, clanking his upper arm as she passed, ponytail whipping so hard it nearly caught him in the face.

"Right," Cyrus said, watching her go forward. "And now for a hand motion everyone can understand." He raised his arm and dropped it in the signal that commanded the army to march, and he heard them follow the order as he hurried to catch Vara, who was already on her own march. "Would you care to lead a detachment down that avenue to our right?"

"While you steal all the glory that is to be had from wrecking the slave markets?" Vara asked, tossing a casual look over her shoulder, ponytail flitting as she did so. "Very well, then; I suppose turning out the homes of the wealthiest trolls would be a task fitting for a holy warrior, after all."

"You'll find they're not much different from the homes of the very poor trolls," Vaste said, "save for a paddock out back for—"

"Goat buggery, yes," Cyrus said.

"Well, they also eat the goats," Vaste said. "You know, presumably after their grotesque and wandering eyes have moved on to a younger, prettier nanny."

"Much like J'anda, I could do without the details," Cyrus said, taking his march left around the square in a slow, circular arc. He spared a glance to his right and saw Vara waiting, impatiently, for the first ranks of Cyrus's army to clear the edge of the square. A second division was splitting off, he could see; so well orchestrated were their maneuvers that no orders had been called. They marched entirely on the motion of a hand. *Handy skill to have in the event of a lockjaw curse.*

The flat, mud-built huts down the avenue gave Cyrus little impression of the peoples inside. The yellow sky, tinged almost green, came from a glow that had settled low over the buildings to his right. Every building carried a browned look, like sun baking had hardened the mud against the elements. They were tall enough, he realized, bigger than the mud huts he'd seen fishermen use in the Riverlands or the sand-glassed buildings of the desert dwellers of Inculta. They were troll-sized buildings but made of the dirtiest material he'd ever seen used. There was none of the artifice of elven stonecutters here, nor of dwarven tunnelers, nor of human craftsman with their brick and wood. This was something of a low art, a functionality that bordered on the basic, like a house a child could build on a city street, doomed to be washed away in the next rainfall.

"How long have these homes stood?" Cyrus asked, unintentionally aloud.

"Ten years, perhaps," Vaste said. "The oldest twenty, maybe?"

Cyrus looked down the desolate, abandoned street. "Why?"

"Quinneria destroyed Gren," Vaste said. "Leveled it to the ground."

Cyrus blanched. "But the people—"

"Oh, they had a chance to flee first," Vaste said. "After the second battle of Dismal Swamp, the one where she broke our defense with a single spell, she marched in at the head of the allied armies. In a booming voice, one that swept over the hillside and down to the town below—not that far off from what you just did, actually—she commanded them to leave, and then lit the plains outside the gate with the most fearsome display of spellcraft you could probably imagine. Then she advanced it toward the city a few feet at a time, warning the people that if they did not run before her, she would leave nothing remaining of them."

"And they left," Cyrus said.

"But of course," Vaste said. "They may be slow, but they're not entirely stupid. Word had reached the people of Gren when their broken army came fleeing back to the homeland. It was a smaller city then, we were spread around the coast and further out. Dwellings in the higher parts of the swamp, and even as far down as Nalikh'akur. All of them, the refugees, they'd been driven north, hiding behind the—well, there no walls at the time." Vaste stroked his chin, and let out a short, barking laugh. "We didn't think we needed walls. In any case, the people fled. Grabbed their children—and their goats," he sent Cyrus a cockeyed look, "and they ran. Hid in the fields, in the swamps. And they watched ..." He hesitated, face suffused with a sort of awe that Cyrus could see came from deepest memory, "... watched the once-wondrous city of Gren, a marvel of the ancients and the elves, as that witch's magic leveled it into near nothingness." He looked at the center of the square, to the broken pillar, covered in vines, which remained.

"So it wasn't always mud huts and swamp grass," Cyrus said, and they started down the avenue toward the slave markets. There was nothing in the air but the lingering of Vaste's words and the march of the army; the street ahead was as abandoned and lifeless as the one left behind. Not a single resident of Gren remained out of doors.

"No," Vaste said, with a note of regret. "The death of my people's imperial ambitions signaled the end of their cares for outside influence. Where once there were spires and grandeur here, the remainder of an outpost of the ancients turned into elven town, abandoned by time and added to by the foremost minds of our people—" he cut off. "Now it's mud huts. Mud huts and pig pens, here and there." He glanced to his right and indicated with a wave of the hand exactly that: hogs in a wooden enclosure, stinking, sulfuric mud mixed with the reeking air. Cyrus caught a whiff of it as he passed, and the faint oink of one of the hogs was audible over the sound of the army's marching.

The glare of the yellow sky matched Vaste's eyes, and Cyrus found himself struck by the glare of the troll's anger. His face fell to a sullen expression, resentment mingled with regret in a combination Cyrus had not seen from his friend before. "You fit in better before the fall of the Troll empire, didn't you?"

He glanced sideways. "We were still a slaving people then. Vicious, violent, gleeful in the destruction of others."

"The Society of Arms is all those things," Cyrus said quietly. The relentless march of the Sanctuary army filled the air around them.

Vaste paused before saying any more. "Yes. I fit in better here before. At least then there was hope, there was aspiration, growth and a future for the trolls. There was an intelligentsia that either died in the last war or was killed in the upheaval and recrimination that followed our failure. They believed we could be more instead of scrabbling to be less. Now we are the lowest form of life on Arkaria, and there is no doubt we will remain so. Even the hated goblins have a better chance of a bright tomorrow than we do." His face flickered with anger as the road widened ahead into a market. "We no longer even try. Servants of the Sovereign, that's all we're fit for because we have no brains of our own."

Cyrus held his reply, casting an eye over the market ahead. Cages were present, iron-wrought, strong in their construction. They seemed out of place in the midst of all the mud huts and low buildings. Their dark metal was intercrossed in small squares, big enough only for a human to squeeze a hand out, perhaps. Latticed bars an inch wide and with a thickness that hinted at their strength. There was a sound of chains, a sound of metal rattling, as Cyrus entered the great market. A few clumsily hung cloth tarps were strung carelessly over a cage here and there, meager protection against the rain and chill for those fortunate enough to be under one.

As Cyrus drew closer, he realized that the silence was the most shocking part of it all. There were figures huddled in the cages, bodies of hundreds or thousands of beleaguered. The nearest cage stood right in the path, and he could see the eyes more than the thin frames. They found him, they watched him, they were near disbelieving as they followed him. Followed the army on his heel.

"Not possible," came a whisper on the wind. The voice of a slave in a cage.

"Don't dare to hope," came a woman's reply. He could tell it was female only by the highness of the voice.

They were all of them dirty. Black hands, soot-stained faces, hair matted and filthy. He could see that some of them had had their hair shorn off like sheep. Cyrus grew closer and the smell of human filth was near staggering, worse than the troll streets and houses. It filled his nose and mouth, gagged him, and made him want to cover his face with a blood-stained gauntlet.

"The man in black," came another whisper, childlike.

"Cyrus Davidon—"

"—of Sanctuary—"

Cyrus felt his pace slow, felt his feet draw into short steps. "Set them free," he said, but his voice sounded choked to his own ears. "Smash open the cages, break their chains." Silence fell. "Set them free," he said, louder this time. "Let them loose." Even his own voice sounded slightly thick with emotion, desperate emotion trying to claw its way out of his mouth and eyes.

"Free—?"

"Don't dare to hope," came the voice again.

"This is a dream, isn't it?" came the child-like voice under the sudden, rising sound of low voices. "This isn't real, is it?"

"This is as real as it gets," Vaste said quietly, more for himself than for the speaker, Cyrus realized.

Cyrus watched his army move forward, snaking into lines, running through the gaps between cages like water running into the cracks in a patch of dirt. They moved with spirit, and he saw them breaking open the cages, forcing fine steel swords into the gaps and prying the metal free. The cages swung with squeaks, muted surprise from the occupants who still murmured among themselves. Some came running out with glee, others rested on the floors within, dull eyes not seeming to take in anything of their surroundings.

Others watched him, emotionless, no thought or reason or action behind their irises. *The living dead, truly.*

Cyrus stood in the middle of the surging army, heard screams and cries of battle on the far side of the square, and felt no call to join them.

"Slavers putting up a last fight," Vaste said. "Probably what that is, anyway."

Cyrus nodded. He looked into the center of the market, where a lone pillar stood. It looked familiar, and he knew instantly it had been one of the few spared by the wrath of the Sorceress. *A construction of the ancients.* He wondered at her intention, and an answer came to him: *She wanted them to remember. Wanted them to remember how she'd humbled them. Beaten them. Wanted them to remember the price for what they'd done.*

"She took everything," Vaste said, as though he were reading Cyrus's mind. He was only inches away, and his quiet voice stood out over the sound of the army. The battle clamor had died away at the far end of the square, and now there were slaves mingling with his own people. His height gave him clear view of the whole spectacle.

And the pillar.

"She wanted to make us feel alone," Vaste went on. "Wanted us to feel like we were isolated in the world, bereft of any assistance. She destroyed the portal, of course. Cut us off. The humans and the elves would not trade with us, and almost no one else would come here. Why bother, after all? It is not as though the swamp is a place of great import." He gave a mirthless chuckle. "Or great exports. We have nothing of value to add to the rest of Arkaria. Nothing but our violence." Vaste bowed his head. "We are alone."

"None of us is ever alone," Cyrus said, his voice dull and dead, the words spoken by rote instinct, driven forth by the sight in front of his eyes.

"That's poetic, but false," Vaste said. Cyrus could feel the troll's eyes burning into the side of his head. "You've been saying that a lot lately. Is that your new motto?"

Cyrus started slowly forward, his legs barely moving with every halting step. "Not new."

"Old, then?" Vaste fell in beside him, and the crowds of soldiers and slaves parted for them as Cyrus wove his way slowly between the cages. "Your old motto?"

"Advice from an old friend, I suppose," Cyrus said. The cages were arranged in a circle with the giant pillar at the center. It stood tall as a titan, a centerpiece for the slave markets, a sight for all to see from wherever they stood.

"Oh?" Vaste said. "And who gave you this piece of feel-good advice that would warm the coldest heart on the most frigid eve? Was it Alaric? It has the ring of something he would say."

"No," Cyrus said, ducking his head slightly to avoid an overhanging cloth. It brushed the top of his helm and he could hear it tear as he proceeded onward. "This was before Alaric."

"So, there was hope for the man in the black armor before he came to Sanctuary," Vaste said, trailing in his wake. The crowds parted, and Cyrus saw the base of the pillar ahead, old stone like that of the Citadel in Reikonos, but more weathered. Vines sprouted from the ground and crawled up the sides like a thick tapestry woven around the base. There were long, shredded tracks where the vines had been torn away, worn by the movement of ropes and chains along the length of the pillar.

"Always," Cyrus said, brushing the cloth overhang free from where it caught his helm. The sky swelled above him at the removal of the dark cloth, the sunset shades growing more orange all the time, fire casting the pillar that stretched above him in shadow, blotting out the sight of its apex to the point he could scarcely see it.

But he could still see it.

"There is always hope," Cyrus said quietly, "all the way until the end." He almost hoped Vaste did not hear it.

"No hope for this poor bastard, then," Vaste quipped, gesturing to the figure atop the pillar. "This is where they make the examples for all the slaves to see." He made a rough gesture. "They cut him up before they put him there, but the odds were good he was alive for at least a day after it happened." There was a snuffling of anger in the troll's words. "Where was his hope, I wonder? Not in Gren, I suspect, for as you heard before we opened the cages, no one dares to hope here. It is a lost place, suitable only for the forsaken." Vaste's voice lowered and hardened, and he pointed at the spectacle of the body chained atop the pillar, an example to all. "And as much as I hate to contradict you, my friend, this man died alone. We all die alone."

"Perhaps you're right," Cyrus said, voice faint, near to cracking. He looked up, and saw in the shadow cast by the pillar, the faint darkness where once there had been the eyes of Cass Ward, hidden under the shorn head and mutilated chest of a warrior true.

Chapter 44

19 Years Earlier

"None of us is ever alone," Cass said to his assembled team. They listened, they hung upon his every word, this twelve-year-old leader of men and boys and girls and women.

And behind them, in the darkness, Cyrus Davidon, also twelve years old, listened for himself and imagined the words being spoken directly into his ears by a caring voice, one that left off all the malice.

No one spoke to Cyrus save for the Society instructors. Speaking to him was forbidden; he was outcast, with no Blood Family to call his own.

Cyrus stayed in the shadows, held to the shadows, hoping no sight of his face remained. This was not a time of testing and yet, here in the Society, every moment was a test. He kept to the shadows as much of the time as he could. It was easier that way, to remain out of the way of the older children in the Society. They were not allowed to kill him in plain view of the instructors, after all. And the instructors were about often, but not all the time. The shadows had become a habit, and looking over his shoulder had been a talent he'd learned in the last few years.

The smell of cooked meat filled the air, tickling Cyrus's tongue and making his stomach rumble. They stood in the mess hall, the place where the assembled Society ate and spoke, met and talked. There was fellowship and the filling of bellies, Blood Families sitting across from each other, huddled over the bowls, taking a drink of their tankards, clinking them together in companionship.

Cyrus stayed in the shadows. He ate on the floor. The hall was divided neatly in two, half the tables for the Able Axes, half for the Swift Swords. He knew his place, and it was to sit against a wall out of the reach of flickering candles and watch that which he never had. He would take his food quickly, sullenly, not a second to be spared, and he would leave the hall as soon as he was done. Sometimes he missed directives, orders handed down from the instructors. That was the price he paid for staying alive, for being clear of the hall before the rest of the trainees got done. He had already found his bedding place for the night by the time the first of them left the hall, and it was always, without exception, somewhere that he could not be approached without considerable noise. He liked to creep about on the tall beams of the dining hall after dinner, sleep against the rafters where he could not be seen, tucked against the red pine so tight that if he rolled so much as an inch in the other direction he would lose contact with the former tree trunk that he wrapped himself around. He had grown accustomed to no blanket.

This was the way of things, the reality and the cold truth. It was the life of Cyrus Davidon, outcast of the Society, and he had hardened his heart to any possibility of hope.

"None of us is ever alone," Cass Ward repeated, speaking to a whole table of those his own age and older. He was a leader, strong-backed and tall. He fled no one and nothing, did not have to pick his battles like Cyrus. Cass Ward never doubted that he had a family at his back, a Blood Family to be the currency that backed his every statement and threat.

Cyrus did not make threats. He chose moments to strike when needed in exercises. He fought singly wherever possible. He had no gold to back a threat if he made it, and his enemies were legion and would overwhelm him with numbers should he antagonize them too greatly. They had already tried on more occasions than he could count. He had defeated them every time they had come, exacting a terrible cost that made them want to stay away from him.

Still, it was a lovely thought, the idea that he was not alone. He finished the last of his stew and left the bowl in the shadows. The kitchen staff never complained about it, which was a minor and nearly unbelievable gift in and of itself. In the Society, every misstep, however slight, was catalogued and thrown back at the transgressor.

Leaving his bowl was an affront to the Society and to the discipline of keeping your own space clean. Still, Cyrus did not push his luck and simply said a prayer to Bellarum that he'd get away with it for another day; leaving the shadows to place this bowl in the spot where the other dishes were collected would have tipped his departure to the entire hall. His shroud of secrecy depended upon it, and it was luck, sheer luck, or perhaps a kind member of the kitchen staff, which spared him this particular disadvantage that could lead to death.

He crept from the room, threading his way through the darkened hallways of the Society. In the hour following the end of his dinner, Cyrus went to the arena, the area of challenge. Tonight was no exception, and—in the shadows, of course—he used a wooden sword to practice the latest movements that had been taught today. With no enemies about to hobble him, he was able to plan, to work the moves into his mind before the tests on the morrow. He imagined a swordsman across from him, fast and agile, testing him, laughing with him, practicing as they drove each other to greater heights of skill.

But there was no laughter here in this place with him; he was alone, always.

When the first laughing voice reached his ears, he put the sword back on the rack without leaving the shadows and fled the arena. Others would come, as they always did. Cyrus watched them, but never once did they pick up swords. They gathered and gabbed, talking their hearts out as they sat in the seating around the arena. Never once had he seen them enter the dirt floor itself, the place of trial and learning, at least not while he was there. They practiced in the day and left their nights free for spoken glee and shared jest; they were a lazy and complacent lot to Cyrus's eyes, but they outnumbered him as a plague of flies outnumbers the wasp. He was content to stick to the darkness and hide from their eyes, counting the days and months and years until he would be free. *Free of this place. Free to seek my fortunes unfettered by people constantly eyeing me with ill thoughts.*

Though I suppose the outside world will leave me just as alone and threatened as I find myself in these walls. He heard Cass Ward's ringing words in his ears and scoffed mentally. *Not being alone is a hobble for the weak; my strength is my lack of attachment. No one to drag me down, to slow me. No one to rely on me, to bind me to them.*

I am alone, and it is my power.

He made his way through the halls as silently as any thief. When he reached the dining hall, he avoided the doors and climbed the nearby stairs. Pausing on the landing, he listened for any sound of glee, or mirth, or breathing. Hearing none, he climbed using the layered bricks, carefully and quickly, squeezing through the small gap in the wall at the top. His feet touched silently upon one of the beams that stretched across the top of the hall. It was only a foot wide and paralleled on each side by matching ones. Ten of them provided the support across the hall, with a much larger one intersecting them in the middle and holding them up.

The candles in the hall were all dimmed, only one in five now lit. In the dinner hour, they shed their flickering light in nearly every direction, forcing him to seek out the farthest place from their radiance. Now the place was all shadows, his domain. He made his way across the beam as silently as he had stolen through the halls and pivoted adeptly at the center beam. It was three feet wide, made from a tree larger than any he had seen with his own eyes. It was long and straight, a sword with ten crossguards. He made his way to the far end, over the massive doors that led out of the hall.

He was almost to the end, to that narrow bed where he slept, when he realized he was not alone. He heard more than he saw, could sense more than his eyes could inform. He froze, the fear of being discovered in this place wrenching his still-full stomach, and he hoped that his senses deceived him. *No. This has been the best, by far of my hiding spaces. I can't—*

Cyrus looked over the side, down to the hall below. There was a figure in the dark, a brown-haired male still lurking in the back of the hall, where Cyrus had eaten his meal. There was the slightest sound of a clatter, and the figure emerged into the candlelight in the middle of the room bearing a bowl—Cyrus's bowl.

Cass Ward made his way slowly to the kitchen, the bowl in hand with his own. He carried them toward the kitchen, where the scent of the ovens' still-burning embers persisted. He placed both bowls on the counter with the rest, making nearly no sound.

Cyrus watched with amazement and dread, suspicion clouding every sense. *Why ...?*

Cass Ward, his task finished, made his way back to the entrance of the dining hall quietly, with nary a step turning up more than near silence. He paused at the entry, his head slightly bowed. "None of us is ever alone," he said into the empty hall.

With a single look skyward, his eyes fell on the place where Cyrus stood in the darkness, and Cyrus felt a chill. *He knows.*

Cass disappeared through the door quietly, shutting it behind him, the slight thump of the wood on wood echoing only for a moment after he had passed.

Cyrus lay awake that night, and the next, and the next, fearing the worst. He watched the shadows, waiting for the inevitable attack to come creeping out of the dark. When he slept, it was fitful and brief, coming in spells that were brought on by extreme fatigue and ending when he awoke from his nightmares in a cold sweat.

It was two weeks before he realized that the attack was not coming, and over a month before his sleep returned to normal, deep and placid, his only refuge.

It was not long after that when Cyrus realized that every time Cass Ward said, "We are none of us alone," in his presence, he was always—without exception—looking at Cyrus when he said it. After that whenever he heard them, Cyrus thought of them differently, a strange resonance plucking at a string deep within him, and it gave him the faintest flicker of hope.

Chapter 45

Cyrus stared up at the desecrated corpse of Cass Ward, feeling empty inside save for one, lone note, the pluck of a chord in his soul, the resonance of it echoing within.

Fury.

It coursed through his veins, reckless, hateful, consuming him with anger that ran like a river current over him. The shadowed body above shuddered with the foul wind off the swamp, and Cyrus shook in his armor, his hand vibrating to that pitch coming from inside.

They are hateful, spiteful, disgusting, worthless, destroyers of all that is worthwhile and good. He looked up, remembering the righteous rage that had flooded him when Narstron had died. It came back with a new face, red eyes shining down from Cass's head.

"Cyrus?" Vaste's voice was a distant sound, the call of a friend on a clear summer's day, far from the deepening sundown in which he stood on the edge of the world, in a place that was home to the beasts that had killed his father, destroyed his childhood, left him at the mercy of people who hated and drove him and flayed the decency out of him.

I have no decency remaining.

His hand found Praelior, and the world slowed around him.

"Get Vara," Vaste said from somewhere behind him, a dragging sound like he was stretching every word for comic effect.

The world was awash with that color yellow, turning red as the sun sank further behind the pillar. It was flame on the horizon, flame the like of which he'd seen Verity turn loose. *Flame like I'll see her turn loose again.*

Soon.

Cyrus drew his sword as he stared, taking a slow circle around to see his surroundings. The only troll in sight was Vaste; but there were bodies, people, as far as his gaze could see. Half or more of them were bedraggled, haggard, creatures wearing cloth or less, fresh scars, fresh wounds, old wounds, infections, puss-laden sores and worse visible on their bodies. They were barely recognizable as the living, barely knowable as people—gnomes, dwarves, humans, elves, the occasional goblin, even. He felt no hate for the goblins; he had known too many of them by now, known them as friends and foes, in war on both sides of the fight.

Cyrus's eyes fell on Vaste, and he saw the alarm in the troll's eyes. It was wisdom, wisdom in the yellow eyes, wisdom that told Cyrus that the troll knew his mind.

"Why Vara?" Nyad asked, from behind Vaste's elbow. "Don't you think it should be Aisling? Or Curatio?"

"*Get Vara*," Vaste said, certainty and alarm flowing in equal measure. Nyad disappeared into the crowd behind Vaste, heading swiftly back the way they had come, robes rustling as she moved down the avenue.

Cyrus took a breath of the dank, foul-smelling swamp, slave-market air, a breath of disgust and vitriol that cleansed him of any doubt. He had fought trolls, more than he could count, and only one had been worth a damn. "Get behind me, Vaste," Cyrus said.

Vaste's hands came up, palms facing the warrior, his staff resting against his shoulder. "Don't do this."

Cyrus spun once more about, taking in the refuse, the wastes, the dregs of the market around him. They stared, the drifting, aimless flotsam barely alive. His eyes fixed on an elven woman who caught his gaze, her brown hair twisted and ragged. Her nose was slightly angled, but she had been pretty once. Under the dirt, under the markings of the whip that showed on her bare shoulders, there was a hint of something familiar. He brushed his way through the crowd as gently as if he were stirring aside the cloth that had hung over the cages, careful not to knock anyone over.

"Elisabeth," he whispered, and the elven woman looked up at him in faint surprise. "Elisabeth, it's you."

She opened her mouth slightly, and there was a flicker of recognition. "I know you," she said.

"It's Cyrus," he said. "Cyrus Davidon."

"Cyrus Davidon," she murmured. "I knew a Cyrus Davidon once. A long time ago."

"It is I, Elisabeth," he said, and he reached out with his left hand to brush her cheek. She pulled away abruptly with a gasp, jerking her hands up as if to defend herself from his touch. "I'm Cyrus. The Cyrus you knew."

She squinted at him, shaking her head. "No," she decided finally. "He's long gone by now. Long gone. They're all gone."

"Who is all gone?" Cyrus asked, staring at her. The rage was curdling within, rising with her every word. He longed to strike out but not at those around him. It was the ones beyond that, the ones in the mud homes and buildings around the square. His mind was clear enough to recognize the victims, to separate them from the tormentors.

And, oh, how he wanted to greet the tormentors. To open their arteries, to make their necks sing through new and gaping holes that he himself did carve. His world was chaos and pain, conquest and fury, and he knew it well. He spoke the language fluently, and it spoke back to him through the sword in his hand.

"They're all gone," Elisabeth said sadly again.

"Cyrus," Vaste said.

"Not now," Cyrus spat bitterly back at him, not even bothering to turn.

"Cyrus." This came from Erith, tinged with loss, and he wondered when she had come into the square. He did not turn to look at her either, afraid that his fury might be loosed on one of them unintentionally.

Cyrus made to touch Elisabeth's arm, but she shuddered, flinched away again, blanched at the hint of his motion, falling to her knees and out of his path. He walked past her as the newly freed slaves made way for him, ducking away as though he were an overseer or the lash, reaching out for them. They parted like gates allowing for his passage. And pass he did, through the square, around the cages, threading through the knot of living beings that had been reduced to this; unthinking, unfeeling, frightened, bloodless creatures that knew naught but pain.

Cyrus knew pain.

Oh, but he knew pain.

He dared not look back; not at the pillar, not at his army or officers, not at the friends he knew tread behind him like they were tied to his very heels.

"Cyrus," Andren said, and he heard him and ignored him with the rest. The word was part plea and part warning, and it went utterly unheeded, drowned in the river of fury that still pushed Cyrus along in its wild currents.

At the edge of the square stood mud buildings, bigger than huts, bigger than the others. Slaver dwellings, he figured. Cloth hangings separated them from the open street, and they rustled. From breeze or fearful hands, he did not know. He reckoned there must have been some of the latter behind them, and he meant to find their owners, carve them free of said hands—

"This is not the way," Vaste said. "They'll answer for their crimes, but this is not the way—"

"It's *my* way," Cyrus said in a low, thunderous voice. It crackled and writhed, a living thing where it should have been dead. "It's the way of the warrior, don't you know? Of the conqueror? Of the lone combatant, who falls upon his enemies like a hawk on a field mouse or a rabbit. Well, I am the raptor and these—these vermin are quailing before me." Cyrus held up his sword and let the fury settle on his bones. "I know what I have to do."

He pictured the rage of his father in that moment, saw the grave in his mind's eye, a specter rising from it clad in bone and rotted flesh like it came from the darkness of the Waking Woods, moaning voice and death rattle echoing as it came for its prey. He saw it rise in his mind, fearful eyes, glowing red, fury of the ages and the righteous unleashed, the fury of a son who had never really known his father because of *them*, laying waste to his enemies, and he knew what he was—

His hand clutched Praelior high above him, and the cloth of a door separating him from one of them, one of the unworthy, one of the prey, was only inches from his grasp, waiting to be torn aside, weapon plunged in, screams ripped free from heinous, slaver throats—

"Cyrus." The voice was clear, rattling through his sword as though it struck the blade with lightning. It rattled down his bones, into his soul, ripping away the anger like a cloth covering denuding his door, leaving him exposed to the message and the voice, *that voice*, full of wisdom and knowledge and carrying so much strength even in death—

"Cyrus," Alaric's voice said, "... don't."

Cyrus felt his grasp slipping, felt his hand shaking, not from rage but from some strange relief granted by the sound. He turned, hoping to see the face of the aged paladin. He wanted to see the hope in the eyes, the wry smile that told him without words that everything was going to be all right, that gave unspoken comfort the like of which he had not known in any of the remembered days of his life.

"Cyrus ... don't," Vara said, and she was there before him. He blinked, looking for Alaric, but he was gone. Had he even been there at all? It was her though, silver armor shining, blond hair as yellow as the light disappearing over the horizon even now. She was sweet, and soft, and gentle, and he felt his sword return to the scabbard by instinct alone, his desire for blood as easily put aside as a meal once his belly was full. "You are better than simple vengeance," she said, and in her voice he heard the echo of Alaric Garaunt's words, and of other words, as well, from farther back—soothing and lovely, and that reminded him somehow of something his mother had once said.

"I am better than simple vengeance," Cyrus repeated, and it gave him strength. His fingers lingered on the hilt of Praelior, but the desire to strike out with it was as gone as Cass Ward. His eyes drifted up to the pillar once more, and where moments earlier he had felt the hatred flare, he now felt only sorrow in its place.

"General," Curatio said, now curiously in the front of his mind. Had he been there a moment earlier? There were others, too—Vaste, Nyad, Larana, Belkan, Andren. They formed a semi-circle with Vara at the center, and a square of refugees and Sanctuary members filling it to the brimming beyond. It was silent, and Cyrus could hear the blood rushing in his ears; not from anger any longer, but from an emptiness that followed in the wake of his decisive wrath. "Their portal is destroyed," Curatio said. "We are quashing the last of the resistance in the fields now. Gren is conquered." His voice came low, a whisper of triumph. "They are beaten."

I feel a strange lack of desire to cheer, Cyrus thought. His eyes found Vara's still watching him carefully, looking for a sign of what he would do, some hint that he intended to turn and strike out at the occupants of the building behind him. "Clear the city," Cyrus said in a strangely choked voice. "Building by building. I don't want it burned, but I want it cleared. Let them remember being driven out, and then let them come back once we've left. Gather up every slave and … get them back to Sanctuary for now. We'll feed them, we'll clothe them, we'll repatriate them as needed." He swallowed heavily.

"That will be … quite expensive," Vaste said quietly but not accusingly. "In time and gold."

"We'll find a way to make it work," Cyrus said and turned to give the cloth hanging behind him a last look. He saw it rustle, faintly, the wind at play.

"And what of the trolls?" Vaste asked.

"Let them remain here in their homeland," Cyrus said and turned his gaze to the pillar once more. He turned his head, letting out a final, poisonous breath as he felt the last of his hatred leave him. It was a curious sensation, and he thought of the creatures lingering in the hut behind him. They were about to be left without the labor to work their fields, to feed their hogs, to have the basics of life done for them. "They're no longer a threat to anyone." He passed Vara, avoiding her shoulder so as not to crash his pauldrons into hers.

"Where are you going?" she asked. He heard her as he passed, a voice of infinite regret, a careful sadness, all currents under the river of her words.

"I'm going to bury my friend," Cyrus said, making his way toward the pillar with slow, dragging steps, as though a lifetime's weight were upon him. "Going to show his body the respect it deserved."

He cut the body down and dug the grave himself, refusing any help offered. Hours passed, darkness fell, and Cyrus took note of none of it. He dug a grave deep, and placed the body inside with care, arranging it in the right order as near as he could. The smell was punishing; the flies had been at work for days and there were gaps that could not be made up. As Cyrus threw the first shovel of dirt on his friend—the only one he'd had at the Society, ever—he reflected that the hope offered by Cass had been like a light in the dark, a candle blown out by a draft on a cold night. The warmth promised was soul-felt, and gone all too quickly.

"We are none of us alone," Cyrus said as he finished, patting the top of the grave with the shovel, wishing it was Praelior in his hand, wishing it was blood on his fingers instead of dirt. "Except when we are."

He stood in the shadow of the pillar, the night nearly fallen. With a last look around, his menace driving back all nearby, Cyrus drew his sword. Breaths were taken in surprise, but he had a wide enough berth.

Cyrus felt the first cool wind come down off the hill behind him, night's fall at his back, blowing under his helm and stirring his hair. He raised his blade and sunk it into the pillar hard; he pulled it out and chopped into the stone again. Pebbles clinked against his armor, chipping away from the monolith by his effort.

The first grunting creak warned him to remove his sword. He circled around to where the pillar showed its weakness, and with his hand on the hilt of his sword, drawing the strength from the blade, he pushed. It gave, then gave some more. He put his shoulder into it and heaved against it. With a crack the pillar broke and lost its battle against the pull of the earth. It came crashing down across the emptying square, all those who remained standing far from the warrior in black, far from the vengeful man who stood alone.

The pillar had fallen perfectly atop the grave. Cyrus took his hand from the sword and tested the weight, pushing it from the side with all his might. The ancient stone did not so much as move, anchored in place by a strength that was beyond the understanding of even men and elves.

"I don't think anyone will disturb him now," Vara said. He turned to find her there, closest of everyone, standing only twenty feet away. *Has she been there all along?*

"No," Cyrus said and found he was having trouble forming the words. The labor had been long, and all color had long since seeped out of the sky. Candles and lanterns lit the square around him, Nessalima's light spells shining from the fingers of the spell casters interspersed among the masses. "No, they won't."

"You could have had our help, you know," Vara said.

"I didn't want help," Cyrus said numbly. "I just needed to …"

"I know," she said simply.

Cyrus gave the square one more look. He saw none of the bedraggled refugees, the slaves chained to this place by chance and fate. He glanced at the fallen pillar. *That could have been me. If only I had been the unhated one, if only I had been the one with the grace to not run afoul of the guildmaster of the Society.*

"Our business here is concluded," Vara said. "The majority of our army has left, and every troll has been removed from the city and told not to return until daybreak tomorrow."

"Do you think they'll listen?" Cyrus asked ruefully.

Vara remained expressionless, her pale skin lit by the thousand different twinkling sources. "I think … if you'll pardon the expression … you scared the shit out of them. I don't think they'll be rushing back even at daybreak. I have never seen trolls so submissive and agreeable to suggestion." She was straight of back, serious. "I think we are done here."

"Then we should go," Cyrus said, giving the shattered pillar a last glance. It had broken in one long piece, uprooted and fallen like a mighty tree—like the one that held aloft the roof of the dining hall in the Society of Arms.

"We await your command, General," Vara said, strangely formal.

Cyrus blinked. *We are none of us alone* echoed in his mind. *But you were, weren't you? At the end? We are all alone in the end, Cass.* He found no warmth in those words.

And a leader is the most alone of all.

"Get us the hell out of here," Cyrus said, and he caught the small motion of Verity somewhere to his side, grey cloak rippling as she made to cast a spell. A light appeared before him, before every one of them that remained. A thousand blinks, a thousand flashes, and he watched them fade.

He waited in that quiet place as they disappeared, one by one, until only a few were left. The orb hovered in front of him, awaiting the touch of his hand.

"General," Vara said quietly. She stared at him, her own orb hanging before her.

Reluctantly, Cyrus nodded. There were only a handful of faces remaining now, all of them watching him. Curatio. Andren. Vaste. He knew they wouldn't leave until he had.

Aisling. He caught sight of her in a motion at the corner of his eye, just barely visible in the entry of a mud hut.

With a last look, Cyrus took hold of the orb as he saw Vara do the same; the chime of the spell magic washed over him, sweeping him away and leaving him with a terrible sense in his gut that they were, all of them, alone, even in spite of the evidence he had just seen to the contrary.

Chapter 46

The passing of the hours was a sweet blessing to Cyrus, listless in the days that followed. Guild business seemed to be on hold, the army in a state of flustered success over the victory at Gren. They seemed to Cyrus like the teenagers he had known at the Society who had embraced the mythical, wondrous and ephemeral first love; glowing in each others' presence, holding hands like it was a mark of pride. He'd seen the behavior, thought it curious in his isolation, much the same as he viewed his soldiers now. Their voices hushed when he was around, their embarrassed relief and proud tones rang loud when they did not see him. They had done something truly worthy of note in their own minds. In the mind of most of Arkaria, Cyrus would have conceded, in that strangely detached way that he had, had anyone asked.

The days ground to a slow close, no meetings to snag them in their passage like blade on cloth, the dull tearing noise of sundered material. They slipped by and Cyrus watched them, a ghost in the halls of Sanctuary.

But not *the* Ghost.

Aisling attended him and he let her, without emotion or enthusiasm. The lack of feeling came as dutifully to him as it had in Luukessia, though he did not quite feel the soul-deep weight now that he had then. This loss was more personal, he conceded, but he kept it at arm's length, away from his day to day emotions, dwelling on it only at day's end or day's beginning. But there was so little business to handle, with the everyone's breath seemingly held for the approaching election, that he felt—for once—surprisingly unfettered.

He knew that he had changed in the eyes of his army, knew they had seen something in him in the square at Gren that had put rumors on lips. For good or ill, he did not know, but he suspected. He'd heard the whispers of the fury in his own mind, after all, and others had read it in his eyes. He'd meant to wipe the trolls out to the last, and that was not a secret. The thought of the barely averted slaughter weighed on Cyrus in those quiet moments, that and the voice of Alaric telling him not to succumb made him wonder if he had simply lost his way or if he was losing his mind.

On the day before the election Cyrus found himself in the gardens, steps almost preordained. He walked over the bridge, noting how like the Realm of Life it looked, even without the snows blanketing the ground. This gave him a spur of a sort, a little poke to his consciousness. Alaric Garaunt had been a man who kept his mysteries close, who embraced them in a way that he had never embraced anyone that Cyrus had seen.

The day was golden, one of those days of fall where rustling leaves and the brisk air made even Cyrus, in his current state, feel alive. He could smell cider on the air and remembered how someone—had it been J'anda?—had mentioned a nearby orchard. He wanted to pluck an apple from a tree and sink his teeth into the sweetness, taste the life as he drained the juice from it. He wanted to walk under red and orange leaves, watching each of them die just so he could remember that he was alive.

But instead he came here, crossing the bridge over the still waters in the Sanctuary gardens, to the place almost at the wall at the back of the grounds. There were still green trees here, the message of summer's end not yet spread to their boughs. He could still hear the satisfying crunch of his metal boots on blades of grass as each step marked his passage.

He stood before a stone monument almost six feet high, six feet wide, but not nearly so deep. It was brilliant stonework, but simple, with an alcove carved into the middle of it big enough that Cyrus could have set his helm.

But it was not his helm that stood in that place of honor.

The helm that rested there was rounded thing, with slits for the eyes—the one eye, really; the other was pointless—and a carved-out space for a mouth to speak wisdom from beneath. Cyrus felt a sharp intake of breath as he laid eyes on it, disregarding the words written on the stone monument. For a moment he believed he could see movement inside the helm—hoped he could see movement inside the helm. It took half a breath for him to realize that some inspiring soul had lit a candle within it, letting light shine from within it.

"Here I am," he said. He cast a look back; there was no one in sight of him.

Cyrus stared at the monument, at Alaric's helm held carefully within it. The helm stared back, the flame within fluttering as a gust blew from over his shoulder. It did not, however, answer him in return.

"I failed you," Cyrus said after a long moment. He had a tight grasp of the emotions at hand and did not let them out. "I didn't believe when I should have. I led us against Mortus, and my arrogance—my unwillingness to follow your lead, to let my guildmates make their own difficult decisions, sacrifices—it cost a whole people their land. I failed you more completely than anyone I have ever failed. I believe I have made the single deadliest error in judgment in the history of man, elf—gods, in all history. When you called me on my error, I embraced an opportunity to run from my humiliation, to run into the open and willing arms of another land that knew me not. But my foolish errors followed me there because they are unforgiving things, and I was able to watch firsthand as my hubris came back to visit people who had not earned it. I watched a land die because I failed to follow your lead. I watched a land die because I was unwilling to make the sacrifice that you, as the leader—the Master of Sanctuary—called for."

He waited, silent for a moment, emotionless, as though the monument would pronounce some judgment upon him, as though the candle within the helm would spit out a spirit and endow the empty vessel with a fire that would bellow condemnation at him. He stood, unflinching, a deeper part of him hoping it would.

"I failed you, Alaric," Cyrus said. His voice sounded neither humble nor proud, nor contrite nor boastful. It lay right in the middle, flat as the plains upon which he stood. "I failed you, and you stepped forward to give your life to keep my foolish mistakes from destroying our own home."

He waited again for condemnation, but none came. "Now I set my sights upon replacing you." He cracked a smile, but it was humorless. "Can you imagine a more arrogant man than I? I have trouble with it myself. I have led Sanctuary into war with the dark elves, into a siege that nearly cost us everything, into a battle with a god—the consequences were a disaster on an order of magnitude larger than any earthquake ever even considered—and now I mean to expand my influence." He stood silent, pursing his lips. "Does that even seem right? I've heard the whispers of the soldiers. My wrath almost emerged once more in the troll homeland, and it was only the faint whisper of your memory that spared their women and children from utter death. I nearly unleashed a slaughter ... and now I mean to lead the largest independent army in Arkaria."

Cyrus honed in on the light dancing within the helm. "Does that not chill you? It chills me. What is a leader to do but believe in what is right to him and lead from that strength? The direction should always be certain, it should not be a matter of question. But I question." He took a step forward. "I doubt. It lingers. I have failed in such mighty ways—and such petty ones as well. They number beyond my counting. I do not know what my job should be, but I question why I would be a leader to anyone."

Cyrus's hands found the sides of his greaves, producing a subtle clatter. "I am a buffoon. I am a destroyer. My judgment is suspect, my methods are foul to your eyes, and I question every decision I have ever made. If I am a leader, we are all surely doomed for fools, and if I am to take us on any path, I am almost assured it is the wrong one. Alaric ..." he felt himself swallow heavily, "... it should have been me that died on that bridge, not you."

He waited, staring at the lit flame, willing it to speak as he'd heard in Gren. The orange light danced as the wind blew, but the monument merely stood, stone, motionless, staring back at Cyrus as he stared at it. He gave it a few more minutes of consideration before turning his back on it, confession done, and just as rudderless as he had been when he arrived.

Chapter 47

Cyrus rose before the dawn on the day of the election, forwent any thought of breakfast and headed down the stairs. His mind was in a muddle, but he kept it clear enough to let his feet guide him down and toward the door. He smiled faintly at the suggestions of luck, few and far between in the crowded foyer, and had almost broken through the grand doors when the acerbic voice reached him.

"Not planning to sit around and await your crowning?" Verity's wit landed upon his back with little effect; Cyrus felt like his skin was thick as hardened leather, and he merely stared at her. "Shouldn't you be running a campaign or something of the sort?" She clacked her wooden stave against the stone floors carelessly as she made her way to him. She came from the lounge, and for a brief moment he wondered if wine or ale had loosened her tongue before deciding that she would probably have given voice to her thought anyway.

"I'm not staying," Cyrus said.

"A man of action," Verity said, adjusting her pointed grey cap. "So very admirable; a quality found among leaders."

He watched her warily, hearing her words as a critique backed by sarcasm but caring not at all. "I could use a teleport."

"Far be it from me to refuse the request of General Davidon," Verity said, bowing. "Where would you like to go, my captain?"

Cyrus felt his tongue grow thick. "Emerald Fields."

Verity raised an eyebrow at that, then shrugged as if to say she might have guessed. "Emerald Fields it is, then." She whispered something in half a breath, and the world dissolved in shimmering green light. A blue sky washed in as the light faded, forcing Cyrus to blink away his disorientation.

He stood before a great portal, wide stone gaping at him, with spears on all sides. He raised both hands in false surrender, but already the weapons were lowering.

"General," Samwen Longwell said, his lance in his hand. "What brings you to the Emerald Fields on this …" he choked off his words, "… this day?"

Cyrus wondered what description he might have applied to the day but did not wish to impose by asking. "I needed some fresh air."

Longwell had the most curious look, as though he could not quite believe what he'd heard. "I daresay you'll find it here."

"Good," Cyrus said with a nod. The small army gathered around the portal was less than five hundred men, Luukessians all by his counting, and some of them plainly not members of Sanctuary. He felt their eyes upon him and wondered how they judged him. He fell into a quick step, heading down a well-trodden, somewhat rutted road.

"Shall I wait for you here?" Verity asked.

"Come back for me before dinner if you would, please," Cyrus said, not turning around. He passed between the separating rank of soldiers, parting before him without a command needing be uttered from any soul.

"Better than waiting about, I suppose," Verity said behind him, loud enough to be heard. "By your leave, then." He heard the tinkle of magic being used, echoing louder than the sarcasm she had left in her wake.

Cyrus looked down the road. Buildings sprang up within a couple hundred feet. New, wooden, lacking in the timeless appearance of stone-crafted dwellings, they sprung from the horizon like moss growing from a rock. They hung close to the earth at first but increased in size the further his gaze roamed toward the place where the sky met the ground.

He could smell the fires burning, the smoke coming out of the chimneys. It was a town, full-fledged and sprung from the earth just as sure as the moss he had thought of before. He could see hints of the so-called Emerald Fields for which the place was named. The ground had been plowed, and the green had been taken up in harvest. Now Cyrus saw the late fields of corn to his right, a crudely made fence stretching off into the distance. Black dirt from one of the fields was the perfect exemplar of his mood, just dark enough to stand in contrast to the lightening sky beyond.

Cyrus walked toward the town unchallenged and could see the burgeoning efforts, the accumulation of so many little exertions over the last months. He had not been here for quite some time, and the change was breathtaking. Where last time had been little plots, now stood houses, storefronts, the veneer of civilization. Still, beyond, he could see the cloth tents yet pitched for those who had no dwellings, and the bones of houses yet unfinished at the far end of the town.

A rooster's crow was answered by another. The sun was already peeking over the horizon at his back, running later than Sanctuary's sunrise by only a few minutes, Cyrus figured. He looked to his left and saw mountains on the southern horizon. The foothills began within eyesight, within a few minutes walk, really, marching up in a slow incline to a mound of boulders and rocks that was the absolute opposite of anything Emerald or Field-like.

With a gentle start, he was reminded of what lurked in those hills, the quiet giant whose strength was as undisputed as any rock from which his kind took their name. "Fortin," he said with a breath, wondering where between his eye and the top of the hill in sight the rock giant was.

"Lord Davidon!" A harried voice reached Cyrus's ears and he turned his attention back to the dusty road through the town. He blinked his surprise at the figure hurrying toward him, her honey-brown hair at loose ends and her movement something between a walk and a run.

"Cattrine?" Cyrus felt a frown crease his face, the weight of emotion pulling down his brow. "What are you doing here?"

"I might ask the same of you," she said, breathless as she came to a stop before him. Her shirt was slightly dusty, and her pants were a blackened mess, as though she'd sat in the residue of a city oven. "We were not informed you would be visiting today, and we are completely unready—"

"I'm not here in any official capacity," Cyrus said with a wave of the hand. "I just ... wanted to look around." He took a breath, hoping that the words did not sound as silly to her ears as they did to his.

"I ... what?" Cattrine seemed genuinely perplexed by his answer, her mind shifting through several expressions he knew all too well to land on a half-smile. "You're here out of curiosity, then?"

Cyrus pondered his answer for the space of a sword stroke. "I just ... needed to ... go somewhere."

"You've been a great many somewheres of late," Cattrine said. "If even half of what I've heard is true, you're the hero who freed an enormous number of slaves and put an end to a great, trollish treachery."

He waved her off again, dismissing her compliment. "I needed to be somewhere ... that didn't involve fighting, I think. Or lauding."

Her eyes found his; they were more piercing than he recalled. "Is there something vexing you, Lord Davidon?"

He did not try to look away. "The sheer stinging of all the things presently vexing me is enough to poison a modest-sized elephant, I think. And you should call me Cyrus."

"I have never seen one of these elephants," Cattrine said, taking a moment to dust some of the coal residue off the front of her pants as she stood there. It billowed off her in a light cloud. "But I have heard tales of them; taller than you, are they not?"

"They are," Cyrus said.

"And very strong, I believe?" Cattrine asked.

"Stronger than ..." Cyrus paused. "Stronger than most animals, I would say."

"Stronger than you?"

He thought it over. "When I'm without my sword, most certainly. When I have my sword in hand, I still wouldn't care to test their strength against mine."

She shivered slightly as a breeze blew down with a chill that followed. Cyrus felt it, but only dimly, like the sun on a winter's day. "Perhaps we should move our discussion somewhere warmer."

He stared down at her. She looked small, rubbing her shoulders, stamping her feet, and he suddenly felt very sorry for her indeed. The memory of his own actions, of the chain of events he'd loosed that led her here ... "Of course," Cyrus said. "Where did you have in mind?"

"I have an office," Cattrine said, just a little sheepish. "Over one of the shops." She waved a hand behind her, indicating a wooden storefront. "It's not much, but it is warm."

"Lead on," Cyrus said, smiling slightly. As warmly as he could manage. He followed her as she trudged through the dust. They climbed rickety stairs that whined at each of Cyrus's steps. For her movement, they seemed magnanimous; for his, they whinged and squeaked at his every footfall. "It's the armor," he said with that same smile; it was only on the surface, though.

"You seem ... sadder than when last I laid eyes upon you," Cattrine said once they were in the office and the door was shut tight. The wind made its lonely howl outside, sweeping down off the hill, but it felt only half-hearted now that he was out of its gust. A fire crackled in a hearth in the corner, and Cyrus found his eyes drawn to it.

"I'm mourning a friend," Cyrus said, tearing his eyes from the flames.

"That means you're blaming yourself, I suspect," Cattrine said. She stood behind a waist-high desk, a rickety old thing that looked like it had come from the Elven Kingdom, something that would not have looked out of place in the government center in Termina. It had long burns on the top surface, and Cyrus found himself staring at the woodworking along the sides. It was elven, without doubt; no human would spend that much time on a purely utilitarian object, and it was far too tall for a gnome or a dwarf.

"I don't know that I'm blaming myself, but I do feel an odd sense of ... responsibility?" Cyrus shook his head, but it did not free him of the thought. "My friend—his guild—they were captured on patrol for the Confederation, far from our borders and interests. Trolls did the deed, back to slaving again." He shrugged. "In this, I am blameless. I can find no cause to put this one on myself. Yet there are other, nagging things that I have done that revisit me now. A long chain of events, of choices, the consequences of which make me look at myself in the mirror and ask, 'Is this man a leader—?'"

She cut him off. "Yes."

He blinked at her. "I didn't finish."

"You asked a question that was easily answered," she said. "I answered it for you, so as to terminate your inward struggle."

He made a sound that recalled to his mind the whicker of Windrider. "I don't find the answer quite so easy. Bad choices should not inspire confidence in a leader."

Cattrine stared at him shrewdly. "Today is the day of the Sanctuary election, is it not?"

"It is."

"Shouldn't you be … shaking hands and making promises you don't intend to keep?" she asked with a sly smile.

"I don't know, *Administrator*," he said with a slyness of his own, "is that what it takes to be elected to high office?"

"Touché." She grinned. "People look for decisiveness, yes, even when it sometimes comes in the form of bad action. Leadership means standing tall, being the guidepost for others, bearing the burdens no one else wants. I think—not as a member of Sanctuary, obviously—that whoever is chosen for Sanctuary's Guildmaster—well, they better have damned broad shoulders if you're going to put that much burden on them." She ran a hand over a crinkled piece of parchment, straightening it to align with the corners of her desk. "It's quite a weight, I would imagine."

"I don't think it's just about bearing a burden," Cyrus said, "otherwise we'd find an elephant and be done with it."

"I know a creature that's stronger than your elephant," she waved her hand toward the window behind her, to the rocky hill that filled the view, "but he's no leader."

"Fortin?" Cyrus asked. "That's true."

"He wants a leader, though," Cattrine said. "He's seeking someone to follow, someone to believe in."

Cyrus inched away from the fire, feeling a flush that came either from the heat or another source. "What do you think he's looking for?"

"Someone stronger than him, but not just in a physical plane," Cattrine said. "Someone to get him what he cannot get by himself. Someone who can … drive him to be better." She held her silence for a moment, and the sound of street noise—of conversation, of friendly shouts, of men and women at work and bustling—reached Cyrus's ears. The smell of the sweet wood smoke reminded Cyrus of the Sanctuary Council Chambers. "What was it about your former Guildmaster that made you follow him?"

"I believed in him," Cyrus said, and it flowed up from a wellspring within, easy as if it were water coming to the surface. "He inspired with his words, wisdom flowed out of him like honey from a fresh comb; he had a somber energy, a fearsome countenance when provoked, and an absolute certainty in the rightness of his cause." Cyrus bowed his head slightly. "He was everything a man wanted to be."

"Many a man I've met wishes to be you," she said.

Cyrus looked at her out of the corner of his eye as he rested a hand on the mantle, inching closer to the fireplace again. "I've been told I came back from Luukessia changed."

"Most people very definitely change after a decapitation," she said. "But their change is that their story ends. Yet yours goes on, and that is, I think, perhaps the least of the things that affected the man inside that armor," she gestured toward his chestplate, "in that time. You feel guilt for things you didn't truly cause. You made choices to counteract consequences of actions you couldn't have foreseen."

"I made some ill choices," Cyrus said, holding it back, saying it lightly. "I erred, and countless people died."

"Yet you did all you could to correct for them," Cattrine said. "You can, of course, blame yourself. Luukessia did, naturally, change you. You cannot have seen what we saw at the end of my land—my home—and assume that you are the same carefree person you were before. But ... to bring this 'round ... you are a leader, Cyrus. People follow you because you are stronger than them, mentally and physically, because you project the aura of quiet charisma and you convey an absolute certainty even when I think you are not feeling it." She stayed behind the desk, a gulf of miles between them. "And, speaking from experience," this brought a smile to her lips, "your shoulders are agreeably broad."

Cyrus looked up the hill beyond her, peering into the rocks as if he could see movement. There was none. "And my failures?"

"You keep trying to make them right, do you not?" She raised her hands to either side of her, to indicate the room in which they stood. For the first time, Cyrus noticed a wall hanging, a tapestry with the crest of the Kingdom of Actaluere. It hung in the between two others, ones he had seen in both Syloreas and Galbadien, the old kingdoms of Luukessia. "This building in which we stand is proof of your commitment in that regard. It would not be here if you had not taken the people of my land under your wing and protected them, stewarded them with gold and effort." She shrugged. "I would follow you. I *do* follow you, though not in war, obviously."

Cyrus looked back to the hills out her window. "Where is Fortin?"

She blinked. "Up the hill." She pointed and Cyrus moved closer to see what she saw. His eyes fell on a wooden structure of some sort. "The Syloreans have begun mining on his land, aided by a group of dwarves that you rescued from Gren." He looked at her in surprise. "Your guild runs without you, it would appear; a group of slaves without homes, who had skills we were very much in need of—they were brought here by Vara and some of the others. I assumed you knew." Cyrus shook his head. "They've been quite helpful thus far. More workers for the fields, farmers with expertise but no land, tradesmen with homes lost in the war … the Emerald Fields offer a fresh start for all who come."

Cyrus took in a low, steady breath. "I should feel pleased at the good work we've done." He pricked his own emotions and found that there was, somewhere within, just such a feeling. "I suppose it's harder for me to see most of the time, given how ill things have gone in Arkaria of late."

"Take heed of the good," Cattrine said. "You do much of it. You and your people."

Cyrus gave her a slow nod. "All right, then." He steeled himself and then marched for the door, the floorboards of her office squeaking behind him.

"Where are you going?" she asked.

He paused at the door. "I'm going to go convince a rock giant to follow me the way he followed the man who came before." Cyrus looked back.

There was a quiet, muted shock on Cattrine's face, but she hid it well. "I see. And how are you going to go about this feat?"

"I'm going to beat him into pebbles," Cyrus said, yanking the door open. "Send one of your healers up the hill in about ten minutes, please." He shot her a dazzling smile as he shut the door behind him. It was made all the better by the stricken look on her face, and he barely noticed the squeaks of protest from the stairs as he walked with certainty to the ground, and then out of the town to the hills.

Chapter 48

Cyrus's ascent up the hill was quick and energetic, legs filled with a spring and determination that he had lacked for the last weeks. He charged, happily and willingly, as though the craving for battle he had felt for so many a year were upon him again. The wind hit him in the face, slapping his cheeks, tugging his hair from under the metal binding of the helm that encased it. The smell that came out of that southern wind was fresh and clean, the scent of wilderness untamed.

Cyrus felt the anticipation tingle across his flesh, the unanswered call to battle stirring that pit in his stomach. The call to war had driven him for years, a fearless, careless and reckless desire to do harm. He had lost that feeling in Luukessia and replaced it with something else entirely. *Something Alaric taught me.* But here, in this hillside charge, the faint stirrings of it were back, albeit in a different condition. Now it was mere anticipation, the desire to charge headlong into a problem to get it over with.

He reached a crest, a small hillside overlook, and glanced back only for a moment. The view of Emerald Fields was stunning, and he made pause to remind himself to enjoy it further when he came back down. The town had sprung up within the valley in less than a year and already looked big enough to swallow up most of the towns of the Plains of Perdamun, towns that had been there for hundreds of years.

The footing was slippery and the gravelly hill gave up stones with every step. Cyrus turned his attention back to where he was going, felt a chill that had little to do with the weather cool his flesh. No, this was pure anticipation; a fight was coming, one that would tax him, would roil his blood in his veins, stir him back to life again. No war of thousands; this was a battle of one against one, his mind against his foe's, his sword against the rock claw of his opponent.

This is my sort of fight.

Cyrus caught sight of motion to his left. The overlook ran a few hundred feet to the side of the hill, a flat plateau of ground that was trodden and worn from constant transit. Cyrus saw where the traffic came from now: a mine cut into the side of the hill. Men stood about it jawing, their laughter catching him by surprise, as peculiar a sound to him as a babe crying. Men and dwarves, he took a moment to realize, some only waist-high to others, their beards nearly as long as they were tall.

He altered his path, heading toward the mine, looking for another sign of a hole in the hill where his quarry would be waiting. It was not immediately obvious, though, and so he directed his steps toward the mine. As he approached, burning with purpose, the men stopped their conversations mid-word. He knew he was a sight, his black armor rolling in from the northerly approach like a storm cloud on a clear day. They must have known him; it seemed of late that everyone did.

"Lord Davidon," one of the dwarves said as he approached. The dwarf was of a height with his kind, chest-high to a human man. His beard was threaded with obvious care, a braid and locks that matched the twisted arrangement atop his small head. He looked to be of middle age, and his eyes were kind. Cyrus had nearly forgotten what kind eyes looked like. "What may these humble servants of yours do ... uh ... for you?" The dwarf reddened as he threw himself to the ground, his dark, dirt-encrusted skin a contrast against the pale gravel of the hillside. Ten other dwarves—the whole lot of them—hit the ground in a bow following this one. The men of Luukessia—Syloreans, he knew by the beards and the rough look of them—watched on with amusement, but there was no danger of them bowing, he knew.

"Rise, sir dwarf," Cyrus said, and the dwarf came to his feet. "All of you, rise. There is no need to be formal. What is your name?"

"Keearyn," the dwarf said, bowing his head. "You have saved my life and that of my family, rendered us free from the chains bound upon us by the trolls. We are miners all, and I am ever at your service."

"I seek the dwelling place of the rock giant," Cyrus said, staring down at Keearyn the miner. The dwarf met his gaze, those kind eyes smiling at merely being recognized. "I have business with him. Could you direct me to where I might find him, please?"

"Och, the manners," Keearyn said. "It is a measure of your greatness that you could be so kind to someone who you need not show a whit of it to."

Cyrus felt an eyebrow raise involuntarily, and his response was delayed. "That's ... nice of you to notice. Still ... I seek the rock giant. Would you be so kind as to—"

"I will show you to his dwelling meself," Keearyn said, bowing repeatedly. He hurried to Cyrus's right, across the plateau, a run that strained the miner's legs. Cyrus kept up with a mid-length stride, walking all the while.

"You saved my kin, you know," Keearyn said, turning his head back to speak. His long braids swayed in the wind coming down the hills.

"You mentioned that," Cyrus said. "Where did the trolls capture you?"

"The trolls didn't capture me," Keearyn said. "'Twas the dark elves. My band of miners came into the port of Aloakna after an expedition to the southern lands to aid the elves of Amti in extracting their minerals."

"The dark elves sacked Aloakna," Cyrus mused. "Were you there when it happened?"

"Aye," Keearyn said with a downturned brow. "We were brought back to Saekaj, taken down into that dark hell of a city. I am well acquainted with the underground, having lived and worked in mines my entire life. The beauty of the earth is a gift from Rotan, our god, but what the dark elves have done in that place defiles the good deity's works. It is a shallow hole, filled with desperation and poverty. Our homeland, Fertiss, is also built in the ground, but I assure you, it is a wondrous land of beauty and care. Saekaj is a black pit of despair from which their own people cannot even gain life and sustenance."

"I see you feel strongly about your captors," Cyrus said dryly.

"The day I was taken from that city in the ground was the happiest day of my recent life," Keearyn said, looking back at Cyrus. "And that is even with the consideration that I came to Gren, which is an open-sky hell of its own."

"What is it about Saekaj that is so bad?" Cyrus asked, the gravel crunching under his boots, tiny pebbles crushed under his weight.

"There is no hope in that place," Keearyn said as they started up a slope. Cyrus could see another overlook above, a hundred feet along a steep embankment. "They have a prison called the Depths, a farm where they grow mushrooms and roots. It is, without doubt, the cruelest captivity I have ever suffered."

"Been in many prisons?" Cyrus asked.

"Only the ones I have seen since my capture," Keearyn said with a shudder. "But I've been in more than a few caves, and these were … an utter despoilment of the earth. A desecration, a sacrilege."

"Sounds like the dark elves," Cyrus said as they reached the ridge of the overlook. Cyrus could see a cave, a dark, gaping mouth extending into the earth. "Sounds about like everything they do under the guidance of their Sovereign."

"Aye," Keearyn said, looking at the entry to the rock giant's cave. "Do ye wish me to await you here, perhaps?"

"No," Cyrus said with a shake of his head. "Your kindness is appreciated, but perhaps you should wait with your friends, out of the range of possible harm."

The dwarf swallowed visibly. "Possible … harm?"

"There's about to be a fight for supremacy," Cyrus said. "When the healer arrives, tell him to wait with you lot until the earth stops shaking."

The dwarf's eyes were wide as wooden shields. "Ye mean to … fight?"

"I mean to fight," Cyrus said, and felt the smile spread. "Go on, Keearyn, servant of Rotan. Rejoin your people with my thanks."

The dwarf swallowed heavily again and bowed. "I wish ye greatest luck, Lord Davidon, and thank you again for the gift of my life."

Cyrus listened and a thought occurred to him. "Make a gift of it, then." He glanced back at where Keearyn began to retreat. "Do good service with your life; help these people in Emerald Fields carve a place in this valley that will protect and sustain them from harm. Do good works to make them independent and proud. Give your fealty to them and you'll repay me more than any other act you might perform."

Keearyn's eyes looked slightly moist, the corners of his eyes glistening like morning dew pooling on the freshly broken earth. "It will be as you say, Lord Davidon."

"Go on, then," Cyrus said, dismissing him, and starting toward the cave mouth with his purpose firmly in mind. "Go forth and do your work."

The dwarf disappeared down the slope, and Cyrus glanced back only to ensure he was clear of the area before entering the mouth of the cave. In the darkness, he could hear a gentle breathing, reassurance that he was in the right place. With a quickly drawn breath of his own, Cyrus smiled and felt the shadows creep long around him as he entered the place where the rock giant dwelled.

Chapter 49

"Cyrus Davidon," came the rumble as he entered a wide chamber. It was circular, bigger than Fortin's cell in the Sanctuary dungeons, and wooden shelving stood in one of the corners. Slaughtered goats hung from hooks in the ceiling next to the shelving, dripping slowly into pails set out to catch the blood. The smell of the blood was rich in the air along with the scent of the earth. It was surprisingly fresh, the entry only twenty feet or so, and it did not possess the stale air of a long-shut or deep chamber.

"Fortin the Rapacious," Cyrus said, his eyes adjusting to the slightly darker chamber. There was enough light from beyond the exit to allow him to see the shape resting in a natural cleft of rock. The eyes were red, of course, and faintly glowed in the dark.

"You have come seeking challenge," Fortin said. He rose, his craggy skin rumbling as he did so, the sound of an avalanche moving down a hillside.

"I've come to subsume your will to my own," Cyrus said and placed his right hand on his scabbard. "Come to challenge you for the right to govern your fate."

"You seek to make me your slave?" Fortin asked, an aura of menace threaded through his words.

"I seek to show you who is the master, who is the strongest among us," Cyrus said. "What you choose to do once that is established is entirely in your hands."

Fortin breathed into the quiet, an ominous sound. "I told you I would remain in my own service until the day you found someone who could best me in single combat."

"I found someone who can best you in single combat," Cyrus said, still maintaining his hold on Praelior. "But I am no master to your slave; I am merely the strength that offers to be your guide."

The red eyes considered him, and the answer came simply, just before the first movement. "Prove it."

Fortin sprang through the chamber without warning, his only hint of what was to come the simple invocation he had offered Cyrus. Cyrus, for his part, was ready, and his blade was drawn before the rock giant was even halfway to him. His feet planted, Cyrus prepared, and when he judged the range right, he swung a mighty slash of his blade that caught the rock giant's arm hard at the elbow. Cyrus ducked and moved, swinging low and reversing, and he caught Fortin with a slash of the blade to the hip that drew a grunt from the rock giant. Unable to change his direction, committed to a charge that would have wiped Cyrus across the floor of his cave in a bloody smear had he succeeded, Fortin stumbled on and landed face-first in the corner of the wall just behind Cyrus.

Cyrus followed his attack without waiting, driving the point of Praelior into the rock giant's hindquarters. A rocky buttock caught the tip and Fortin roared in pain, lashing backward. Cyrus ducked low, removed his blade and drove it into the rock giant's knee. Cyrus rolled quickly to his right as Fortin toppled, wiping out a small wooden table in the process.

Cyrus did not waste his time with a boast or an idle taunt. Fortin was face down upon the ground, and Cyrus struck. He drove his blade swiftly into the back of the rock giant's head, sparing neither mercy nor thought for what he attacked. The blow delivered, he withdrew his sword and stepped back, maintaining a defensive posture.

Fortin did not move, did not stir, remaining still as stone. Cyrus waited there for a moment, then another, circling toward the mouth of the cave. He did not come within arm's reach of the rock giant, keeping a safe distance. Still, Fortin did not move, and Cyrus edged his way out of the cave until he heard steps behind him.

Cyrus turned and saw a human in white garb hurrying along, the thin, silken vestment draped over his shoulder in a line. "Your name?" Cyrus asked.

"Ah, uhm, Jacub Smythe," the man said, young and nervous as Cyrus might expect from a healer sent into the den of a rock giant.

"Cast your resurrection spell, Jacub Smythe," Cyrus said, with a nod toward the fallen body of Fortin. "This is close enough."

The twitchy young man stopped, blinked, eyes moving from Cyrus to the body and then back again. "This is close enough," he finally decided, as though he had heard something truly wise. He closed his eyes, hands moving quickly, words coming out under his breath. A white gleam appeared from his hands, draping the corpse of Fortin, and the healer sighed, words spoken.

Fortin roared into the earth, surging to his feet so quickly he slammed his head against the ceiling of the cave. Dust and pebbles rained down and the rock giant screamed in pain at the fresh harm to his wound. He hit his knees as Cyrus watched, placing himself between the healer and the rock giant, who staggered, finally catching sight of Cyrus in the entry to the cave.

"I have bested you," Cyrus said, still in a defensive posture, blade at the ready. "Do you yield?"

"You … killed me?" Fortin asked.

"I killed you," Cyrus said. "Healer Smythe resurrected you."

Fortin stood silently, swaying just a bit against the dark background of the cave. "I have only fallen in battle once before. This is … disconcerting." The rock giant made a rumbling noise within his chest, something guttural that did not encourage Cyrus to step forth.

"Do you yield?" Cyrus asked again, an edge to his voice.

"I yield," Fortin rumbled. "You have bested me, Warlord Davidon."

"I'm not a Warlord," Cyrus said, never taking his eyes off Fortin. "You will aid Sanctuary once more?"

"I am at your disposal in battle," Fortin said, red eyes curiously not finding him in the dark. They seemed to be swaying with the rock giant, and Cyrus suddenly remembered the resurrection effects. "I will follow you into war." There came another strange rumble from the rock giant. "Though I am not certain that was a fair fight."

"Fighting fair is for paladins," Cyrus said.

"Winning is for warriors, however it must happen," Fortin agreed, sounding … woozy? "I will remain here, awaiting your command, ready to render assistance when you call for me." He took a knee, dipping his head toward Cyrus. "If that is acceptable, Warlord?"

"I'm not a Warlord," Cyrus said again. "But you may call me General."

"I call you what you are," Fortin said.

"As you wish," Cyrus said, bowing his own head in acknowledgment. "I am afraid I must leave you for now, Fortin. I am sure we will see one another again 'ere too long."

"I look forward to joining you in battle once more," Fortin said.

"All right, then," Cyrus said and began to back down the tunnel. He almost bumped into Healer Smythe before remembering that the man was there. "Come on, Smythe, let's leave the Lord of Rockridge in peace."

"I suspect you should leave me before I lose control of my ..." Fortin rumbled, then shook, a mighty bellow following after.

Cyrus froze, waiting to see what happened, and regretted that he did.

An explosion emanated forth from the rock giant's mouth, a whole carcass of lamb that Cyrus only recognized by the configuration of the ribcage, strung together by pieces of cartilage. The smell—gods, the smell, it hit like a punch to the face. Liquid bile followed, flooding out of the rock giant's mouth in a foul waterfall down his chest and to the cave floor below. It soaked the gritty ground, a wave of stench issuing forth that sent Healer Smythe to his knees, vomiting forth his own breakfast immediately.

Cyrus assessed the situation, hand rushing to his nose, clanking against the blocking of his helm as he struggled to keep from making his own contribution. "I wish you well, Fortin, Healer Smythe," he nodded to each of them in turn, not daring to sheathe Praelior, not yet. "And I bid you farewell, for now."

Without another word, afraid to remove his hand from his mouth for fear of losing control of his own stomach, General Cyrus Davidon beat a hasty retreat from the rock giant's cave, the stench of his own victory chasing him away from the scene of his great triumph.

Chapter 50

"You look none the worse for a battle with a rock giant," Cattrine commented as Cyrus made his way back into town. The main street was flush with activity, and Cyrus had watched the considerable goings-on with interest as he had threaded his way down the hill. He had avoided the overlook with the dwarves, preferring instead to take a long path to give his stomach time to settle. He thought the stench of Fortin's upheaval hung with him, but part of him wondered if perhaps it was all his imagination. When he reached the base of the hill, he had chanced to look up, and saw Healer Smythe beginning to work his way down, green face stark against his white robes, with a dark liquid stain oozing down the front.

"I won," Cyrus said, "and quickly."

Cattrine made a most peculiar face. "What is that smell?"

Cyrus thought about it for a moment before answering. "The stink of victory."

"Ancestors," Cattrine said, her delicate nose wrinkling, "what would losing smell like?"

"Less potent," Cyrus said.

"I congratulate you on your victory, then," Cattrine said, pinching her own nose and waving a hand, as if to ward off the smell. "Perhaps you should bathe, though?"

He took her advice, letting her lead him to a creek nearby. She made herself scarce while he removed his armor, letting the water run over it only briefly, hoping to wash the scent clear of it. He made a reminder to himself to oil it later, give it a good going-over to insulate it from the elements. He waded in to the chill creek himself, felt the goosepimples rise on his flesh as it ran to the waist, and then he ducked his head under.

The water rushed by his ears, the sound of it blotting out the outside world. It was replaced with a quiet thrum, the noise of his own heart. He looked up into the blue sky above the surface, the world distorted by the water, and felt a strange, quiet peace settle over him. It was not born of contentment, for the stings and nettles of all that had passed were still there, at a distance but on his mind. The creek ran over them like a balm, though, quieting them, and as he stood, breaking the surface of the water and drawing breath, he found even the death of Cass was no longer quite as vexing as it had been just that morning when he'd awoken. The cold breath he drew in next was sweet invigoration, life flooding back into his lungs, and he felt tall as he stood in the stream. He waited there for a few minutes before wading to the shore and dressing again.

He found Cattrine again in the town, in the thick of things. He watched for a while, damp hair dripping occasionally on his armor, a faint tapping that drew him out of his thoughts. She was firmly in command of the goings-on, issuing light orders that were taken with grace, redirecting wagons filled with timber toward their eventual destinations, telling work crews where they needed to be. She even warned children out of the path of a coming convoy, sending them back to a safer locale.

She saw him watching, met his gaze with a smile, and broke from what she was doing to come greet him. Wordlessly, she led him to a field at the edge of town where trestle tables were being unfolded in a number beyond his counting. Cyrus helped, setting them upon a hillside of green grass. She told him that they ate a meal as a community once per day, at the noontime hour. Everyone came, from every work crew and business and shop. It was a massive undertaking.

"Soon enough I suspect it will have to end," she said, "but for now it anchors our day. It gives purpose to those for whom there is not enough work to occupy them, something to put their efforts toward every morning. We eat as individuals and families in the morning and evening, but at noon each day we take our meal as a community."

He stood on the hillside and watched once the tables were set up. Spell casters from Sanctuary moved among the tables, filling each with fresh bread. Cooks came along and supplemented the offering of the spell casters with small, carved wooden bowls of some porridge spooned out of cast iron pots. The smell reached Cyrus and he realized it was weak. Perhaps fish bones or marrow from some creature helped to give it more flavor, but there was little but water in its base. "It's what we have," Cattrine said with a smile, and he noticed for the first time that more than a few of the settlers of Emerald Fields were thin.

He ate with them, listening to the subtle and pleasant buzz of conversation. He heard no griping at the thinness of the stew, nor of the flavor of the conjured bread or the water that had been hauled in buckets from the nearby stream and from the well. The sound was all amiable, children playing in the background with yells and yawps of joy, laughter at jests. It reminded him of the days of Sanctuary before he'd left to go to war. The pall over the Great Hall had been thorough of late, but it had not always been so. Once, there had been joy in meals, happiness and shared humor. A lightness at being together in fellowship that made him wonder at its absence.

"What are you thinking?" Cattrine asked him, sitting across the table after he had finished his meal. The noonday sun was sinking in the sky, and Cyrus reckoned it was growing late, perhaps even toward the dinner hour at Sanctuary.

"Thinking about the way things were," Cyrus said. "The way I'd like them to be again."

"That sounds like the task of a leader," Cattrine said. "Boosting morale."

"Morale is a difficult thing to control, what with the war," Cyrus said. "With the famine."

"Send the world's greatest farmer into the desert for a year and all you're reap is a prodigious crop of sand," Cattrine said.

Cyrus pondered the meaning for a moment before acknowledging defeat. "What is that supposed to mean?"

"It means that sometimes you can't win given the circumstances," she said. "That sometimes perhaps the morale battle is lost. But I don't think—judging from those of my people who live and work with you in Sanctuary—that you're trying to farm in the desert. I think the morale is fine, that the company is good and true. I think you simply see through darker eyes now yourself. Perhaps what is a desert to you is a green field to another." She glanced toward the emerald hillside, taking it all in with the sweep of her gaze. "Bare and barren are two separate things, after all."

"I see it as more work," Cyrus said, leaning his elbows on the table. "Things I need to take handle of, even if I'm only the General of Sanctuary. Things I need to get my hands around."

"I am sure that whatever you turn your eye to will burgeon," Cattrine said. "Your talents, when applied, will make short work of most problems."

He watched her carefully. "Your words are kind."

She returned his gaze. "You are suspicious of my motives?"

"I suspect gratitude is your motive," Cyrus said. "For what we've done to try and help you." He let out a sigh. "And nothing else."

"I will always be fond of you, Cyrus Davidon," she said, a shadow of disappointment visible in her eye, "but yes, it is mostly gratitude for what you have done for myself and my people. Perhaps just a hint of that which was between us, also expressed in the form of gratitude."

Cyrus lowered his eyes. "I'm sorry, Cattrine."

"You have nothing to apologize for," she said simply, and he knew she was sincere.

"You have my apologies nonetheless," Cyrus said, and he stood. "I thank you for your kindness, for your counsel."

"You are most welcome, any time," she said, and rose. She smiled at him, deep and true, and he knew she meant every word of it. "Give me warning in advance when next you plan to visit, and I will arrange a tour of the far-flung reaches of our valley, our fields, and show you all the good you have done."

He cast an eye over the fields filled with tables, with people and families, with the whole of the town gathered near and chatting, gradually drifting apart as they moved off to their afternoon labors. "I think, for today, I have seen the good I have done." He took a breath of that fresh, clear air, felt just as awakened by it as he had when he emerged from the stream. "And it has made a world of difference."

She looked at him, corners of her mouth tugging outward in a smile. "Are you ready to return to your battlefield, then, Lord Davidon?"

He thought it over carefully, just for a moment. "I didn't leave a battlefield behind." He straightened, feeling unburdened for the first time in a while. "But I am ready to return to what needs to be done. Back to my guild." He felt the first hint of his own smile. "Ready to get back to my duty."

Chapter 51

Cyrus teleported into the foyer of Sanctuary with his eyes closed, opening them only as the flash began to fade. He took in the columns and the balcony, swept his gaze around to see the fading light coming through the enormous stained glass window that stood above the grand doors outside. It had taken him some time to hike back to the portal where he met Verity, and he knew sundown was approaching even Emerald Fields by the time he left. He could see the faint hints of sunset stirring orange beams across the stone floor of the foyer, cascading ochre that reminded him of everything good in this place.

It felt like home.

"Sir," came a thin voice from over his shoulder. Cyrus swung 'round, taking in the guard stationed around the seal on which he stood. Cyrus's eyes fell upon a youth of Luukessia, obvious by his sash of Galbadien, the Garden Kingdom. He wore the armor of a dragoon, like Samwen Longwell. A shock of bright, hay-colored hair sprouted atop his head like a fountain of gold in contrast to his sun-tanned skin. He had only one eye, though, a scarred pit replacing his right one, a strange, out-of-place detail on an otherwise youthful visage. It reminded him, in placement and detail, of Alaric.

"Dragoon," Cyrus said, using the cavalryman's formal title. "What can I do for you …?" He waited for a name.

"Rainey McIlven, sir," the young man said with a bow of respect. His lance stood at his side, pointed toward the ceiling. All of the guards had their weapons pointed at the ceiling now, though Cyrus knew they had not been when he first began to appear.

"What can I do for you, Rainey McIlven of Galbadien?" Cyrus asked with a smile.

"You have done all I needed already, sir," McIlven said, bowing that blond head again. "I wanted you to know I have voted for you, sir. I trust you to lead us as steady as you ever have."

Cyrus felt a faint twitch as an eyebrow rose of its own accord. "I thank you for your belief in me, Rainey McIlven, and I hope I will do credit to that faith should I win." With a slight bow of his own, Cyrus broke and turned toward the entry to the Great Hall. He could see the full tables laid out within, could hear the buzz of dinner already in progress.

"You did get one thing wrong, sir," McIlven called to him as Cyrus had just reached the doors of the Great Hall. He turned back, looking through the patch of men standing 'round the great seal, curious about the answer. "I may be from Galbadien, but I am Rainey McIlven of Sanctuary, sir." He snapped off a crisp salute that scraped the butt of his lance against the stone floor as he came to attention. There was a clatter and clink of metal as every one of the soldiers in the formation matched the young calvaryman of Luukessia. Cyrus froze, uncertain of how to respond for a moment, and finally returned the salute a few seconds delayed, his own armor making only a whisper of noise in the process.

Cyrus entered the Great Hall, easing into the wash of conversation like he was taking slow steps into a stream. It ebbed around him, a hush falling on those nearest him as he passed through the main aisle, keeping his gaze straight ahead so as to avoid any chance that someone might stop him to congratulate him the way young McIlven had. He had accepted the compliment, but uneasily, wearing it the way he might wear unfamiliar armor.

He made his way without comment, amid a sea of whispers, to the officers' table at the front of the room. It was a simple, circular thing, not unlike the one in the Council chambers, but situated as near to the far wall as it could be—and far from the kitchens, Cyrus reflected. He did not tilt a gaze in that direction, knowing that Larana would surely have made something for him. His stomach, though, was surprisingly sated with the simple stew and bread, lighter fare that had settled him. Even a meat pie held little appeal at the moment; he feared he would look into it and imagine how many mouths it might have fed in the Emerald Fields.

"So kind of you to join us," Vaste said from his place at the table. They were all there, waiting, plates in front of them in various states of disassembly. "It almost feels like there was some reason you should have been here today, something you might have missed by your absence."

"The voting is done?" Cyrus asked, his gaze drifting over a silent Vara and a surprisingly bubbly Ryin. He took note of Erith, fidgeting in her chair, and then realized J'anda was sitting in his seat, still and silent, trace of a smile upon his thin lips.

"I don't suppose you thought to cast your ballot before you left this morning?" Vaste asked.

"I did not," Cyrus said, taking his seat beside Vara. It made no protest at the addition of his weight, and she made no move to acknowledge his presence. Her meal was barely picked at.

He met Curatio's gaze across the table, the elder elf with a cup in his hand. He raised it to Cyrus in silent salute, and Cyrus bowed his head in acknowledgment of the quiet gesture. Once he had settled it, the healer kept his gaze on Cyrus. "And what mischief have you been up to today, General, that has your eyes as lively as I have seen them in some time?"

"I went to the Emerald Fields to inspect the results of our patronage," Cyrus said, staring at the empty place in front of him, curiously satisfied with the lack of plate and cup, "and I found things there much to my liking."

"It is not all gloom and darkness the world over, then?" This from Longwell, who wore a canny, surprisingly sly smile, his dark steel helm riding on the table next to his meal, which was entirely finished.

"I am pleased to report that there are places where the sun shines and the crops grow, unfettered and unchallenged by this war and this famine," Cyrus said, that trace of a smile matching Longwell's own. "Where people eat in fellowship and celebrate each other's company, grateful to have what they do, remembering that there are many who have none." *Including their lives*, he did not add.

"I find a healthy pinch of gratitude leavens the bread of life," Curatio said, his cup in hand. "Is that not so?" He looked to J'anda.

The enchanter stirred. "The contrast provides all the glory to the painting of life; what is brightest day without blackest night? What is the light without the dark? We should celebrate our lives, our moments, for those who cannot." He raised his own cup at that and drank deeply from it.

Cyrus thought about saying something, about asking the question on his mind, but Nyad pre-empted him. "You haven't asked about the election."

He let his eyes drift to the wizard, her blond hair arranged in careful ringlets around her bronzed skin. "I assumed someone would tell me if there were anything of import I needed to know."

"We were just about to announce the results without you," Vaste said. "Should we tell you first, or make it a surprise?"

Cyrus blinked, considering it. "I enjoy a good surprise." He looked at Vara, catching her eye, then to Ryin. "I wish you both the very best of luck, and I want you to know that I will follow either one of you and serve this guild as best I can, regardless of the result."

Ryin almost flinched. "Well. That is … magnanimous."

Cyrus watched him carefully. "Do you know who won?"

The druid shrugged. "Of course. But I accept your kind words for what they are—the sincere gesture of a true servant of Sanctuary." He met Cyrus's gaze evenly. "Which, I hope you know, I have ever been as well."

Cyrus gave him a slight nod. "I believe that with all that is in me."

Ryin smiled faintly, and Cyrus turned to Vara, who did not look at him. "I wish you all the best as well, Lady Vara," Cyrus said.

"I know that you do," she said.

Cyrus turned his gaze to J'anda, upon the cup he held in his thin and creased hands. "What brings you to our table this night, J'anda? Spying for Sovereign?"

"Indeed, he shows great interest in this election," the enchanter said. "However, I have other business to discuss with you; but it can wait until the morrow."

Cyrus began to frown, but Curatio rose at his place and a silence fell in the Great Hall. Despite the assembled crowd, it had a curiously vacuous feeling, as though all the air had been purged from the chamber. "I stand before you now," the healer began, "in my role as interim Guildmaster of Sanctuary, to declare the results of the vote placed before the membership this day."

Curatio cleared his throat, a curiously dramatic sound. Cyrus noted the presence of a twinkle in his eye and wondered whether it was relief knowing his time as Guildmaster was at end or excitement at the prospect of what would follow. He had little time to judge, though, as Curatio went on: "The self-determination of Sanctuary is our greatest uniqueness. Other guilds may beat us in sweep of power, but we are tied to no city, have our loyalty and fealty irrevocably sworn to none, and our Council rules at the behest of our members. We chart our own course, our choice of destination is entirely of our own making. To that end, I directed our officers to carry out a vote to determine the members' wishes on the following matters:

"One, the disposition of several candidates for officership in Sanctuary.

"And two, the candidacy of three officers deemed worthy to ascend to the role of duly-elected Guildmaster."

Curatio cleared his throat again, and this time Cyrus realized it was a theatrical trick; a moment's pause to let his words sink in for desired effect. "The election was carried out in compliance with the procedures laid down in the Sanctuary charter," Curatio said, "and administered with the impartial supervision of Erith Frostmoor, Samwen Longwell, Nyad Spiritcaster and myself." He straightened his back.

"The following individuals were elected to officership in the Sanctuary Council—Andren."

Cyrus blinked, scanning the crowd until he found the bedraggled elf, who was halfway to a sip of his flask when the attention of everyone in the room fell on him. His face was frozen, as if he were listening for something that he had missed, his dark, tangled hair and long beard giving him his usual disheveled look. "I'm sorry," he said, in his drawling, lower-class elven accent, "did someone say my name?"

Curatio's eyes twinkled. "Congratulations on your election to officer, Andren."

There was a stark silence, which was broken by Andren's half-shocked cry of protest. "I didn't even put my name forward!"

"Your name was submitted by the membership," Curatio said, "and approved by a seventy-five percent vote."

There was a ripple of laughter that ran through the crowd, and Andren made an audible gulp, his flask forgotten. "Oh, you lot are in for it now." His face turned to a scowl. "What a dirty trick, giving me responsibility."

"If I may continue," Curatio said, back in full command. "Other officers approved, without delay and in full haste—Thad Proelius, Odellan, Mendicant." Cyrus found each of them in turn, quickly and quietly. He watched them receive their congratulations, more quietly and less comically than had Andren. Mendicant, in particular, looked pleased. Odellan, humble as always, simply looked rather shocked.

"Here endeth the officer candidacies," Curatio said, "and we turn now to a decision of the utmost import." His eyes surveyed the room, grey, serious, gravity apparent with every syllable. "Of our three august candidates, only one could be chosen, though all are loyal servants of Sanctuary and able in their own ways."

"Get on with it!" came a bellow out of the back of the room, followed by a loose laugh from all quarters. Cyrus frowned at the blatant disrespect, but Curatio showed only a faint amusement.

"As you wish," the interim Guildmaster said with a muted smile. "The winner and Guildmaster of Sanctuary is—"

"Congratulations," Vara said, leaning to his ear the moment before the announcement was made. Her breath was warm, her voice was cold. His eyes flicked to her, caught her as she left her seat and disappeared into the crowd as a roar filled the Great Hall, a throng from every table on their feet and cheering with such noise that Cyrus wondered if his eardrums had burst.

Dully, he felt the slap of hands upon his back, his attention still focused on finding Vara where she had vanished into the assemblage. He found Vaste suddenly at his side, a sea of motion to his right as the entirety of the guild loudly celebrated his ascension.

He looked up at the troll, who wore a satisfied look. "How did you do that?" Cyrus asked over the clamor.

"Let's see," Vaste said, speaking just loud enough for Cyrus to hear him, "you did extremely well with the goblins, the gnomes and Luukessians."

Cyrus felt his tongue stick to the roof of his mouth. "Why?" he barely got out.

"Apparently they're still grateful to you for saving their lives," Vaste said with only a little irony. "I try not to get hung up on those trifling details myself, but …" He paused, suddenly serious. "Also, someone circulated a rumor that you had a best friend who was a dwarf, and that he died."

Cyrus frowned. "I did."

"Honestly, you make this so easy," Vaste said. "That got you the dwarves. You also won the rock giant vote, I hear." He nodded his head out over the crowd, still applauding with thunderous approbation. Cyrus cast his gaze out to find Fortin, who nodded to him once he caught the red eyes. "Not sure how you pulled that off," Vaste said.

"I killed him," Cyrus replied, giving Fortin a nod in return.

"If only it worked that way for everyone," Vaste said. "You lost the elves by an overwhelming margin, since one of the other candidates is something of a religious icon to them. If they were like rock giants, you could have had them line up and then kill them one by one." Cyrus watched him for a hint of joking, but the troll delivered it all with a straight face. "Ultimately, they were irrelevant, though. You won the whole thing handily." He proffered a massive, green hand. "Congratulations ... Guildmaster."

His eyes met Vaste's yellow ones, and he took the outreached hand in his own. "Thank you."

The volume swelled around Cyrus as he went from officer to officer, taking their congratulations. Ryin shot him a tight smile from where he stood, Erith wrapped him in a hug, pulling him down to her, whispering something laudatory that he could not hear over the roar of the crowd. J'anda raised his cup to Cyrus, unmoving, still seated.

The room blurred around him, and Cyrus became dimly aware that Curatio was standing at his shoulder. He stopped and faced the healer, the smooth, alcoholic scent of a cleanser filling his nose as the interim Guildmaster offered his own hand to Cyrus. Cyrus took it and they shook. Curatio pulled him with a surprisingly firm grip into a careful, one-shouldered hug. "Now, the weight of all this is on you," the healer said with a measure of glee. Cyrus broke from him embrace to find Curatio's timeless face stretched in a wide grin. The healer reached under his robes and brought out a winding necklace upon a chain, circular pendant on the end of it. "Lower your head, if you please." Curatio paused, then frowned. "Actually, it might be best if you knelt."

Cyrus took a knee, feeling every eye in the room upon him as a silence fell. He closed his eyes and felt the weight of a chain—light, cool to the touch—fall around his gorget as the healer carefully placed it around his neck. The pendant fell down the front of his breastplate, clinking there as Cyrus returned to his feet. The cheers swelled through the hall again, echoing with a jubilation he had nearly forgotten until that very afternoon.

He raised his hands in signal for the assemblage to quiet, and they did in an instant. Seats were taken, and within moments no one but Cyrus was standing in the hall. Even Fortin's considerable bulk was lowered as he sat down in the corner.

"When I came to this guild five years ago, I was searching for a place to make my mark," Cyrus said, trying to decide exactly what to say. It came out surprisingly easily. "I was looking to become … powerful. To grow my strength. To obtain better armor, to fulfill …" he let his voice trail as he searched for the right word, "… to fulfill a destiny that I thought was rooted in power alone. I wanted to be the foremost warrior in Arkaria." He blinked, looking out across earnest faces. His eyes found Andren's, and on the bearded healer's face he saw the scarred expression of remembrance. "I drew a tight circle around those I cared most for, and I fully intended to keep it small.

"That plan of mine did not last a week in Sanctuary. I lost one of those friends, one dear to me, and in his absence I gained … countless more." Cyrus's eyes swept to Erith, Nyad, Vaste and J'anda. "My circle widened of its own accord, the familial ties I lacked by circumstances of my childhood forged by the caring of those who came to me as strangers. My time in Sanctuary has been marked by a change in my ambitions. Where before I cared only for becoming the strongest, my aspirations were tempered by a voice of reason, a mentor who taught me more than anyone I have ever known.

"I still hear his voice in the quiet moments before a tremendous decision. I hear his urging, caution and moderation, his wisdom and temperance, warning me against the rashness of action that is in my very nature. I hear his words about purpose, about power being granted to those who can best use it for the good of others, not themselves. These words stay with me long after the man himself has passed." Cyrus turned to look at the empty seat where Alaric had once taken his meals.

"When my friends and I considered coming to this place, we spoke of perhaps staying for a short while, filling our pockets, and continuing to ascend elsewhere," Cyrus said, each word a confession that he signed with a little bit of his soul. "Now, I cannot imagine ever leaving. What Sanctuary has become is what each and every one of you have brought to it. The care and consideration of this army, bound for greatness, carrying a purpose nobler than any group of mercenaries or climbing guild, is what makes it special." He placed his gauntleted hands flat on the table, knuckles down. "I am proud to serve as your General, and I will do my utmost to lead you as Guildmaster. I thank you for your support and bid you all good night. A long day awaits us on the morrow, with decisions to make for our next steps." He smiled. "I look forward to seeing the new officers—and the old—tomorrow morning in Council."

He rapped his knuckle sharply against the table once, signaling the end of his speech, and was met with uproarious applause. He rushed to leave, shaking a few hands as he made his way down the aisle through the surging crowd. He brushed off a few more with a smile and a mumbled word of kindness, scrambling out into the foyer where he caught a flash of blond hair moving up the stairs.

"Vara!" he called, hurrying after her. *She must have stayed to listen at the back.* He took the steps two at a time up the long, winding spiral, but she moved as though she had Praelior itself in her hand.

He caught up with her on the floor of the Council quarters, sprinting out of the hallway to see her retreating back only two doors from her quarters. "Don't run," he said.

She paused, straight of back, stiff of bearing, before turning to look at him. There was no measure of discomfort there, just stiff resolution. "I don't think there is much to be said."

"I accept your congratulations," Cyrus said, a little stiffly himself, "but ..." His eyes searched the corridor as if the words he needed were written somewhere on the stones. "Dammit, Vara, I don't want to lose you over this."

A flutter of eyelids was her response. "You cannot lose what you have never had."

He felt the sting most acutely but hid his response under neutral reply. "Sanctuary cannot afford to lose you."

"Sanctuary will not lose me," she said. "Not at this time, in any case. I remain at the command of the Council and the Guildmaster."

He felt his eyes close, relief expressed involuntarily. "Thank goodness."

"You wish my counsel?" she asked, still formal.

He opened his eyes, and she still stood there as stiffly as she had before. "For the sake of … yes, Vara, I wish your counsel."

She took an almost imperceptible breath. "The Princess of Pharesia, your ranger who dallies with endless sticks, and Erith the frosty dark elf—all of them are, so far as I know, more promiscuous than the dark elven quencher of your loins. Yet you never hear me cast aspersions upon them. Why do you think that is?"

He tread lightly, sprinkling familiarity and levity into his response. "Because you're jealous, of course."

She bristled, though it was barely visible under her facade of unmoving, steely calm. "There is a deeper problem with this thief of yours. I sense deception from her, some hidden scheming, some mean purpose that she would never admit to."

Cyrus felt a rush of discomfort, a swell of weariness that lay upon him like a weight. "Or it could be your overwhelming …" he stifled the first choice of word, "… emotions … clouding your judgment in regards to her."

"I would think you would be more complimentary of my judgment, given how many times it has been the only thing that kept me from disemboweling you." She arched an eyebrow, and he saw a faint glimmer of amusement—the old Vara—peeking through. "As I said, I am here to serve the guild of Sanctuary and her Guildmaster. You make take my counsel however you like, and if you desire to throw it out the window like a discarded napkin," she made the slightest motion toward a shrug, but in her reserved state it was almost as expressive as if she had broken into a dance, "so be it." She bowed her head at him. "Good night, Master of Sanctuary. I shall see you on the morrow."

"On the morrow, then," Cyrus said and started for his door.

She clucked her tongue at him then wagged a finger. "Your quarters are upstairs now."

Cyrus blinked; he had quite forgotten that Alaric had had his own quarters. "Right. I suppose I should …"

"It seems only fitting," Vara said, and she opened her own door quite stiffly, just as she had done everything else thus far in their conversation. She paused just before she shut the door. "Congratulations, Cyrus," she said and then disappeared behind the wooden planks and black-iron castings that made it a seemingly impenetrable barrier between the two of them.

He stood there for only a moment before turning. He opened the door to his old quarters and gathered his things wordlessly. There was little enough to gather, he found, just his clothing and few possessions. He placed them all into a bag, regarding his massive bed with one eye. *I'll have it moved tomorrow.*

As he turned to leave, he saw a fleeting shadow in the arch of his door. He recognized the figure, thin and slight, her white hair glistening in the torchlight. He gave her only one look and felt something sink within him. "Not tonight," he said and walked past her without another word. She did not follow.

Cyrus found his new quarters already opened, an entire floor with four massive, sweeping balconies open to the night air. A strong breeze blew through as he settled his bag upon the stone floor just above the terminus of the winding staircase. The night wind blew upon him, chilling him under his armor, and with a glance he saw a fire start in the hearth, roaring, filling the room with its warmth and a sweet, wood smell. The torches lit at his presence as well, casting their illumination over the quarters of Sanctuary's Guildmaster.

Cyrus stood there, in the middle of the floor, in the dark of night, stars glistening in four directions around him as though he were standing out on the plains themselves. He walked to the nearest balcony, passed through the doors that were opened and anchored, the breeze not disturbing them at all.

His hand found the railing with a gentle clink, and he took off his helm with the other. The wind swept through his hair with force, blowing it behind him as he looked—north, he realized. He could see the outline of the Waking Woods in the distance, the moon shining down on still plains. Fires were lit in a line along Sanctuary's curtain wall, and he could hear the voices of the guards, the watchers, at their task.

And now watching over all of this is my task, he thought, one hand on the rail. It was a heady sensation, being up this high. The sense of weightlessness that had found him in the stream at Emerald Fields was gone, replaced with something else entirely. He did not feel weightless, that was certain.

We are none of us alone. The words came back to him again, unbidden. Uninvited.

The Guildmaster of Sanctuary stood there until dawn broke over the eastern horizon, watching the day leach the darkness from the Plains of Perdamun bit by bit. He had duty, he knew, he had tasks before him.

And he had never felt more alone in his life.

Chapter 52

When Cyrus strode into the Council Chambers at the hour appointed for their meeting, he found the entirety of the Council, new and old, already assembled and awaiting him. Applause greeted his ears, soft and congratulatory, not quite the deafening roar he had heard in the Great Hall the night before.

Cyrus demurred, trying to show them by word and expression that he was not worthy of the pomp and circumstance. It was all velvet draped on his shoulders to him, unnecessary, unwanted. He circumnavigated the big, round table, deftly avoiding the habit of gravitating to his old seat, which was now taken up by Odellan. Instead he wove around, passing each officer in turn. He strode by Longwell, Vaste (who harrumphed significantly as he passed), Thad, Nyad and finally Vara before arriving at the high-backed chair that he had stared across the table at for … years.

Cyrus hesitated at the arm of the chair, pulling his gauntlet off, letting his fingers run down the time-pocked surface of the chair's arm. He felt suddenly self-conscious, as though aware that he could never quite fill the seat, embarrassed to even try. He had a vision of himself sitting in Alaric's chair the way a child would sit in an adult's when they were absent; he saw his legs dangling, failing to reach the floor, arms not long enough to even touch the rests.

He coughed, breaking the spell of the vision, and pulled it back from the table. He found it surprisingly light and lowered himself into the seat without allowing for any more hesitation to settle upon him. It fit him well, and he scooted it forward on the stone almost noiselessly, removing his helm and settling it on the table, quite naturally, before even realizing that he had just mimicked a most familiar action.

"Here we are," Ryin said from his place three seats to Cyrus's right, "ready for the coronation of our new king."

"I'm not a king," Cyrus said, and his voice sounded hushed and hoarse to his ears. "Just the same ass you've always known, with perhaps a bit more weight lent to my words now." He tried to smile, to take in the whole table, and swept his gaze left until his eyes found Vara at his immediate side. She was watching, not coldly nor warmly, simply there, attentive, the perfect officer at watch.

"I think we can all agree with that," Erith said from across the table. A little rumble of levity ran through some of the newer officers, and Cyrus felt the mood in the room lighten.

"It would seem we have begun to settle some of the outstanding business lingering upon our door," Curatio said from Cyrus's immediate left. "Though obviously our recovery of the Daring did not go perhaps as well as we might have hoped."

Cyrus felt his cheeks grow dark, his forehead flush at the thought. "How many of them did we account for?"

"Nearly all," Erith said from across the table. "Some are in better condition than others." She played with a strand of her white hair as she spoke. "Elisabeth is still in the Halls of Healing, her mind a bit … addled. Most of the rest have either joined us, taken their leave, or gone to Emerald Fields." Her head bowed deeply, as though she could not face the dark thoughts swirling in the wake of her pronouncement.

"Wow, that's a bit grim this early in the morning," Andren said from beside her. Cyrus looked at the elf and realized for the first time that he no longer had a beard. His cheeks were pink, his eyes were baggy, but his beard was completely gone.

"Did you wander into a sheep's pen last night and awaken to the shears this morning?" Cyrus asked, studying the elf.

Andren's face flushed a deeper scarlet. "I figured that I should look the part of a reputable officer of Sanctuary."

There was a pause until Vara spoke. "I suspect the next event of note 'round here will be the Goddess of Life not only returning, but declaring her candidacy for officer and offering to man the Halls of Healing."

"That does bring us back to the search for her," Cyrus said. "We've made precious little progress in this matter—"

J'anda broke into a wild fit of coughing, hands over his face. It was horrible sounding, wracking and deep. Cyrus watched the enchanter, who seemed a darker navy than usual once his hands came away from his face. Curatio rose and started to move to him, but J'anda waved him off. "I ... apologize," the enchanter choked out. "I am afraid that I ... sometimes feel ... utterly wretched."

An uncomfortable silence followed the enchanter's words. *No one wants to talk about his failing health*, Cyrus thought. He tapped a finger upon the table, only once, and caught a meaningful look from Curatio. *So that's the specter lingering in the corner of the room that everyone pretends not to see.*

"Vidara?" Cyrus asked, diverting attention back to the matter at hand and away from J'anda's coughing spell.

Mendicant spoke up finally, his small voice a curious presence in the Council Chamber: "We are children playing in a ground that is inhabited by giants. We know nothing of that which we investigate."

Cyrus let that grim pronouncement hold sway for a moment. "I agree. But that does not absolve us of at least giving our best effort to finding her."

"I think we have given that effort," Vaste said. "Some of us made great sacrifices, if you recall, in terms of rodents and genital biting—"

"A pleasant change from goats, no?" J'anda asked.

Vaste ignored him. "This investigation is at an end without further information. A snowy, forbidding realm filled with wild and nasty creatures is not much to go on."

"We also have the testimony of the Gatekeeper," Vara said quietly.

"Which is nothing to go on," Vaste said. "Less than nothing, perhaps. He could very well have been lying. Every word from his mouth is suspect."

"Fine," Cyrus said, dismissing the entire matter. "There is one thing left in regards to the Daring, though, before we consider that one closed." He eyed the faces around the table. "Someone allowed those trolls to operate in human territory."

Curatio adopted an inscrutable expression. "That is ... quite a bold accusation. You have no proof, I assume?"

"I have no proof, only suspicion," Cyrus said, lowering his own head to stare at the nubs and knots in the table. They were different than the ones in front of his seat. "And my suspicions run immediately to the villain of my choosing—Rhane Ermoc was in charge of the Wardemos portal when I teleported there to join the search in progress."

"Casual cruelty is one thing, and obviously something Ermoc has proven himself eminently capable of," Vara said, "but this is … something else entirely. He would be betraying the entire Confederation by allowing trolls to operate within their borders."

"It has the ring of nonsense," Vaste said, "which probably means it's true, since Cyrus is spouting it."

Cyrus felt his face crinkle in a frown at the troll. "What is that supposed to mean?"

"You always put these things together," Vaste said. "Like the goblins raiding the caravans, and Ashan'agar's spiders stealing the godly weapons. You see the threads that lead from point to point and connect them before the rest of us. I would call it wizardry, but we all know you are bereft of magic. In any case, perhaps you do see the thread that we do not; I would not care to wager against it being so."

Cyrus blinked in surprise. "Truly?"

"Truly," Vaste said. "Though I will take odds on whether we'll ever be able to prove it. That is such a tall order, it makes titans look minuscule by comparison. It would require having a human witness, because no one would believe a troll."

"Or the wizard that teleported them," Cyrus mused.

"Most likely a dark elf," Vara said quietly.

"Good luck tracking down one dark elven wizard in the midst of countless," Erith said.

Cyrus turned his head to look at J'anda. "Has word reached the Sovereign's ears about the fall of Gren yet?"

The enchanter stirred in his chair, looking as though he were coming back to life. "I do not believe so; his eyes are elsewhere, keenly centered on his eastern offensive at the moment. If it has gotten to him, he is keeping it very quiet, presumably to retain his tight leash upon the troll armies at his command."

"Because they'd come running at Sanctuary if the truth came out?" Ryin asked, a small measure of alarm in his voice.

"Because they'd go running home," Vaste said without expression. "They'd abandon his offensive as quickly as if he mandated compulsory bathing." He waited a moment as the silence hung in the chamber. "They don't like baths," he added helpfully. "Well … mud baths, I suppose. Sulfuric ones—"

"This adds nothing to the conversation, dear Vaste," Curatio said gently. "It would seem our best interest would be in finding a way to get word of this particular coup into the ranks of the dark elven army, then, in hopes that it spreads to the trolls."

J'anda looked at Curatio warily. "I will … see what I can do. However, I have something else more pressing to attend to that may speed things along in this regard as well."

Cyrus looked at the enchanter, whose lined face was carefully neutral. "What's that?"

J'anda waved a hand. "I must discuss it with you in private after the meeting. Suffice it to say … we must take a journey."

Cyrus tried to keep the frown from showing. "All right." He shook his head, dismissing it. "Any other business?"

"Something rather surprising this morning," Thad Proelius said, his face almost as red as his armor. "We received an envoy about an hour before the meeting."

"From who?" Andren asked.

"From 'whom,'" Vara corrected him.

"Oh, feck off," Andren said. "From *whom*."

"The dark elves," Thad said. "They're requesting the return of the bodies of their soldiers lost during the siege last year."

"Tell them to feck off," Vara said, obviously quite put out. "Where was this request seven months ago, after the battle itself?"

Cyrus watched her, splashes of red mottling her cheeks. "I agree, though perhaps not as adamantly as Vara. We burned those bodies months ago. Why would they come looking for them now?" He turned to look back to J'anda, whose face was covered by his hands.

"The Sovereign …" J'anda began, taking time in selecting his words, "… is in the midst of many initiatives. One of them is the repatriation of all the corpses he can possibly get his hands on."

"Is anyone else extremely disturbed by the thought of the God of Darkness trying to collect corpses?" Vaste asked. "It just sounds wrong."

Curatio took the news with what almost seemed like amusement. "Long dead corpses are irrelevant. It's most likely related to the famine. We know his people are starving, yes?" He looked to J'anda for confirmation.

J'anda stirred. "It is true that Sovar is in dire straits, and that the army has consumed a large part of the mushroom and root crops that have been used to feed the poor until recently. The surface farms above Saekaj are working at their capacity, the slaves toiling harder than ever to try and keep up with the demands for increased food production. With winter coming soon, it will likely become more of a squeeze than before."

"There you have it," Curatio said. "Famine drives curious behaviors, as a starving man will do desperate things for food. But we have no bodies to give them in any case, so there is no cause to fret."

"I have an idea about that," Vaste said. "We could step outside the walls and piss in the dirt. That will clump it together, and then we shovel it into barrels and send it back to him." He made a flourish with his hand. "And thus, we send the Sovereign of Saekaj Sovar our piss in a barrel. With his dirt. And ashes. But mostly our piss."

Cyrus spoke first. "Vetoed. We may be at war with Yartraak and the dark elves, but we needn't throw pointless, petty insults their way."

"Oh, yes," Andren said, "because we wouldn't want to step on their toes, would we? They might lay siege to us or something similarly terrible."

"It's such a shame," Vaste said, taking up where the elf had left off, "because when it comes to stepping on toes, there is no one better than I."

"Thank you for giving me an excuse never to dance with you," Vara said.

"I don't see you doing much dancing in the nowadays," Vaste said. "Or ever, actually."

"Thad," Cyrus said, "please deliver a diplomatic reply offering our regrets, but that in order to keep disease and rot at bay, we were forced to dispose of the dark elven bodies with fire." He waved a hand. "Something of that sort."

"It will be done," Thad said, "diplomacy and all."

"Excellent," Cyrus said, and his gaze swept the table. "Any other business?" He waited for a count of three under his breath. "Let's call it a day, shall we?"

"Sounds like a brilliant idea," Andren said, "as I've developed quite the thirst."

"Yes, you wouldn't want to miss your morning drink," Vara said icily.

"No, I wouldn't," Andren agreed, missing the irony. He popped out of his seat as though moved by a spring, and disappeared through the doors faster than anyone else.

"I find myself rather famished," Vaste said, "though not perhaps for the whiskey that Andren is."

"Few are," Erith agreed, disappearing through the door with the troll following shortly behind.

"My compliments to the new Guildmaster," Ryin said, standing behind his place at the table. His piercing eyes met Cyrus's. "I may have opposed you, but you can be assured of my wholehearted support."

"And occasional passionate disagreement?" Cyrus asked, amused, drumming his fingers on the table.

"But of course," Ryin said, with a bow of the head. With a smile, he left.

"Off to deliver bad news," Thad said. "This dark elven envoy, I don't think he's going to take it well."

"Oh?" Cyrus asked. "Was he fearsome? Should I send assistance?"

"He seemed rather pitiful, actually," Thad said, scratching his head, red helm cupped under his arm. "I don't think he's going to be pleased to return with our message."

"The Sovereign is rather notorious about failing to discriminate between messenger and message when responding to displeasing news," J'anda said quietly, also still seated.

"Perhaps the envoy will need some of what Andren is partaking of," Curatio said with a slight smile as he rose from his place to make his way to the door.

"More likely he'll run off and never be seen outside the bandit lands again," J'anda said with a shrug. "I heard there is a booming trade for wizards willing to teleport dark elves to distant portals—Gradsden Savanna, the Inculta Desert, Fertiss, the Mountains of

Nartanis and the last portal on the southeast beach are popular destinations."

"Is that so?" Cyrus asked. "Interesting."

"Perhaps we'll offer him a wizard to take him wherever he so chooses as well," Curatio said with mirth, leading Thad through the door.

Cyrus made a quick survey of the room; Vara, Nyad, Longwell, Odellan, Mendicant and J'anda all remained. None seemed in a hurry to leave, each lingering in their own way. Vara was staring at the table, apparently lost in thought. "Someone will eventually have to either speak or I'm going to assume you're all waiting for me to leave and carry out my perception of your wishes."

"I have nothing that cannot wait," Vara said, awakening from her daze. She stirred and moved from her seat to the door with an easy gait, not even looking back once.

As soon as the door was shut behind her, three of the remaining Council members began to speak at once—Nyad, Longwell and Odellan all halted after barely getting anything out; Cyrus did not comprehend any of it. He turned his gaze to Mendicant and gave the goblin a warm smile. "What do you need, Mendicant?"

"I only wish to express my thanks for your belief in me," the little goblin said with a bow, his deep blue robes in most odd contrast to his green, scaled skin. "You have always treated me as an equal in the halls, even when I was the only one of my kind here, even when you had cause to hate us, and it has been that treatment that has drawn so many of my people to these halls—and gotten me elected as an officer."

Cyrus looked at the goblin impassively. "You have proven by your merits that you are worthy, Mendicant."

The yellow eyes found Cyrus's, and he could see gratitude there. "But you gave me a chance to prove I was worthy when no other guild would have me—you and Lady Niamh, may the Earth-Father guide her soul to her rest."

Cyrus gave him a subtle nod. "That is what Sanctuary is, for you and me—a haven when no one else would have us. You honor us with your presence, Mendicant, and you honor your people with your service." He bowed at the waist to the goblin, who, bereft of a reply, merely returned the bow and headed for the door.

Cyrus turned his attention to the remaining officers. "I hope you're not all going to thank me, because if so … it's hardly necessary."

"I'm not here to thank you," Nyad said. He looked at her carefully, and she seemed a bit red in the face.

"Then I'm saving you for last," Cyrus said, turning his attention to Odellan.

"I *am* here to thank you," Odellan said, apparently a little embarrassed. "But not as floridly as Mendicant, perhaps. I just wanted to offer my congratulations on your new post, and say that if there is anything that this former Endrenshan can do to aid you, in my capacity as officer or in regards to the army of Sanctuary, all you need do is ask." He snapped to attention and offered a crisp salute, which Cyrus returned. With that, Odellan turned, his sculpted, carefully crafted armor clinking quietly with each step, and retreated out the door.

"J'anda?" Cyrus asked. The enchanter had closed his eyes and leaned his head back against the wooden rest on his chair.

"Save me for last," J'anda said, not opening his eyes, "after the wizard's complaint or remonstrance. I could use a mild dose of amusement before I am forced to ask of you … what I am to ask."

"Fine," Cyrus said, looking between Longwell and Nyad. "Longwell?"

"The people of Luukessia overwhelmingly supported you in your election," Longwell said, beginning cautiously.

"And I hope they know I am very grateful," Cyrus said, equally cautious. He feared where the dragoon's overture would head.

"I wanted to talk to you about it," Longwell said quietly, "because I have heard rumblings … that you blame yourself for what happened to Luukessia. That you might think we blame you." Cyrus remained silent, slightly dumbstruck, unable to even muster a "Who told you this?"

"The people of Luukessia do not ascribe blame," Longwell said, formally, "and certainly, even though well aware of our misadventure with the God of Death, do not connect that event with what happened in our land."

Cyrus stared at him, feeling his eyes narrow slightly. "This goes against human nature that I've seen; most people look for someone to blame."

"Yet they do not blame you," Longwell said. "They blame the old kings at times—usually the ones that are not from their own land—they blame fate, they blame ancestors … anyone but the man who tirelessly fought to lead us to safety against the onslaught." Longwell stood, picking his own helm off the table and placing it upon his head. "I only thought you should know." Without another word, he retreated from the chamber, shutting the door behind him.

"Well, that was not so entertaining," J'anda mumbled under his breath.

"Hold on to your robes, because this should be more promising," Nyad said a little shortly.

"Oh, Lord of War," Cyrus muttered, "I've barely assumed office; what have I done?"

"Do not adopt that pretense of being deliberately dense in my presence," Nyad snapped at him.

"There is no pretense in this instance, I can assure you," J'anda said.

"That's helpful," Cyrus snapped.

"What?" The enchanter shot him a mischievous grin, which wiped years off his aged visage. "You don't have the faintest idea what she's angry about."

Nyad turned her glare from J'anda to Cyrus, the rosy cheeks of her ill humor finding rest under the cold eyes. "Fine, let me declare it so we are clear: your poor treatment of Aisling is simply breathtaking."

"My—what?" Cyrus found his mouth agape and wondered how it had gotten that way.

"Goddess knows," Nyad said, building up a formidable momentum, her words coming with less warning than a flurry of sword strikes from a troll, "I have held my tongue through your various and sundry sexual misadventures as an officer—"

"You're the only one, then," Cyrus said under his breath.

"—but you are the Guildmaster now," she went on, undeterred. "I acknowledge that you are both young and foolish, but make a decision, leader. You cannot continue to lead the poor girl on. I fail to see how you can make such quick decisions under threat of death in battle yet let this linger as though you have all the time in the world to manage her—"

"I am not having this conversation with you—" Cyrus said, his reserve run over, nearly sputtering as the outrage bubbled within.

She cut him off. "I will have my say as your elder."

"I will listen to her have her say," J'anda added, eyes very slightly open and watching the whole exchange, "because it promises much amusement."

Cyrus shot him a fiery glare. "Whose side are you on?"

"Oh, but you forget," J'anda said, "I have seen your heart's desire, my friend. I remember it well, though you may try and deny it. I doubt very much it has changed since that day."

"Do you not recall that day upon the riverbank four years ago?" Nyad had parked her hands upon her hips, her robes tangled around her figure.

Cyrus felt his eyes flutter. "I remember being naked. Is that the conversation you're referring to?"

"The very one," Nyad said.

"This keeps getting better and better," J'anda said.

"You remain a sad and tangled heap of a man," Nyad said, "and have scarcely advanced since that day. Again, the aura of indecision that hangs about your love life is perhaps suitable for an officer and a General of Sanctuary, though there is surely some debate to be had about that." Her arms folded in front of her. "But no longer. You are too old, too advanced in position, to continue with these … half measures."

"Half measures?" J'anda repeated. "Is she talking about your …?" He waved a hand lower, toward Cyrus's faulds, the armor around his waist and hips.

"NO!" Cyrus said, and heard Nyad echo it a half-second behind him.

J'anda held up his hands in apology. "Carry on, then. A curious mind merely wishes to know."

"I have not been adopting … 'half measures' … with Aisling," Cyrus said. "I have not had time to have a proper conversation—"

"You have used the girl for your own pleasures while failing to tell her that you are doing so," Nyad said.

"She wanted to be used in such a fashion," Cyrus said. "She made it clear she would take whatever I was willing to give—"

"And you gave it to her over and over, did you not?" J'anda's tone was quiet but accusatory.

"I say again, whose side are you on?" Cyrus turned on the enchanter.

"That of the truth, as ever," J'anda said.

"I would think that a master of illusion would be keenly aware of the shifting nature of 'truth' depending on who one speaks to," Cyrus said.

"The truth is the truth," J'anda said with a shrug. "And the truth is that you are still in love with Vara. This does not change. The only thing that does seem to change is who you give your … 'half measure' to."

"I do not have a 'half—'" Cyrus caught J'anda's smile and stopped. "I have had conversations with Vara about this very matter, I'll have you both know. She remains steadfast in her position that we will not be intertwined. Not that it's any of your business. I plan to have a conversation with Aisling about this given the next opportune moment." He felt himself flush, drew himself up. "I will end it with her. You have my assurance." He felt his eyes roll. "Now … can we please … be done with this infernal conversation?"

"She deserves more than being a runner-up and a consolation prize for your affections," Nyad said.

"Which 'she'?" Cyrus asked.

"Both of them," Nyad said. "In spite of whatever arrangement you think you have with Aisling, she is not here merely for the use and convenience of Cyrus Davidon."

"It was mutually—" Cyrus stifled his reply, half-given, before catching that smug glint from Nyad again. "Never mind." He felt the words rush out with more than a little hostility. "Is there anything else?"

"I am finished, provided you keep your word," Nyad said with a last nod.

"I am finished with her," Cyrus said, more than a little hotly. "I will share that fact with her immediately. Good enough?"

"Good enough," Nyad said and started toward the door.

"Not so fast," J'anda said. "I require a favor of you, Nyad."

She gave the blue-skinned enchanter an eye. "And what is that?"

"A teleportation spell," J'anda said, eyeing her, still seated. "Cyrus and I require passage to Huern."

"The gnomish city?" Cyrus asked. "Why in the name of the gods would we go there?"

"Because I have asked you to accompany me," J'anda said seriously, beginning a slow rise from his chair. It looked like a tiresome effort, the movements of an old man. "I can tell you no more until we are there."

Cyrus debated throwing his anger back in the enchanter's face, tossing those ill feelings right at the wrinkled skin of the dark elf. He took a breath, then another, and looked to Nyad. He saw written on her youthful features a canny look that told him she expected him to do it, and supreme disapproval waited should he yield to the temptation. "All right," Cyrus said instead. "Let's go to Huern."

Chapter 53

Huern was a curious sight, like a city on the horizon with a perspective trick. It looked distant, small, as if it were miles away, or perhaps a town of dollhouses the like he had heard wealthy children played with.

It was no trick, though, and he stood in the square outside the mighty portal, which towered over the whole of the city. The buildings all reached his waist at highest, stone-carved and wood-built together. It was a curious architecture, what the gnomes built, which borrowed from the humans and the dwarves in equal measure with little elvish influence.

"Here we are," Cyrus said, casting a wary eye over the small structures that ringed the square. The place was not built with humans in mind, let alone humans of his stature. Gnomes passed through the square giving wide berth and suspicious looks to the tall folk in their midst. Cyrus, in particular, felt the gaze of the locals upon him. They reached only to his knee at the best of times. "I'm going to have to look at the ground every moment I'm in this city or else I'll commit accidental murder."

"We shan't be here for long," J'anda said, giving a nod to Nyad. "Would you kindly wait for us here? We must take a meeting in the outskirts."

"A secret meeting that I'm not invited to," Nyad said, slightly sullen. "Oh, certainly, I'll just wait here for you like a horse tied to a post, ready whenever you appear."

"That's the spirit," J'anda said, ignoring her irritation. "Come along, Guildmaster. We don't wish to be late."

Cyrus shot Nyad a look that was short on sympathy; her diatribe was still fresh in his mind. "Can't be late," he said, as though it were any sort of explanation, and followed behind J'anda as the enchanter carefully picked his way down a side street that led out of town.

"You know she'll be able see us over every one of the buildings, right?" Cyrus asked, easily falling into step beside J'anda. Huern had little of the disgusting smell of other towns this size that Cyrus had visited; he wondered if it was because gnomish privies were undoubtedly smaller than those used by larger folk.

"We're going to a hillside just over the horizon," J'anda said. "She won't see us—or our guest—there."

"Would it matter if she did?" Cyrus asked.

"Very much so," J'anda said, inscrutable. "She would almost certainly come rushing in, agitated, throwing a distinctly princess-y fit, and we would waste hours of our time having to hear her tunnel to the bottom of her rage rather than simply sifting through yours and going on with our—in my case, considerably shorter—lives."

Cyrus cocked an eyebrow at him. "Who are we going to meet?"

"You'll see," J'anda said.

"Gods," Cyrus said, "nobody wants to tell me anything, but everyone wants to tell me what to do now."

"Everyone wants to have your ear," J'anda said, "to believe they have influence over your actions. There is a difference, and I hope you see it."

"Right now all I see is short people," Cyrus said, taking another suspicious glare from a gnomish couple that passed him on the dirt street.

"The thing that always struck me about the Gnomish Dominions," J'anda said, "is all the little differences between their cities and ours." His lips pursed in a smile.

"Was that supposed to be a joke?" Cyrus asked.

"A small one, I assure you."

Cyrus chuckled. "Nyad would be most upset with you for being insensitive about the little people."

"I feel a tiny pang of regret."

Cyrus snorted that time.

They followed the path out of the little town, Cyrus marveling at the scale of things. He had been to Huern before, years earlier when he tried to recruit gnomes to Sanctuary. It had struck him as a fairly insular place at the time. The smells were curious; he passed small chimneys belching puffs of smoke no larger than his fist, the faint aroma of bread misting within them. He stuck his face into one and breathed deep, the smoke filling his lungs, the smell of the cooked, ground meal nearly choking him.

"Just because everything is smaller, don't assume it is any less potent," J'anda said.

Cyrus kept up with the enchanter, medium strides that left indentations in the dirt road an inch or two deep. He wondered if he might be causing real damage with his mere steps as he saw a small wagon drawn by dogs go rustling by. It bumped in the slight ruts in the dirt.

"Just try not to touch anything," J'anda said.

They wended their way up a nearby hill. It was a very slight slope, but it carried them high enough that Cyrus could easily see Nyad waiting in the center of the square, a small crowd gathered around her, as though she were a statue for them to admire. "That doesn't look promising," Cyrus said.

"She knows the ways of the gnomes," J'anda said. "I'm sure she'll be fine."

They crested the hill, a small green grass field stretching forth below them. Cyrus caught sight of a normal-sized figure waiting below, a heavy cloak and cowl covering them from top of the head to the tip of their toes.

"Son of a—" He whipped his head around. "Did you bring me to a meeting with Malpravus?"

"No," J'anda said sharply. "Who do you take me for?"

Cyrus continued down the hill with the enchanter, studying the figure as he approached. Clouds swept by overhead, a stiff breeze blowing the stranger's cloak as they drew closer. Cyrus squinted, wondering why there was a strange elevation about the man's—he felt sure it was a man—shoulders within the cloak. Still, the figure stood somewhat sideways, providing little but a silhouette for him to go on.

There was a mighty tree, three times Cyrus's height at least, lingering overhead. As they drew under its boughs, J'anda's pace slowed. "I need a staff, I think," the enchanter said. "A walking stick.

Something." His breaths came with a little more labor than they should have given the leisurely pace, Cyrus thought.

"At least you can just teleport back," the cloaked figure said roughly, voice a low sound, familiar to Cyrus's ears. "Rather than walk back to town."

"I know you," Cyrus said, staring at the cloak. It dawned on him just before the cowl was swept back to reveal navy flesh and dark hair, with spiked pauldrons that stood tall on each shoulder. "You sonofa—"

"I wasn't exactly expecting a warm greeting from you," Terian Lepos said, his once-ubiquitous grin strangely absent. "But I hope you can at least put aside your anger for this meeting ... because we desperately need to talk."

Chapter 54

"Were you anticipating a blade to the face?" Cyrus asked, his hand hovering on Praelior's hilt. "I saw you fighting against us in the field at Livlosdald."

"Have you gone blind?" Terian asked. "Because I sat on my horse during that battle and never cast a spell nor drew my blade. So I find it curious you would have seen me fight against anyone."

"I know the two of you will need to sort through your warring emotions," J'anda said, "but I hope you do it swiftly so that I may be granted the grace to have the necessary conversation here before I die of old age."

"Why do I need to have a meeting with this traitorous filth?" Cyrus asked.

"Because maybe I can help you," Terian said archly, lips pursed in obvious disapproval.

"Help me … what?" Cyrus asked with a laugh. "Die? I'll call upon you if ever I want to go slowly and painfully."

"I could also do it swiftly and painlessly, if you'd like," Terian offered. "But that's not why I'm here."

"You cannot believe this man has any aid to give us," Cyrus said, whirling on J'anda. The wind tugged at the wisps of the enchanter's greyed hair, the once stark white faded with his aging. "He offers a blade hidden in his sleeve while he proffers a hand."

"He is placed to assist you," J'anda said, "in ways you don't even know. He is also favored of the Sovereign, and has the ear of Malpravus."

Cyrus turned to look at Terian, focusing his full attention on the dark knight. "And why would he help me?"

"Because on the day Alaric Garaunt died," Terian said hotly, "you weren't the only one that was left broken and mourning."

Cyrus felt a curious flush on his face. "Oh?"

"He may have called us 'brother,'" Terian said, voice shot through with wistfulness, "but you and I lost a hell of a lot more than a guildmate when that bridge collapsed."

Cyrus stood there in silence for a long pause, the wind whipping around the three of them, tree rustling in the autumn breeze. "What do you want, Terian?"

Terian's ire broke, and his face split in a mirthless smile that looked somehow haunted. "The son of a humble warrior leads one of the greatest armies in Arkaria. Oh, how the times do change."

"And have you changed?" Cyrus asked, still waiting.

"I have changed," Terian said without a trace of emotion. "But that's irrelevant. There are forces at work here, bending and shaping the world in ways I don't care for. There are things I have seen …" the dark knight shuddered, an impressive effect that rattled his armor, "… that make me fear for the future, should I live so long as to see it."

"You're in over your head." Cyrus spoke it aloud as soon as the realization hit him.

Terian's lips formed a tight smile. "With the very, very wrong people. In so deep, I fear to open my mouth to take a breath, to speak a word. I regularly stand in the presence of a god, take his orders, carry out his wishes. And I do it all with the Guildmaster of Goliath close at hand."

Cyrus stared at him coolly. "You should choose your friends with greater care."

Terian's eyes flashed, but his response came back calm. "I didn't have that many options to choose from."

"Sounds like poor decision making," Cyrus said, not even bothering to hide the slap.

"Perhaps," Terian allowed, barely a whisper. "But how I got here is completely irrelevant. I can help you."

"Why?" Cyrus asked with a burst of laughter at the absurdity of it all. "Why now? Why risk your life, which I know is precious to you? And to help me, whom you wanted to kill not so very long ago?"

"Because ..." Terian said, and the words spilled forth in a very practiced manner, as though he had repeated them often enough to hear them in his sleep, "'Redemption is a path you must walk every day.'"

Cyrus just stared at him. "That is possibly the most ludicrously simplistic bit of idiocy I've ever had mouthed to me. What addle-brained moron came up with that trite bit of nonsense?"

Terian let a low guffaw. "It was the previous holder of your august office."

Cyrus felt his skin cool a few degrees. "Alaric."

"None other," Terian said. "It was something he repeated to me before the bridge went down." The dark knight turned his head so that Cyrus saw him in profile. "He coupled it with the reminder that he still believed in me." Terian looked at Cyrus, dark eyes hidden in the shadows cast by the branches of the tree above, yet Cyrus could see the burning within them nonetheless. "I walked the wrong path. I followed the wrong people. It took a considerable distance for me to come to that conclusion with all certainty, but I am there now." He stared at Cyrus. "Now I offer you a choice—do you want to help me start walking back, or would you rather just watch me fall?"

Cyrus stared at the dark knight. "You once taught me the lesson of facing down that which you fear, even when you can't see it. Of fighting past the legends and rumors and bullshit and striking directly at a foe. But when the day came that you considered me your enemy, you did not afford me the courtesy of coming at me straight on. Why should I believe that you're facing me head on now?"

"Because," Terian said, and he sounded choked, "you are not my enemy."

"I killed your father," Cyrus said.

"Did you?" Terian asked, and there was something ghostly, a lightening of blue shade of his face, as though he had suddenly gone a bit pale. "I could only wish you had killed him."

Cyrus felt his brow furrow hard at that. "I stabbed him to death and left him to rot on the bridge in Termina, Terian."

"Of course you did," Terian said, his expression wavering. "But it doesn't matter anymore."

"You spent the better part of a year following behind me as a friend until you found occasion to betray and kill me," Cyrus said. "But now it's ... bygones? Water under the—"

"Fallen bridge, yes," Terian said, his face still curiously absent some emotion and dotted with the specter of another. "Deep water under a fallen bridge, I'd say."

"You told me it wasn't over between us," Cyrus said. "At the end of that very bridge."

"It's over now," Terian said, simply and definitively. "Unless you want to revive it."

Cyrus waited, trying to discern any hint of deceit. "That easy?"

"It may only have been a few months, but I've lived a lifetime of fear since that day," Terian said. "I have other things to concern myself with now. Much more frightening things than the new Guildmaster of Sanctuary."

"You dangle under the nose of the God of Darkness and want to betray him to me?" Cyrus asked. "To what purpose?"

"To the ultimate purpose," Terian said without hesitation. "I want the dark elves to lose this war. I want the Sovereign to leave Saekaj again, for good this time."

Cyrus watched him. "And you think I'm the means to that?"

"You're the only one who's beaten him," Terian said, and at this Cyrus caught a hint of displeasure. "If there were anyone else—the King of the Elves, the Council of Twelve—I'd be talking to them. But he's got them on the run. Reikonos reels under assault from our armies, and even now we make inroads into the east. The Elves cower across the Perda, watching the world of man burn. The Riverlands are weeks away from a determining battle." Terian raised his arms. "You are the only opposition. The pebble in his boot."

"A pebble in the boot is hardly fatal," Cyrus said.

"The scorpion in his boot, then," Terian said, and his facade broke. "Do you want my help or not?"

"What help do you offer?" Cyrus asked.

Terian lapsed into a sullen silence. "For now, there is little I can tell you."

Cyrus laughed. "I thought you were sitting at the right hand of the Sovereign."

Terian did not look amused. "I know much. But I can tell you little, for the same reason as J'anda." He gestured at the enchanter with a flip of the arm. "If you suddenly were to make your decisions in possession of tightly guarded information, my head would swiftly be separated from my body, and I would be of no more use to you."

"You're of little enough use right now that I'd scarcely notice the difference," Cyrus quipped. "Except as the aforementioned suicide aid."

"Give me time," Terian said, and his words carried a hint of pleading. "There are things happening now that will become widespread enough knowledge soon. I'll be able to tell you everything once that happens, without fear of reprisal."

"Or you could just … surrender yourself to my custody," Cyrus said with a shrug. "Give yourself up, return with me to Sanctuary. Then you could rat your guts out as loud as you wanted, squeal your secrets."

"And you would protect me?" Terian asked with a smile.

"Sure," Cyrus said. "You'd be safe enough in the dungeon."

"The dungeon," Terian said with a slow nod of acknowledgment and a faint smile to match. "Of course."

"That's more for my safety, I'll admit," Cyrus said. "But if you want to help—"

"It is not only my life at risk," Terian said. "There are others, people I care about, who I would not put in the way of harm."

Cyrus looked at J'anda. "And you? Do you share the secrets of which he speaks?"

"I do," the enchanter said with a nod. "And I keep them for the same reason—to prevent harm from falling on Terian's loved ones."

Cyrus felt a cool scorn blossom within. "I find it hard to believe you have anyone who loves you left at home."

"So do I," Terian whispered, "but apparently I do. Their lives matter to me."

"Then why not root for the Sovereign to win this war?" Cyrus asked. "Surely they'll be fine if he does—"

"No one will be fine if he wins," Terian said, hard as quartal. "Arkaria will drown in bones."

"You can't tell me anything that can help," Cyrus said. "I have to trust you until such time as you feel open to telling me what you say I need to know." He shook his head slowly. "Of all the truly stupid things I have done and been accused of, this vies for top prize."

"I can tell you one thing," Terian said, glancing at J'anda. "There is a spy very close to you. We think they're on the Council."

Cyrus looked from the dark knight to J'anda, who nodded. "A spy that is not me," J'anda said. "Obviously, I am a spy."

Cyrus felt his expression sour. "Obviously."

"The Sovereign knows much of the inner workings of Sanctuary," Terian said. "More than he should simply from J'anda's reports."

"He knows things *before* I report them," J'anda said. "His source is quite good; they have firsthand knowledge of your adventures in Luukessia."

Cyrus felt his mind blaze at that thought. "There were a thousand members of Sanctuary with us in Luukessia. Not counting the Luukessians."

"Whoever it is," Terian said, "they're probably on the Council. The things that Dagonath Shrawn knows about you, about our ways …" Terian shuddered. "If I were still within the walls, I would fear for my life."

Cyrus felt himself looking at Terian with smoky eyes. "Do you fear for mine?"

Terian took his time answering, and when he did, it caused a subtle chill to run down Cyrus's spine. "Yes. I fear for your life. Watch your back, Cyrus Davidon. In the name of the man who was father to us both … watch your damned back."

Chapter 55

The knock at the door sounded with all the authority of a thunderclap on the plains. Cyrus looked to the dull, wooden separation at the bottom of the tower stairs. He was still unused to his new quarters, though now his mighty bed rested in the middle of them. It was a curious thing, the open doors at each point of the compass, and in spite of his gloom he could still appreciate the delightful airiness that they brought; sweeping night wind, stars shining down from the sky, a moon somewhere overhead and out of his sight.

Cyrus sat at the table, staring down the steps toward the doors to his quarters, as though the door would simply open itself. "Come in," he said finally, resigned to the fact that the knock would doubtless come again in mere moments.

She slid in soundlessly, her leather armor failing to produce so much as a squeak; her boots whisper-quiet on the stones that composed the floor. She tilted her head, frost-white hair falling down on either side of the night-blue face like the moonlight shone down above her instead of somewhere outside. Aisling made her way up the stairs, taking it all in. "So … this is the Guildmaster's tower."

"Obviously the whole central tower is not mine," Cyrus said, feeling a swell of relief at the unanticipated diversion, "only the top floor. Though there does seem to be a rather thick layer of stone between me and my officers."

She looked sly as she came up the stairs to his level. "You did it."

"I was merely elected," Cyrus said, gauntlets pressed together in clenched fists. He held his hands together as though the tension between them could be worked out by a firm grip. He found little relief with this, though, and finally pulled them apart, placing his palms flat against the table. He could feel the sweat soaking the soft cloth that lined his armor. In spite of the breeze wafting through his quarters, Cyrus felt quite warm.

"You put yourself forward and allowed the guild to show you how much they love you," Aisling said, doing her slow, stalking walk toward him. He was keenly aware that it was part of the seduction; he had seen it enough times by now to know what it entailed.

"I don't think that it extends as far as 'love,'" Cyrus said. "Belief in my leadership, perhaps. A lack of good alternatives, maybe." He felt himself smile, but it was not heartfelt and it dried up as quickly as a discarded skin of water in the desert. "We need to talk."

"Do we?" She slid around him, her hand sliding up his arm. Even through the plate, it had some effect, like the wind had picked up and run goosepimples down his flesh. She paused behind him, and he kept himself facing straight ahead only with great effort. She leaned down and wrapped her arms around his chest. "Can we do it after?" Her warm, cinnamon breath rushed into his ear and he felt himself stiffen involuntarily. In more ways than one.

"We cannot," Cyrus said, standing abruptly. He realized a moment too late that had she been slightly less graceful, he would surely have caused his skull to collide with her chin. As it was, by the time he came around, she had dodged his sudden movement and rebounded back to him, catlike, sliding up against him with both hands wrapped around his neck. He felt her fingers run through his hair at the back, kneading the back of his neck in such a way that he felt his tension decrease by a significant margin immediately.

She tugged gently upon him, drawing his face down toward hers. "It can wait."

He felt his eyes begin to involuntarily close and through great effort he snapped them open and stopped his slow bend toward her lips. "No."

He watched her eyes flutter open, slitted pupils that gazed at him in violet wonder. "What?" she asked.

"I cannot do this any longer," Cyrus said.

"A tired refrain," she said and began to pull him to her again, "you'll feel differently after. You always do."

"I don't want to feel differently," Cyrus said, grasping her hands and pulling them off his back. Her eyes registered muted shock. "I don't want to keep using you to soothe my aches while imagining you're someone else." He turned his back on her, letting go of her arms. "You and I have done this dance for far too long, and I have been a fool and a weakling letting myself think that this could be more than it is." He looked to her. "I use you selfishly, and it has to stop."

"It doesn't have to stop unless I want it to stop," she said, her face composed in straight lines, devoid of emotion. "And I don't wish it to."

"You hold out hope for something that will never happen," Cyrus said. "My feelings for you are gratitude—for what you've done for me, for saving my life, for the guidance you've provided, and the thousand times you've been a balm. But no more than that."

"You don't know that it couldn't be more," she said, and now she looked a little like he'd slapped her. "You haven't given it time—"

"You've given it a year," Cyrus said, trying to keep his feelings at a distance, assessing them analytically, like a battlefield he was about to send his army upon. "Nothing has happened. In spite of the muddling of things, in spite of the desires of the flesh, the call of my heart has not changed since the day I first took my relief in you. I respect you, I find great comfort in your kindness—that much has changed. But I do not love you, Aisling." He said it with great pain, as though he were pulling a knife from his own heart as he said it. "I wish I could. But I do not."

She took it stoically. "You do not know what you are saying."

"I know what I am saying." Cyrus maintained the distance between them out of careful consideration. However much he wanted to reach out, to offer her support, he knew that this thought was folly that would lead him astray, back to the bed, to her arms, to her bosom, to all else. He imagined his feet rooted to the ground by invisible vines growing out of the stone, as if a druid had cast a spell on him. "It must be over."

"It can't be over," she said, emotionless.

"It is," Cyrus said, studying her face, looking her in the eyes. Her reserve was glacial, a wall of ice so thick it muted the purple of her eyes. "I am sorry, Aisling. I cannot keep doing this to you." He let out a reluctant breath, life rushing out of his body. "To us."

"You can do whatever you want to me," she said in that throaty whisper, the one she used when she tried to sway him. "For as long as you want. This is an offer that has no limits." She took a step toward him and he countered it, imagining vines pulling him away to maintain the distance between them.

"I have limits," Cyrus said, "and we have reached them in regards to my sense of responsibility. I feel as if I have been preying upon you, and it does neither of us justice. It shames us both."

"There is no shame in what we do," she said, and he caught the first hint of anger from her.

"There is shame for how I feel as we do what we do," Cyrus said. "I don't imagine you as we linger together. I close my eyes and—"

"Stop," she said, closing her own. "It doesn't matter."

"It matters to me."

Her gaze found him again. "Let her go."

"I cannot," Cyrus said. "I ... won't."

There was a calculation performed behind her eyes in that moment, something he had never seen from her before. She did not move for a long moment. "Are you certain?" she asked finally, a low whisper that carried not even a hint of seduction.

"I am," Cyrus said. "And I am truly sorry."

She glanced away, lips pursed, and when she moved, it was toward the stairs. "You need not feel sorry on my account." Her shoulders were straight, her walk as silent as ever as she stole down the steps.

"But I do anyhow," Cyrus said.

She paused at the door, turned to look back at him as he stared down at her. A flicker of emotion came over her, then another, and another. They passed in succession, each no more than a fragment, but each something that Cyrus had never seen from her before, and it stirred his curiosity. "Farewell," she said finally said and disappeared through the door without another word.

Cyrus watched the darkened door for a moment, pondering what he had seen. Unable to make any sense of it, he eventually retired to the balcony that looked to the south and stared out at the moonlit waters of the river Perda, running wide across the empty plains. He almost felt as though he were gliding across the water himself, running as weightless as if he had the Falcon's Essence upon him, free of some burden he had not even known he had carried.

Chapter 56

The light autumn fell upon the Plains of Perdamun with as gentle a touch as it always did, turning only the occasional tree red and yellow with its kiss. The bluster of a north wind settled in, blowing for weeks at a time. Cyrus did not count the days, nor did he try to track them at all, save for by the news that blew in as though carried by the winds. It always seemed to come out of the north as well, and sometimes with as much bitterness as the wintry gusts.

"Reikonos is under heavy siege," J'anda told Cyrus as they walked through the grounds. Cyrus had eschewed the Council Chamber on this occasion as the enchanter had promised things that were for his ears only, safely away from those who might be whispering them directly back to the Sovereign of Saekaj. It still made Cyrus uneasy, the thought of a traitor in their midst, but he was able to keep this malingering disquiet to himself. *Who else would I tell at this point?* he wondered to himself without amusement. "They have only a few miles before the dark elves will be at their gates," the enchanter went on.

"That bodes ill," Cyrus said. "The Big Three are unable to stem the advance?"

"Amarath's Raiders have pulled out of the city's defense completely," J'anda said tonelessly. "Burnt Offerings and Endeavor hold the line with only the aid of the Confederation's soldiers."

"Hells," Cyrus murmured. "It truly is an ill wind out of the north."

"Not the north," J'anda said. "Thanks to your defense of Livlosdald, the Northlands remain safe. The Riverlands, on the other hand …"

"That front goes ill as well?" Cyrus asked, his steps growing more uneven with each bit of news. "The Confederation has little in the way of glad tidings, then."

"It could be worse," J'anda said with a shrug. "The Confederation still controls several vital defense points on that front. All is not lost yet. And the siege of Reikonos could be a very long and costly one for the Sovereign, should he continue to gamble on that front."

"It seems like he's making sound bets," Cyrus said, "though I would love to know the origin of his seemingly endless font of troops."

"The truth will come out eventually," J'anda said, and Cyrus could see the discomfort even in the lines of the dark elf's face, wrinkles set upon with an unhappy expression. "Soon, I hope."

"Before this war is prematurely ended, I hope," Cyrus said.

"Terian also asked me to convey his hopes that we will be able to have a more thorough conversation within the next week," J'anda said.

"Lovely," Cyrus said, "I'm certain that will be a productive talk, since neither of you are able to truly discuss the secrets of the Sovereign."

"We are making preparations," J'anda said. "Details need to be attended to before we can make our move."

"A move you can't tell me anything about," Cyrus said.

J'anda looked only a little pained. "It is a tricky business, being a spy whose loyalties are supposedly in flux. I have maintained illusions for more minds at a time than almost any other enchanter in Arkaria. But the illusion I maintain now I do without the benefit of my skills, which are useless in building this particular facade."

"How do you do it, then?" Cyrus asked.

J'anda's expression slipped for just a moment, and Cyrus caught something from the dark elf he had never seen before; a cold, burning fury that almost made him want to take a step back. "I have motivation. Debts unpaid that need to be settled before my end."

Cyrus considered pulling on that small thread, seeing what else came out, but something in the very back of him told him not to. "I trust you."

The fury passed, replaced by the enchanter's usual, amiable mien. "As well you should."

They left it at that, the bluster chilling Cyrus enough that as soon as he'd seen J'anda disappear into the light of a return spell, he turned his course back onto the path around Sanctuary, headed to the front doors. He kept his cloak tight around him to ward against the chill but found it did little. It was a low agony, a slow, biting wind that nipped, stealing a little of his warmth at a time.

When he opened the door into the foyer and felt the warmth spread over him, it was like the relief of a bath after the aches of battle. He took in the breath of sweet smoke that wafted from the massive hearth to his right, running along the side of the room. The assembled guard standing encircled around the seal only gave the briefest of looks toward him as he shut the massive door behind him. He gave a nod of greeting and received several hundred in return.

"Ah, so there is a fool willing to brave the day's chill," Vara said from his left, emerging from the lounge with a leather-bound volume clenched in her silver gauntlet.

"If a fool's required, you always know where to find me," Cyrus said with a tight smile that was returned only a little. "How goes it, Lady Vara?"

She raised an eyebrow to him. "It goes, Lord Davidon. Have you any news to report?"

"Rumors, mostly," Cyrus said, with a twinge of guilt. Much as he wanted to immediately share what he'd heard from J'anda, he drew the circle tight around himself, allowing no drop of knowledge to spill out of it. "Have we heard anything from the Confederation of late?"

"Nothing substantial," Vara said, peering at him curiously. "My sister has been inconsistent with her updates of late. Have you heard anything?"

"Nothing of Endeavor," Cyrus said, suddenly mindful of the hundreds of eyes around them. "On a different subject, might you consider … joining me for dinner tonight?"

She frowned at him. "I eat dinner with you every night."

"Not in the Great Hall," Cyrus said, suddenly feeling a bit like he'd always imagined the teenagers in the Society felt when preparing to ask other members of their Blood Family to the occasional formal events. "In my quarters."

There was a batting of her lashes, but it came and left quickly, with no other sign of emotion. "I am afraid I must politely decline, Lord

Davidon." The formality of her reply made him think of the falling snow in the Realm of Life, blanketing hope with something cold and damp and lifeless.

"Of course," Cyrus said with a nod and started toward the stairs as she made a move to do the same. They both stopped, pained, and he gestured for her to go first. She hesitated, then finally moved to do so, circling around the garrison of soldiers in the center of the room.

Cyrus, for his part, watched her go without moving to follow, considering alternative courses he might take instead. His eyes went from the lounge to the doors of the Great Hall, anything to keep from a long, uncomfortable walk up the stairs following in Vara's close company.

"You look like a man in desperate need of somewhere to go." Andren's voice fell upon him from his left, and he watched the healer emerge from the front doors.

"I would honestly take a drink right now, willingly and gladly," Cyrus said.

Andren shook his head. "Can't."

Cyrus peered down at the clean-shaven elf, so different in bearing than the friend he'd known for so long. "Who the hell are you?"

"I would normally be the first to offer you a drink, and gladly," Andren said, a little too appeasingly for Cyrus's taste. "But we can't right now. A messenger came a few minutes ago, a herald if you will."

"Heralding what?" Cyrus asked with a frown. "The end of all dispensaries and ale consumption in the southern plains?"

"The imminent arrival of Pretnam Urides on urgent business," Andren said. "I'm sending word to the rest of the Council now. Says he needs to speak with us immediately."

Chapter 57

Cyrus waited in silence in the Council Chambers, head against the tall wooden backing of his seat, the rest of the Council silent around him. The doors to the outside balcony were propped wide, faint gusts stirring the hearth's fire every now and again. The smell of home was moderated by the fresh breeze, and Cyrus felt a tickle of anticipation as they waited in an unnatural silence, as though on a death watch.

"Someone say something." Ryin broke the room's silence, the only other noise the stirring of the doors in the breeze and the crackle of the fires.

"Humans can be bled for almost five hours before they die if you do it correctly," Vaste said.

Into the shocked silence that followed, Erith spoke. "How do you know this?"

"Terian told me," Vaste said, looking Cyrus right in the eye. It took him only a moment to realize that the troll was watching for a response, and Cyrus did his utmost not to give it to him. *How does he know?*

"Before or after he attempted to slay our Guildmaster?" Vara said, archly as ever.

"Long before," Vaste said. "Though I imagine he's had enough practice to have refined his technique since."

"You always know just the thing to say." Curatio was muted in his reply, wry as always in his observation.

The knock at the door was a welcome diversion for Cyrus, and he nearly fell over himself to speak. "Come in."

The door was opened for Pretnam Urides, who walked in with a little less swagger than he'd had last time, Cyrus thought. *I wouldn't have though it possible to see the man this … bloodless.* His usually chubby jowls looked thinner, and Cyrus had to concede that the head of the Council of Twelve had seen better days, weeks, months and years.

"I come to you with a proposal once more," Urides said without preamble.

"We'll just skip the greetings and ask how much gold is involved, then," Vaste said.

Urides looked at Vaste with his usual disdain. "Perhaps it might be best to spell out the duty involved before discussing the money."

"Oh, all right," Vaste said. "I suppose a good whore does at least provide some idea of the service involved before mentioning how much it will cost." Cyrus blanched at the comparison and found himself inadvertently looking at Vara when he recovered. She had an arched eyebrow just for him.

"Yes, well," Urides said. "Have you heard Deriviereville?"

"A town in the Riverlands," Cyrus said. "Nice place." He pictured it in his mind. "Not very defensible, though."

"It is just as well that we do not plan a defense there, then," Urides sniffed. "Deriviereville sits upon the Merone River, a key shipping lane and the first gateway to the Riverlands. Swampy roads control the approaches to the town; the only reasonable road runs under the eaves of a keep called Leaugarden some hundred miles to the southwest."

"I have been to Leaugarden," Curatio said. "It is eminently defensible."

"All right," Cyrus said, peering at the head of the Council of Twelve. "So why don't you defend it?"

"I will need to mass the soldiers currently holding Livlosdald in order to provide that relief," Urides said, a little nastily. "Our forces defending the road to Leaugarden are presently in retreat, harried by the full weight of the dark elven army."

"I don't know about the full weight," Cyrus said, a little slyly. "I heard they're throwing some reasonable tonnage at Reikonos."

"Did you?" Urides said, every syllable conjured of purest ice. "Then you understand why we are unable to provide relief to the Riverlands at the moment; the bulk of our army is doing all that is possible to keep our capital from falling under some considerable onslaught."

"When would we be able to expect relief at Leaugarden?" Cyrus asked.

"One week," Urides said, sounding unusually subdued.

Cyrus glanced at Curatio, waiting to gauge the Elder's reaction. He caught a nod, but a cautious one, before turning to Vara, who looked stonily neutral but nodded her head once as well. "We can do this thing," Cyrus said, eyes on Urides's thinning face, "but it will be costly."

"We are willing to offer two times what we paid you last time," Urides said. "Half up front, as before."

"Three times as much," Cyrus countered easily, "and three-quarters up front."

"That is highway robbery," Urides said with even more frost.

"Oddly, this is not the first time you've accused me of that," Cyrus said evenly, "but at least this time it has the virtue of being true, after a fashion."

Urides was unmoved. "It is an extortionate amount."

Cyrus leaned forward. "Let us speak plainly—I have little hope of collecting the full amount. Your capital is likely to be under total siege in the immediate future, which means you'll be cutting off all teleportation in and out in hopes of weathering the storm the dark elves are going to bring down around your ears."

"They cannot continue to pour troops into battles at the rate they have been losing them," Urides said, a little less firmly than Cyrus might have hoped. "Eventually they will reach their snapping point."

"I hope for your sake—and all of Arkaria's—that they do," Cyrus said. "But in case that day comes after they have had a chance to sack Reikonos and take all the gold from your vaults, I want my due now."

The Councilor's jaw wavered as he stood there. "Your proposition is accepted, simply because I have no other choice. Seven days, this is what you promise me?"

"Seven days," Cyrus said.

"Very well," Urides said. "Your gold will be here within the hour."

"That was awfully fast," Vaste said.

"He already had it prepared," Cyrus said, watching the Councilor carefully. "I did not bargain him up nearly so hard as he expected, all his protestations to the contrary."

Urides paused, eyes narrowing. "A decent sort might have done it for less."

"My decency is surprisingly restrained with people who have accused me of criminal action in the past," Cyrus said thinly, "no matter how noble I may find their aims. Also, I have mouths to feed."

Urides tipped his head to Cyrus ever so slightly. "Be that as it may, I will not forget this moment."

Cyrus raised an eyebrow. "That I came to your aid in your hour of need or that I asked for payment in exchange?"

Urides's expression cooled once more. "Perhaps both. Perhaps one more than the other, though which I decline to say." He raised a hand and disappeared in the light of a spell, the sparkling light of which remained in Cyrus's eyes, the shaded outline of a man standing between the seats of Odellan and Erith.

"That was certainly a quick decision," Ryin said.

"Once you've taken money to be a whore once," Vaste said, "it's so much easier upon subsequent engagements."

"You speak from personal experience, then," Vara said.

"If only," Vaste sighed longingly. "No, I'm afraid there's just not enough demand for my services; very few can handle this much manliness even once, let alone twice."

"Very few can handle the smell, I rather suspect—"

"We'll need scouts on the ground at Leaugarden," Cyrus said, interrupting the banter between the paladin and the healer. "Nyad. Take Forrestant with you, have him assess the field." Cyrus turned his gaze to Odellan. "Any idea if his new machines are in working order yet?"

Odellan's pained expression was obvious between the twin, flowing golden rivers of hair that framed his face. "Not all of them, no. But some."

"Get him to Leaugarden," Cyrus said to Nyad. "Once you've done that, teleport to Emerald Fields and have them send a messenger to Fortin that we'll be needing his assistance in glorious battle."

"Will it truly be glorious?" Nyad asked, skepticism obvious by the thin line of her lips.

"Gloriously brief if you don't get done what I've asked," Cyrus said, and she gave him a wary nod before disappearing out the door.

"Longwell?" He caught the gaze of the dragoon. "We will most assuredly need the cavalry for this."

"I shall prepare them," Longwell said, a look of rough satisfaction lighting his face.

"I will make ready with the army," Odellan said, "unless you have further orders?"

"I don't remember Leaugarden," Cyrus said, shaking his head. "I'm not sure I've passed through there."

"You're unlikely to forget it after this," Curatio said with a faint smile, "as it should be a rather well-known battlefield following this victory."

"I find it interesting that you assume we will win before we have so much as set the first foot upon the field," Vara said.

"I always assume we will win," Curatio said, drawing his robes about him as he stood. "I plan for defeat but try not to let it become much more than a weak suggestion." He gave Cyrus a nod. "I will assemble the healers and prepare them to do their duty." He breezed out the door with the aid of his robes, the white fabric catching the wind from the doors behind them. Andren, Erith, Vaste and Mendicant followed in his wake, with Longwell and Odellan out the door just after.

"Will I be left in charge of Sanctuary's defense in your absence?" Thad asked, rising from his place at the table.

"You're the duly-appointed castellan, Thad," Cyrus said with a smile. "You're always in charge of Sanctuary's defense. I think it would be wise to leave you here to do what you do better than anyone else, though, yes."

"As you will," Thad said, scooping up his helm and saluting. Cyrus returned it from a seated position and watched the red-armored warrior retreat from the room.

Cyrus did not look at Vara, instead turning to Ryin, who remained seated. "Any words of gloom or warning you'd care to sprinkle upon the occasion like water upon a flame?"

The druid's expression was dour, a flat, pensive gaze fixed on the empty air at the center of the round table. "I hope Curatio is right and that we win. I hope you are wrong and that Reikonos does not fall." He gathered his own robes about him and stood, looking glummer than Cyrus had ever seen him. "All else, I reserve my judgment on."

"That is … a decidedly more … quiet … opinion than you usually render," Cyrus said.

Ryin blinked at him. "I was raised in Reikonos as well, you know. I have no interest in seeing it overrun with dark elves. I may be here to provide a contrarian opinion, but what am I to say in this moment? If we do not do this thing at Leaugarden, the Confederation's food supplies will be cut off, Reikonos will starve and fall, and we will become the next convenient target of the Sovereign of Saekaj." He shrugged. "All roads lead to our facing the dark elves at this point; there is no more waiting it out and hoping for the best." He swept his robes behind him and the air felt curiously still. "The best we can hope for is to be the block upon which the Sovereign stumbles." He disappeared out the door.

"And what do you say, Lady Vara?" Cyrus asked, still watching the door as it closed behind Ryin Ayend.

"I say you should do what you do best," Vara said, standing and striding toward the door. "Pretend the Sovereign is a certain dark elven slattern, bend him over the nearest handy object, and fuck his unshapely arse into submission."

She did not look back, and left the door to the Council Chambers wide open as she left Cyrus in the silence, nothing but a gust of wind to stir him out of his stupor.

Chapter 58

Dark clouds hung over the field of Leaugarden, a hummock high on a swampy plain that dipped into the water at regular intervals. It looked a little like it had been transported out of the ground near Gren and plopped into the eastern Riverlands of Arkaria, the beating heart of the Human Confederation's farms and fields. From where he sat atop Windrider, the horse whinnying at the activity all around them, Cyrus could see one of the countless streams that crossed the land. It was a wet place, especially now, the skies threatening to turn loose a deluge at any moment. Cyrus could feel the droplets every now and again, first signs of what was surely coming.

"Grim day, grim deeds," Curatio said from his place in the line of officers. They were as ready as Cyrus assumed they could be, given the short time they'd had to prepare. The smell of the horses and the greenery mingled with the wet air in his nose, making him remember days long gone by when he'd felt soaked and chilled. *Not a good combination for battle, that's sure.*

"Let us hope our grim deeds include a number of beheadings," Vaste said. "I, for one, would like to see Malpravus's head on a pike, displayed for all to see."

"We don't do that," Cyrus said absently, stroking Windrider's neck and mane, garnering a whicker of approval.

"We should make an exception in this case," Vaste said. "I don't feel like I'll believe he's dead until his head is separated from his body and most of him is burned to ashes. Then, perhaps later, we can burn the head as well."

"That is truly disgusting," Nyad said, "and in violation of Sanctuary's charter on many levels."

"Tell me you wouldn't feel safer having that necromancer spread to the four winds," Vaste said, looking pointedly at the elven princess. Nyad did not respond for a long moment. "I'm waiting to hear the staunch denial, that you'd be okay with him lingering in a prison cell. Perhaps directly under your chambers?"

"I did not say we should leave him alive." Nyad was a little flushed, and she did not meet the troll's eyes. "I simply think that putting heads on pikes is barbaric."

"Lucky for us that our General is something of a barbarian, then," Vaste said.

Cyrus felt the frown come from annoyance and surprise. "How the hell did I get dragged into this?"

"I still haven't forgiven you for not telling me about your plans last time," Vaste said.

"I'm just hoping that we're up against a dark elven army only," Cyrus said. "After all, with what the Sovereign is trying around Reikonos, it feels like he'd need his magical talent working on that front. Maybe we'll have a nice, easy roll-over battle with nothing but a few angry trolls."

"Army on the horizon!" Ryin called from above.

"Are there trolls?" Vaste called.

"Some," Ryin returned. "Not as many as last time."

"Looks like you get at least some of your wish," Vaste said. "Happy now?"

I'll be happier once we're done with this, Cyrus did not say. "That's hardly a complete picture of the threat at hand," he said cautiously.

"The threat at hand is the annihilation of every bastion of free peoples in Arkaria," Vara said, weighing in at last. She was positioned directly next to Cyrus in the line, though she had yet to look at him. Her eyes were firmly fixed on the horizon, leaving Cyrus to wonder if she did, indeed, see anything there. "The complete picture is relevant only so far as strategy and tactics are concerned; we make our stand here or we damn everyone by our failure."

"Yes, let's not go damning anyone," Vaste said. "Least of all ourselves."

Vara shot him a careful look, sideways, without turning her head. "That was less joking and more concerned than you are usually capable of."

"Well, I've heard the stories of the damned which you all faced in Luukessia," Vaste said. "I don't care to become anything close to that." He seemed genuine, Cyrus thought, waiting, just waiting, for the jibe to follow. It did not.

"Let us all take a moment to recover from our shock in Vaste's staidness," Curatio said.

"Hey," Vaste said, "I can be serious, too. Like that time in the Realm of Life, for example."

"When the chipmunks went after your groin?" Cyrus deadpanned, staring ahead at a distant horizon that was partially blocked by trees. If there was an army there, they were down the road quite a ways.

"That was serious business," Vaste said without a trace of humor. "If they had impaired my functioning, why, I don't know what I'd do."

"Bitch and whine until you realize you don't actually use those parts?" Vara suggested.

"Admittedly I'm no Cyrus Davidon," Vaste said smugly, "but I'll have you know that they see use. Plenty of use."

"Again, he drags me into this," Cyrus said aloud, "as though I'm not even here."

"He makes a valid point," Vara said, "you are the exemplar of using those parts to ill purpose."

Cyrus made a noise of sheer frustration with his throat, a *tsking* sound that rattled the back of his tongue, driving up hints of the flavor of the eggs he'd had for breakfast. *Not lately*, he thought, trying to still his reaction. He did not give an answer aloud.

"I thought he ended it with Aisling?" Vaste asked.

"He did," Erith said. "Or so the rumor goes."

"She's quite dispirited," Nyad said, sounding a little gleeful about it. "She had to leave for a few days to get over it, I hear."

"I expect it would take more than a few days to get over the hero of Termina, wouldn't it?" This from Andren, who was peering down the line.

"You all are annoying me beyond my capacity to express it," Cyrus said under his breath.

"Take it out on the dark elves," Curatio suggested. "I heard he even summoned her to his quarters to do the thing right; messenger and all. Then delivered the axe blow—"

"Curatio!" Cyrus snapped, sending a fiery gaze at the healer. "You are over two hundred centuries old; this common, small-folk gossip cannot possibly still be interesting to you."

"Indeed, the follies of you short-lived people in your mad scrambles to bed everything that is not nailed down is the source of much amusement to me," Curatio said with a twinkle in his eye. "It helps while away the dull days as few things do."

"Perhaps we should spare the 'hero of Termina,'" Vara said acidly, "and discuss this after the battle, in a more appropriate locale, where the subject of your ferocious rumor-mongering is not around to be irritated by your insipidness."

"Thank you," Cyrus said cautiously. He waited for her to make another jab, but she did not. He lowered his voice so that only she could hear him. "You still run rather hot and cold on me, you know."

Vara let out a long, irritated sigh. "I am easily angered. You know this, and yet still you seem to put special effort into *making* me angry of late."

"I don't mean to," Cyrus said.

"I suspected it was unwitting," Vara said, "but that makes it no less irritating." She lost a note or two of anger, and her next reply came out much softer. "Still, I know what it feels like to have others talking about you incessantly behind your back. To have them do it in front of you as well, as though you were not even here—well, it's more than a bit of a plague upon decency."

"Thank you," Cyrus said. "And thank you for refraining from making any … choice comments … about my decision to end things with Aisling. I know it would have been easy to say something gleeful and unkind—"

"Such as?" Vara asked, and he noted the raised eyebrow. It was the only hint of any emotion she gave.

"I'm sure you can think of something uncharitable given half a chance," Cyrus said. "But thank you for not expressing it."

"General," Andren said from down the line, in a high, slightly gleeful murmur, "you have a visitor."

Cyrus turned his head to look in the direction Andren had indicated and found Aisling upon her horse, out of formation and approaching him from behind the lines. She was between the front rank of the army and the line of officers at the fore, her horse making a slow approach. "Gods," Cyrus said under his breath.

"Can I talk to you for a moment before the battle?" Aisling asked. She was hooded, the cowl not doing much to hide her face even in the grey light of the day. He could tell by looking at her that her heart was heavy. The usual light was gone from her eyes, the smooth slyness ever-present on her lips was missing, replaced by a weight of emotion that Cyrus felt from ten feet away.

"Can it wait?" Cyrus asked. "We're moments from the start of a battle."

She blinked, and he saw the greyness of the day reflected on her face. "Not really," she said, almost a whisper.

Cyrus cleared his throat. "All right. Can we make it quick?"

"Certainly," she said, and led her horse into a trot.

"Go on," Vara said quietly, "harken to the crack of your master's whip." Even as low as she spoke it, he could hear the amusement radiating from every word.

"There we go," Cyrus said, "gleeful and unkind all in one." He let out a thick sigh and started Windrider to moving, following Aisling out into the field before them.

She rode her horse into the field twenty feet, then fifty. Each step that carried them away from the lines of battle deepened Cyrus's discomfort. Still, he followed and brought Windrider to a halt when she stopped. She dismounted and he heard her feet make a slight slopping noise as her boots touched down on the muddy field.

Cyrus lingered on Windrider for a moment, staring down at her, clutching the reins of her animal, before making the decision to follow her lead. He dismounted, his boots hitting the soft ground with a sucking sound. It wasn't horribly wet, but he did sink into the soil a few centimeters. He pulled one of his boots free with a very subtle slurping noise and stepped closer to her. He looked her in the eyes, standing only a foot from her. "Well?" he asked.

"Have you reconsidered?" she asked, voice a ghostly hollow.

This is not good. "No," he said as gently as he could. "Aisling, it's over. Nothing is going to change my mind."

She turned her head slightly, and he saw her lips purse. He looked away from her face, not wanting to see her cry. "Okay," she whispered. "All right." She rustled, just slightly, as she moved toward him. He stood there, frozen, deeply uncomfortable. He felt her arms wrap around him as they had so many times, circling his breastplate, drawing him ever-so-slightly down to her. He felt his armor adjust as he slanted his body to comply with her desire, ready to put the halt to it should she try to kiss him. A final embrace was not so unwarranted, he thought.

Then her hand slipped up his backplate, under the chain mail, something cold finding its mark just to the side of his spine, and he started to react, his senses dulled by her presence, the comfort he usually experienced at her touch making him just a hair slow to answer her movement—

Then the chill of metal against flesh turned to the agony of fire slipping into his back, and he realized too late that she had a dagger in him, in his—

Every muscle seized and screamed, surged and cried out, and for a second he felt paralyzed, his knees barely able to still bear his weight. "I'm sorry," she whispered in his ear. "But once I told him I had lost your ear, he told me that I had to do this."

Cyrus pulled his head up to look her in the eyes. He could barely see them, hidden under her white hair. "Wh-who?"

She raised her head, ever so slightly. "The Sovereign, of course." She sounded dead, the iron in her voice every bit as cold as the steel she'd just slid into his back. "He's the one who told me to get close to you."

"Y-you," Cyrus said, feeling his head bob, his strength fade. "You were ..." He felt her holding him up, keeping him from falling to a knee. The pain was astounding, an agony in symphony, four parts, eight parts, more parts than he could count—

"I'm sorry," she said, "but you have no idea what he's like. What he can do. How he—and his servants—can compel cooperation." She did not smile, and her face was all regret. "There's a reason you never heard his name until now."

"They'll ... heal me, you know," Cyrus said, every word struggling to get out. He tried to fight back against her, to summon his strength to push her down, knock her over. He could not quite manage it, the shock at her betrayal still causing him to blink in astonishment. "I'm not ... finished."

"My blade was coated in black lace," she said quietly, still whispering in his ear. "If there was ever a man strong enough to survive, it would be you." She pulled it out, and somehow the pain increased, compounded, grew like it had little agony mites planted under his skin that spawned their own nest that was spreading all over him. "I hope you do. But your battle is over, I'm afraid, and that's what he wanted." Her face was a blank mask.

"You won't ... get away with this," Cyrus said. He could hear movement behind him, looked over his right shoulder—

Something exploded, a blast of fire that turned into a wall, an inferno ten feet high that descended like a falling curtain upon the officers of Sanctuary. It crackled and burned with all the fury of a dragon's breath turned loose, and Cyrus watched, helpless, his body overcome by the wracking pain, as his friends disappeared in the flames.

Chapter 59

Cyrus could see the dark elves on the horizon, the marching, orderly lines of battle coming from before him, and the storm of flames sweeping in a circular motion behind him, holding in place over the officer's line like a tornado of fire had descended from Enflaga's own hand to burrow its way into the wet ground beneath. From the Sanctuary lines came a rider in grey, hat slightly askew as she rode with her staff still pointed at the fire. Verity came forth from a stunned army that was in disarray, the wizard's work startling the horses that comprised the front ranks and quelling any immediate response.

"Surprised to see me?" she asked as she brought her horse around Cyrus in a neat circle. She stared down at him from higher than Aisling, a faint smile on the elf's lips.

"Serving the Sovereign?" Cyrus was wracked with pain, and the taste of blood was upon his lips. "Not the usual ... choice ... for an elf."

"But before I served him, I served one of his friends," she said, and her expression darkened as she stood off from him, whirling her staff so that the tip faced him dead on. "For Mortus," she said, and he could see the energy of her spell turn the crystal red as she cast.

A thunderous shock ran across the earth, causing Cyrus's legs to quiver, and he turned his head in time to see Verity thrown from her horse by a shockwave that rippled the air. Vara's horse was charging across the ground between them, the paladin herself with hand outstretched, the spell she'd heaved already landed for its full effect. Curatio sat upon the back of his horse, his hands raised, a dark expression upon his face, the air crackling with some undefined energy, and Cyrus saw nothing of the dilettante who had been gossiping about him only moments earlier. He was replaced with something that seethed with raw power, something drawn from the air and the ground, the fire that had surrounded him only a moment earlier, and it was as though his eyes glowed across the scorched black ground of the plain around him.

Verity hit the ground with a fearsome sound, her horse landing atop her. The violence of the impact was sudden but muted by a flash of cerulean that nearly blinded Cyrus. A ball of blue energy hovered before her and Aisling, and Cyrus watched numbly as the wizard grasped it, moaning as she did so. She disappeared into a flash of light that consumed her as well as her fallen horse.

Cyrus swept his gaze to Aisling, letting his hand fall to Praelior, finally, his instincts finally coming back to life after the stunning weight of pain and emotion had kept him on his knees and at her mercy for entirely too long. "I trusted you," he rasped.

"I'm sorry," she said, and he was left with the impression she truly was. She did not wait for his reply, however, snatching the ball of light out of the air and vanishing in the power of the spell.

"Cyrus!" Vara shouted as she was nearly upon him. The skies were dim, now, and his hand was upon the grip of his sword, sweating profusely within the lining of his gauntlet. The pain was still sharp, the taste of blood still present but slightly diminished. The hoofbeats of Vara's horse came to a halt feet from him, drawn to a sharp stop, raring to its hind legs. "Are you all right?"

"I'll be fine," Cyrus lied as he fumbled for Windrider's reins. He felt slow, diminished even with his hand on Praelior. He turned to look at Vara as he did so. "She tried to kill you all," he said dumbly.

"And what did she do to you?" Vara's voice whipsawed past him. "Because it looked as though she stabbed you in the back under your armor."

"She did," Cyrus said, keeping the pained expression off his face. "But that'll keep."

"Fool," she said mildly, her heart plainly not in the remonstration. She raised a hand and he saw the twinkle of spell-light. "Have Curatio heal you as well; mine do not carry nearly so much curative power as his."

"Okay," Cyrus said cautiously. His head already felt light. He put his loose left hand upon his flank and brought it forward; it was covered with dark liquid that shone against the black metal palm. His mind was strangely blank, and only one thought recurred: *I cannot lose this battle.*

"Are you coming?" Vara asked, still ahorse. She had the reins tight in her hands, staring down at him.

"Yes," he said. "Okay." Windrider snorted at him, whinnying loudly as he tried to place a foot in the stirrup and failed the first time with a grimace. The pain was manageable, he told himself. He landed his foot on the second try and hoisted himself up with a grunt that contained a scream only by the judicious application of his teeth to his lips. He made it, though, and swung himself over to balance atop the horse, who held incredibly still under the sway of his considerable weight.

"Hurry," Vara said as he slowly brought Windrider about, "unless you'd like to become fodder for the dark elven army's spiders."

"I'm hurrying," Cyrus said, spurring Windrider into a trot, every step of which hurt. The grey sky clung above him like a blanket, and made him crave a long sleep in which he could tuck himself under it. He could still taste the blood, but his mouth felt strangely dry.

He returned the to chaotic lines, reforming behind the Sanctuary officers. The ground was scorched and glassy, the wet, trodden grass completely burned away by Verity's spell. Cyrus stared at the line, neatly made, each officer standing where they were before the incident. Cyrus steadily guided Windrider back into place, easing into the line. "Are you quite alright?" he asked, looking down at each of them, their horses blurring together and forcing him to shake his head to clear it.

"We are fine," Curatio said seriously. There was a tightness to his expression that belied the fury Cyrus had seen radiate from the healer moments before. "In spite of a serious betrayal."

"Tell me about it," Cyrus said, and realized he had said it somewhat hoarsely.

"Are you quite well?" Curatio asked. "Do you require a healing spell?"

Cyrus waved him off. "Vara took care of it."

"Damnation," Andren said from his place a few horses down the line, "she bled you good."

"What's that?" Cyrus asking. He could feel himself sway atop the horse. Windrider whinnied loudly.

"You've bled all down the back of Windrider." Andren pointed at the flank of the horse. Cyrus tried to turn and nearly passed out from the pain.

"Nothing to be done for it now that I've had a healing spell," Cyrus said, stringing together the lie as best he could.

"They're coming," Longwell shouted from down the line. He hoisted his lance in the air, high enough for Cyrus to see it.

"Okay," Cyrus said, "remember this ... is a battle of maneuverability. From what we know, they're an ... infantry-based army." His head swam, and he could see the lines of the dark elves, blurry in the distance. It was as though the sun was shining directly in his eyes, without the glare. "We'll hammer them with cavalry when they close, break them up with a charge, then go about disassembling them once their ranks are broken and ... disorganized." He managed to get it all out, stringing together thoughts as though he were threading a piece of twine between trees in a forest.

He looked to his right; Vara peered at him with narrowed eyes. "You are not well."

"I'm as well as I'm gonna get," Cyrus said, putting on a wolfish grin that was all facade. "Is Forrestant ready to do his part?"

"He stands ready," Curatio said. "Perhaps you should stay out of the fray until you recapture yourself."

Cyrus started to argue and turned just a degree, far enough to feel a scream of pain that nearly caused him to lose his balance and topple. "Not a bad idea. Odellan," Cyrus caught the soldier's attention, "you'll lead the infantry into the field while Longwell moves with the cavalry."

"Aye," Odellan said, and Cyrus did not miss the odd tone in the elf's voice at his choice.

"Leading from behind is not exactly your usually stratagem," Andren said quietly.

"What is wrong with you?" Vara said, but it was not harsh; it almost sounded caring, warm concern stretched over urgency.

"I've just been stabbed in the back by someone I trusted," Cyrus said, waving his right hand lightly at her to dismiss her concerns. "Forgive me if I'm slightly rattled." He looked at her, and could tell she was not convinced. The first rank of dark elves was only a few hundred feet away now. "Ryin, signal for Forrestant to begin his bombardment."

"So ordered," Ryin said from his place in the air, and a barrage—roughly a third or less of what had been fielded at Livlosdald—broke overhead a moment later. The explosions rocked the battlefield just shy of the advancing enemy, which stopped just outside the first round of falling bombs. Cyrus blinked at the maneuver, the sudden stop of the army opposite them. It took him a moment to realize—

"That's Malpravus behind the first rank," Vara said, her eyes now thankfully shifted to the battle. Her voice hardened. "And Terian."

Terian. Cyrus's eyes blinked, watering, as he stared across the field of impending battle at the massive dark elven army. He felt as though he were too tall for the world, too tall for his horse, and he bobbed with Windrider underneath him. The horse moved to compensate, and he managed not to fall.

The dark elven army began to move again, to charge across the blackened field of battle, men in armor easily hurdling the small fires left behind after the explosion of the projectiles Forrestant's segment of the army had sent forth. They ran across the field in a mad hurry, and they seemed so very many to Cyrus, like they stretched beyond the horizon. He squinted, trying to focus his attention on them, trying to determine a count. *Isn't this usually easier?* He found himself unable to concentrate, the pain welling up and displacing every thought he attempted to form.

The second wave of projectiles launched overhead to mixed effect. It hit in pockets, wiping out segments of the charging army but failing to slow them. Body parts flew through the air with each impact, small craters left where each landed.

"It's not stopping them like last time," Vaste said from somewhere down the line. Cyrus did not turn to look.

"Ready the army," Odellan said, presumably to someone behind him.

"Perhaps you should head to the back of the lines," Vara said. It took Cyrus a moment to realize she was talking to him.

Cyrus still held his grip on Praelior, but he could feel his hand shake uncontrollably with even his light grip upon the hilt. "All right," he said. He looked down the fore of the charging army and could form just enough thought to realize that if he could barely remain ahorse, dismounting to fight would be an exceedingly poor idea. He turned Windrider and started the horse on a slow canter back to the nearest break in the lines that would lead him away from the fight.

"Cavalry, ready!" Cyrus could hear the shout, and turned his head to look. He could see the dark armor of Longwell on the left flank, lance held high. *They'll wait until the dark elves are good and exposed, until the snake is fully uncoiled.* Cyrus stopped his horse about two-thirds of the way back of the army's ranks, surveying the battle. He could feel eyes on him, watching him, wondering and questioning why he was not at the fore. For his part, he simply tried to keep drawing breath, which was becoming more and more of a challenge.

The clouds above were exceedingly dark, the wind whipping bitterly around him. He could smell fire on the air as well as taste the blood in his own mouth. The noise was chaotic, a cry, a roar, a hubbub that all blended together in a faint cacophony under the sound of wind or blood rushing in his ears; he could not tell which.

"Lord Davidon, are you all right?" a faint voice asked. Cyrus found he could not answer. He felt as though the beads of sweat that ran down his forehead were as big as his gauntlets. He felt both cold and hot at the same time.

He had a perfect view of the front rank of dark elves slamming into his forward army, and a stench washed over him that reminded him of death. They were clad in armor from head to toe, light armor that extended to leather masks and guards for every part of their body. It was a fearsome effect, he reflected, and was surprised he had not noted it until now. It gave them the look of lightly armored knights, churning up the field in their uniform appearance, an army sweeping in time toward his; the tide rushing in.

They hit his lines and there was chaos, immediate and certain. The dark elves broke through in places, crashing like waves on the rocks and slipping into every gap. He watched it as though it were happening in a fever dream, his people falling here and there even as they struck down dark elves. The bombardment added a chorus to the thing, low roars here and there, a drum pounding in the background.

Arrows flew. Had he noted them before? They shot from a formation of archers on the right flank to little effect, sprinkles of spices dropping through leaden air upon an army so thick that they did not seem to fell a single soldier. Cyrus watched the chaos hew closer to him, watched it as though it were unfolding miles away even as the dark elves slashed their way through the front ranks of the Army of Sanctuary.

Cyrus saw Curatio, still atop his horse, swinging his mace down upon unsuspecting enemies. One of the dark elven helms flew through the air as though it were a ball thrown by a strong arm. It made a low, lobbing arc and rolled into the left flank.

Cyrus looked up and saw the horses of his cavalry in motion. He imagined he could smell them, hear them champing and stamping, churning the wet Riverland sod as they made their charge. They came all in a spear, riding hard toward the body of the dark elven army. There went a ripple through that side of the dark elven formation, and he thought it curious.

Curious. Almost as if it had been preplanned. As if it indicated something.

Something important.

Cyrus found himself wanting to shout, but a hoarse whisper came out instead, deep and throaty, almost unrecognizable. "Stop the charge. Stop the ... charge." He coughed, a wracking spasm that almost caused him to fall from Windrider. He tasted the tang of blood upon his lips, wet and rolling down his chin, a warm slobber of his lifeblood.

The air grew still around him as the cavalry closed their distance on the dark elven army's right flank, the axe ready to fall upon the enemy. He watched it grow closer and closer, watched it fall home—

As the first of the horses hit that edge of the dark elven formation, he watched them fall as though their legs had been cut from underneath them, and every horse and rider that slashed their way into the depths of the dark elven army disappeared under the swords and axes and clubs of an enemy that stopped their charge as though it were nothing more than a child toddling into the midst of a bloodthirsty horde. In helpless horror he watched them fall, line after line, and he could not even raise his voice to make it stop.

Chapter 60

Cyrus watched the horses disappear in wave after wave, ripples radiating out from the right flank of the dark elven army as they sunk almost without sight under whatever assault the dark elves were making. He felt a panic rise within him and urged Windrider forward unthinking even as he realized his army was falling back in front of him. Chaos tinged the air, screams and cries of battle mingled in his ears. The dark elven horde was surging, the Army of Sanctuary was wavering; the failure of the charge of the cavalry ahead was at least obvious to most of their number from the slightly higher ground which they occupied.

Every step of the horse brought Cyrus stinging pain. He drew his blade and urged Windrider forward. There was a whicker that almost sounded like a denial, but the horse continued steadily on, up to the disintegrating front lines.

Dark elves saw him and started for him when he was but a hundred feet from the beginnings of the ever-expanding battle. The Sanctuary formations made a ripple of their own, warriors and rangers bowing out to precede him, to fight the seeping precursors to keep them away from their General and Guildmaster. Cyrus respected the gesture but said nothing; he could not muster any words.

He stopped the horse and slung over his right foot to dismount, keeping his torso from twisting to aggravate his wound. As he stepped down, the agony speared him again, nearly causing him to sink to his knees as he folded in half at the midsection. He recovered, though, and raised himself back to standing. He held Praelior in his hand and turned to face the advancing ranks of dark elves. Their dark armor, their faceless masks, they filled his view as far as his eye could discern.

He made ready for the onslaught coming. He swung his right arm experimentally; he managed several strong strokes without twisting his torso and making his wound do little more than murmur in pain. *This is manageable. I can do this.*

He took slow steps forward. Dark elves emerged from the increasingly swirling lines, throwing themselves at him. They were not as slowed by his sword's magical effect as they usually were, but they were slow enough. Praelior cut through them—and their armor—as though they were boots running over soft sod. He watched them fall into the mud, dark blood draining out on dark ground.

Cyrus heard a chorus of cheers from behind him; his army, watching their General take the field. The horde of the enemy was still swirling as far as his eye could see. There was not a single troll in view.

"What are you doing?" He heard Vara from his right and turned his head to look, turning it back just in time to slash through another small wave of dark elves. She was there in the fray, looking at him questioningly, silver armor slick with red—her own blood, or that of one of another member of Sanctuary.

"Fighting," Cyrus managed to say loud enough for her to hear. "Do we have a cessation spell out?"

"No," she said, "but the dead are not exactly rising."

"Good." Cyrus turned his attention to a dark elf that broke free of the line in front of him and slashed the beast's head off. "Then we'll be able to unleash some spells. We need to work our way out to the fallen cavalry."

"Are you barmy?" Vara shouted. "We're not even holding them back here, let alone in any position to start trying to drive them back!"

Cyrus blinked, taking three dark elves in turn, the last rushing him from the left and forcing him to turn slightly. It hurt, a knife of pain in his side that caused his sword stroke to miss slightly low. It still decapitated his foe, but it was not as clean as he would have preferred, an extra inch of shoulder taken off with all the extra effort that required.

Cyrus turned his eyes back toward the place where the cavalry had disappeared; long lines of them were still visible, halted in their charge and standing off at a distance from the battle. Cyrus thought that wise; whatever the dark elves had deployed—caltrops, probably, judging by the way the horses had fallen once they hit the line of battle—there was no attacking the dark elves on that side from horseback. Nor, he had to concede, was there room to maneuver over to the other flank, assuming the dark elves did not have caltrops ready to deploy on that side of their formation. *Which would be a poor assumption.*

Cyrus saw an empty circle in the far section of the dark elven army, a break in their charge, their forward surge. He could see something moving around within it, keeping them at bay. He watched a lance go skyward for a moment before sweeping in a circle, and he knew who was at work within their army. *Longwell. He's still alive. Gods be with him.*

"We need to turn the tide," Cyrus muttered. His sword was moving slowly but automatically; still, slow to him was fast to those without the weapon of a fallen god in their grasp, and he fended off every comer in his place just behind the front Sanctuary rank, slashing holes in any dark elf that dared to try and slip through to wreak havoc. The forward line was strong, healers keeping their charges hearty. The soldiers were covered in their own blood by this point, the flaws in their armor exposed and obvious by the bright red signs left behind, stains of wounds long since healed.

"You'll have a hell of a time with that!" Vara shouted. "This is a holding action, General, and we are barely holding."

Cyrus blinked. They were still coming, that constant horde, that forever and swarming army of the enemy. "Need to break them somehow." He looked out ahead. "Spells, maybe." He stared over the full battle, unfolding before him. *I'm the leader*, he thought. *I need to lead us through this.*

The way Alaric would have.

He felt a sound building in his throat, a cry of rage and pain that had little to do with his wound. He raised his sword high and put one foot before the other. He pushed his way through the line in front of him and waded into the enemy fray, whipping Praelior around. He sent heads and swords and arms hurtling away, clearing a circle with his swing. He swung again and again, slashing his way through the dark elven army as though they were some foul undergrowth, something that sprung up from the ground in the wretched Realm of Life gone wild. He contained his motion to avoid twisting himself but swept as wildly as he could, catching a dark elf that came low under his swipe with a boot that sent him twenty feet through the air in a low arc.

Enemies. Foes. The death of Arkaria if left unchecked. He swung and felt blood spatter across his face from the strength of his attacks. His armor was dripping with the signs of his fight, and he felt his lip curl with fury. *I cannot let them win. I cannot let us fail.* He thought of Vara's words, spoken before the battle, of how all Arkaria's fate rested on this battle, and he swung his blade unyielding, splitting armor and helm, sword and shield, driving back his foes.

The way Alaric did on the bridge.

His legs felt heavy but he pushed on. Every breath came as a struggle, every swing of his sword felt like he wielded a lead weight. Dark elves fell before him like wheat before the thresher and he watched them fall with little emotion. There was no joy, no feeling, just the bare will to push on through a fatigue that was threatening to wrap him up and carry him off. It was unlike anything he'd felt in battle before. The skies were darkening, and he wondered if sunset was at hand.

"Cyrus!" the shout came from far, far behind him. He turned his head to look back and saw that he had carved his path out of the lines a little too well; they were well behind him now, a small bulge in his army that had surged out to follow him was being chipped away, only three warriors in leather armor at his back now, the dark elves closing in. He watched two more fall in the space of seconds, and he was left with one at his back.

"What's your name?" Cyrus asked as the warrior placed their back to his. He kept his blade on its task automatically, slashing down the next wave of attackers before him.

"Grenene Eridas, sir." the voice was a little higher than he expected, and it took a moment for him to realize that behind the armor was a woman. She kept her sword hard at work, fending off three dark elves but failing to kill any of them. Her blade was plain, dark steel, the sword of a line warrior without anything mystical to it.

The same sword the chaff in front of me carries. Cyrus widened his arc of interest as much as he could, trying to cover her flanks as well as his own, but he faltered on his left. His killing strokes turned more defensive. "We need to work our way back to the line, Grenene. I need you to begin walking back while I cover you, all right?"

He heard a choked sound and turned to see her holding her throat, blood slivering down over a leather gorget. He watched four different blades pierce her chest piece, the overzealous enemy finishing her before his eyes, and he swung 'round in a wide sweep that not only killed three of the four of them but neatly cut the remains of Grenene Eridas in half in the process. He would have perhaps felt regret had she not already been truly dead, with her killers already moving into position to finish him.

Cyrus felt the first blade sink into him at the knee, piercing the chain mail between the joints of his armor. It was a sting, an asp laying a single tooth into him, but it made him jerk away in response, twisting his back and torso in reply.

The fiery tendrils of pain did not hesitate, screaming through his back and dropping him as though the blade had run all the way through his leg and out the other side. He lashed out blindly and had the satisfaction of seeing his attacker catch a sword across the mask; it split the leather and he caught sight of blue flesh flushed the color of sky, with white eyes as blind as an old human beggar's meeting his from beneath the remains of the mask. Teeth showed in a terrible rictus, lips cut wide open in some sort of horrible scarring that exposed tooth and jaw. For a moment, Cyrus wondered if he had punched his blade through and opened up the dark elf's face, but he had no time to wonder at it because the enemy attacked again.

Cyrus felt this attack at his hip, a sword driven low, breaking the chainmail and causing him to fold left. This drew a scream of pain, another flail of defense, and he took the leg from his attacker. His foe dropped to the ground, light blue flesh with white bone beneath. Cyrus imagined he saw maggots crawling out of the earth to devour his enemy, and he felt his breaths draw low.

Is this it? he wondered. The world slowed around him, as though dipped in water. He felt it around his ears, the feeling of being drowned again, submerged, fighting against a current too strong for him by half. The pain was a constant, it was there and yet distant, as though it stretched from him out unto the whole world. It encompassed all, the pain, and there on his knees there was no escaping it, no matter how many times he railed against it with sword and armor.

Death comes for us all.

Just like it came for Alaric.

Cyrus stared at the endless hordes of dark elves before him. He could distantly remember Vara's prophecy about the fall of Arkaria, could almost see it happening. He felt aware of the world, of everything. There was a single blade of grass in the burned and upturned dirt of the battlefield, and it looked like a sword planted in the soil. He wondered if it would grow more blades, blades enough to impale his enemies upon.

They were all around him now, moving like they were underwater, hampered by the flow of the currents against them. *This is the end*, he thought, and it was well that it was. His hand grew heavy on the hilt of his sword, and he wondered how much longer he could hold to it.

A single dark elf broke from the crowd surrounding him, deep blue armor spiked upon every surface. It was fitting, Cyrus thought, that death should come in this form, for the dark knight did look more like death than almost anyone Cyrus had ever seen.

"Terian," he whispered, and looked upon the dark elf's face, grim, his helm's faceplate up so that he could look Cyrus in the eye.

"Cyrus," Terian said, and he hefted the axe—didn't he have a red sword, Cyrus wondered?—high above his head. It was a blued steel and looked fearsome to Cyrus's eyes, the weapon that would surely kill him.

Cyrus watched as it descended and could not seem to do so much as lift his sword to see it stopped. It came fast, like—

Chapter 61

"Today, Terian?" Cyrus managed to get out as the axe fell.

The axe stopped mid-descent, whipping sideways with a shocking speed, splitting the head from an unwitting dark elven soldier as Terian whirled into a spinning attack. "Gods damn you, Cyrus Davidon!" he said, whirling into his own formation with a speed that made Cyrus's eyes struggle to keep up. "No, not today."

"I'm not sure ... there'll be another," Cyrus managed to get out. His head was woozy, spinning, and the pain—

Oh, the pain.

The dark knight spun, countering attacks and splitting limbs from bodies with stunning alacrity. "Why did you have to get yourself beaten in battle for the first time ever today, of all days?"

"Aisling ..." Cyrus said, trying to struggle back to his feet. He could see the dark elves surging in around him and whipped his blade around, a sword clanging off his back armor with enough force to send a shock of pain through him. "She ... got me."

"She was the spy," Terian said as he swept low with his weapon, chopping several foes off at the knees. "Son of a bitch. I should have seen it."

"She was the ... traitor," Cyrus said. His lids were heavy, and he coughed, drawing more pain, blood bubbling down his chin. He tried to rise but failed. A heavy thud hit the earth behind him. He could not turn to see his death coming.

"You bloody fool," Vara's voice split the air around him. "What did she do to you?"

He could see her, armor glinting, moving behind him, but he could not turn. Cyrus had a palm down against the earth, sinking in, trying to hold himself upright but losing the battle. "Knife ... black lace." He coughed harder and watched dark strings of liquid splatter on the ground, crimson highlights on the blood-stained soil. "You can say ... you told me so ... both of you." He looked up to see Terian driving his axe through the helm of a dark elf, exposing a bloodless skull that grinned at him.

"I told you so," Vara and Terian chorused. Cyrus caught the shared look between the two of them, the fury on Vara's end and amusement twisting Terian's lips in the gap of his helm. They did not pause for more than a half-second; they moved again in a whirl.

"We're going to get overwhelmed," Terian said, calling over the clangor of battle. "Cyrus, on your feet!"

Cyrus tried to rise and failed. "Can't." He looked at Terian and coughed again. His mouth was all blood. "Just ... go."

"Idiot," Vara said.

"He is rather a dunce, isn't he?" Terian followed. "Any chance of help?"

Vara paused. "Perhaps some," she said, and then Cyrus heard the thunder, felt the shake of the ground through his palm and knees.

He turned his head and saw the wrath coming. It was as though a battering ram were slewing its way from the Sanctuary lines on his right, carving a path unchallenged through the dark elves as cleanly as if an elephant were leading the charge. It was no elephant, though, he knew as he saw the red eyes, and it stopped only inches from him, the near-purple blood of dark elves smeared across the craggy, rock-hewn legs.

"Fortin, get him out of here," Vara said crisply. "He's been poisoned by that dark elven slattern."

"Poison is a coward's weapon," Fortin pronounced and brought a hand down upon a charging dark elf so hard that it crushed his head and upper torso as though it were a melon. "I should like to show these cowards what I think of them."

Cyrus started to reply to that, but he saw movement against the ground. A dark elven body was lying there, where Terian had chopped its head cleanly off. It stirred, hands moving in some sort of bizarre puppetry. It rose to its knees, then to its feet, a weapon still clutched in its hands. Another rose beside it, a torso cloven in half, ribs exposed. Cyrus could see others rising, a few corpses here and there, sprinkled throughout the field of battle, and it made him feel oddly colder than he had even a moment before.

"Shit," Terian said. "We need to get out of here."

"Get the General behind the lines," Vara ordered, and Cyrus felt a strong, rocky hand lift him from the ground, cradling him under an arm. It was an odd perspective, and he had a firsthand view of Fortin's other hand smash one of the rising dead into pieces with a backhanded thrust. It looked like he'd thrown a clod of dirt that disintegrated into smaller pieces midair, and Cyrus watched them in awe. "We need to pull in tighter."

"You don't understand," Terian said, "you need to withdraw the Sanctuary Army now. You cannot handle the numbers Malpravus has without a strong front line and a more organized spell caster front. You—we've already lost."

"A convenient thing for someone in the opposing army to say," Vara snapped at him.

"It is," Terian agreed, "but no less true. Have you not noticed what you've been facing all along? Have you not seen what is hidden behind the armor of the dark elven troops?"

"Dark elves," Fortin said, and a swipe of his hand wiped out a line of advance.

"Dead dark elves," Terian said, smashing a few opponents of his own. "And not the sort Malpravus is raising now, either. You face a limitless army of the dead, raised from every soldier the dark elves have lost in battle whose corpses they were able to recover."

Cyrus's eyes flitted back to Vara, whom he could now see from his perspective under Fortin's arm. She swung her sword, clean and smooth, lightly taking the mask from a dark elf without killing him. The leather fell away to reveal that same light-blue skin, strangely bloodless, a deep rot already set in upon the cheek, maggots festering in a wound and running down the face—

With horror she struck its head, then turned her blade on the next one in line, impaling it through its mask. She threw it off and the mask remained on her weapon until she flung it down. The dark elf fell to a knee, gaping wound in its cheek from where she'd struck it, but it did not bleed. Instead a cascade of white maggots ran out of the wound where the blood should have been, the white eyes as lifeless as any corpse Cyrus had ever seen, but more focused. The dark elf started to rise, and she ended it with a decapitation.

Cyrus watched as the horror hit home for her, ran across her face and the battle fury deteriorated. He saw her gaze quickly at the horizon, trying to count. "Retreat," she whispered then said it louder. "RETREAT!"

"This battle is not lost," Cyrus said, but he could barely hear his own voice. There were many of them, that much he could see. The world was darkening, though, darkening with dark elves.

"RETREAT!" The call was taken up, and Cyrus felt Fortin spring into motion, sprinting back toward a line of Sanctuary's army in the distance. He caught sight of Terian following behind, swinging his axe and giving a solid run for his efforts.

"No …" It was only a whisper, but Cyrus managed it. It was a sound of drifting words in the chaos of the storm. He saw bodies on the ground as the rock giant ran him past. Sanctuary bodies. Corpses of his people, fallen in battle, some still speaking, whispering into the storm at him with bloody lips as he flew by overhead, born of a strength that was not his own.

Cyrus thought of the fallen cavalry somewhere out there, of Longwell's spear making its way through the army, and he wondered where it—he—was now. How many had died?

The pain was a seeping darkness of its own. The skies had turned black, and Cyrus felt every jolting step the rock giant took. He had only the presence of mind to take Praelior, still faintly clutched in his fingers, and thrust it back into his scabbard. His fingers lingered on the hilt for a moment more, feeling the symbolism of what he'd just done.

I just surrendered. Gave up the battle.
Alaric would never have done this.

He took his fingers off the hilt as he saw a light flash before him. It was a warm, green glow, like sunlight on summer grass, and it offset the chill he felt spreading from his fingers. He embraced it, hoping it would lead him somewhere better—home, perhaps—as he drifted into the dark as the light faded around him.

Chapter 62

He awoke in pain, the sort that had followed him through his dreams and nightmares to bring him back to this place. White curtains wafted in sunlight, a gentle breeze swelled around him, and Cyrus could feel a slight chill around his shoulders even though his body was warm. He came back to himself in light, a powerful light that made him wonder if he was in the middle of a sunlit day. The smell of home, of a hearth burning, was heavy in the air. When he opened his eyes he could see beams of wood running out of a central radius. It looked familiar, like he'd seen it before, and he realized he was in his quarters atop the central tower of Sanctuary.

"Welcome back to us," came Curatio's voice from his bedside. He turned to look and felt the pain in his back as he did so. Cyrus gritted his teeth together; his head felt clear save for the searing spikes of anguish that his motion had triggered. He turned his eyes instead to find the healer seated by his bedside. "It would be best if you did not move just yet. I consulted with our friend Arydni in treating your wound—which I was unable to fully heal even after spreading rotweed into it, since the time had nearly passed before I could address it." He leaned forward on his chair, eyes hard. "What you did was incredibly foolish. You nearly died."

"I was … trying to lead," Cyrus said, but it came out as a whisper. He coughed lightly, and Curatio brought a skin of water to his lips, drops of refreshment running into his dry mouth like life returning to a desert parched by heat.

"I cannot fault you for your intentions," Curatio said once he had withdrawn the skin. Cyrus watched hungrily as drops of water ran down the dried bladder, catching the sunlight coming in from the open balconies. "Obviously, the Sovereign has been planning a rather comprehensive response to deal with us, something a bit more treacherous than we were expecting."

"Then we lost?" Cyrus asked, watching the healer as he turned to set the bladder down.

"Completely," Curatio said, turning back to look at him, not one ounce of hesitancy. "We lost thousands unresurrected in the retreat, mostly our front-line warriors and rangers, as well as several hundred cavalry and their soldiers."

"Longwell?" Cyrus asked, coming up with the only name he could think of.

Curatio smiled faintly but only for a second. "He made it back to our lines before the escape. We are unlikely to get a full tally of the dead, and it is entirely possible that some still living were left behind in the retreat. Though you would not ask, Martaina managed to save your horse from being left behind."

Cyrus frowned. He had forgotten about Windrider completely. "A curious decision, fighting to spare my horse. Was she not in the battle on the right flank with the other archers?"

"Apparently she crossed the lines," Curatio said without expression. His white robes nearly glowed in the sunlight. "She saw you fall and was fighting her way over to help. She was unable to reach you in time and thus rendered what service she could. She covered the retreat until the last possible second, firing arrow after arrow into that ..." Curatio's voice fell and his lips pursed, "... that godsdamned undead army."

"What happened there, Curatio?" Cyrus asked, squinting at the healer. "How could have they have managed to raise their dead?" He waited for a response, but the healer's lips remained firmly pressed together. "Those soldiers weren't freshly resurrected; some of them had been dead for weeks or months—"

"Have you ever heard of a soul ruby?" Curatio asked, and Cyrus caught a hint of weariness at the corners of his eyes.

Cyrus felt a sick sense of nausea descend upon his belly, twisting it. "Yes."

"This is the product of that dark magic," Curatio said, staring straight ahead. A cloud crossed the sun and a shade fell upon them as the breeze stirred the hangings once more. "A soul ruby applied to a dead body produces a creature between death and life; all the skill and memory and ability of the deceased, but with a will that is easily subverted." Curatio was stiff in his seat. "Easily bent to the control of one who is master of the dead."

"Malpravus," Cyrus said.

"A general for the dead," Curatio agreed. "There are others, of course, necromancers who can command just such a legion. But such a legion has never been seen before, because soul rubies are impossible to produce without the sacrifice of another's soul. The power inherent in that essence allows a spell caster such as Malpravus to fuel such powerful, dark magic."

"How did they come up with so many soul rubies?" Cyrus asked, staring at the dark ceiling beams overhead. They looked like a masterwork of carved wood, impressively done, smooth and glossy, varnished to gleam in even the reflections of sunlight that were hitting them. "Who did they sacrifice?"

"Every soul in Aloakna, perhaps?" Curatio shook his head. "I do not know. It would be a ridiculous task, raising an army of that size. No one with any decency would do such a thing."

"Which is why Malpravus and Yartraak are directly involved," Cyrus said. "How did you know about all of this?"

"Terian told the Council the same story that he gave to you and Vara upon the field of Leaugarden," Curatio said, once again impassive. Cyrus looked in his eyes, but could derive no sense of the healer's feelings about the dark knight. "Once he had said his part, I was able to fill in a few of the things he did not know through my own rather considerable knowledge." He sighed. "Though it is knowledge I wish I did not have."

Cyrus looked past him, out over the plains. He could see green grass in the distance, stretching out the north, uninterrupted. "How do we even fight something like that?"

Curatio's silence was rather damning in and of itself. "The Council conferred while you were invalided and came to the determination to do nothing immediately save for close the portal both here and at Emerald Fields. Those orders have already been carried out." Cyrus started to sit up in bed, but Curatio stopped him with a heavy hand upon his chest. "We still have constant communication between the two places; two spell casters, with their return spells linked both there and here, carry messages back and forth as needed. They are fine there, and we are fine here. The Sovereign has ... other concerns at the moment." The menacing way he said it made Cyrus shiver slightly.

"And the rest of Arkaria?" Cyrus asked. "What of them?"

Curatio turned his head to look away from Cyrus. "Our failure at Leaugarden has resulted in a rather spectacular forward attack of the dark elven army upon the Riverlands." He made a sipping sound with his tongue. "Their crops are being spared, but little else is."

Cyrus felt a desire to smash something, to slap something, and tensed his back. A wave of pain crested and ran over him, tearing a grunt out of his throat. "Son of a bitch."

"The Sovereign is son of no one," Curatio said wryly. "You should rest. In the coming days we can confer about this; there is little to be done now, though." He stood and gestured to the balcony doors with a hand. They closed slowly with a click.

Cyrus looked at him in surprise. "What magic is that?"

"Not the same as that used on the field of Leaugarden, that much is sure," Curatio said, more than a little dour. He started down the stairs and Cyrus heard his footsteps halt. "Hope is not lost, you know."

Cyrus could not see the healer, but he could sense his presence. "Sanctuary just watched their General and Guildmaster brought low just before the dark elves fielded a seemingly unstoppable army that beat us with tactics I would have found hard to counter even if I'd been able to command the battle." Cyrus stared at the swirls in the wood beams above him. "We may not be hopeless, but our hope has certainly been dealt a rough blow, Curatio."

There was a moment of silence, and then Cyrus heard the feet upon the stairs again, followed by the whisper of hinges opening a door. "And yet it remains, so long as the Guildmaster says it does and acts as though it does. Remember that." The door closed.

Cyrus lay there, staring at the ceiling. It only came to him later that Curatio had said something that had sounded almost as if it had come directly from Alaric.

Chapter 63

"I've scraped more lively looking turds off my boot," Terian said, staring down at Cyrus with Vara standing watch over the dark knight. Two other guards stood nearby as well, both paladins; all three were watching the dark elf with a level of scrutiny and suspicion Cyrus had rarely seen outside of the Reikonos market when the suspected pederast wandered past.

"Thanks to you, I'm alive to be scraped," Cyrus said. He was still flat on his back a week after awakening. Two of the balconies were sealed at the head and foot of his bed due to a heavy crosswind this morning, but the breath of the autumn day still made it through the room in spite of the best efforts of the hearth to keep the chill out.

"I'm just sorry I couldn't tell you who the traitor was before she nearly gutted you from behind," Terian said, rattling the chains wrapped around his wrists.

"That's all right," Cyrus said, and cast a look at Vara, who was staring at Terian impassively. "I ignored the warnings of the only person who did." She gave him little other than a prim look that held no emotion. "You mentioned when last we met that you had people in Saekaj that needed assistance ..."

"I had them moved out before the battle," Terian said. "Saekaj was turning into a prison camp; I couldn't wait any longer to act on it."

"Is not Saekaj always a prison camp?" Vara said with a healthy dose of sarcasm.

"Not Saekaj, no," Terian said seriously. "Sovar, yes. Sovar is where the underclass live; Saekaj is where the wealthy are. Even they are currently feeling the squeeze of the Sovereign's war. Travel restrictions, diversion of crop land formerly devoted to luxury foods such as corn turned to wheat for the army instead, the expensive threads and imports market drying up completely ..." He smiled viciously. "Yes, the wealthy are feeling the pinch of war this time, and the griping that's following is so loud I wouldn't be surprised if even the Sovereign can't ignore it."

"He's the Sovereign," Cyrus said, "and the God of Darkness. Does it matter how much people complain to him?"

"Oh, they wouldn't have the balls to complain to him," Terian said, "because that's a sure path to losing those balls. Yartraak may be many things, but merciful is rarely one of them."

"'Rarely'?" Vara asked, eyes jaded. "I am surprised if he is capable of so petty a thing as mercy; it seems beneath him."

"He's capable of it," Terian said, almost impassive, his chains and manacles a dark steel against his even darker skin. He wore faded cotton clothes, clean but weathered, something that looked like it had been in a trunk for a long stay. "He's capable of many things, as well you now know."

"How's he doing it?" Cyrus asked.

Terian turned to look at Cyrus out of the corner of his eye. "Powering his army? That is an excellent question, one to which J'anda and I have been searching for an answer without much success."

"So you were not exactly deep in the enemy's confidence, then," Vara said.

Terian's eyes lit fire, catching the morning sun. "Oh, no, we both were firmly ensconced in his inner circle, which should give you some idea of exactly how secret this must be."

Vara stared flatly at the dark knight. "I find it hard to believe that the Sovereign is foolish enough to trust two men who have essentially betrayed him before with his deepest secrets." Her hand was on her sword hilt the entire time, Cyrus realized, but she emphasized this by sliding it slightly out of the scabbard, exposing an inch or two of blade before letting it click back into place. "At least, not without some assurance of their loyalty."

Terian's face was covered in a dark grin that Cyrus saw no humor in; he wondered if the dark knight felt any. Somehow he doubted it. "We provided assurances, trust me. We both left Saekaj in the past under ... unpleasant circumstances, but were at best considered to have committed affronts against the Sovereign—personal betrayals, not treason." He shuddered slightly, holding his wrists together. "There is no going back from treason."

"Which is why you are quite content to sit in our dungeon," Vara said.

"Which is why I'm positively overjoyed to sit in your dungeon for now," Terian said. "I won't be quite so enthused on the day that the Sovereign finishes his business with the Confederation, because he'll be turning all his attention to you before he mounts an invasion of the Elven Kingdom."

"And he'll just leave the dwarves, the goblins, the gnomes, the desert men and the bandit lands at his back?" Cyrus asked.

Terian made a scoffing noise. "Do you realize what he has at his disposal? An insanely difficult to kill army—because they're already dead—that he can regenerate at will. They're fearless, they're skilled, and every dead body left on the field against him becomes fodder for him to replace the few in every battle that are fallen to so many pieces he can't stitch them back together again." He shook his head as though he were in disbelief. "Do you know what this means to the war? It's over, unless you can find some way to stop him. You might as well take the portal right to the Ashen Wastelands and start hiking south in hopes of finding something past the dragons, or get on a ship and brave the Torrid Sea, because as of right now, he will conquer Arkaria. It is destiny, unavoidable."

"Unless someone stands against him," Vara said.

"No one's standing against him," Terian said, looking darkness at her. "No one can. Toe to toe, he destroys every army because he had a bigger one starting out and it's only growing—save for that time you cost him nearly a hundred thousand soldiers and burned the bodies afterward."

"That's why he's been sending envoys to retrieve the dead," Cyrus said.

"Yes," Terian said, "and kindhearted idiots that you all are, everyone's been giving them back to him rather than destroying them the way he would have done for any of you."

"This is a new thing, then," Cyrus said, chewing his lower lip.

Terian paused. "What?"

"It's new," Cyrus said. "Them asking for the bodies back. They didn't send an envoy after the battle of Sanctuary. They sent their first after Livlosdald. They didn't even do it after we kicked them out of Prehorta."

"And so?" Terian asked, eyes wide, pulling his hands apart as far as the chain keeping him bound would allow.

"What changed?" Cyrus asked.

"What do you mean, 'what changed'? You're getting your asses kicked!" Terian said.

"Why was he suddenly able to do this only a few months ago?" Vara asked slowly.

"Get Curatio," Cyrus said to one of the guards. The guard resisted, holding his position until he caught a nod from Vara, then stormed down the steps at a run.

"I guess this is my opportunity to escape," Terian said with exaggerated humor.

"Try it and I will send you out of the tower on a blast of air without more than a thought," Vara said.

"All right, then, I guess I'll stay here," Terian said. "Not like I have anywhere else to go."

They waited in silence, until finally there was noise of footfalls upon the stairs and Curatio appeared at the side of the bed, his white robes looking slightly dirtied. "You know, I do occasionally have other duties to attend to besides—"

"Could Yartraak be powering his army by soul rubies ripped out of one soul over and over?" Cyrus asked without preamble, cutting him off.

Curatio's frown was instant. "You do understand that a soul ruby is produced when the subject of the soul sacrifice dies, yes?"

"What if they couldn't die?" Vara asked.

"Everyone dies," Curatio said, clearly a little put out.

"You haven't," Cyrus said.

Curatio sighed. "Every mortal dies, then." His expression changed, mouth falling slightly open. "Oh." His eyes darted backward and forward quickly, calculating the possibility. "Yes. Yes, that would—oh, you soulless bastard—"

"He did it," Cyrus said, shaking his head. He caught the stricken look from Vara, the cold flush of white up and down her neck, followed by the red mottling that always appeared when she was in a fury. "He damned well did it."

"Did what?" Terian asked, standing with his arms as wide in front of him as he could get them to go without removing the chains. "Anyone care to take a moment and explain to your poor, tortured prisoner what you all seem to know …?"

"He was the one," Cyrus said, shaking his head. "All along, we've been looking for the answer, and it … was right there." He turned his eyes to Terian, who looked near apoplectic, ready to explode with frustration. "Yartraak is powering an infinite supply of soul rubies by draining one person, one person with power—a soul—far beyond that of a mortal.

"He's draining Vidara. He kidnapped the Goddess of Life … and now he's using her to destroy the whole damned world."

Chapter 64

Cyrus left the bed without help several days later. The pain stuck with him, fits of it that seemed to shoot through him without warning when he moved in certain ways. Curatio pronounced him "fit enough" when forced to render an opinion, but also suggested he avoid battle for at least another month. "Give yourself time to heal from such a brutal injury."

Cyrus did not hold his tongue. "Which part, the physical stabbing or the emotional one?"

Curatio gave him a pained look as they stared at each other, the Halls of Healing silent around them. "Both."

Cyrus walked with the aid of a staff that had appeared at his bedside one morning, hobbling along with one hand on the top of it for support and the other on Praelior to give him strength to endure the still significant aches. He caught the glances as he worked his way down the stairs all the way to the foyer for the first time in a month.

There were greetings and glad tidings hurled at him from many a well-wisher, hushed voices commending his motion, telling him how good it was to see him about again. He took them all with the grace of a smile, one that he had worked on forging to hide that bubbling pool of rage and disappointment that had taken up residence in his belly. He could feel it when he thought of Aisling, imagined her face. *For years she played me. Years she watched me, looking for her opening. And then she opened me.*

This never would have happened to Alaric.

Cyrus made his way out the front door, feeling the burn inside his chest and along his back and craving air fresher than even his open tower could provide. He forced his way through the front doors with a hard shove, down onto the lawn and found his gait straightening as he went. The pain was still there, but his care for it diminished. It was here and there, stitched through his muscles in the place where the black lace had gone untouched by the remedy Curatio had used. He'd felt this peculiar agony once before, though it had been lighter then, the healing more complete.

He tossed the staff aside somewhere around the middle of Sanctuary. The stone wall of the building loomed high to his right, and he hobbled along without support, hand clutching Praelior, his pace slow but the pain entirely manageable.

He could see the garden ahead, the bridge extending over the water. He longed for the peace of the stream. He had seen it run past off the balcony that looked south, but he wanted to see it run beneath his feet. Wanted to see it ripple and reflect, wanted to see the wind stir the surface.

I want to feel alive, not locked in my own high dungeon the way Terian is trapped in his low one.

He made it to the bridge, the grey stone stretched over dark waters, the greenery framing the whole setting. He saw her a bit late from atop the crest of the bridge, standing in the corner of the garden at the monument. He ignored her at first, looking down into the waters below, placing a bare palm on the stone guardrail that was there to keep him from toppling in.

"You are surprisingly mobile," came Vara's voice from behind him. He did not turn. "At least, for a man who was nearly dead a month ago."

"Couldn't stay in bed forever," Cyrus said, looking down. There was a ripple, and he watched it intently. "Couldn't keep pacing my tower; I was wearing holes in the stone."

"You look ... very different without your armor," she said. She took a step nearer; he could see it in the reflection of the water, which had grown still once more. "I see you still have your sword, though."

He did not turn to face her, merely stared at her reflection. He could not recall if her eyes were always that blue or if it was a reflection of the sky and water lightening them. "Seems like I have need of it. I should keep it by my side lest someone else try and betray me."

She was silent for a moment. "Do you fear I would betray you?"

"No," he said quietly. "Which is why you are seeing my back." He turned his head enough to look her in the eyes. They were that blue, indeed. "You know something of this feeling."

"I do," she said and slipped into place, leaning on the rail beside him. "Very much so."

He felt his jaw tighten. "Does it ever go away?"

"The very tangible, stomach-churning sense of betrayal?" She had her arms folded upon the stone, and she moved slightly, producing a scraping noise as her vambrace moved against it. "No, it does not go away. It does, however, fade in time, until you are left with a mere sense of unease rather than the roiling series of emotions you are no doubt feeling at the moment."

"Roiling sounds about right," Cyrus said. "I can feel them all come in sequence; shame that I was fooled, and that it happened before so broad an audience. Regret that I ever allowed myself to lower the veil for someone who was plainly playing me all along. Embarrassment that I let her …" He felt his eyes close involuntarily. "… let her tempt me in ways that I did. That I ruined other things by foolishly going along with her without so much as a fight. She played my every emotion as skillfully as a flute player hits the high notes." Cyrus clenched his hand around his sword. "And she may have cost us this war." He lowered his voice. "*I* may have cost us this war."

"Oh, I well remember these feelings," Vara said. "Of course, mine only cost me every friend I had."

"I didn't lose all my friends," Cyrus said, staring into the middle distance. "Yet. But lives were lost. Lives of people I lead."

"You trusted the wrong person," she said stiffly.

"I didn't listen to you."

"It is hardly a requirement for you to listen to me," she said.

"Aren't you elves supposed to be wisest and fairest?" Cyrus said, not really feeling much amusement in the way he said it.

"That's really only me," she said, a little droll. She waited for him to look up, he could see, slight hint of a smile. "Gods, you are feeling it, aren't you?"

"We can't free her, can we?" Cyrus asked.

Vara paused. "My namesake? The Goddess of Life? I don't know; perhaps you should ask Terian. I don't think it would be wise to attempt it until you are able to battle again."

"Where would he even keep her?" Cyrus asked, feeling the drift of dark feelings upon him. "Saekaj? The Realm of Darkness?"

"Probably Saekaj," Vara said after a moment's thought. "He would need her in a place where he could easily supply the rubies, after all."

Cyrus gave it a moment's consideration. "Storm the city of Saekaj, face all their armies and then the God of Darkness at the end of it all." He shook his head slowly. "I don't think Alaric would embrace a plan like that, not any part of it."

She let out a light breath. "You have got to stop asking yourself what Alaric would do and start doing what Cyrus Davidon would do." He blinked and looked at her, but she was staring out across the water. "Alaric Garaunt did not build Sanctuary into a military army upon which you could safely hang the fate of all Arkaria. He wanted to, true, but he did not do it. The General of Sanctuary did."

"That's ... complimentary," Cyrus said.

"I was merely repaying the one you gave me earlier about being wise and fair. Do not read too much into it."

"Alaric also didn't lead us into hideous defeat," Cyrus said.

"He didn't lead us into battle most of the time, or have you forgotten?" Vara asked. "Alaric was a leader, and that meant that he delegated the role of General to a man he deemed better at strategy, tactics and overall militarism than himself. His intent was to protect Arkaria. If ever there was a moment when Alaric's mission for Sanctuary required Cyrus Davidon's ability to lead people in battle, this is it. He was entirely about garnering the preferred result; he left the rest up to those of us to whom he trusted the mission."

Cyrus glanced over at her, and her blue eyes glistened. "He told me not to go after the gods, Vara. He made me promise, before I left for Luukessia."

"You are the man in the head seat at the Sanctuary Council table now," she said. "If you see going after the gods as being against the best interests of our mission, then do not do it. But sometimes a leader has to hold to a higher loyalty than his mere word, given two years ago to a man now ... dead." That word came heavy, and she shuddered as she sidled slightly closer. "Our whole land is at risk. Terian is right: we will fall; it is only a matter of time. We cannot stand against an infinite army, no matter how much we might want to. You are brave, and you are daring, and you are decent—"

"I don't remember giving you this many compliments."

"—and I trust you to lead Sanctuary where it needs to be led." She stiffened and let out a low breath. "You have my sword, for as long as you need it." She stood there, curiously stiff for a moment, then relaxed. "You daft jackass."

Cyrus frowned. "What the hells?"

She shrugged. "As you said, I gave you too many compliments; I took one back by negating it with an insult."

He found himself chuckling, low, almost under his breath. "You'll be the death of me."

"I am no dark elven harlot," Vara said, "and I suggest you avoid those in the future."

"I'll be listening to your advice more carefully in the future," Cyrus said, leaning upon the sword hilt. He paused, contemplating. "How do we do this? Such a thing … it's … impossible?"

She stood there, stiff, her eyes drifting across the rippling surface of the water before settling on him. "Then this task is in the right hands." She moved past him with a click of her metal boots against the stone bridge until she had reached the other side. He watched her go, the armor catching the reflection of a yellow sun overhead, the silver shining in the daylight. She continued on, turning back for only a second. "You are still a gooberous dunderhead."

"Offsetting that last compliment?" he asked.

"No," she replied, turning to walk off, "merely speaking the truth." But he caught a smile before she turned away.

Chapter 65

Cyrus stood upon the bridge for a while longer, gazing into the distance. The sun was high overhead, but the chill of autumn had set in on the ground in a way he did not feel in his tower, not even when the wind whipped through at its hardest. Without his armor, he felt its bite keenly. Clouds rolled in slowly overhead, making the skies overcast, highlighting them yellow where the sun tried to break through.

Cyrus started back toward the entry to Sanctuary, but now the weariness from his long walk set in. He made it almost halfway down the long wall before he needed to take a moment. He looked to his right and his eyes fell on a wooden building that stood out in the yard between Sanctuary itself and the wall. It was a solid color, a dark-stained brown like the beams of his tower roof.

A chimney puffed wisps of black smoke toward the heavens, and he stared at the door, cracked slightly open. It was almost inviting him onward, to step inside.

He took the invitation, crossing the lawn and pushing the door back. The hinge made a squeaking noise as he did so, heralding his entry. The room was dark, and the smell of smoke was thick, something less sweet and more choking than any hearth in Sanctuary. "Hello?" he called tentatively.

A soft, orange glow caught his attention as his eyes adjusted. He saw the movement of a shadow behind it, a small, dark figure that shifted when his eye ran across it. He concentrated, focusing in, and distinguished the shape of a woman.

She stood behind an anvil with a glowing bit of steel upon it. She stared at him for a moment before raising the hammer and bringing it down upon the glowing metal. The sound jarred him, reminding him of battle. Like the crashing of blade against bone, the anvil and hammer beat together.

Larana brought the hammer down again, and again. She flipped the hilt of the sword upon which she worked then hit it again. She glanced at Cyrus, only for a second, then dealt the weapon two more swift blows before tossing it into a wooden barrel. Cyrus heard it hiss in the water and watched the steam rise in the dark.

"Hello," Cyrus said again, walking through the dark of the workshop toward her. She was barely visible in the low light of the glowing fire behind her. He could see the frizz of her hair, the orange radiance highlighting dark strands, showing just the hints of smudge upon her face from the coal smoke that hung in the workshop.

"Hello." Her voice was so small it almost escaped notice. She did not just whisper; she failed to project the word more than an inch from her lips, and Cyrus felt almost as though he had to lunge forward to catch it before it fell from his reach.

"This is an impressive smithy," Cyrus said, looking around. "I don't think I've been out here before." He watched her, waiting to see if she would say anything. "You know, I could have used a good smith a couple years ago. There was this whole thing where I needed a sword—"

"I wasn't much of a smith then," she said, and he caught a glimpse of her eyes for just a flash, in the dark. They were a deep green, he thought for a moment, but then she disappeared back to looking at her anvil, its dark surface empty of anything to concern her.

"You learned in the last three years?" Cyrus asked, turning his head to look at a full suit of armor plate that stood in the corner. He'd seen its like on the warriors of Sanctuary; upon inspection he'd deemed it quite good, though he'd not thought to ask who had supplied it.

"I learn quickly." She said it as quietly as a mouse.

"Apparently," Cyrus said. He felt the jab of his wound. "You know, I could use some help with my armor."

She answered quickly with a little more force. "The problem isn't your armor."

He blinked in surprise; her vehemence was an immense improvement over the near-silence of before. "The problem is the wearer?" Cyrus asked, jesting slightly.

"No," she said, a few shades under a normal tone, "it's your chainmail."

"Well, it's just normal stuff," Cyrus said, "like any other, bought in a market. I repair the links myself where I can—"

"You shouldn't do that," she said, and there was force there. She still did not raise her eyes to his.

He wanted to ask her age, get her to look at him, say something about Belkan, but all the inquiries he could muster seemed somehow rude. "Well, I didn't know we had a smith available," he said, trying to soften it as a joke.

"I am whatever you need me to be," Larana said.

Good gods, she is in love with me. "I hate to impose," Cyrus said.

"It would be no imposition." Near silent now, her voice seemed to have retreated even further.

"I would not complain if you wanted to make an attempt at better chainmail for me," Cyrus said, treading lightly. "But neither would I want it to get in the way of your other duties."

"Seems like preserving the life of our Guildmaster should be one of my highest duties." A little stronger, this time.

"You say that now, but miss one dinner and you'll catch enough hell to change your mind," Cyrus said. He felt oddly at ease, even in spite of her reserve. "I'd be much obliged for any help you can render." His hand found the wound on his back without thought. "Anything that can help me overcome my own … failings … would be appreciated." He gave her a nod of thanks and turned to leave, the smoky air in the workshop hanging heavy around him.

"I voted for you," she said. It was almost a normal volume.

"Why?" Cyrus asked, letting it slip before he realized he had done it. He began to amend his question but stopped himself. *Why, indeed? I'd like to know, actually.*

"Because I believe in you," she said, matter-of-factly. "I always have." She looked at him again, just for a moment, and the green eyes were like glittering emeralds in the dark.

Cyrus stood at the entry, the daylight flooding in through the cracks. "Thank you," he said and retreated from the dark, unsure what he could say other than that.

Chapter 66

Winter's grip settled upon the Plains of Perdamun, laying its frosty fingers upon the green grasses and leeching them white on every morn. The new year came in with the news that Reikonos remained under siege, that the Riverlands were still being rolled through by dark elven hordes beyond counting. The skies hung grey like they had above Leaugarden, and Cyrus kept his head down as he practiced incessantly, regaining his strength day by day. The wound still hurt, but the pain was fading over time. The day after the winter solstice came the first bit of good news in what had seemed like months.

"The trolls have deserted the Sovereign's army," Nyad said in the Council Chambers, the leaden skies hanging outside the balcony windows. Cyrus had shifted in his seat to give them a glance but turned swiftly back when she spoke.

"How do you know this?" Cyrus asked.

"They surrendered to my father," Nyad said, face slightly aglow. "Their entire army. They broke from the Sovereign's forces without a fight before Leaugarden and ambushed a dark elven squadron that had a wizard. Caught him in the night, kept him hostage, forced him to take one of their envoys to Pharesia to negotiate repatriation."

"Repatriation?" Cyrus asked.

"It's a large word," Vara said, "but it means they want to go home."

"I know what it means," Cyrus said with a frown. He caught her sly smile. "Stop trying to get my goat."

"Yes, leave that to the trolls," Vaste said. "So, did he allow them passage back to Gren?"

"In small numbers over the last days, yes," Nyad said. "Evidently they fled back into the swamps quite gladly, leaving their weapons and armor behind in Nalikh'akur."

"I hope you immediately moved them elsewhere," Erith said, "so as not to have them recaptured by a horde of angry trolls bent on deceit."

"I doubt this is a deceit," Vaste said.

"Because your people are too stupid to pull it off?" Ryin asked.

"They're honestly not that dumb," Vaste said, "just very different in their desires and tastes—"

"Such as the taste for human and elven flesh," Odellan muttered.

"—and what they consider acceptable behavior," Vaste finished. "They want to go home. They're not stupidly adventurous, and the homeland is of paramount importance. The fact that it was invaded, that some of their kin died … it's a bit too close to what happened in the last war. It left scars that run deep, and they'll be in a protective mode for some time." He delivered this all without much in the way of emotion. "No, I think they're done for now."

"Good," Cyrus said, a perfect vision of the slave markets floating to the top of his mind; he saw the pillar, saw the remains of Cass hung upon it in his mind's eye. "Now we have but one unstoppable enemy left before us."

Vara hung her gaze carefully upon him. "And when will we endeavor to stop them, pray tell?"

Cyrus swallowed something that tasted like bile. "I don't know."

Chapter 67

Another two weeks came and went with stunning alacrity, and Cyrus felt himself nearly returned to form. His muscles were strong, the wound's ache was just that—an ache, nothing more—and the winter air stung his bare skin as he practiced thrust of sword and form upon the faded grasses of Sanctuary's side yard. The air held the chill that seeped up his nose, threatening to invade his chest and make it twinge with the cold. He had built up his fitness once more, turning his power loose in attack after attack against the empty air. There was not a soul in sight save for one, who watched him with all the interest he might have accorded to a seamstress going about her business.

"It's all very impressive, this thing you do," Andren said. He was still bare of cheek and still red of face, though now it was from the winter's cold. Though it did not seem to be below freezing, the air still held a bitterness that came from the north. "Especially considering you were on the mend only a month ago."

"I need to mend quicker," Cyrus said, thrusting at an invisible foe that he imagined was a dark elf. "I need a plan."

"Have you spoken with your resident dark elven traitor?" Andren asked. Cyrus thought he looked peculiar, as though something was missing. It took him a moment to realize that there was a lack of ale or flask in his hands; that they were covered with gloves alone.

"I've spoken with Terian, yes," Cyrus said. He smiled darkly. "He highly encourages us to invade Saekaj. Which gives naturally gives me pause."

"Can't imagine why; it's not as though he's been trying to kill you these last years or anything." Andren stamped his feet, drawing his cloak tighter against his white robes. He lowered his voice. "Do you think he's sincere, that it's the right course? Or do you think he still wants you to run your guts into a waiting blade?"

"I don't know," Cyrus said absently as he struck another blow against an imaginary foe. "But it's not as though we've heard a whisper from J'anda, which ... is concerning. With no idea what we'd be up against, it gives me pause."

"Vara wants us to attack, doesn't she?" Andren asked.

Cyrus paused, looking over at the elf. "Told you that, did she?"

He shook his head. "She hasn't said a word."

"Then how'd you know she wants to invade?"

"You can read it in the way she holds herself during the half-arsed discussions we've had in Council," Andren said. "Been around her long enough now to tell when she's keen about something."

"Oh?" Cyrus asked. "How can you tell?"

"She has the same look in her eyes as when she talks about you," Andren said, and Cyrus missed his target wildly.

Cyrus held position for a moment and did not turn to look at the elf. "Not funny."

"It was a little funny."

"We'll just have to agree to disagree," Cyrus said, honing his attention in on the next target in his line. He did not have his armor on, and he could feel the sweat running down his flesh, catching the frigid air like icy fingers tickling down his chest and arms.

"It was also true," Andren said as Cyrus made his next attack, and once again he went wide of his intended mark.

"You ass," Cyrus muttered.

"I've been called worse," Andren conceded. "So what is it really? What's holding you back from driving down into the tunnels of Saekaj at the head of an army big enough to wreck most peoples' days? From doing what you did in Enterra and the Realm of Death, some perverse mix-up of your greatest victories wherein you build your legend even more?"

Cyrus felt his brow pucker. "I am not here to build my damned legend."

"And yet it gets built even still." Vara's voice interrupted, and he turned to see her walking across the browned grass toward them. "They're attributing the freeing of the troll slaves to you, did you know that? As if the rest of us weren't even there."

"I did not know that," Cyrus said. "I've been a little too busy to go looking for rumors about my own exploits."

"But if he'd been able to walk at the time, you can bet he'd have been in the thick of them," Andren said.

"Yes, being an invalid is probably something of an impediment to seeking out conversations that might build one's ego," Vara said.

"I am not an invalid," Cyrus said and brought his sword around in a violent chopping motion that caused his back to twinge in pain. He halted his advance and brought Praelior back to center. "What do you want? Here to jab a few needles in me?"

"I heard my name as I was walking over there," Vara gestured toward the corner of Sanctuary in the far distance, "and came to see whether the gossip was flattering or not."

"Gods, with ears like that I don't know how you sleep on the same floor as Vaste," Cyrus said.

"His snoring was the least of the obnoxious noises I dealt with this year," Vara said, catching his gaze with something like reproach. "Though at least your night sounds did end fairly quickly as opposed to his continuous ripping of tree branches into small chips."

"How quickly?" Andren asked with obvious glee.

Vara rolled her eyes. "I heard my name. What are you discussing?"

"Invading Saekaj," Cyrus said.

"Your amorous intentions toward the liberator of Gren," Andren said.

She rolled her eyes again. "That would be a short conversation."

Andren had a twinkle in his eyes. "Longer or shorter than—"

"Invasions take quite a bit of planning," Cyrus said, trying to drag things back on track.

"More time than our leader apparently takes in the bedchamber," Andren said with amusement.

"You're both the most maddening sort of idiots," Vara said.

"It's why we work so well together," Andren agreed.

"Are you still stalling on this invasion?" Vara asked, turning her attention to Cyrus, who realized quite suddenly that he'd abandoned his exercises some time ago and was merely standing still, chest heaving as his breath steamed in the air.

"I am not ... stalling," Cyrus said, catching a look from Andren. "I have perfectly valid reasons for my hesitancy."

"Such as?" Andren asked.

"Because the last time we killed a god, we unleashed consequences that killed a whole land," Cyrus said, lashing at Andren.

"That was the God of Death, who held captive the souls of the departed," Vara said, drawing his gaze back to her. She was implacable in this, giving her answer in seconds. "It seems unlikely that were we to kill the God of Darkness—which might not even necessarily need to do in order to accomplish his defeat—it is hardly a foregone conclusion that we would unleash something as preposterous as a perpetual night."

"Or day," Andren said, nodding along. "Could you even imagine that? A day that never ended? It just drags on and on—"

"Like a conversation that did not have the good grace to die?" Vara asked, shooting him a sharp look. "I am imagining something of that sort just now." She transferred her attention back to Cyrus. "Fear of what might happen should not cloud you to the truth of what will happen should the Sovereign continue his work unimpeded."

Cyrus stared at her, blue eyes aflame, the only spot of light in a grey sky, and the truth tumbled loose from his lips. "I know you said I can't lose what I never had, but ... I remember the sight of Mortus swinging that hand at you. It descends in my memory as though it were pulled through hardening sap by some unerring force." He watched her eyes flicker with uncertainty. "I remember how it felt, watching it fall. How it compelled me to jump into the path of his swing." Cyrus drew a deep breath, felt his chest heave with the effort, saw it mist before his lips. "We killed the God of Death, but it was hardly bloodless. In spite of riding the teleportation out of the Realm of Death without injury, I may be more scarred by the events of that day than any other before or since."

"Which says something, because that's a right good one you've got going on your back there," Andren said.

Vara was silent for but a moment. Then she spoke, low: "You cannot hide behind your scars and use them as a justification to keep from doing what you know should be done."

Cyrus's eyes fell toward her belly, where the armor's gleam was not so bright. "Can't I?"

She traced his gaze, and her eyes narrowed. "That is not the same. You are to lead this guild, not merely follow the desires of your—"

She halted and made a noise of sheerest frustration. "Also, that suggestion is a gross oversimplification. It is not my scars that keep me from you."

"I am ... confused," Andren said. "What just happened here? I thought we were talking about invading Saekaj, and now we're on about scars ...?"

"What keeps you from me?" Cyrus asks.

"Good sense," Andren said.

"Caution," Vara said then glared at Andren. "Do not presume to speak for me."

"You've said worse yourself," Cyrus said.

"Yes, *I* said it." Vara folded her arms in front of her. "It was not said on my behalf by some newly-sober elven officer bent on using me as puppet for his own jokes."

"I—" Cyrus began, and then saw Vara jerk her head as though she'd been kicked. "What?"

She wheeled, looking toward the front of Sanctuary. "There's someone at the gates."

"From here?" Cyrus asked. "Really?"

"No, I hear it, too," Andren said, and the elf was struck with a look of concentration. "A messenger, announcing himself." He paused, and Cyrus caught a sudden, stricken look on Vara's face, her jaw gone slack. "Oh, they're saying that Reikonos is being sacked."

Cyrus felt the chill drop through him, run from top to bottom in a mere second, even as he saw Vara turn her head to look at him, fear of some sort frozen upon her face. He knew that fear, knew its origin; it came from the depths inside, from the place he knew of all too well—

"I'm sorry," Andren said, whispering, his red face blushing deeper. "I shouldn't have said it like ... like that. I didn't know that's what it would be."

"It's all right," Cyrus said, swallowing heavy, feeling like he'd just passed a boulder down his throat. "It's ..." His head felt light, the grey skies seemed to close around him, and Vara's pale face and blue eyes were right at the center of it all, the anchor that kept him from falling over as one word ran through his mind over and over.

Home.

Chapter 68

"I need to get inside Reikonos," Cyrus said as he stormed into the foyer. There was no buzz of activity; the place was as sedate as though nothing were happening. He had seen the gate opening for the messenger as he entered, but did not wait to hear the details.

"Don't be a fool," Vara cautioned, two steps behind him.

"It's arguably a little late for that," Andren said, following behind them both.

"Shut up," Cyrus and Vara said in unison. He stopped abruptly and turned to face her. She barely stopped in time to keep from colliding with him, surprise sending her faint eyebrows north. "I can't just let this pass," Cyrus said. "No more than I could let Termina simply fall."

"Far be it from me to stop you from throwing yourself wholeheartedly into what is surely a hopeless battle," Vara said, her blue eyes finding his, "but ... actually, yes, let me stop you from this. This is madness. If the dark elves have indeed breached the wall, even assuming you could get in, it would be utterly fruitless to do so." Her eyes flitted downward from his, a little hint of nerves causing her severe expression to waver. "Also, you are not wearing a shirt. Of any sort. At all." Each addition to her speech grew fainter in volume, and finally her gaze averted, moving above his head to the blank walls.

In spite of himself, Cyrus felt a grin appear. "It's a peculiar time to note that, wouldn't you say?"

That caused the ice to flare with heat as she looked back into his eyes. "You are rather large; it is difficult to miss."

"Sure," Cyrus said and turned away from her to stalk to the center of the foyer. "I need volunteers for an expedition into Reikonos. One hundred strong fighters willing to teleport into the mouth of death itself." He cast a furious gaze over the foyer, trying to communicate his mood without letting it drip over everything said. "The weak of will and those afraid of death need not bother even appearing."

Silence reined for several seconds. "Well, that's an affront to my manhood," Andren said.

"Only a small one," Vara said.

Cyrus did not wait to hear the rest of their bickering; he could hear his call taken up, making its way into the Great Hall on other voices, wending its way up the stairs at the shouts of runners. He made a run of his own, sprinting up the stone steps, passing two druids who were stopping to shout the news, to spread it to the five towers of Sanctuary. The challenge he'd delivered in the foyer took on a seeming life of its own as he heard it echo down the halls of Sanctuary.

Cyrus reached his own door in the tower, the stairs still ringing with loud shouts behind him. There was motion, movement, people being turned out of their quarters by his mere command. He had ears for little of it, unstrapping Praelior and throwing it upon the bed as he turned toward the freestanding dummy that held his armor. He paused, tilted his head in curiosity, noting for the first time that which had been left beneath the plate mail. He pulled the strap on the breastplate and let the backplate fall to the ground with a crash as he pulled the breastplate forward, holding it in front of him like a shield.

He had not put on his armor in weeks. Some time between his last battle and this moment, someone had come to his quarters and replaced the old, weathered, stripped and broken iron links with something entirely different. These links were forged tighter into tiny circles not even big enough for a gnome's dagger to find a gap. He let the metal flow beneath his hand as he ran his fingers over it. *That does not look like steel or iron* ...

He shook his head, clearing the curiosity aside, and started to dress, throwing on a cloth shirt from his wardrobe then following it with the chainmail. He had just begun to strap on his leg armor when the door was flung wide and he heard metal steps upon his stairs.

"You are a bloody fool," Vara said.

"You already said that," Cyrus said, finishing with the straps on his greaves. The plate fit perfectly over the new chain, its color black as his armor.

"You can't teleport into Reikonos right now," she said, a soft glow of exertion and satisfaction upon her cheeks. "The portal is closed for the siege, if you recall?"

"I recall," Cyrus said.

She stared at him dully then looked skyward before making a sound of utter exasperation. "Auuuughh, Vidara, why must you curse and afflict me with this man?"

"She can't hear you," Cyrus said, working on his greaves. It was slow going, the straps on the inside and outside of his thighs.

"You buffoon," Vara said with another sound of frustration and took a step toward him. He half expected a slap, but instead she dropped to a knee and pulled the straps on his leg tight enough that he thought he might have lost the blood in his thigh even through the chainmail. "You sit, idle, on your hands, for the last month—"

"I've been indisposed for the last month," Cyrus said, now working on his vambraces, strapping them to his wrist. "I couldn't very well lead a battle from my bed, after all."

"*Now* you wish to lead a battle?" Vara asked, pulling the metal that girded his waist tight. "Try leading it where it will do some good."

"I need to see Reikonos," Cyrus said, and it came out lower and more menacing than he'd intended, but also soul-deep. *I do need to see it.*

"What do you get for the man who has it all?" She stood, taking hold of his breastplate and thumping it against the chainmail that girded his chest. "Torturous misery, apparently." Her eyes lost some of their fire. "Take it from someone who knows; seeing your homeland burn does nothing good for you."

"I need to see," Cyrus said quietly, matching her movement with the backplate. She held his breastplate in place while strapping them together. "I just ... need to."

She took a gentle breath as he sat there on the bed, looking up at her. She was different from this angle, from below, her nose sharp, cheeks high, and her hair barely visible under her helmet. She looked less imperious, he decided, even with her eyes closed. "Very well, then."

Cyrus stood, taking his helm and placing it upon his head then strapping Praelior back to his waist. "How do I look?" Now he was looking down upon her again. Her eyes still closed, she looked as if she were struggling to be patient, like she was working through some emotion of her own.

The blue eyes opened, the sky shining down on a sunny day—though Cyrus knew there was no sun to shine on this day. "You look …" she said warily, letting out a slow breath, "… you look ready."

Chapter 70

They found madness, full and unchecked, waiting on the staircase. Only the shout heralding Cyrus's coming parted the way for him, men and women in armor both leather and metal shoved themselves to each side for him, mashing themselves either into the wall or teetering on the edge of the open spiral leading to the foyer below.

"They follow you," Vara breathed from just behind him as they passed the fifth floor.

"Good," Cyrus said, "because I'm about to lead them somewhere worthwhile."

He entered the foyer to find it packed from side to side, the gaps rapidly filling from the emptying staircase and the hallway leading to the rear towers. Cyrus stalked across to the small staircase and up to the balcony. He could see the other officers up there, waiting in the place where the guild was addressed in times such as these. *Dark times*, Cyrus thought.

He took each step with a confidence born of the fury that had settled within. It was a sure thing, his sense of anger and righteousness, and it kept his hand on Praelior without a thought for the caution he usually felt when grasping it. He made his way down the line of officers standing back from the short, stone railing that kept the balcony from opening into the empty air between it and the seal on the floor below.

"Reikonos is invaded," Cyrus said, noticing after he had begun speaking that silence had fallen without any suggestion from him. "I am going to ... assess the situation. Who will go with me?"

The answer was a roar, a sweeping wave of motion from wall to wall.

"No shortage of volunteers for this suicide mission, then," Vaste said.

"I don't hear you volunteering," Vara snapped at him.

"OOH, PICK ME, PICK ME!" Vaste bellowed, loud enough to cause a ripple of quiet to fall on the floor below. "I WANT TO DIE AT THE HANDS OF PILLAGING DARK ELVES!" Cyrus looked back at the troll, who was moving his shoulders and torso in some sort of enthusiastic dance, eyes shut. When he opened them again, he appeared slightly startled at the silence that had fallen over the room. He blinked and looked at Cyrus. "Well, I would go with you."

"How could I possibly deny your request to die after that helpful display?" Cyrus asked, annoyed. He turned back to the waiting crowd. "This will be a small force, tightly knit. No more than a hundred, all veterans of the Trials of Purgatory with the armor and mystical weapons that entails." He looked down and saw more than a few crestfallen faces. "I do not judge your courage to be lacking if that is not you; but we are walking into the heart of an army that has invaded the largest city in Arkaria and thwarted its defenses. I must have a force elite in experience in order to fight our way out if necessary." Cyrus turned to Odellan, who stood at attention down the line. "Assemble the force; use your own judgment."

Odellan did not even react in surprise at being so suddenly called up. "As you would have it, Guildmaster." He saluted crisply and broke into a trot, passing down the line of officers and descending to the floor below, already barking orders about formation and calling out names to assemble on the seal.

"How do you plan to enter Reikonos?" Curatio asked, sidling up to Cyrus and speaking low.

"I'm at a bit of a loss on that one," Cyrus said. "My first thought is that we teleport to the nearest open portal, the one outside the walls at—"

"The dark elves will be watching it with a considerable army," Curatio said shrewdly, shaking his head. "You would die before you even drew a blade to defend yourself." He wore a slight smile. "In fact, they will be watching every portal for a hundred miles in any direction of the city walls—save one."

Cyrus looked at the healer with more than a little shrewdness of his own. "Save one, you say? Where might this one be?"

"Allow me my aura of mystery, Lord Davidon," Curatio said, and the smile broadened just slightly. "Suffice to say that Alaric and I are not so far apart in our love of a good secret. I can get you into Reikonos."

"I guess you'll be coming with me, then," Cyrus said.

"I'm coming with you, too," came a voice from behind him, and Cyrus turned to see the spiked armor, bathed in shadow, lingering between two columns that held up the ceiling.

Vara drew her sword. "Who let you out, traitor?"

"I could get out any time I wished," Terian said, boots clanking as he made his way forward. "I lived in this guildhall for more years than I can count, always in the darkness. I know more ways in and out of the dungeons than anyone else save for Alaric." Cyrus saw his eyes gleam. "Let me come with you."

"So you can try and kill him when his back is turned?" Vara asked, sword still exposed.

Cyrus put out a hand to stay hers; Terian had yet to make a threatening motion. *If he could have truly escaped the dungeon at any point ...* "All right," he said to Terian. "You can come along."

"You—" Vara said, whipsawing around to him.

"Fool, I know," Cyrus cut her off. "I'm always a fool, a dunderous moron—whatever."

"If you trust him, you are more than that," she snapped.

"I trust him," Cyrus said, realizing it was true. "I don't think he means to kill me any longer." He stared at the dark knight. *What was it, Terian? What prompted you to let go of that grudge? Somehow I doubt it was anything I said or did ... yet the change is within you, as sure as if someone had cast light into the darkness you showed me in Luukessia, as sure as if they had driven it all out.*

"Finally, someone listens," Terian said under his breath.

"Finally, he takes leave of his senses once and for all," Vara muttered.

"The only way to avoid all betrayal is if we refuse to trust," Cyrus said, turning to look at her. "To shun all company, to stand alone." He looked at Terian. "And I still believe that we are none of us alone; or at least that we don't have to be."

"What a stunningly naïve piece of silliness," Vara said under her breath. "But as you wish; I only hope this does not come back like a thrown gnomish boomerang to clip us solidly in the back of the head."

"Gnomish what?" Cyrus asked, befuddled.

"It's a wooden device, roughly the size of your thumb and forefinger," she said. "You throw it and it turns in the air to come back to you. Annoying little thing, especially when you're caught in a hailstorm of them."

He cracked a smile. "So that's why you don't like gnomes."

"I don't like *you*," she said. "Gnomes I detest."

"Guildmaster," Odellan called from below, drawing Cyrus's attention to the seal. Neatly ordered rows of ten awaited, with a gap of six in the front. "Your striking force awaits."

"Vaste, Vara, Terian, Curatio and … Mendicant," Cyrus said, jutting a finger at the goblin, who made a startled noise. "Let us away, my friends."

"Surely," Curatio said, taking the lead down the stairs, the hems of his white robes swishing as he descended.

"Yes, let us hasten unto death," Vaste said with excess enthusiasm. "Where are we going again?"

"Reikonos, you fool," Vara snapped. She eyed Terian. "The heart of treachery and darkness."

"No, we're not going there quite yet," Terian said. "Maybe later, though."

Cyrus caught his look and shook it off as he stepped into his place in the line. "Curatio … where are you taking us in Reikonos?"

"Oh, I'm not taking you into Reikonos," Curatio said airily. "Under it, though, that sounds like an idea."

"Better question," Vaste said, "how is a healer going to teleport us anywhere?"

"I think I still remember the spell," Curatio said, facing forward, staring at the space above the entry to the Great Hall. He lowered his voice so that only those nearest him—and perhaps some elves in the hall—could hear him. "Probably shouldn't mention this to anyone, though; technically, as Vaste suggested, it is heresy, after all …"

"What?" Mendicant's high-pitched voice squeaked.

A green light flashed around them, blinding Cyrus, and he felt the world disappear around him as he was swept into a current of magic and taken far, far from where he'd been only a moment before.

Chapter 71

The world distended around him, and a darkened, grim chamber that Cyrus was all too familiar with appeared around him with the last of the flash. He blinked the surprise out of his eyes and checked his surroundings with speed, trying to see if there was any foe within proximity. There was not; only the small army of Sanctuary in a tight formation around him.

"Oh, this place," Vaste said in disgust.

Cyrus looked behind him and saw the portal standing tall above them, realizing finally where they were. "This is where you took us to the Realm of Life."

"Yes," Curatio agreed. "I doubt anyone else recalls how to do that, though, so we should be quite safe until the dark elves get bored with their business upon the surface."

"So ... years?" Terian quipped.

"What now?" Vara asked, turning a pointed gaze upon Cyrus. The room was dim, but the portal glowed faintly in the dark.

"No squirrels," Vaste said. "No chipmunks. Hedgehogs are right out."

"Is that an improvement over goats, would you say?" Curatio asked in a musing tone, as though he were genuinely weighing the alternatives.

"I would not say," Vaste replied, nonplussed.

"We need to get to the surface," Cyrus said, casting his attention to the exit at the far end of the room.

"There are easier ways," Curatio said and stepped out of line, walking toward a nearby wall.

"I hope this involves more heresy," Vaste said drily. "Because one simply can't have enough offenses punishable by death chalked up to one's name in a single day."

"Speaking from experience," Terian said, "after the first few, you start to care less and less."

"Thank you for that charming blueprint into the making of a murderous killer," Vara growled.

"This way," Curatio called. A door had appeared beside him, a staircase visible behind it in a lighted passage.

"How do you know these things?" Vaste called to him as Cyrus started them forward.

"If you want to know all of a city's secrets," Curatio replied, leading the way into the staircase, "it helps to be around when everything is built."

They circled in an upward spiral for some time, the smooth rock walls of the staircase chamber glowing a faint, unearthly blue. Curatio led the way, tireless. Cyrus looked up and saw the end approaching, a final spiral that ended upon a stone balcony overlooking the steps.

"Where now?" Vaste asked as they reached the balcony, a half-circle that jutted out from a blank wall.

Curatio did not speak, instead walking to the wall and running his fingers over it. Runes lit up with the same glow as the walls, only brighter, highlighting an archway that looked strangely familiar. The wall parted as easily as if it were two doors being slid open, and Cyrus found himself looking into a chamber filled with the dead bodies of human guards.

"Yay!" Vaste said into the shocked silence. "We're here!"

Curatio extended a hand in invitation, and Cyrus stepped through first. He heard the sound of something and saw Curatio with his mace in hand, inch-long spikes deployed from its perfectly circular head. The healer nodded, and Cyrus stepped into a wide chamber that he knew all too well.

"The Citadel," Cyrus murmured, looking up. It was the familiar entry to the place, and he had emerged from what had always seemed to him to be nothing but a blank wall, part of the massive, towering structure that had been the defining building of Reikonos for as long as he had been alive—and longer.

"Indeed," Curatio said, coming to his elbow. He looked up; the Citadel was some thirty stories tall. "I can hear a war party above us doing their work, and there are at least a few guards stationed outside. Where shall we go, Guildmaster?"

Cyrus blinked, thinking it over. "Up, I suppose."

Curatio watched him carefully, but his face betrayed a hint of approval. "A wise suggestion, I think. We'll need to climb." He gestured to a door on the far end of the room, and they found a staircase beyond, the remains of human guards and government officials strewn all over it.

The stairs spiraled neatly around the circle that was the Citadel's outer wall. On every floor they passed an entry door; without exception, it was thrown open and utter slaughter was contained within. Cyrus spared only a cursory glance after the first few floors. *Bloodthirsty animals could not have wreaked more havoc*, he thought. *Though I suppose the dead soldiers of the Sovereign are animals and worse.*

"They'll sweep their way to the top," Terian said, only a few steps behind Cyrus. "They'll have sent their elites up first, trying to catch the Council of Twelve before they can escape. They'll almost certainly have failed, but they'll try anyway."

"Interesting how you know their strategy, dark knight," Vara said. "Or at least how these creatures think."

Terian answered her with but a shrug. "No more interesting than you not knowing it, white knight. Pure as the winter snow, aren't you? Never had a dark thought of revenge in your life?"

"I find myself having a few dark thoughts at this very moment," Vara said, "specifically about how I'd like to apply that axe of yours to your own genitals from now until dawn."

"You clearly don't have that many dark thoughts," Terian said with a smirk, "as you've already threatened me with that one before."

"Silence would be better as we march up to a certain confrontation with the enemy," Curatio said soothingly. "There will be plenty of time to argue later, I hope."

They fell into silence as they continued to make their way in the long, repetitive loop around the Citadel. Their ascent was dizzying, and Cyrus kept his eyes on the blue stones that made up the walls, realizing once more than the lower staircase to the portal had been of almost exactly the same construction.

"Something on your mind, Guildmaster?" Curatio said to him in a low murmur, as if he could sense the thoughts directed his way.

"Now that I am the Guildmaster, any chance you want to spill some secrets for me?" Cyrus asked, giving him a glance back.

Curatio smiled thinly. "I will take it under consideration."

"That sounds a lot like your version of 'in the fullness of time.'"

"I would suggest you come up with your own particular phrase that expresses those sentiments," Curatio said, and Cyrus once more found him utterly inscrutable.

"Why?" Cyrus asked. "I don't have much in the way of secrets."

"That is almost certain to change," Curatio said. "And the time between now and when it does is not likely very full, to twist Alaric's preferred phrase."

Cyrus started to question him further about that, but they reached the apex of the staircase just as he opened his mouth. They came to a sharp halt just before a door to his left.

"Not a single visible dark elf on the floors below," Terian murmured, low. "I guess they've finished their business there."

"Likely not many people there to torment and terrorize," Curatio said. "This siege has been going on long enough that the government had probably suspended most of their functions."

"Be ready for anything," Cyrus said and paused before the door.

"Anything, you say?" Vaste asked. "How about—"

"Not now," Vara and Terian chorused.

"No fun," Vaste said.

Cyrus came around the corner of the room with his sword drawn. He saw dark elven armor before him and struck both of his foes down with little in the way of thought or mercy. Bones cracked at the swing of his sword, bodies flew to either side, and Cyrus was left staring into a room where he had been on several occasions before.

It was almost peaceful within the chamber holding the Council of Twelve's meeting room. There was a surprising lack of damage, and the dark elven forces within were—

Not so dark elven. At least, not all of them.

"Cyrus Davidon," came the voice of the man who sat in the center chair behind the Council of Twelve's seat. He was flanked by a few others, each of which Cyrus knew a little too well. But he hung his gaze on that one in the center, stared him down, ignoring the half a hundred soldiers that were scattered throughout the room. "It is a true pleasure to run into you—though of a bit of a surprise to see you in this place, I must admit." A thin smile stretched over blue lips. "Still, a pleasure."

"I wish I could say the same," Cyrus said, staring at the dark elf playing at being king of Reikonos, "but I can't ... Malpravus."

Chapter 72

"I cannot tell you how much it pleases me to see you again, dear boy," Malpravus said, thin fingers pressed one against the other just below his skeletal chin. "I was worried that the spy the Sovereign sent to your bed would be the end of you."

"It takes more than some snake with a little knife to put the end to me," Cyrus said, sweeping his gaze over the mighty desk at which Malpravus sat. "As your friends there should know."

Cyrus looked at each of them in turn; Orion stood to one side, the ranger still garbed in green, his metal helm covering all but his eyes. Carrack, the wizard, stood directly to Malpravus's left, gaunt and attired in something that looked like sackcloth. His eyes were sunken, his tattooed chest was displayed through a slit in his clothing, and Cyrus suspected he had been pulled out of prison just moments earlier. Then, to the other side—

"I knew you were lying sack of shit, Rhane Ermoc," Cyrus said, looking at the human warrior who stood at Malpravus's side looking much like a loyal dog sitting at the hand of its master, "but I didn't go so far as to assume you were treacherous enough to betray the entire Confederation."

"Why, dear Rhane here is the reason we sit before you," Malpravus said, not bothering to conceal his malevolent grin. "He opened one of the gates for us himself."

"Bloodlessly, I'm sure," Cyrus said with a full measure of sarcasm.

"On our side, yes," Malpravus said. "I can't say the same for the poor humans he was forced to gut in the guardroom."

"This is a staggering level of treachery," Vara said.

"Oh, not to worry," Malpravus said, "we had other help as well." He gestured to Terian, forcing Cyrus to look at the dark knight. "For example, your good friend there was responsible for an idea that allowed us to send forth some two thousand armored knights over the wall riding vek'tag."

"Is this true?" Vara's pitch was too high, and Cyrus started to move toward her, albeit slowly.

"It was my idea," Terian said neutrally. "I can't say I knew it would be used in this way, but I certainly bear the blame."

Cyrus took a few steps forward, allowing more room for his army to file in behind him. By his reckoning, they had Malpravus's small group overmatched, but only in numbers. "So now you have the city of Reikonos at your feet."

"Dear boy," Malpravus said, "now we have all of Arkaria at our feet."

"You should have joined us, Cyrus," Orion said. The ranger sounded strangely choked with a glee of his own, muffled beneath the helm. Cyrus cast a withering glare at his armored visage but could not even see a hint of humanity beneath the mask.

"It is not too late," Malpravus offered. "Surely you see the direction in which the wind is blowing—"

"And smell it, too," Vaste said, "because of all the corpses you've just left rotting."

"—there is no hope for those who stand against us," Malpravus said. "The Confederation is all but vanquished. With our full armies turned loose, every keep that still stands in the north and the Riverlands will fall within weeks. Soon, the Kingdom of Elves will follow, then one by one the smaller principalities, until all of Arkaria knows but one master."

"This has a familiar ring to it," Cyrus said, shaking his head at Orion. "Sounds like the same line of bullshit he tried to fill my ear with when he sold his soul to the Dragonlord." Cyrus pointed a finger at Malpravus. "The same line you tried to push on me when you wanted me to betray Sanctuary. 'Give up all hope; you have no chance.'"

"You truly don't," Malpravus said, and he seemed almost … sad. "There is no possible way to thwart the army that stands before you. You will die trying."

Cyrus stared at the necromancer's dull eyes. "Then I will die trying. I will die as a free man, with a blade in my hand, the master of own damned fate and not some simpering dog that licks the boots of another in hopes he'll be spared."

"It is a poor choice that you make," Malpravus said, drawing himself up to stand. "Poorer for the fact that your friends shall have to suffer death with you for it."

"Oh, let's face it, we've suffered death for worse reasons," Vaste said.

"Why would you assume that we would die, Malpravus?" Curatio asked. He was smiling enigmatically.

"You cannot stand against our power," Malpravus said. "I hold control over death itself." He made a motion with his hand and the enemies within the chamber champed their jaws together with a loud clack. Cyrus's eyes were drawn to the nearest of them; the face was familiar, that of a young lad of Luukessia that had introduced himself to Cyrus on the day of election. What had been his name? *Rainey McIlven*, Cyrus remembered with a flash of rage. *Lost at Leaugarden.*

He turned his eyes on Malpravus.

Lost to him.

"Do you?" Curatio asked. "Do you indeed?" The healer stood tall and brushed past Cyrus, his mace in hand. "I know more about death that you could possibly even imagine, Malpravus." The elf's voice was low and deadly, heavy with menace of a like Cyrus had rarely heard.

"Your power is limited, healer," Malpravus said.

"Actually," Curatio said, and Cyrus could hear the smile in the way he said it, "it's yours that's limited." He raised the mace high above his head and a blinding flash of white light blasted through the chamber. A shrieking whine deafened Cyrus, leaving a hissing in his ears even as the light faded before him, forcing him to blink the flashes away.

The dead bodies at Malpravus's command stood motionless, and then, one by one, began to tumble to floor, lifeless. Cyrus watched them crumple, puppets with their strings cut loose, until the only ones still standing were those behind the Council of Twelve's desk.

"Intriguing," Malpravus said. Cyrus could see the tendrils of hate behind the necromancer's impassive expression. "It seems that I am not the only master of death within this chamber."

"To the contrary," Curatio said, "I am much more versed in the power of life and am well studied in guaranteeing its end." He made another motion, tossing a ball of purest spell energy of a sort Cyrus had never even seen. It cascaded with living will across the chamber, like a bolt of lightning covered in glowing red water, forking and flowing toward their foes. The desk in front of Malpravus exploded in a shower of splinters even as a light swallowed him whole into a return spell. Carrack followed into a green light of his own as Rhane Ermoc and Orion both lunged for the man, disappearing along with him.

Cyrus watched them go with a barely contained fury, the smoke from Curatio's attack settling in the fore of the room even as splinters of wood fell before them like rain.

"What ... the hell was that?" Vaste asked. Curatio did not answer; he slumped slightly as though he were feeling suddenly weak, bent at the waist. The troll waited a moment. "Oh. Let me guess. More heresy."

"Have you ever seen a healer do anything like that before?" Terian asked Vaste, in a voice that plainly accorded him the respect due an idiot. "No? Probably heresy, then."

"I have never seen such a thing from any caster of spells," Mendicant said, voice squeaking in awe. "That was ... wondrous."

"Wondrous, yes," Vaste said, "and also carries a death sentence."

"They can only kill you once, fool," Terian said. "Stop whinging."

"Perhaps you don't know this, being a dark knight," Vaste said, "but there's this spell called resurrection, and with it they can kill you over and over. I know, because I can cast it."

"Where did you learn that spell?" Curatio asked, speaking at last, sounding more than a little drawn. "I hope it wasn't anywhere that would get you in trouble for heresy."

"Touché," Vaste said. "So ... what now?"

Cyrus walked a slow, steady path to the back of the chamber, to an exit he had seen when last he had been here. He walked across the rich carpeting, pushing his way through the wooden doors that led to the rope-pulled box that transported guests of the Council from the bottom of the tower to the top. To his right stood an open balcony. He steeled himself and swept out upon it.

Reikonos was burning.

Black smoke stretched in heavy clouds across the horizon, pillars puffing blackness into the sky. The wood and brick construction of his city lay before Cyrus's eyes. Dark armies ran through the streets, visible to his eye even from here, like little globules of blood running whichever way gravity pulled them. The screams were one cacophonous horror all melded together, the volume muffled by his distance from the fray.

"My gods," Vaste said from his side, staring at the spectacle.

The smell of burning flesh was upon the wind, and burning other things, too. The wind whipped and the ash was falling. Snow was on the ground, on the rooftops, but the soot of the fires was turning it dark already. He could almost taste it on his tongue. Cyrus put a hand upon the railing of the balcony and stared upon his city, burned, ruined, ravaged.

"Cyrus," Vara said gently from beside him. He had not noticed her arrival. "It will do you no good to look upon this. There is nothing to be done here."

"Nothing?" Cyrus's voice was a harsh whisper, a deathly one, and fury filled it to brimming.

"That's not entirely true, is it?" Terian asked, easing into place at his other ear. "You know it. You can't defend this city now, that's sure; there's no wall you can put up, no bridge you can guard and let them run against you, match their power against yours in a futile, foolish grind to their death. They are inside, they are everywhere, and wild with the taste of blood and slaughter, these dead."

"Because of you," Cyrus said, and his head turned slowly to take in the dark knight who spoke into his ear.

"Not only because of me," Terian said quietly.

"They like the taste of blood and slaughter?" Cyrus asked, and he could feel the craze of rage force his lips wide into a smile that was near-madness. "I'll drown them in it."

"For once," Terian said, eyes a little wild, "don't be the fool warrior who thinks with his gonads that I always—falsely, I might add—accused you of being."

"It wasn't that falsely," Vara murmured.

"Use your shrewd mind," Terian said, ignoring her, "calculate the odds against you in this fight."

"And let my city burn?" Cyrus finished the natural extension of the thought, watching the black smoke of the fires drift just ahead of him.

"You can end this," Terian said. "But you won't end it here, and not by throwing yourself into a battle you can't hope to win. If you want to turn this army around, you need to provide them with a reason to walk away so compelling, they cannot possibly stay for another moment of pillage."

"You magnificent bastard," Vara whispered.

"Pretend for once I need you to do my thinking for me," Cyrus said, leveling his gaze on Terian. "What would you have me do?"

"We go to Saekaj," Terian whispered, and Cyrus caught a hint of fear in him from the mere statement. "You have a dagger matched against a sword. Saekaj is the exposed neck. Open it and watch the sword lose its menace."

"You want me to invade your own home," Cyrus said quietly. "To stomp down your doors, settle your scores—"

"I want you kill the God of Darkness!" It burst out of Terian in a fury. "I want you—you wielder of that," he pointed at Praelior, still clutched in Cyrus's hand, "I want you to free my damned people, because no one else can. I want you to turn loose your rage and set us all free in one stroke of the sword."

"Killing Yartraak will take more than one stroke of a sword," Curatio said from behind them, his voice still drawn. Cyrus looked to his face and found lines there, age that he had not shown moments earlier.

"I want you to save my home," Terian said, and there was weight behind the words that forced Cyrus to look upon the dark knight. His expression was soft within the helm, a quivering lip visible, buried in all the spikes and steel. "I want you to save us, Cyrus Davidon ... to save *our* people. Mine and yours."

Cyrus looked out across the horizon, across the fires, across the burning, the killing and the war. The stench of death was with him, hung in his nostrils, the smoke lidded his eyes and made him want to blink them clear. *But there is no blinking them clear, is there? No washing them clean of what I've seen, no swing of the sword I can make anywhere in this city that will end this, stop the killing.*

He looked south, past the massive city walls, and saw an army there, still filing into gates like maggots bursting from the dead bodies that comprised it. Somewhere beyond his sight was an end to that army, but he could not imagine it in any of the endless fields that he knew rested beyond the gates of Reikonos. The end was far beyond, far to the south ... somewhere in a cave, beneath the cool earth, where darkness made its home.

The decision was made, and his heart nearly screamed for joy at it. He looked to his right and saw Vara there, cool with certainty. Her hand was upon his arm, as though she had intended to restrain him somehow from Terian. It moved even as he watched, pulled back, with a final pat of ... reassurance? She pulled it back and drew herself to her full height. Her eyes were certain, too, and mirrored his own.

"We go," Cyrus said at last. "Mendicant ... take us back to Sanctuary, if you please."

"And?" Terian's voice cracked. "Then?"

Cyrus felt the sweet chill of his fury, so righteous in his anger, so delicious it masked the fear perfectly, felt it raise the bumps on his flesh. "And then ... we go to Saekaj ... into the halls of infinite darkness that Yartraak calls his own—" He looked Terian right in the face,"—and I stab that godless son of a bitch right in the eye until he's nothing but a shrunken corpse." Cyrus's words crashed from him like a righteous fury, burning the air with vengeful certainty. "Just like the last one we killed."

Chapter 73

"I need Fortin with us on this," Cyrus said, already issuing orders before the spell energy had dissipated to fully reveal the Sanctuary foyer. "Use whatever chain of teleportation you must to get him here." He caught an acknowledgment muttered from Mendicant before the goblin skittered off between the towering legs of those around him to disappear into the crowd. Cyrus took in the waiting throng with a glance, still swelled to full from his address just an hour earlier, spearmen standing encircled around the great seal. They seemed to relax as he and his small force appeared.

"What news, General?" Longwell shouted from the balcony above. The torches crackled on the walls, and the hearth roared over the sound of the silence in the cavernous room. Longwell held his lance tight, at attention, like a tower hanging over the room. *Like the Citadel*, Cyrus thought, oddly.

"Reikonos is fallen," Cyrus said, trying to keep his voice and face from betraying his emotion. "The walls are overrun, the armies are in the city."

"Do we ... retreat?" The voice came quiet and scared from somewhere in the crowd. It was followed by an uneasy silence that told Cyrus everything he needed to know about where his guild was standing. The fear was palpable, the sense of inevitability that came from watching the foundations of your world crumble around you.

"You're asking if we should run?" Cyrus spoke to no one in particular, to everyone he could see. He jutted his jaw, gave it consideration. "It is a reasonable question, to be pondered by reasonable men. When the world is fully arrayed against you, why should you go out and greet it with sword and spell, knowing that you will almost certainly be struck down?" He took the whole room in with an easy sweep of his gaze. "Why fight? Why fight when you feel you cannot win? When the fear of what you are facing is so swelling as to cripple you? As if it could grab you by the face and shake you until your heart quails at the thought of opposition. They're reasonable feelings, for reasonable men. Retreat? Aye, most would."

He looked forth, upon his waiting audience, gaze sweeping over countless eyes spellbound and hanging upon him. "BUT WE ARE NOT MOST," Cyrus said, raising his voice to the rafters. "For whatever reason you joined this guild—gold, power, strength—you are here now. You are one of us, now. And I am here to tell you that our purpose is not simple enrichment, that our strength is not gathered in days of glory to be rattled like a saber to impress those around us. Sanctuary is no mere army for hire to the highest bidder so that our vaults may overflow and our purses may clink when we walk. We were meant to be more; a bulwark against the forces of darkness that threaten to swallow the land—"

"Darkness, like Yartraak, see?" Vaste muttered under his breath. "So clever."

"Hush," Vara said.

"I know the fear that you feel," Cyrus said, "looking at the overwhelming odds mounted against us. They have an army of the dead. They have raised some of our own against us. I take this as insult, and I hope you do as well. Fear them? A reasonable man would—"

"But not a woman," Vara muttered.

"Now you hush," Vaste replied.

"—but this is not a place for reason," Cyrus said.

"Also true," Vaste said.

"Not now," Cyrus said under his breath then let his voice return to its previous sweeping volume. "Reason tells us to run in the face of fear. Reason would tell you to withdraw from the battle. But reason is not needed here, not now. Courage! Courage is what we cry for. Courage will bring you to the front of the battle lines, will see you against the monsters, the dead and the God of Darkness himself, and see you back safely! Do not fear that which stands before you. Do not run in the face of your enemies. They are not unstoppable, no matter what they may have you think." Cyrus drew his sword, whirled it in a tight circle once, and held it aloft so that the soft blue glow shone upon the assembled army. "I once looked in the face of a man who was an enemy and I said we accepted none but the brave to roam within these halls. I call upon that bravery in every one of you now. I call upon you to look within, to dive deep into yourselves and find your courage. Courage to stand against the insurmountable. To go into the darkness without fear, because your fellows are with you. We are none of us alone, and as we descend into the darkness of Saekaj Sovar—" He caught the ripple of surprise at that announcement, "—we will be there for each other. We will strike into the black heart of our enemy, and we will kill Yartraak—and end this war."

A stunned silence had swept the room throughout the entirety of his speech, and Cyrus felt himself swallow heavily, hoping it was not visible under his gorget. He waited, surveying the eyes, not quite sure what he saw within them—

"LET'S KILL THE RUDDY BASTARD!" Andren cried, and his shout was swept up in a chorus of approbation so loud that Cyrus felt as though he might be deafened. Armor rattled, swords were held aloft and shaken, and the cry of fury among the members of Sanctuary was such that Cyrus could scarcely believe it.

"Looks like they're willing to follow you into blackest death," Vara said into his ear.

"What about you?" Cyrus asked, not taking his eyes off the cheering crowd. "Will you follow me into darkness?"

"If you can find a way to get us there," Vara said smoothly, prickling a thought in Cyrus's mind.

"Dammit," Cyrus said. "Their portal is bound to be guarded." He searched for Curatio and found him standing beside Terian, only a few feet behind him. "I don't suppose you have a secret path into Saekaj?"

Curatio smiled. "Well, actually …"

Chapter 74

They appeared in a small flash, a group of only ten. The room was barely large enough for that, a confined space that reminded Cyrus of the sort of closet in which one might store brooms, but slightly larger. Cyrus's eyes did not adjust but to show him dark walls, stone-like in origin; finally his eyes brightened through the aid of magic so that he could see the grey stonework that surrounded him from floor to ceiling.

Cyrus looked over his shoulder, trying to find a portal. He glanced down, looking at the floor then to Curatio, who stood at his right. "It's in the ceiling," Curatio said with a smile. Cyrus looked up and saw wooden beams stretching off in either direction; if there was a portal up there, it was wider and taller than the room, and they had to have been right in the middle of it so as not to see a single trace of its stone, runed border.

"How do you know about this?" Vaste asked.

"I have lived a very long time," Curatio said, a little mysteriously. "Long enough to have been acquainted with someone who dated Marei, Goddess of Night, before her death."

"And they just happened to give you the spell to teleport to this portal?" Vaste sounded a little suspicious.

"Indeed," Curatio said. "It was a sad thing when she died; I doubt Yartraak even knows that someone else can come to this portal other than him."

"Wait, what?" This came from Terian. "Ohhhh … this is how he returns to the palace."

"Yes," Curatio said. "With this here, he can keep his soul bound in his realm, able to use the return spell at any point."

Cyrus felt a slight shiver. "The gods use the same magic as you do?"

"Most people use a very basic version of the magic the gods use," Curatio said, sounding like he was breathing more than a word of caution. "You would do well to remember that; it is not as though even the fiercest wizard in Arkaria could step into easy battle with the likes of someone such as Yartraak and win. He would overwhelm you with both physical strength and his magic."

"Don't fight him alone," Cyrus said, "got it."

"I will need to bring in the army a few at a time," Curatio said. "I would advise staying as close to this room as possible; wandering about the palace would be exceedingly foolish."

"You could teach someone else the spell," Cyrus said. "Couldn't you?"

Curatio sighed. "Unfortunately, not easily. The way that magic is taught in these days in order to avoid the blocks that we call heresy is quite appalling to someone like myself who was around when the fundamentals of magic were discovered and expanded upon." He pursed his lips in the dark. "Or, as I have heard others say … 'Kids these days.'" He smiled, and vanished in the twinkling of light from his return spell.

"We need to clear the room," Cyrus said, and there was a sound before him of a door squeaking open. He looked ahead and saw Odellan peeking out through the ever-so-slight light that came through the crack. After a moment he opened it wider, enough for them to pass through into a hallway.

Cyrus stepped out, long walls stretching in two directions. They stood at a right angle, a turn of the hall; it stretched before them and to their right, curving off into another turn some hundred feet ahead. There were other doors before the turn of the hall, and Cyrus found himself wondering where they led.

"This is lovely," Vaste said, "so dark and homey. Like living in a cave. Oh, right. It is a cave. Forgot that."

"This is actually quite a bit more opulent than most of our peoples' living conditions," Terian said, and Cyrus noted Erith standing beside him, shuddering slightly. "The Sovereign's palace is an impressive bit of construction, tunneled into the back wall of Saekaj, which is where the favored and wealthy live."

"It all looks constructed," Cyrus said, glancing at the walls. They were carved just the same as any castle he'd ever been in; the only difference was the utter lack of sunlight.

"It's meant to," Terian said.

"Should we not be worried about guards?" Vara asked.

"Well, we're standing in the middle of the most heavily guarded place in Saekaj, so … probably?" Terian said with a smile.

"You don't seem afraid," Vaste noted, "or terribly aware of exactly where we are."

"The Grand Palace of Saekaj is a sprawling place," Terian said. "Think … twisty dungeon. It's deeper than anyone knows. I'm told even the butlers are assigned specific sections that they aren't to deviate from, because they may get lost or stumble somewhere that they're not supposed to be." The dim light would have completely shrouded him if not for the spell that granted Cyrus his sight. "I have no idea exactly where we are."

The door behind them opened and a few more figures were disgorged. The ground shook with the steps of one of them.

"Fortin," Cyrus said.

"Lord Davidon," Fortin said. "It is agreeable to see you walking once more."

"Been walking for a while," Cyrus said.

"It is the fighting that matters," Fortin rumbled. "To see a great warlord humbled by such dark treachery as was perpetrated by Ice-thing …"

"Her name was Aisling," Cyrus said.

"Her name means 'Traitorous Whore,' as far as I'm concerned," Vara said.

"I find myself curious about the origin of your human names," Fortin said, voice rumbling quietly. "I had heard your people name their offspring meaningless collections of syllables they deem pleasing to the ears."

"Hey," Cyrus said, "not all of our names are meaningless." He saw a flash of green eyes from behind the rock giant's leg, a tangle of dark hair, and pursed his lips as he realized Larana stood in the shadow of Fortin. *On the second wave, Curatio? Why not bring a newborn gnome at the same time?*

"Oh?" The rock giant stared back at him. "What does 'Cyrus' mean?"

"It has an archaic meaning," Cyrus said with half a smile, pulling his attention to the red eyes, "'Kicker of Rock Giant Arse.'"

Fortin let a low, rumbling laugh that elicited a frown from Vara at the noise. "We should try to keep quiet," she said.

Cyrus saw motion behind the rock giant as another flash heralded the arrival of another wave of their forces. A cloak moved swiftly out of the room, rustling as it approached him. He caught a flash of long dark hair, whipping with the fast pace set by the person beneath it. "Martaina," he said. "Good to see you."

"I wish I could say the same." He felt her fingers upon his wrist as she slapped something into his hand.

"What the ...?" He lifted it, squinting his eyes at what she'd handed him. "What is this?"

"I figured you'd forgotten," she said with a glint in her eyes. "It's the treasure of the Mler. You may recall you died to find it."

He had a sudden remembrance of drowning in the dark, the feeling of the water flooding his lungs and crushing in on him, of his consciousness being swallowed by the blackness of unbeing. "I'd quite forgotten it; the dying was still ever present, I'm afraid." He stared at it then searched for a pouch on his belt, tucking it within the soft leather and closing the flap. "Good thinking. You're like my right hand, Martaina."

He sensed discomfort radiating from her. "I am not," she said. "There are things your right hand likely does nowadays that are better left to a more willing elf." She looked pointedly into the darkness, and he followed her gaze to Vara, who appeared not to notice.

Another flash, another small grouping flooded out of the closet.

"Sir," Odellan said quietly, just loud enough that Cyrus could hear him, "we are terribly exposed here. We need to establish a guard of our own or we will inevitably be found out and killed before the bulk of our forces arrive."

"Right," Cyrus said. "Martaina, take your eagle eyes and watch 'round that corner. Bow out, make sure anyone who comes within view does not have another breath leave their lungs." He watched the weapon appear in her hands, and she stalked quietly to the corner, peering out with only a fraction of her face exposed.

Cyrus turned his attention to the passage in front of them. "Then there's this." The next corner was far in front of them, at least three hundred feet. Countless doors lay to their left and right. "If we can establish a guard at the corner, the rest of us need to start securing these rooms so we don't get surprised by someone going about their business and screaming in shock at being surrounded by an army."

"This reminds me of Enterra," Andren said, and Cyrus realized that he hadn't even known that the healer had arrived. Another flash from the closet signaled the arrival of another wave, and Cyrus realized he had also lost count of how many times that had happened.

"Fortin," Cyrus said, and the rock giant rumbled acknowledgment, "get to the corner—but step lightly; stop anyone that comes around it."

"Also quietly, I presume?" the rock giant breathed then started toward the corner. He seemed to be moving on the tips of his toes, light enough that while Cyrus could feel some vibration, it was not quite the shaking of the earth sensation that the rock giant produced when running.

"Time to turn out the rooms," Cyrus said and looked around himself for assistance. He counted Odellan, Vara, Terian and Ryin in close proximity. A fair host of other Sanctuary members were in close attendance as well, but he could not see them nearly as well the farther away they were.

"Like morning's end at some of the dirtier establishments," said a familiar voice, somewhat accented with the tones of the Northlands.

"Is that Menlos Irontooth?" Cyrus looked for the northman, squinting in the dark. He caught a glimpse of the dirty fellow, waving from behind the shoulder of Samwen Longwell, face partially obscured by the dragoon's lance. "No wolves?"

"They're here," Menlos said. "You need them?"

"I need them quiet," Cyrus said. "If you can deliver that, I can find a use for them to chase down anyone who might run."

"Oh, I can provide quiet," Menlos said. "And they're always up for a good meal."

"They may have to grab them on the run," Cyrus said, "though I suppose that'll get a bit loud."

"I would advise against loudness," Vara said. "Save it for your bedchamber."

He stared at her in the dark. "That almost sounded like something that would be said by—"

She glared at him. "Do not ... finish that statement."

He let it go, instead turning his attention to the first door on their left. He gave a quick count and stopped after fifteen before them. "Damnation. Terian?" He waited to see the dark knight appear next to him. "I know you don't know this part of the palace, but what would you think that is?" He gestured at the first door.

"It could be the keeping rooms for the Sovereign's harem," Terian said with a broad shrug. "Guard quarters, though I would think they'd be a bit more lively. Treasure rooms, perhaps. Dungeons? I really have no idea."

"Into the dark," Cyrus said.

"Find your courage," Terian said with a wide grin.

"Maybe it's back here," Cyrus said and ripped open the first door, the dark metal handle shaking in his hand as he pulled upon it.

He stared into a pooled darkness within, a chamber bigger than the hallway, bigger than he would have guessed by the door next to him, bigger than it had any right to be from its outside appearance. It extended to a small, three-step staircase a few feet in front of him, the outer perimeter of the room leading into a pit. Glancing up, he could see the ceiling carved upward in a similar pattern, pyramiding upward in a stair-step effect.

Inky blackness lingered in the depths of it, and he felt himself shudder involuntarily.

"CYRUS!" Martaina's shout snapped his head around; the ranger was standing at the corner, arrows flying from her bow as quickly as she could pluck them from her quiver. Shouts echoed down the hallway beyond her, furious, screams of pain and rage. "A whole godsdamned army division is marching down this hall!" The normally calm elf was moving with a frenzy, retreating a step at a time—

"WARLORD!" Fortin's rumbling cry echoed down the hallway from the other end, and Cyrus barely turned in time to see him with a flood of tiny soldiers around him. The rock giant's arms were in motion, spattering bodies, shearing bones, and throwing corpses against the wall with a fury. Doors began to open in the spaces between Cyrus and Fortin, bodies pouring out in armor, helmeted heads swiveling to find the army in their midst. They flooded into the halls and the Sanctuary force went forth to greet them, Odellan at the fore.

The split was automatic, and Cyrus did not whisper a word, the chaos and clangor so loud he would have had to shout to be heard in any case. He watched Andren fling a white, glowing hand at Martaina just as she failed to block a sword-strike with her bow and was impaled. She shrugged the sword out of the wound and was healed, Longwell coming to her aid with lance in hand as a dark elven squadron came around the corner in a fury.

Cyrus hesitated, just a moment too long inside the door. It was a curious thing, that which held him back. It was a compulsion, a question asked by the darkness—

"Cyrus Davidon ..." came the voice. He felt the words shudder along his spine, the armor little protection from the power of the voice that spoke them. He turned, looking into the dark, watched it shrivel and fall away to reveal a grey-skinned figure with three horns sprouted from its head, thin legs and arms. It was a tall thing, rising up above his height even on the lower footing offered by the pit.

"Sovereign," Cyrus said, using the thing's official title. He stared at it—at him, he supposed—the red eyes looking terribly familiar as they glared out at him from within Yartraak's own bedchamber.

"Come in ... and close the door behind you," Yartraak said. It was polite, it was a suggestion, but one that carried with it all the menace of a threat. *Come in and close the door behind you ... or your entire army will be flanked by a god and splattered down the hallway in mere seconds.*

Cyrus took only a moment to contemplate it. The smell of sweat and blood was heavy in the hall already; he could see floors slick with the dark, crimson liquid, saw the flash as Curatio arrived again bearing reinforcements that would be forced to immediately pour into the fight. He caught a glimpse of Terian in the midst of the soldiers flowing out of the doors down the hall, of Vara fighting among the ones pouring around Martaina's corner. The battle was truly joined, the Sanctuary force was already overwhelmed, and there was little enough he could do save for wade in with Praelior—

And bring behind him the God of Darkness, into a battle that they were already losing.

He listened to the shriek of swords upon metal, the screams of the wounded and fallen, and he took one silent step back into the

Sovereign's chambers, shutting the door behind him. The sound of battle faded as he did so.

Cyrus stood there, and the darkness swelled around him, closing in like the night falling at the end of day.

Chapter 75

"We meet at last, Cyrus Davidon," Yartraak called into the darkness. The power of the spell that gave Cyrus sight seemed to have been ripped away, flooded by the black seeping from the god who held it in his sway. "Master of Sanctuary. Favored of Bellarum. Holder of Drettanden's … trinket." Cyrus heard the rumble in the Sovereign's voice. "Now you stand before me, outside the assistance of your guild and your god. What have you to say for yourself?"

"It's kinda dark in here," Cyrus said, smarting off.

There was a low rumble of gleeful laughter. "This is what happens when you step into the domain of darkness, yes? All … alone." He sounded immeasurably pleased.

There was a sound of the door opening and closing behind him, and then a flame lit in the darkness, a glowing blade wrapped in fire. Cyrus saw it illuminate the blue eyes, the high, pale cheekbones, and saw a small spatter of blood in a thin line across her cheek. "Oh, there you are," Vara said casually. "I thought you'd wandered off. And in the middle of a battle, no less."

"Vara, get out of here," Cyrus hissed. He had Praelior in his hand, drawn the moment he'd seen her appear. The blue glow was a pittance of light compared to her flaming sword.

"And miss the chance to glare into the darkness, see the heart of its cowardice hiding within the ignoble black?" She taunted without fear, and he knew that she was aware of what they faced.

"The fabled Vara," Yartraak said from in the pit, "the Goddess of Life's own dear one. The two of you together, standing before me. What a day this is. Do you know what I call you?"

Cyrus blinked and found an answer immediately sprang to mind in light of what he'd seen of the God of Darkness before the black swept in and shrouded everything. "Damned good looking."

"Puppets," Yartraak said, an ounce of displeasure creeping into that dark tone. "Proxies."

"I think you were closer to the mark, personally," Vara said to Cyrus with just a bit of a stage whisper.

"And funny as well," Yartraak said. "I'd heard that about you."

"Well, now you've heard it with your own ears," Cyrus said and felt to his belt for the pouch that contained the treasure of the Mler. He concentrated, just for a moment, and light flooded into the darkness. "And seen it with your own glorious eyes, gorgeous."

There was a screech of surprise as the chamber was lit from the artifact in Cyrus's hand. It glowed with a brightness not unlike the midday sun, sprinkling radiance in every direction. Cyrus was already moving when it flared, jumping into the pit with his sword at the ready. He saw Vara at his side, matching his movements with her own blade raised.

The treasure of the Mler—a light so powerful it could shine into the depths of the deepest ocean—blasted the swirling darkness shrouding Yartraak and gave Cyrus a full view of the creature. It was grey, as he'd seen before, and the horns that wrapped its head came around like elephant tusks to point along both sides of the God of Darkness's elongated jaw. The third horn seemed to originate at the back of his head and ran in a low arc over his forehead, offering his nose some protection. Red eyes squinted into the sudden brightness, and the creature was tilted back, unnaturally bent at the torso, as though he possessed not one waist at which to bend but two.

Cyrus came low as Vara went high; his blade slashed into the tough skin at the god's hip, opening a two-inch gash. Vara, her ambitions higher than his own, went for an impaling strike and was turned aside as Yartraak batted a backhand at her. He missed by less than an inch, and Vara was forced to fling herself aside, slamming into an oversized wooden couch that lay against the inside of the pit wall.

"First blood's mine," Cyrus said, coming out of his attack in a defensive stance. Yartraak already looked smaller than he had when Cyrus had first seen him. He was down a few inches in height but was still a commanding presence, taller than Cyrus still by a considerable margin. The red eyes seethed with the anger of a being not used to being physically attacked; the fear was mingled in there with the rage, and they were both almost tangible, coming off the Sovereign of Saekaj like hot breath.

"All your blood will be mine," Yartraak said in a low fury and raised his three-fingered hand. It was aglow, and Cyrus did not hesitate, diving to his left behind an oversized bed. A gout of flame followed him and struck his feeble cover, causing it to explode from the sheer force.

"I could use some magic," Cyrus muttered to himself. Splinters rained down on him, tapping upon his helm and pauldrons as he stayed behind the destroyed piece of furniture. A small fire crackled in his ear. The treasure of the Mler had fallen from his grasp, glowing faintly where it had skittered, about ten feet away, shedding only a fraction of its previous light and growing softer by the moment.

Yartraak appeared above him and Cyrus came out swinging. Using the glow of the artifact and the burning pieces of the bed, he dodged around the wreckage between them, the God of Darkness's red eyes following him just slightly more swiftly than the grey flesh could. Cyrus rolled, something he'd practiced, aided by Praelior's speed, and he came out of it on his feet. He tried to cast a look at Vara, but she was not visible—

A blast of concussive force hit Yartraak from the blind side, knocking him forward. He did not lose his footing, but Cyrus watched his red eyes close for a moment in the growing half-light as Vara's sword lit into flame once more, this time behind him. Yartraak swayed on his feet like a drunk staggering down a Reikonos street, and Cyrus leapt at the opportunity. He raised Praelior high in his hand—

And a thunderous blow caught him midair, slamming into his breastplate and pitching him into the back wall with world-ending force. There was a crashing, thundering noise in Cyrus's ears, the sound of all manner of things breaking, and then the darkness was complete, as though he had fallen completely to pieces and the world had gone with him.

Chapter 76

Cyrus awoke feeling as if he were drowning, like he could not get a breath into his lungs. He forced air in painfully, the darkness shrouding his eyes like it was choking him.

This is what Alaric felt like ...

Air surged into his nostrils, the pain increased, and he realized he was drawing breath. Painful breath, true, but breath. He could feel his fingers, his toes somewhere down in his boots. He took another breath, felt the pain that encircled his ribs.

I'm alive.

He felt himself blink, the world resolving into focus around him. He was in a room, dim light filtering in from two torches high upon the wall.

I'm alive ... and Alaric is not.

Vara.

Somehow that thought gave him the strength to move. He pushed himself to all fours. His back hurt, his ribs ached, but still he drew breath. He looked up, to the height of the chamber. *Some sort of throne room?* He glanced back and saw a wall caved in. *Did I fly through that? Gods.*

He blinked. *Forget the gods.*

Only one of them matters at the moment.

He could hear the rough scrape of blade against flesh somewhere in the darkness behind him, through the wall. He stared into the darkness, searching for any sign of his weapon. He could see Vara's blade lit inside, moving in the inky black, floating as if wielded by a disembodied hand.

"Cy ... rus ... David ... on ..." The voice was a whisper behind him, and he turned to find the speaker. The room was dim, dark, but there was something in the shadows against a nearby wall. There was a throne not far from where he stood and the speaker was next to the wall beside it, a shadow huddled against it.

His eyes tried to penetrate the dark, and he saw a shock of wispy white hair, like straw in the torchlight. Wrinkled flesh was visible beneath it. "Cyrus ... David ... on ..." the voice came again, weak and feeble. "Do mine eyes de ... ceive me?"

"My name is Cyrus Davidon," he spoke to the shadow, keeping an eye on Vara's sword, moving in the dark. "Speak quickly; I'm rather in the middle of something." He turned his gaze back to the dark and saw Vara evade, edging ever closer to the massive hole his body had made in the wall when he'd been smashed through it.

A face emerged from the shadows, aged and pale, lined so heavily it looked like something so bereft of life as to be found on an embalmed and half-rotted body. He could barely tell that it was female, the lines holding no hint that it had ever been anything other than a crone. She looked either human or elvish, something pale that did not belong in the depths of Saekaj, and her eyes were milky white, her blindness as obvious to him as the fact that she was aged beyond all counting of years. "Free me," she whispered, and it was more than a plea.

"Vidara?" Cyrus asked, nearly astonished.

"Yesss," she hissed and launched into a hacking cough. "Freee ... mee ..." her voice dissolved into the coughs of the aged, life seeming to drip out of her with each of them.

"I'll get right on that," Cyrus said and tried to put the thought of her out of his mind. Vara was in there, was in need of his help; she was holding off the God of Darkness by her lonesome, after all, and that was no small feat. His eyes gazed through the black, catching sight of something glowing faintly blue in the rubble—

He rushed forward and scrambled for it, brushing aside crushed stone and broken brick, finally laying his hand upon the hilt of Praelior, seizing it, taking it up again. All but the worst of the pain was washed aside, and what remained was dulled. This was not so terrible; not nearly so bad as the stabbing that Aisling had lain upon him. This was pain, certainly, but not insurmountable.

He saw the flash of a spell within the dark and then saw Vara's blade shoot through the air toward him. She hit the ground next to him, coming out of a quick, graceful leap like those he had seen her make more times than he could count. She grunted as she shot past him, stumbling slightly as she made her landing. Whether she had been forced into this direction or chosen it, he was unsure, but the sight of her sailing toward him was enough to gladden his heart, bracing him against what he knew would follow within seconds.

The God of Darkness came barreling out at him, the torchlight catching him as he swept through the wall. Cyrus stood waiting, Yartraak only slightly taller than him now, and Cyrus braced as a hand swept toward him. He extended Praelior at the last second, sweeping it around exactly the way he had with Mortus, letting the blade catch the god's swipe—

Cyrus felt himself launched from the force of the blow once more. His hands were anchored on the hilt of his blade this time, though, even as the pain shot through him from top to bottom. He flew in a high arc through the air and hit wooden doors at the front of the hall, knocking them open and tearing one from its hinges as he landed. He somehow rolled through the landing, tucking his blade against him as he tumbled over heavy red carpet.

His ribs screamed their displeasure, but they were still with him to scream. His left arm felt curiously painful, but he attempted to bend it and it moved with all of its usual utility. He stood, though it took him a moment. The taste of blood was thick in his mouth, he could feel the warm liquid running out of his nose, and he knew he'd been in a battle. He wiped his face with his left hand, prompting a cry of pain from his arm at the movement. *No matter*, he thought. *I'm not dead yet.*

There was a flash of powerful spell energy from within the throne room and something hit the door to the chamber in an explosion of force. Grey flesh smashed the doors in half, ripping the remaining one free of its hinges as Yartraak tumbled to the ground before Cyrus. His horned head was smaller now, the God of Darkness driven to his knees by the landing. The ground shook as he rumbled, a snort of fury that Cyrus ignored as he reversed his grip on Praelior and drove it into Yartraak's back, burying it to the hilt—

The reprisal was instantaneous; a blast of force sent Cyrus rocketing backward as though a barrel of Dragon's Breath had gone off under his feet, his armor splitting another set of doors as he was propelled through. He slammed to the ground and found himself in a roll once more, flopping near-uselessly as a world of caves and hard rock tumbled around him. He rolled over a bridge at high speed. Before him appeared a wall with an open gate, guards in armor swarming over it. He hit the ground and rolled under the gate, bowling over three dark elves in armor as he passed through like a projectile hurled from an angry fist.

Cyrus rolled to a stop in the middle of a street, walled estates visible on either side of him. He felt the drunkenness that followed a hard punch, the wooziness that told him he'd been struck hard upon his head. He tried to lift his neck, tried to stand, but failed. He realized dimly that he lay upon a bed of dark elven guards, their bodies broken by his landing upon them. He wondered at that, but his cognition was slow from the battering. His ribs screamed endlessly, and there were other pains attacking him now, more than he could count. He made another effort to move and failed as the agony dragged him down. Even breathing was a chore, the darkness closed in around him, each breath coming heavier than the last.

There was a crunch as something landed nearby. He could see the gate through which he'd rolled, and the grey-fleshed, red-eyed, horned fury that was Yartraak, God of Darkness, stood at his feet, staring down at him. The faint hint of a glowing, blue blade's tip poked from his breast, protruding from between ribs that showed beneath his flesh.

"Cyrus Davidon," Yartraak rasped. "You are in *my* city. You have broken through my palace, despoiled my walls and humiliated me in front of my people." His breath carried an oily stink even from this distance. "You have failed in your foolish quest, and now I will destroy you before I go forth and finish your elven wench and all the other fools of your ilk—"

One of the long, three-fingered hands snaked down and grasped Cyrus around the neck, ripping him from the hard ground's embrace. It hurt, and he rattled within the bounds of his armor. "You will pay for this affront," Yartraak whispered. "Your friends will pay for you, in pain and blood."

Cyrus spat in his face, blood oozing in a wad across the grey flesh. "You first." He swiped at the God of Darkness with a weak hand, landing a gauntlet on a horn, grasping at it with weak fingers.

"You should have been my servant," Yartraak said, the red eyes glaring out at him. "But instead, you die a fool's death." He raised Cyrus high in the air above him, and the air was cut from his throat as the grip tightened. "You will be the first to feel the end of your peoples' day ... it is coming, and soon ... to all the corners of Arkaria ..."

Cyrus fought it, fought the pain, fought the struggle to draw a breath, but he could not seem to grasp it, as though it were the hilt of Praelior—so near, yet so very far from his reach ...

Cyrus fought the darkness, but it came to claim him, screaming, crying, and finally dragging his eyes shut as it took him into its foul and empty depths.

Chapter 77

"You are not alone," the voice whispered to Cyrus in the dark.

The pain was strangely absent, and Cyrus could feel his fingers. They scraped against something, against stone or steel, producing a low, scratching noise that perked up his ears. The scent of blood was gone from his nose, the taste missing from his tongue, and he could see a faint glow of white light around him.

Cyrus sat up, the darkness fading. He was in a place shrouded in white, something strangely familiar about it. The light began to fade, and lace curtains flapped in the wind. He heard the crackle of a fire behind him.

The tower of the Guildmaster, he realized at last.

Sanctuary.

Cyrus sat upon the floor, his armor pressing against the hard stone. It felt immovable, strong, and his fingers idly traced the line of the irregularities in the surface, like waves upon the surface of the water. It stared back at him, grey, and he could see a bright, sunlit day outside each balcony.

"You are not alone," the voice came again, and he realized that someone stood before him, a silhouette against the background of the open windows, the skies so clear that he could see the outline of the Heia mountains far to the south.

Cyrus stared at the shadowy figure as it resolved, sharp lines of the armor taking shape before his eyes, the dark splotch over one of the eyes becoming a black patch as he watched.

The other eye, grey as a stormy sky, stared out at him, the edges of the skin around it crinkled from a very slight smile that had stretched from the lips all the way up to it. Sincere and true, and something Cyrus had not even realized he missed.

"Alaric," Cyrus whispered. "You're ..." he felt his balance tip, his head swim as though he were bobbing in the water, "... you're dead."

Alaric's smile faded, but the piercing eye never left him. "Assuming it is as you say ... does that mean that mean that I am no longer able to help you?"

"You're dead," Cyrus said finally. "I'm imagining this."

Alaric nodded his head once as the lace curtain fluttered in the breeze behind him. "A lovely place. Not a terrible one to imagine in time of strife."

"Better than where I was," Cyrus said, and his tongue felt thick with the memory—the blood, the pain.

"Where were you?" Alaric asked.

Cyrus smiled at him, faintly. "Shouldn't you know? You're in my head, after all."

"I imagined it would be a grimmer place," Alaric said, looking around, "it being inside *your* head, after all."

"Was that a joke?" Cyrus asked.

Alaric grinned. "It did have the ring of one, did it not?"

"I was in Saekaj," Cyrus said, all thought of mirth passed in an instant. "I led Sanctuary into Saekaj to fight Yartraak. To kill him." He let his head bow. "I failed you, Alaric."

"You failed me?" Alaric asked, and Cyrus watched the Ghost's boots scrape across the floor as he took slow steps forward. "Me, a figment of your imagination? Is such a thing even possible?"

"I failed the real Alaric," Cyrus said, not looking up, as though even the judgment of this vision he saw would be enough to break his mind the way Yartraak had broken his body. "I failed the guild. All Arkaria. I ... failed. There is nothing more to it."

Alaric's armor made a slight protest as the old knight knelt, knee clanking against the stone floor. "I have failed, you know."

Cyrus looked up and saw that grey eye. "You saved Arkaria. From the scourge."

"But I have failed before, you know this, yes?" Alaric's voice was soft. "I failed the night your friend Narstron died. I failed the day that Niamh was killed." He lowered his voice. "I failed you in the Realm of

Death, and after. Many times in my life, I failed. Some were more painful than others."

Cyrus stared at him. "How did you fail me?" He almost laughed, so absurd was the statement.

"I have hidden so much, for so very long," Alaric said, and his voice carried a scratch of weariness, of troubles that weighed it down, obvious to Cyrus's ear now that he was practiced in the feeling. "At some point after the death of Raifa, I tried to carry everything all by myself. It's a powerful loneliness that can set in, here in this place." Alaric encompassed the whole tower with a wave of his hand. "Curatio could not always help, no matter how he tried. Nor could ... another." He smiled. "Keeping secrets exacts a price. Especially when you keep them from those dearest to you."

"I failed you, Alaric," Cyrus said again. "I failed the guild. Led them into death."

"And I failed you," Alaric said, and now his face was grim. "Failed to trust you, failed to believe in you enough to trust you. There are things going on in this world that I thought were beyond you, and I made my every effort to keep you out of them rather than helping you step into them with your wits about you. I shackled you to my fears, made you slave to my previous experience, kept you in the dark when I should have helped you into the light." His face was impassive. "I did this to you ... and to so many others."

"We made our choices," Cyrus said, watching him carefully. "I made my choices ... and they were poor."

Alaric's blank expression wavered, just for a moment, and Cyrus felt the knight's hand come to rest on his shoulder. It felt warm through the armor, the squeeze of affirmation that he could scarcely even feel. "There is blame enough to go around, but you do not condemn the child for the failures of the parent."

Cyrus felt a weak laugh leave him. "You're not my father, Alaric. Much as I occasionally wish you were."

"No," Alaric said, with a slow nod. "I am not, much as I also have wished that I could have been; you grew to the man you are without a father, shaped by the horrors of war and arms. You did it alone, carved yourself into a fighter in a place that had broken all others."

"I didn't ... do it alone." Cyrus felt his voice fall to a whisper. He looked into Alaric's eye. "But I'm alone now."

"Are you?" Alaric said, and he stood, slowly. Cyrus looked up, the eyes of a child upon an adult, and he saw nothing but light and benevolence shining down upon him. "Are you, truly?"

"Yes," Cyrus said, and his voice sounded small.

"Though you are not my son, you are my legacy, Cyrus Davidon," Alaric said, and he seemed somehow distant, even though he stood right there. A trickle of blood ran from his lips, and Cyrus caught a glimpse of a horrible pallor upon his face, which had seemed so healthy and ruddy only a moment before. "That which I left behind to guide Sanctuary." His head straightened atop his shoulders, and he seemed to look beyond Cyrus, hovering above him.

Cyrus felt himself rise opposite Alaric, felt himself lift into the air above the knight. Alaric flickered, just for a moment, reality intruding, dark cave walls, a grip around his neck, a grey-skinned beast with red eyes—

"You are my legacy, Cyrus Davidon," Alaric said, but his voice was distant, and he was gone, replaced by the red-eyed fury of a god who wanted him dead, "but you are not the only one I left behind—"

Chapter 78

"Turn and face me, you dead-skinned, rat-eyed, fecking arsehole."

Cyrus snapped back to waking, dangling in the grasp of Yartraak. He saw what lurked over the beast's shoulder; a blond-haired fury, cheeks lit crimson, mouth a thin line of vengeful anger, her armor shining silver in the bare torchlight and the furious flame crackling up and down her sword.

Cyrus could feel the blood coursing down his upper lip, could taste it as he opened his mouth and it dribbled in, even as he heard more of it rushing in his ears. His flesh was cold, the aches and pains settled about him. He saw a glow upon her hand and the agony faded more than a bit.

"Shelas'akur," Yartraak whispered. Cyrus noted the presence of soldiers here, dark elves ringing them with others closing from behind him. These wore the clothing of civilians—some fat, some thin, all dressed like they had the finest of finery available to them.

"Fitting you would call me that," Vara said, looking like pure, mauling death, ready to turn itself loose, "since I am about to drive the last hope out of you."

"You talk entirely too big for a mortal your size," Yartraak said, rasping.

"You're not so big yourself anymore," Vara shot right back. Cyrus felt his feet dangling and adjusted them; his toes barely touched the ground, but they did touch.

"You are surrounded by my forces," Yartraak said. "My armies. You are in the heart of my darkness."

Cyrus reached for his blade, still jutting from the God of Darkness's back. He tried not to be obvious about it, but it mattered little; it was beyond his grasp, and the Lord of the Dark still had him firmly by the neck. *One good twist and I'm dead ... but maybe if he's forgotten about me ...* he felt the fingers grip his throat. *Nope. He hasn't forgotten.*

Cyrus's eyes found Vara's, saw the hint of panic from her, only visible because he knew her well enough to see the subtle flicker of her eyes.

Dammit ... the bastard is using me to keep her at bay.

"Is she worth dying for?" Yartraak asked, and Cyrus felt his feet leave the ground again. He turned his horned head just enough to look at Cyrus. "Well?" He loosened his grip, ever so slightly, and Cyrus felt himself cough. "Is she?"

"That and more," Cyrus rasped around the fingers wrapped around his neck. He could feel the toes of his boots touching the ground, just brushing it. *Just a little more ...*

Yartraak smiled hideously. He turned his gaze back on Vara, still standing fearlessly before him, her fiery blade in one hand. "And what do you say, Lady Vara? Is he worth dying for?"

The fury barely flickered, like a breeze blowing across a candle's flame, but for any who knew her as Cyrus did, it was as obvious as if the fire had gone out. "Perhaps," she said simply.

"Perhaps?" Yartraak let out a rumbling laugh. "Perhaps?" He looked at Cyrus and laughed in his face, that oily smell. "Is this love? She answers, 'perhaps'!"

"Perhaps ..." Vara said, drawing Yartraak's attention back to her and halting as though there were more to add, "... but it's not going to come to that."

Cyrus saw the flash in the god's eye just before the spell flared from Vara's palm. He had a split second to realize she'd cast it without words—could she do that before?—and he was swept out of the God of Darkness's grasp. His back hit the ground hard, and he scrambled to his feet as a dark elven soldier came at him with a blade in hand.

Cyrus dodged, grabbing the blade with his gauntlet. Even bereft of Praelior, he was faster than most, instincts tuned in years of combat, forged in the fires of more wars than he could count. He gripped the blade tight and drove it back, snapping it up so that the hilt smashed the wielder in the face. It came free of the soldier's grip, and Cyrus reversed his hold on it, bring it around into the neck of the threat he saw coming out of the corner of his eye. Another soldier of the dark elves, one of a hundred around them, and he caught it across the throat with all the grace one could expect of a razor that opened one's neck.

Cyrus swirled in motion, feeling the lack of Praelior keenly, the speed it gave. He fought in a mad swirl, his blows less effective as the soldiers closed in on him. He saw Vara fending off Yartraak behind him, her hands moving so fast that they were a blur, and it reminded him of the time he'd stood with her beneath a dragon and watched her carve the scales apart, her sword strokes as delicate as a painter's brushstrokes.

There was only some of that here, her sword a frenzy of motion. She dodged the spells cast her way by Yartraak as he drove her toward the gate. Cyrus hurried backward, fending off the attacks of the guards, the warriors as he worked to press himself toward Yartraak. He saw bows pointed at him, fearful to shoot out of concern for hitting their Sovereign, and he exploited it, never daring to move more than a few inches to either side. He could see the hilt of Praelior when he glanced, still hanging out of Yartraak's back as though it were buried in a stone.

I need it.

Cyrus watched Vara's movements slow, watched the God of Darkness hound her relentlessly. She could not help but give ground; he was stronger, there was no doubt. Faster, too, though only by a slight edge. She met his strikes with glancing blows, bleeding him a drop at a time. His thin arms were black with ichor of the sort Cyrus had seen drip from Mortus, a hundred tiny cuts causing him to drip.

He was shorter than Cyrus now, this much was apparent. The guard had ceased to advance on him with furious sword thrusts; he was less than two feet from Yartraak's back and hurrying backward, alternating his gaze fore and backward, trying not to unexpectedly run into the Sovereign should he halt.

The black cave walls hung above them like a sickly night sky, craggy and cleft, glowing faintly translucent as though some living light grew upon them. The walls of the Grand Palace were just there, twenty feet behind Vara, and Cyrus felt a clenching of his gut at what was likely to be waiting beyond; guards, guards beyond counting, sure to ambush her if they were within feet of the gate. The thought of her falling, struck down by spears and swords, flashed heavy in his head. He had a hundred at his back, and suddenly he did not care.

Cyrus lunged at Yartraak's retreating back, both hands outreached, and felt his fingers tighten around the hilt of Praelior. The world slowed at his caress, and he tightened his fingers around the pommel. He forced his hand up the hilt without giving up his grip and yanked, ripping the sword free of the God of Darkness's back—

A howl echoed through the cavern, bouncing off the walls like a wolf had let out a scream to its pack. Cyrus fell as Praelior gave way, lost his footing from his wild jump and toppled, his back hitting the hard ground of cavern. He saw Yartraak's back arch as he bent in that unnatural way, shouting from the pain. He whirled upon Cyrus and stared down with furious eyes, moving with a speed that was frighteningly fast, angry with the pain, drunk on it, spiteful and ready to rain down his vengeance upon Cyrus for the last time. *I can't stop him*, Cyrus realized. *Not from here. I can buy myself perhaps a few seconds and that is all-*

You are not alone.

Cyrus looked upon the face of Sovereign of Saekaj Sovar in all its inarticulate fury, and he tossed Praelior, the weapon that might have given him a few seconds of life, between the grey, skinny legs of the God of Darkness.

He watched the weapon fly as Yartraak registered surprise with those red eyes; of all the things he might have anticipated, Cyrus knew that this was not one. Praelior sailed with Cyrus's throw, aided by the strength it had given him while it was in his hand, sailed in a low arc—

And fell into the open right hand of a very enraged elven paladin.

She stood with a blade in each hand, and Cyrus watched as flames rippled from the crossguard to the tip of his sword, the furious heart of its user poured out onto the weapon itself.

"Your hope—" Yartraak said.

Vara did not even wait until he finished. She came low with her own sword, striking his right wrist before he could get it high enough to issue a spell to stop her. It hacked loose the three-fingered, clawed hand, the strength given her by Praelior enhancing her already righteous anger, and she followed a second later with the blade once wielded by the God of Courage and smote Yartraak's head clean from his shoulders. "Do not speak to me of hope," she said when his body wavered before her, quivering on dead legs as it started to fall, "for you have none left."

Cyrus lay there as the army that had chased him stood in absolute silence. Yartraak's corpse fell to a knee, and something thumped, landing beside him. He turned stunned eyes upon it, and saw the face of the God of Darkness, come to rest on its side.

"He will ... betray you, you know ..." Yartraak said, red eyes already glazing over, the light fading from them. Cyrus stared, mesmerized, unable to take his gaze from the dying face. "You have ... his favor ... now ... but ... the moment your interests diverge ... he will ... kill you." That came out a whisper, the eyes growing duller. "It's what he ... does ..."

The lips ceased their movement, and Cyrus jarred himself out of his trance to get to his feet. He looked at the crowd of soldiers standing awestruck before him, paralyzed, the civilians behind them even more deadened by the spectacle that greeted their eyes at the gates of their Grand Palace.

Cyrus looked back and saw her, then, the fury that had saved him. Vara stood, both blades extended at her side, avenging angel with holy wrath wrought down the metal in the form of scourging fire. She was a spectacle unto herself, death, swift and blazing, the firelight gleaming on her armor, shining in her hair, and her eyes a burning blue like the sky itself was channeled through her with all its glory and grandeur.

"Get the hell out of here," she said to the guards before her, voice low and full of terrible menace. "I am your destroyer, the end of your wretched lives, the fiery death of your god and the burning fear which should consume your every nightmare. Flee from me, give me my due with your screams ... or I will take it from you in the form of your lives."

Cyrus felt as though he should take a step back but instead held his ground, though he swallowed hard. He eyed the dark elven soldiers and civilians standing in the road outside the Sovereign's palace. The first clatter of a spear hitting the ground surprised him, but the next twenty happened so quickly that he did not have time to place them in their proper context. By the time the screams started, he was certain he was near-dead and witnessing something quite otherworldly.

They fled, every witness and watcher, throwing weapons aside, cravenly shoving their way past women and children, disappearing into the wide avenue beyond as though death itself were nipping behind them. The cries echoed off the walls, and Cyrus turned back to see guards fleeing out of the gate behind them, running wide around Vara, hewing close to the walls that circled them, closing off access to the houses on either side. They screamed, these men in full armor, they cried like children, and they, too, ran down the road as though pursued.

He looked back at her, caught the fury in the eyes once more, and shook his head. "That was …" He blew a breath through his lips. "Damn. That was something."

She looked at him coolly. "You may be able to scare a horde of angry trolls with the aid of a wizard and a listing of your deeds, but I can well guarantee that these bastard dark elves will be talking about the night the elven woman with the flaming swords made them surrender their courage and run screaming for years to come."

He nodded his head in concession. "I doubt I'll be forgetting it any time soon, either." He extended a hand. "Can I … have my sword back now?" She looked at him, inscrutable, and then the blade of his weapon extinguished before she turned it around to offer him the hilt. "Thanks," he said, taking up Praelior once more, staring into the destroyed facade of the Grand Palace. "I suppose we should get back to the army, help them clean up what's left of the mess."

"But of course," she said, matter-of-factly. "There is also the small matter of freeing Vidara." She started toward the gate, pausing just outside it to glance around the corner; seeing nothing there, she entered the palace courtyard on her way to the bridge that crossed the moat.

"She's in the throne room," Cyrus said, hurrying to keep up with her. He walked alongside her, still feeling some aches running through his body. "And … by the way … thank you."

She glanced at him sideways for only a moment. "Worry not, Lord Davidon, epic hero … I shan't soon let you forget the night you were forced to surrender your sword to me so that I could save your life."

He felt a rueful smile creep across his lips as they made their way back to the palace. A river ran beneath them, the sound of running waters a soothing, calming thing after the crash of battle with a god.

"Lady Vara ... I cannot imagine anyone I would rather be saved by than you." He saw her cheek redden, but she hurried her pace before he could so much as inquire about it and he was forced to increase his speed to keep up.

Chapter 79

"I feel like I've been batted about like a cat's toy," Cyrus said, tilting his neck left and right as they stepped through the wrecked front doors of the Grand Palace. Wood and stone were broken here, beams split, splinters jutting out. Cyrus could smell destruction all about, the dust in the air from it. He spat blood upon the ground, realizing a moment later it was a gleaming wood floor, shining from a heavy varnish.

"Charming," Vara pronounced, more neutrally that he would have expected. "You did get thrown through quite a few walls and doors. I was impressed with your aerodynamic capabilities; perhaps you should consider offering yourself as a projectile to Forrestant should the need arise in the future."

Cyrus heard the crack of something not quite right in his neck as he moved. "Perhaps after I'm healed, and once we've won the battle—"

He was cut off by the wooden wall erupting as something slammed through it, shattering it into fine splinters. A dark shape, considerably taller than Cyrus, skidded to a stop in front of him and let out a deep, bellowing roar, animal fury in search of challenge.

"Whoa, rock giant!" Cyrus said, pointing his sword at Fortin as if he were a horse that needed to be calmed. "Whoa!"

Fortin breathed down upon him with dank breath that nearly caused Cyrus to tear up. *He's been eating his kills, I would wager.* "Warlord. You have settled your business with the God of Darkness?"

Cyrus stood there for a moment then exchanged a look with Vara; her lips twisted slightly higher in one corner. "She did." He gestured at her with an elbow.

"The blue fleshlings have fled before us," Fortin said. "They are broken. And they taste like gnomes." This he delivered with a certain smiling satisfaction.

"Very good," Cyrus said, not entirely meaning it. "Where is the rest of the army?"

"Cyrus!" Vaste stepped gently out of the wreckage of the wall that Fortin had cleared. "Where have you been?" His eyes fell to Vara. "And you, too." He grinned. "Snuck off in the middle of the battle to test out one of the Sovereign's beds?"

"We killed the God of Darkness, you daft prick," Vara spat at him. "Where were you?"

"I like how you said, 'we,'" Cyrus said.

Vara sent Cyrus a look of exasperation. "I could not have done it without you distracting him by being flung through half the walls in the mansion. Oh, and lest we forget, your sword was also helpful in striking his head from his body."

"I'm just glad I could do my part," Cyrus said seriously, but the smile snuck out nonetheless.

"Cyrus." Terian emerged from the rubble behind Fortin, drawing the rock giant's gaze as though he were prey. "Did you do it?"

"It's done," Cyrus said, once more getting an acidic look from Vara. "Well, she did it. But it's still done."

The dark knight's armor was stained with blood that nearly matched its shade. "Good. You should go."

"Go?" Cyrus stared at him blankly. "Go where?"

"Home," Terian said, stepping under Fortin's shadow as he moved toward the shattered doors behind Cyrus.

"How do you intend to get the dark elven army out of Reikonos?" Cyrus asked, suspicion descending upon him like a cloud.

"I can't yet," Terian said, taking a step back as Cyrus unfolded his hands. Terian held his own up in surrender. "You killed the Sovereign, but he has servants that do his work for him. I can't control the army until I've dealt with them."

"We can deal with them together, then," Vara said, watching the dark knight through smoky eyes.

Terian flashed her a pained smile. "You could. You could run through Saekaj, destroying every great house in turn, killing every soldier, inspiring fear and making them flee before you."

"Sounds like fun," Fortin said.

"But ..." Terian said, looking at each of them, "... afterward there will be little or nothing left, and no one to command the army to return from Reikonos."

"I had better hear a plan take flight out of your lips swiftly," Cyrus said, muted fury beginning to bubble up now. "I came here and did your damned bidding—"

"And you did it beautifully," Terian said. "But the rest of this? It's not your fight." His eyes were gentle, conceding. "This battle is mine, now."

"I want your word, Terian," Cyrus said, trying to soothe the rising anger. "That you will fix this. That you will deliver what you promised."

"I will do it or die trying," Terian said swiftly. *And true*, Cyrus thought by the look in his eyes.

"You will need help, I think." A figure slipped out of the shadows, wearing a familiar face. Cyrus blinked; it was the J'anda of old, before he had become frail and worn, life burned out of him by time and effort.

"Aye," Terian said, nodding. "We will."

Cyrus looked at Terian with reluctance. "Do I even need to say it?"

"If I don't get those troops out of Reikonos," Terian said a little warily, "you won't need to come looking for me. Believe me on that."

"Because there will be nothing left of you?" Vara asked, and Cyrus knew she'd caught the hint of truth in the dark knight's words.

"There are still powerful people invested in keeping Saekaj and Sovar under control," J'anda said. "They will already be moving to exert that control now that he is dead. Fortunately," he said with a smile, "I have set a few wheels in motion myself." He looked to Terian. "Which we should now attend to."

"Fine," Cyrus said, feeling his anger coil back down into his belly like a snake going to sleep. "We will leave it in your hands."

"That's all I ask," Terian said, but he wore a grimace, "Brother."

Cyrus stared at him, unblinking. "Brother," he finally said, and it was an acknowledgment of its own.

Terian began to turn, J'anda at his side, but he paused just for a moment and looked back at Cyrus. "If you're … spoiling for a fight …"

Cyrus looked at him with a raised eyebrow. "Yes?"

Terian stared at him, the wreckage of the palace foyer providing a dark background behind him. The dark knight smiled. "There is … one thing you could do on your way out that would be of immeasurable help …"

Chapter 80

"Cyrus." Curatio's crisp voice drew Cyrus back to the throne room. He climbed the rubble that remained of the broken doors, admiring the place where the God of Darkness had tossed him through the wood. The healer's hand glowed as Cyrus entered, Vara shoving her way through the rubble behind him. "Are you all right?"

Cyrus felt the healing spell run over him, felt the remaining wounds and pains decrease in their forcefulness. His eyes fell from the healer to the ragged figure at his feet, the goddess who had been near-drained. "I'm fine. Is she all right?"

"She is alive," Curatio said cautiously.

"Which begs the question," Vara said, looking to Cyrus, "how are you?"

Cyrus frowned. "He just asked me that. I'm fine."

"No," Vara said, shaking her head.

"No, I'm not fine?" Cyrus stared at her. "Pretty sure I'm okay. The pains are gone, except for those little phantom ones that stick around after a heal—"

"No, how are you alive?" Vara asked him crossly. "The blows of gods shatter mortal men into pieces."

Cyrus stared at her eyes, then looked to Curatio. "This is true. Mortus broke me as I recall; I was only spared by your timely spell." He glanced at Vara. "How did you survive?"

"He never hit me," she said, with a cocked eyebrow. "Unlike yourself, I move out of the way of killing blows."

"How peculiar," Curatio said, drawing the attention of them both as he knelt next to the throne, his eyes dancing to Cyrus only for a moment. "Is that new chainmail that you wear?"

"Yeah, it's—" Cyrus paused midsentence. "How the—?"

"I am no blacksmith," Curatio said, staring at the fallen form of the Goddess of Life, mostly hidden behind the throne, "but I do know quartal when I see it."

Cyrus's fingers ran over the smooth links under his gauntleted fingers. "Quartal?"

"Someone must be fond of you," Curatio said, "that's a fortune in the metal."

Cyrus felt his lips open slightly, and he caught the questioning look from Vara. He abruptly cleared his throat and came around the throne to lay eyes upon the fallen goddess. "How is she?"

"Drained," Curatio said, running his thin fingers through her silver hair. "Though I am at a bit of a loss to explain how exactly this was performed."

"Using this," came a voice from behind the throne. There was the sound of something heavy hitting the floor and rolling, like a rock on stone, the crackle of its surface running toward them. It caught the torchlight as it came to a stop at Curatio's feet, a ruby the size of a head, gleaming, almost glowing even in the faded light.

"Slattern," Vara hissed.

Cyrus caught sight of Aisling holding her place against the far wall, standing in a doorway, silhouetted against the darkness behind her. "What are you doing here?"

"Heard the hubbub," she said, staring at them from a safe distance. Cyrus wondered at the curious way she held her body; not just standoffish but wounded, like she'd had something broken. A thin trickle of dark blue blood ran down the corner of her mouth. "Came running."

"Were you already here?" Cyrus asked, finding his way to his feet to stand next to Vara. The darkness hung in the throne room, and he cast a glance to his side to see others easing into the doors slowly, Martaina among them. Her bow was unslung, an arrow already nocked and ready to fire. She moved for a better angle; Aisling was not exposed, standing as she was just inside the doorframe.

"Does it matter?" Aisling asked, weary. "Take the Red Destiny. See if you can restore some of the souls to her. It might aid her recovery."

"Do you think a pretty bauble will make us forget what you've done?" Vara bristled.

"Why would you forget it?" Aisling asked through thin, unsmiling lips. "It's not like I can."

"Why?" Cyrus asked; he started to reconsider, to ask something else, but he realized that it was the only question that mattered.

"He took someone dear to me," Aisling said. Her eyes were haunted, still, her catlike motions all gone. The way she stood was like a person broken.

"And you very nearly took one dear to me," Vara said.

Cyrus looked over at her, blinking. "Did you just say ...?"

"Hush."

Aisling did not smile, and her answer was bitter. "I could apologize, but I'll be honest—"

"For the first time ever?" Vara asked.

"I didn't mind beating you for him," Aisling said. "Of all the things I was told to do, fighting with you over him was the sweetest, because you don't normally lose." Her eyes flashed purple in the dark. "How did it feel?"

"How will it feel when I kill you?" Vara shot back.

"Like nothing," Aisling said quietly, and she started to fade into the shadows.

"Wait," Cyrus called. "Your ... love? Your friend? What happened to them?"

She half-emerged, face still shrouded in shadow. "I don't know."

"You can't think you're just going to walk out of here—" Vara said.

"Let her go," Cyrus said.

"You cannot be serious," Vara hissed at him. "This is the second person who has attempted to kill you that you have let walk away in the last year. Any more and I will start to suspect that you truly do wish to die—"

"You killed the one who tried to kill me," Cyrus said, peeling his eyes from Aisling to look at Vara. "She was no more than the hand of Yartraak, else she'd have finished the job. She certainly had the chance."

Aisling watched him from the shadows. "Do you expect me to thank you?"

"I'd say you've shown me your gratitude over the last year in every way I could possibly handle," Cyrus said with a twist of the knife. She did not flinch from his words. "I don't ever want to see you again."

She disappeared into the darkness and the door shut behind her. She said something, but he did not catch it.

"Damned right," Vara muttered, drawing his eyes to her.

"What did she say?" Cyrus asked, frowning.

"I need to get the Goddess of Life back to her realm," Curatio said from behind them. He had her clutched in strong arms; she was small, thin, waif-like. *Like Aisling,* Cyrus thought, wishing he could drive the thought out a moment after it came to him.

"Can you do that yourself?" Cyrus asked, staring at the healer behind the darkened throne. It sat empty, but it still stole his attention, making him look it over once before his eyes returned to Curatio.

"Of course," Curatio said.

"It's a little hostile in there, wouldn't you say?" Vaste called from his place at the far end of the room. "Angry squirrels and whatnot."

"With the death of he who I suspect caused the curse," Curatio said, hefting the goddess in his arms, adjusting as though she were more than the light weight she appeared to be, "I do not think that will be a problem any longer. She draws strength from her realm, and her reappearance will help put it back into order." He stared at Cyrus. "The question is ... what do you mean to do?"

Cyrus stared at him and narrowed his eyes. *Did he hear my conversation with Terian all the way in here?* "One last thing," he said, "on our way out." He let his hand drift to Praelior. "One last task left unfinished that we could do to ... make Arkaria a better place."

Curatio nodded once, the hint of a smile at his lips enough of a sign that Cyrus was certain he knew. "Good luck," the healer said, and disappeared in the twinkle of spell light.

"Where's the army?" Cyrus asked, not wasting a moment.

Odellan slipped out of the shadows near the door. "We have roughly one thousand with us, Guildmaster. The rest are waiting in the main hall at Sanctuary, ready to be deployed anywhere we can teleport them." The elven officer stood, stiff, as though waiting for an order. "What are your intentions, Lord Davidon?"

Cyrus settled his jaw then turned to look at Vara, who stood beside him still. *Still.* He smiled, though faintly; she did not return the smile, but neither did she look away. "I think," Cyrus said, looking at the hole in the doors and seeing the wall and gates beyond, "that Saekaj Sovar needs a lesson in civilization."

There was a silence, broken by Vaste. "And how do you plan to teach them this lesson, oh mighty Warlord?" His words dripped with sarcasm.

"By depriving them of something that they desperately need ripped from their vile, clawing grasp," Cyrus said with a grin. Now he a caught a hint of a smile on Vara's lips as well—but only a hint. "Prepare to march; we'll be taking a route through Saekaj and out to the surface, where we'll kill the guards to their portal and bring in the rest of our army."

"And then?" Vaste asked, waiting. "Sack the city? Slaughter their livestock? Grab the Sovereign's corpse and parade it through town with a pike up his ass?"

Cyrus paused. "Maybe that last part, on our way out." *It'll probably keep them from giving us much trouble.*

"That's civilized," Vara snorted.

Cyrus ignored her. "But, no ... that's not the purpose. The purpose is to bring our army in ... and free every slave in this godsdamned land by sheer force of arms." He stared into the assemblage before him and imagined his eyes glowing the way Vara's had, a righteous fury as he laid it out before him. "We finish the job, we end slavery in Arkaria for good, and we do it here, on this very night." He gave a single nod and started them on a forward march, dodging his way out of the wreckage of the throne room of Saekaj with Vara at his side.

"Good speech," she said as they crossed out of the front doors, the army following close—but not too close—behind. "Magic aside, we'll make a crusader out of you yet."

He smiled as they crossed the bridge and entered the city unopposed. Guards quailed before them, faces hidden behind windows, nervous eyes nearly afraid to look at them. Cyrus marched through Saekaj with Vara at his side, unopposed, as they threaded their way into an open tunnel road, on a path for the surface. And the army followed behind them, unstoppable, felling the few enemies that made it past the paladin and the warrior who led them out of the darkness.

Chapter 81

"A lot of people have said over the years that they're going to free the slaves," Andren said as he walked beside Cyrus through the streets of Reikonos, "but no one's really done much about it until the Lord of Perdamun." The elf held up a hand in the air, and brought the other up to smack it down with a loud clap. "Then you go and order your army to knock over Gren, and four months later you force Saekaj to give up every one of their slaves at the point of the sword." He shrugged expansively. "There's talk, and then there's you. Worlds apart. You just do it, don't you?"

Cyrus let his cloak part in the middle. The spring air was swirling through the streets, matched by the construction efforts that were in progress. Roofs were being re-thatched on stone houses that were black with the scorching kiss of fire brought to them in the sack. People still walked with a hesitancy, as though something were going to leap out with them. It was not the same city, this Cyrus knew. It was more guarded, more afraid—but there were survivors. "I wish I could have 'done it' here when it came to saving the city." He frowned. "That didn't sound right."

"City's still here," Andren said. They threaded their way down an avenue that was all too familiar, the sun far, far overhead and barely visible in the gulch-like valley of the slums. "Battered, sure. A little beaten. But you made your deal, and the dark elves pulled out only a day or two after we finished our job in Saekaj." He shrugged again. "I don't think Pretnam Friggin' Urides was responsible for that, do you?"

"No," Cyrus said. "I think Terian Friggin' Lepos was."

"Guess you won't know unless someone finally comes out of Saekaj to tell the tale," Andren said. Not a word had been heard from Saekaj in the outside world since Sanctuary had ravaged the surface farms and gone into the slave quarters under the earth and freed everyone within them. Cyrus could still see the scared faces of the whip-wielding guards, running for their lives with the Army of Sanctuary coming at them in overwhelming numbers.

"Since it's been two months and we've heard nary a word," Cyrus said, "I don't imagine that silence will end anytime soon, do you?"

"Suits me fine," Andren said. He was still clean-shaven, a fact which amazed Cyrus to no end. He seemed different, but Cyrus saw little need to comment upon it for fear it would push him away. "I can do without the dark elves for quite some time, if you know what I mean." He laughed. "You probably can, too, right?" His laugh stopped. "How's your back?"

"Only hurts when it rains," Cyrus said as they came around the final corner. There was construction everywhere, buildings going up, buildings being repaired. The shanties that had dominated the slums had been burned, and the smell of ash was thick in the air along with that of fresh pine lumber dragged from the forests of the Northlands.

"Why did you let her go?" Andren asked. "Every single one of us would have gladly gutted her for you."

He blinked in surprise at the vehemence of the healer's pronouncement. "Even you?"

"Especially me," Andren said and Cyrus saw a pinprick of red anger in his eyes, something he did not usually see from the elf unless he had both drink and provocation. "But she feeds you a sad story, and you just let her walk away."

Cyrus paused, looking in the direction of their destination. *In truth, I don't want to go on; this cannot end well.* "Let us presume ... just for a moment ... that it was not as she said. That she stabbed me and failed, that she was with me for no purpose but that she served the Sovereign." He fiddled with his cloak, the thought of it producing its own sort of discomfort. He felt a bit sick but held it back. "Then she spent years trying to and eventually succeeding in sleeping with someone that she had no interest in. The only way she held my confidence was by sex, and every time I started to slip from her grasp, she was forced to go back to this same well in an effort to reclaim me."

"Yeah," Andren said, nodding, "and we should have killed her for it."

"She had to sleep with me for over a year," Cyrus said, and he felt a swell of pity, "even though she didn't want to, because her master bade her do it. He exercised his power over her to get her to use her body against her will." He shook his head. "No, I wouldn't have her killed for that; he did far worse to her by using her in such a way, and I feel ill that I was complicit in such an act."

Andren's cheeks crinkled in disgust. "You thought you were with someone who wanted you."

"But she didn't, did she?" Cyrus asked. "And I was fool enough to buy her act. Egotistical enough, I suppose." He shrugged. "She should hardly be penalized for that, no matter how ... used I feel." And he did feel used; he woke in the night with a sense of disgust, and showered under a stream of chill water for hours, imagining he could still smell her upon his skin.

"Come on," Andren said, a pity in his eyes that went unspoken.

"Yeah, okay," Cyrus said and followed behind the elf.

"You gonna be all right?" Andren asked as he fell into step beside Cyrus again. A blustery wind, the last gasp of winter, whipped through Cyrus's cloak.

"Eventually," Cyrus said.

"You know, there are other women. Plenty who wouldn't mind—"

"I am fully aware," Cyrus said, unblinking. *Plenty of ... choices. But there's only one I want.*

They came out from behind a lumber wagon, filled to the overflowing with long boards, its axles strained under the load. "Well, I'll be," Andren said aloud.

Cyrus looked in more than a little wonderment himself. The old barn stood before them, untouched; a weathered, run-down thing, the chains across its door intact. It had been their home once, long ago, and though the mark of fire was evident on every building around it, it remained completely unharmed, standing proud in its place on the street.

"Probably not worth burning," Andren said.

"Maybe," Cyrus said, unconvinced. The healer moved toward it with key in hand, ready to open the doors. *Or maybe it's just a survivor* ...

... like us.

Chapter 82

Two days after Cyrus returned from Reikonos, Vaste sat upon the front steps like a discarded bag of refuse upon a slope, the wide part of his middle threatening to pour out of his robes, his head looking up into the sky like it was going to fall on him at any time. Cyrus stared at the troll; he'd been apprised of the healer's unusual behavior by whisper and worry from guildmates. So odd was the troll's state that he'd thought about having Curatio talk to him, but something prickled him about it. *It's not the sort of thing a friend leaves to others*, he decided.

"Oh, hi," Vaste said, not even rolling over to look at him. "Come to deal with the blatantly obvious troll that's lying strewn across your front steps?"

Cyrus thought about doing his usual poke, sending the troll's repartee right back at him, but something gave him pause. "I'm here to talk to my friend, Vaste, who appears ... not himself."

That forced the mammoth green head to turn toward him, neck braced against the stone step. Sanctuary's shadow loomed over them, the front doors cracked just a hint at Cyrus's back, doubtless to allow any number of curious listeners to hear their conversation. "I am not myself," Vaste agreed. "But I'm not anyone else, either."

Cyrus arched an eyebrow. "So ... who are you?"

"Oh, don't be an obtuse shit," Vaste said. "I am who I'm always been, I'm just suffering a bit of an identity crisis."

Cyrus eased down next to him, lowering himself to sit on the step next to Vaste's head. The troll watched him with bright yellow eyes, looking just a bit like he might snap and attack. "My question still stands. You're still Vaste, but what do you think of yourself?" He paused. "Is this because of Gren?"

"No, it's because the damned sky is blue," Vaste said, staring upward. "Of course it's because of Gren. But it's not *just* because of Gren, if you catch my meaning."

"I couldn't have a more difficult time catching your meaning if it were a greased goat," Cyrus said.

Vaste glared at him. "Oh, yes, add your humor to the situation. That's sure to help."

Irony. Cyrus picked his words carefully. "So … what else is it besides Gren?"

"Do you know what it's like to not know your place in the world?" Vaste asked.

"I know something of it, yes," Cyrus said.

"Please don't give me a 'Poor me, I was all alone in a city of my people and hated by everyone around me' story," Vaste said, "because I suspect you and I could match each other tale for tale."

"Probably," Cyrus agreed. "So, we both had difficult childhoods … Now what?"

"So now you have a homeland, albeit battered," Vaste snapped, "and I don't. Poor me. I win."

Cyrus shook his head. "You win. Is that what you want?"

"Will you stop asking me questions and give me a chance to get around to pouring my heart out to you?" Vaste shook his head, neck rubbing against the stone step. "Honestly, it's so difficult to work my way around to a tearful admission with you being so busy being sympathetic and understanding."

Cyrus chuckled then stifled it swiftly. "Sorry. Go on."

"Do you know what gets me the worst?" Vaste spun his head around. "It's not the lack of homeland; Sanctuary fills that. It's not the … pitiful lack of romance, there are books to fill the void." He snuffed his statement and sunk into another stubborn silence.

"What is it, then?" Cyrus asked.

"I'm glad you asked," Vaste said, launching right into it. "It's Goliath. It's Malpravus." He turned his head to Cyrus, and the yellow eyes glowed with feral anger. "You know I've been … different … since I learned from that shaman outside of Gren several years ago. He opened my eyes to things. Gave me an … attunement … with the dead."

Cyrus found himself wanting to say something but stopped just in time.

"Nothing to say to that, eh?" Vaste kept his eyes on Cyrus. "I know what you wanted to ask, though—does it make me like Malpravus?"

Cyrus cleared his throat. "You're nothing like Malpravus."

"No, I'm not like Malpravus," Vaste agreed. "No one is like Malpravus. A necromancer is supposed to speak for the dead. To use the power of the deceased with their cooperation. Malpravus … abuses their power like it's his own. It's not. It's not even in the same city as his power, and he runs roughshod along with it like he worked for it himself." Vaste made a disgusted noise. "And he got away, again."

Cyrus felt himself nodding. "There will be a reckoning. Between us and Goliath. You may bet on that."

"They're not honest fighters, Cyrus," Vaste said, and he sounded quiet. "They're liars and cheats, and they would do to you a thousand times what Aisling did given only a half of her opportunity." He looked up at Cyrus, and the anger was gone. "I fear the day we are forced to go up against them, because even if we outmatch them ten to one, it will not be a fair fight in our favor."

Cyrus stared across the lawn at the sky, white clouds drifting overhead. For a moment, he imagined he saw them exactly as Vaste did, and there was some small measure of peace there amid the dangerous skies far in the distance. "I guess we'll just have to be ready for anything we can imagine they'll pull."

"It's not the things I know they'll do that scare me," Vaste said, and his voice was a hushed whisper. "It's the ones I can't imagine that wake me up in the night and don't let me return to sleep again."

Cyrus could not find it in himself to disagree.

Chapter 83

A meeting that Cyrus had long anticipated came two weeks after his conversation with Vaste under the blue skies. This was to be quite a different conversation, he imagined, and he had prepared himself by summoning the full Council and awaiting the arrival of their guest in the silence of the chamber. The blue sky was still visible out the window, and Cyrus sat at his place at the head of the table, adjusting himself in his seat. The chain that bound the medallion he had received from Alaric had begun to chafe, just slightly. He wondered what it would take to adjust to it, that oddly shaped, circular thing, and sighed when he had to concede that he had no idea.

The door to the Council Chamber opened onto the silent gathering. Everyone was in their seats save one—J'anda's chair was still empty, nearly three months after Saekaj.

"The Sanctuary Council," Pretnam Urides said in abrupt greeting as he entered. His staff thumped the ground in time with each step and he strode to the edge of the table without preamble then fixed his spectacled eyes upon Cyrus. "Lord Davidon."

"Sir Councilor," Cyrus said with a nod. "What can we do for you?"

Urides did not show a single ounce of amusement on his weighty face. "I have come for the gold you owe me."

Vaste made a loud, scoffing sound. "Gold we owe you? We saved your damned kingdom!"

"Confederation," Urides snapped before anyone else could issue the correction.

"Whatever it was, I didn't see you atop the Citadel when we threw out Goliath's chief death-whisperer," Vaste said. "I don't recall seeing your people in Saekaj when Vara made the Sovereign her personal object of anger relief." Vara frowned at him but did not say anything.

"Nor would you," Urides said, "for we were not there."

"But you acknowledge that our actions caused the dark elves to pull their armies out of your capital and the Riverlands?" This question came from Odellan and sounded significantly more polite than any of Vaste's inquiries.

"I acknowledge that we had a contract for you to defend Leaugarden for seven days," Urides said, unflinching, "and that you failed in this regard."

"Someone send the dark elves back to Reikonos," Vaste said. He looked to Erith. "You, go get dark elves. Send them to Reikonos." She gave him a look, and he made a hand motion as if to speed her up. "Now, Erith, we don't have all day."

"Your troll is oh so very amusing, Lord Davidon," Urides said without humor.

"I find his wit keen," Cyrus agreed.

"Thank you," Vaste said brightly.

"Are you going to pay us our due or not?" Urides asked.

"You know I am," Cyrus said, giving Urides a slight shrug of the shoulders.

"Yes, you tell him—*what?*" Vaste's voice changed pitch to a shriek midsentence.

Urides showed the first hint of satisfaction. "I had hoped you would be a man of honor about this."

"I am a man of honor," Cyrus said. "But ..."

"There is no but," Urides snapped.

"There's a small but," Cyrus said, keeping his tone even. "Your Confederation is in a mess. I'm sure your gold is of immediate use to you, and I will make sure it is returned to you this very day, but I require one thing."

"Let it be something valuable," Vaste said, "like all the property those mansions on the heights were on before they got burned and sacked."

"That is not mine to give," Urides snapped without looking at Vaste.

"This is something you can easily part with," Cyrus said. "You recall of course, a couple years ago, right after you made that unfounded accusation that we were plundering those caravans—"

"I vaguely recall something of that," Urides said, as though it were nothing.

"Very faintly, I'm sure," Vaste said. "Probably hidden under a mountain of other memories in which you slandered and blackmailed innocent people."

"Vaste," Curatio said from his place at Cyrus's right, "you really should wait until after the Councilor issues a more staunch denial to thrust the truth of events upon him."

"In the wake of that," Cyrus said, drawing to his feet, leaning his knuckles on the table, "you made Alaric the steward of the Plains of Perdamun. Do you recall?"

"But of course," Urides said, and now his suspicions were raised. "Why—?"

"I want you to renounce all claim to the Plains of Perdamun south of the line comprising Santir, Idiarna and Prehorta," Cyrus said. "Sign a treaty to that effect, right now, today, in front of witnesses in your own capital, and you will have your gold back in your vaults by tonight."

"And if I do not?" Urides cheeks were now purpled with umbrage.

"You'll get your gold back when I get around to delivering it," Cyrus said.

Urides stared at him through the spectacles. "This is how a man of honor comports himself?"

Cyrus leaned forward, and he could feel his brows stitching a heavy line across his forehead. "Two years ago, you raced willingly and happily into a war here in the plains that ended up damned near costing you your entire Confederation." Urides took his words in silence. "Two years. You filled the plains with soldiers so you could provoke a war you felt certain you'd win. Now you're looking out at the wreckage, and I wonder if you have enough soldiers to even protect what you've got left." Cyrus stared him down. "Scratch that. I know the answer. You don't."

Urides made a sniffing noise. "And you do?"

"I'll do a fair sight better protecting the Plains of Perdamun once you've ceded your claim than you did during the time when they were supposedly under your auspices," Cyrus said flatly. "Because, in case you missed it, Sanctuary was there every single time that the dark elves were beaten back—Termina, here, Livlosdald."

"But not Leaugarden," Urides said with some satisfaction.

"That's your own territory, man," Curatio said with disgust. "Try not to look quite so gleeful celebrating our defeat."

"I can afford your defeat easier than I could have afforded your victory," Urides said with a sense of haughty triumph. "Very well. I'll sign your treaty; as you say, we are unable to defend such holdings at this time in any case."

"Great," Cyrus said without feeling. Everything that had been said by the Councilor had left him with unease, and he had a sudden suspicion that this bargain might have been offered in advance. "In the interest of time, might you have such a document upon your person at this moment?"

Urides' eyes flashed behind the spectacles, and one eyebrow crept up. "This is all that you want for the gold? Nothing else?"

"Ooh, I want a pony!" Vaste said.

"That will be sufficient, I think," Cyrus said.

Urides reached within his cloth jacket and withdrew a roll of parchment tied around the center. "I believe you will find this agreeable."

Ryin reached out and seized the paper upon the table before Andren or Erith could quite manage. He unthreaded the string that bound it and shook it open. He gave it a glance and then slid it to Cyrus. "It does cede the Plains of Perdamun to you as the Guildmaster of Sanctuary. It also lists you as Lord Davidon."

"A fancy title for a fancy man," Vaste said.

"Your gold will be returned to you immediately," Cyrus said to Urides.

"What else might you have offered if we'd asked for it?" Vaste asked, prompting Urides to turn back to him.

The light caught his spectacles. "My forgiveness of your demands," Urides said. Cyrus got the distinct impression he was not joking.

"Damn," Vaste said, snapping his fingers. "Should have asked for that. And a pony. Always need a pony for something around here."

"I thought it was goats with you people," Ryin murmured.

"Good day, Lord Davidon," Pretnam Urides said. He disappeared into a twinkle of spell light.

"Anyone else think that whole 'my forgiveness' thing sounds a bit ominous?" Vaste asked. "Bodes a bit ill? Anyone?"

"I think … that Pretnam Urides is a dangerous man to have as an enemy," Curatio said, choosing his words with care.

Cyrus just stared at the space that the councilor had inhabited, waiting for the flare of the spell to disappear from his vision. It did not do so quickly, remaining in his sight like a dark cloud in an otherwise spotless sky. "So am I," Cyrus said. "So are we all."

Chapter 84

It was only three days later that Cyrus received the summons to the Halls of Healing. He wondered at the nature of the invitation, unable to recall a single time that Curatio had bid him to do anything without good cause, and so he came immediately.

The halls of Sanctuary were abuzz with life; the fires burned in the hearths even though spring was beginning to give way to the breaths of southern summer and its warmth. The grass across the fields was darkening in its turn, and Cyrus wondered if a walk might not be in the offing, or perhaps even a ride on horseback.

He entered the Halls of Healing and found Vara waiting for him, her arms folded neatly behind her as though she were ill at ease and knew not where to put them. She looked stern but smiled ever so slightly as he entered, a concession she had made from time to time of late. "Guildmaster," she said crisply.

"Lady Vara," Cyrus replied. He saw the lightness in her eyes; it had been this way since the return from Saekaj, a sort of gentle swordplay between the two of them that carried none of the sting of her old insults. It was refreshing, and yet still he felt … at arm's length with her. An invitation to dine with him in his quarters had been turned aside with a faded smile, and he had caught the gist. They were not adversaries, but they were back to the distance. Though he felt pain at the thought, it was not so bad as it could have been, he conceded.

"Were you summoned to these halls as well?" Vara asked, looking out upon the empty room.

"Indeed I was," Cyrus said.

"Curious, that the Elder would summon the Guildmaster," Vara said.

"Curiosity is why I came," Cyrus said. "That and politeness. I assume Curatio would not have asked if he did not have good reason."

"Indeed, Curatio had good reason," Curatio said as he entered from behind Cyrus. His white robes traced the floor as he walked, hair back enough for his pointed ears to be displayed. "One of our guests is still perhaps a bit weak, and I would prefer not to have her trudge all the way up to the Council Chambers."

"Or my rather substantial quarters?" Cyrus said with a smile.

"Yes, well, that carries a curse of a different sort," Vara said, "what with the discarded undergarments that undoubtedly teem with life of their own."

"Is that why you turned down my dinner invitation?" Cyrus asked with a reckless smile. Hers vanished instantly, and he was sorry he had brought it up.

"I believe you recall Arydni?" Curatio said, and stepped aside for the Priestess of Life. She was not clad in her full ceremonial garb, Cyrus was relieved to see. She looked just a tad weathered, noticeably, and he wondered if this was the beginning of what the elves called "the turn."

"It would be impossible to forget her," Cyrus said with a smile as she brushed his cheek with a kiss as light and delicate as if she'd touched him with a rose petal while passing. "Though I am surprised to see you."

"You completed your contract," Arydni said, not greeting Vara in the same manner.

"Oh," Cyrus said, blinking. "I, uh ... forgot, honestly. There were a few other things going on around that time ..." He started to wave her off.

"Do not make of this something that it is not," Arydni said, smiling at him with her full, lively cheeks. "You have done a good job, and you will be paid. The priestesses are even now transporting our payment into your foyer."

"Well, thank you," Cyrus said and happened to catch a look at Vara, who stood absolutely still, her hands still behind her. "Vara?"

"It's you," she whispered, fixed upon the second cloaked priestess.

"It's wh—" Cyrus jerked his head to look at the other woman, but realized halfway through the turn who he was looking at. Her hair was dark and glossy and shining in sunlight gleaming in from the window. Her cheeks were full where before they had been sunken like Malpravus's. Her skin was supple and new, as though a few weeks ago it had not been so wrinkled as to make crumpled parchment look smooth by comparison.

She carried with her the scent of spring as Cyrus imagined it, the smell of new life blooming from every flower, sprouting from every bough and shoot. He took a breath of it and was intoxicated by its power. He looked into her warm, green eyes and saw the liveliest plains grass waving in the wind. "Vidara," he whispered, and the name was sweet upon his lips.

"Master of Sanctuary," she said in a low, throaty voice that almost made his ears purr at the sound of it. "Cyrus Davidon."

"Why can't everyone say it like that?" Cyrus asked, unthinking.

He turned his head to see Vara glaring at him in warning. "I will smite you," she said.

"I think I'm already smitten," Cyrus said, but it was as low and complimentary as he could make it sound.

"I came to offer you my thanks," Vidara said, letting her cowl back to show her full hair. A green vine was wrapped across the top of her head like a tiara, holding back the flowing brown locks, yellow and white flowers blooming from it like honeysuckle jewels to crown her. "For saving me from the Sovereign."

"You mean Yartraak?" Cyrus asked, and saw the sudden blanch from Curatio and Vidara. "Something I said?"

Vidara looked at him with those green eyes, and Cyrus saw pain in them, and not the pain that was born of ordinary life wending its course but a dark, horrible pain that went deeper. "What he did … was unspeakable among our kind."

"Kidnapping is not looked upon fondly by any of our peoples," Cyrus said.

"She doesn't just mean the kidnapping," Curatio said. "She means running a city. Interfering in mortal business. Starting wars of conquest with mortals."

Cyrus glanced at her and saw something of significance in the way she looked at him. Something she was trying to tell him, perhaps? "But don't the gods regularly interfere in Arkaria?"

"We have rules," Vidara said softly. "Proscriptions for the conduct of our business with mortals. They are strict. They are serious." Something flashed in her eyes. "They are being ... ignored ... in some ways, and yet ... enforced in others."

Cyrus searched for a question, tried to find a way to ask what was nagging in the back of his head. "What rules?"

Vidara crossed her hands in front of her. "I cannot say."

"Because of rules," Cyrus said, and watched her nod. He nodded toward Vara. "Did you interfere with her?"

"Cyrus," Curatio said, one step shy of a snap. It was a warning, pure and simple.

"We all have our favorites, Cyrus Davidon," Vidara said, but she did not smile. "I must leave you now."

"Don't go," Vara whispered, but the Goddess of Life had already lifted her cowl.

"I must," Vidara said, but she paused at the door, cloak as green as summer leaves flowing behind her. "I need tell you both one thing before I go ..." She paused at the door, and he saw her lay a hand upon the frame, the stones that bordered it. Her long fingers traced lines as she stood there, and she was silent for a moment, as though trying to decide what to say. "Be wary," she said at last and turned to leave.

"Be wary of what?" Vara asked, and once more the goddess halted in her steps, though this time she did not turn far enough to let them see her face.

"Of everything," Vidara said, and she disappeared with only the slow swish of her green cloak to herald the passing of the Goddess of Life.

Chapter 85

It came the close of the first month of spring, some nine days after the Goddess of Life came to Sanctuary, and everywhere her touch was visible in the world, so far as Cyrus could see. The temperate winter in the Plains of Perdamun was broken by a streak of warm days so pleasant and fair that he could scarcely conceive of better weather on the Emerald Coast.

The morning Council meeting was done with the balcony doors fully open, and they had nearly wrapped up their day's business, the summer air calling them outside, when the doors to the Chamber opened once more, and an old friend entered.

"J'anda," Cyrus said, the first to see him. "It is … good to see you, my friend."

The enchanter's gleam was still in his eyes, though the lines on his face seemed to have become even more pronounced. "It is good to be back among friends," he said, his cultured voice not hiding that sliver of pleasure that crept into it.

He fielded affections from some, strong handshakes from others, smiles from all. He was settled in his chair with greatest fanfare; the return of a conquering hero could not have been more gleeful or well taken. He seated himself, his blue robe draped over the wooden arms of the chair, the rich stitching at home on a man Cyrus had always thought of as impeccable in all things.

"So," Vaste said, with—did Cyrus imagine it?—just a little deference, "how did it go?"

"Saekaj Sovar is at peace," J'anda said, interlacing his wrinkled hands. "But you already suspected, did you not?"

"Suspected," Curatio said, "but heard no confirmation."

"What happened down there?" Vara asked.

J'anda's eyes clouded for a moment, and he did not look at a single one of them, focusing instead on a spot on the table. "War. Death. Chaos. All the things you would have expected, I think."

"There was a lot of death walking around when last I saw your army," Vaste said. "Is it ... gone?"

"The dead have returned to their rest," J'anda said simply.

"And ... you won?" Cyrus asked carefully.

"We won," J'anda said with a nod, "if winning is possible when your house turns in upon itself."

"Who stands atop the house now?" Vara asked, and Cyrus wondered if she knew something he did not.

"Someone who wishes you to have this," J'anda said, removing a scroll from his sleeve and sliding it toward Cyrus.

This time it was snatched by Curatio, whose fingers knocked Cyrus's aside as if he were trying to teach a child table manners. The healer opened the scroll and read it, eyes bobbing from side to side. "Well ... that is unexpected," he said when he was finished.

"Was it?" Cyrus asked, a little irritated, shaking his gauntleted fingers. The snap had somehow stung, even through the plate armor.

"Congratulations, Lord Davidon of Perdamun," Curatio said, handing Cyrus the scroll.

Cyrus took it with outstretched hands and pulled it open lengthwise, eyes running down the parchment as he read. It was as Curatio had said, a declaration from the Dark Elven Sovereignty of their cession of claim to the entirety of the plains. He raced through it to the end and started to read it again, but was stopped by the signature.

Terian Lepos
Sovereign of Saekaj and Sovar

Cyrus leaned back in his chair, eyes fixed on the seal below. It looked different than the one he'd seen for the Sovereignty before, and his eyes flew to J'anda, who sat with a waiting smile upon his lips. "Truly?" Cyrus asked.

"Truly," J'anda said.

"Truly, the rest of us would like to know what is going on," Vaste said rather loudly.

Cyrus stared at the enchanter, pondering the meaning of the signature, of the parchment, of everything. "Do you suppose ..." he asked, carefully taking his gaze to the enchanter's eyes, which were visible just above where J'anda had steepled his hands, "that this means he and I ... are done?"

J'anda took a breath at this, long and slow, and then he looked Cyrus directly in the eye. "I think he is done."

Cyrus looked back at the parchment and smiled, something full, something deep, like business had concluded greatly to his satisfaction. Like some weight had lifted from him, some validation come down from on high to affirm the moment on the beach when he'd spared the sword and let Terian Lepos wander off into the woods alone. "Good." He gave the parchment a nod, then smiled and looked up at the Council assembled around him. "Now we both are."

Chapter 86

They had celebrated J'anda's welcome return with a feast prepared by Larana. Fatted calves, fresh vegetables, strawberries—all these had graced the table, and the wine had flowed from casks. Far below his balcony, Cyrus could hear the celebration still going on. The curtain wall that separated Sanctuary from the plains was lit by watch fires and torches, and he could see the men moving about on their lonely watches, music swirling out into the night from the open doors to the foyer.

Cyrus watched from above, alone, listening to the notes grow discordant at a distance. He had heard the melodies played fresh when he had stood upon the stair, watching at the distance he felt between himself and the members of the guild. He was the watcher, the silent observer—like Alaric had been—the encourager that walked the walls in the night watches, patting each soldier on the back and breathing kindnesses, but never the host at the center of the party, never the man in the middle of the ring of acclaim.

He stood under a lit, full moon, and regarded it as it regarded him, bone-white glow shedding soft upon the dark land.

I am alone.

I am the leader.

He smiled ruefully. *But I repeat myself.*

The sound of his door opening came as a surprise beneath the soft rush of the lace in the breeze. He'd thought it a curious choice when he'd seen it in Alaric's quarters; now he wondered if it hadn't been someone else who'd chosen it, and Alaric had merely left it there … after.

"Hello?" Cyrus spoke into the dark. The torches' soft glow lit the floor, and the smell of dinner still hung heavy upon the night air. He saw movement behind the lace, ready to grasp his sword out of little more than habit, and then he saw the face of his visitor. "You."

"Me," Vara said simply, brushing through the white curtain, the cloth streaming between her fingertips as the wind caught it, pulling it playfully away.

"Shouldn't you be at the celebration?" Cyrus asked.

She arched the eyebrow. "Shouldn't you?"

He swept a hand toward the balcony. "Clearly I have much to do here."

"Clearly." She walked past him and stood at the balcony's edge, leaning upon the stone rail and looking out.

He felt a strange compulsion to explain himself. "Alaric didn't … partake of events for very long, you know."

She did not look at him. "There were many things that Alaric did not do. Such as go after the gods." She delivered it with a little levity to ease the sting. "You are your own man."

Cyrus felt a little laugh escape. "I'm still following him. I'm following a dead man." He laughed again. "And everyone else is following me."

"I can think of worse examples," she said.

"So," he said after an appropriate pause, "what brings you to the top of the tower?"

"I'm still quite irate that you stole these quarters from me in that election," she said with a straight face as the moonlight leeched the gold from her hair. "I think I might have to demand you cede them and go sleep on your ruddy plains that everyone seems to have given you."

He laughed unexpectedly, and it felt good. "I think I may be bound to this tower now." He felt the laughter disappear without a trace. "I find it ironic that they call me the Master of Sanctuary; for the truth is that leadership, as Alaric did it, makes you as much a slave to your followers."

"He did emphasize that," she said. "But is that so bad? To serve a good people, to help them achieve … whatever it is they want for themselves?"

"No," Cyrus said and looked out with her into the night. "That is not so bad."

"What do you want, Cyrus Davidon?" she asked, quietly.

He felt a great stirring within, as though this might be the most important question he had been asked yet. "I ... don't know." He caught the glimmer of surprise. "Are you asking me as Guildmaster, as a warrior, as a—"

"As a man," she said, looking at him from the railing. Her hair was aglow, soft white, the torches bathing her in warmth on one side and the cold light of the moon sapping her color on the other side.

"I ..." Cyrus stumbled in his words. "I am a Guildmaster, though. *The* Guildmaster. It, uh, governs everything I do ..."

She stared at him, and her lips moved, just slightly, before she spoke. They looked red even in the moonlight. "You are my Guildmaster, and I owe you my loyalty. I am yours to command." Her eyes swept down, then back up, and the blue gave him a glimmer of something—hope. "But I don't just want you to be my Guildmaster."

Cyrus felt his mouth go dry. "A life spent in chains is no life at all."

Vara frowned at him, but it did little to sully her beautiful face. "Kinky. Did the dark elven slattern teach you that?"

"You're the one who said, 'Love will find a slave,' if I'm not mistaken." He chuckled and she matched him. It was perhaps the warmest moment in recent memory he could recall of her.

"Some ties are worth the binding, I think," she said. "Some chains worth the wearing."

She leaned in and kissed him, her soft lips upon his, and it took him back to a moment on a street in Termina when the world had seemed so glorious and bright. He pressed back upon her lips with his own, felt her hand on his face, smooth fingers running down his jaw and the taste of her tongue upon his own.

They broke, and he looked at her, smitten, awestruck. She smiled. "You aren't alone."

He took only a moment to lean back in and kiss her again, more fully this time. It was rich and delicious and something long, long desired. Somewhere in the midst of it, as he rested a hand on those golden locks and she entwined her fingers in his dark hair, he came to believe her—to believe that truly, he might indeed not be alone.

Chapter 87

Alaric

Alaric Garaunt was alone. Truly, desperately, completely alone. The silence persisted for days upon end, then it would be broken by the maddening tap of something slowly trying to steal his sanity. He tried to ignore it, of course, but that never worked for more than a few hours at a time. It would continue, unceasing, unremitting, unrelenting, until finally he would exhibit the first signs of strain. He would talk to himself, in a normal tone at first, then with increasing violence. Had his hands been free, he would have gesticulated wildly, making points to himself. His hands were not free, however, and so he was forced to imagine that he was making his gestures. It was a difficult thing to cope with for a man who had been able to make himself insubstantial at a mere thought to suddenly find himself anchored to the same place, month after month, year after year, with little company but the silence when it was silent, the maddening noise when it attempted to drive him mad, and …

… and the appearance of the others, when he was meant to suffer.

On a usual day of torment it was only Boreagann that would appear. Blunt of face, slow of wit, but skilled in the arts of dealing pain. He could draw the blood so skillfully that the wounds would close in such a way as to yield the maximum suffering before they healed. He smelled of rotten fish, wore a helm that looked like it had been carved from the arse end of a particularly shaggy bear, and when he breathed his foul breath, Alaric felt that the bear's arse metaphor worked all too well once again.

Today, though, Boreagann was not alone. He had company, company of the usual sort. Of course. Because today could not be a day of silence, a day of the maddening noise or a day of simple torment.

No, today was a day for taunting. And those were the worst of all.

"Greetings, gentleman," Alaric said from his place upon the cold, metal table. He was naked, and if he had felt exposed when he had first arrived here, over a year ago, it had not improved in the intervening time.

"Alaric," came the booming voice of Boreagann's companion. Alaric did not even care to think of him by name anymore. His helm was a thing of crafted lines and anger given armored form. The rest of his plate was much the same, hiding almost every part of him beneath it, giving little or nothing away of its wearer. The booming voice did this as well; it was at once jovial, but threatening, good-natured but heavy in its cruelty. Vile anger was a sweet sauce to this fellow, Alaric knew by long experience. "It is a good day, is it not?"

"Having not been outside," Alaric said, level of tone and forcing a pleasant smile upon his lips, "I would not care to speculate. But, being as you are the warden and I am the prisoner, I will simply have to take your word for it."

The companion slowed a step, taking in Alaric's sunny disposition. It gave him pause, Alaric knew, and that made him feel something warm deep inside, in a hidden place where even Boreagann could not carve it out of him with all the implements he regularly employed. "I have to admit, you are in a far better mood after a year here than I had anticipated," the companion said, booming again. "I had thought you would break."

"I have never broken before," Alaric said with a half shrug. "I see no reason to start now."

"I believe you," the companion said, nodding sagely. "I watched you argue your case, plead before my brethren for that non-existent mercy that they claim to hold dear," he guffawed, "watched them buy into your line of thought. Watched them play into your hand, spare the life of Cyrus Davidon ... and I rejoiced, Alaric. In this, after all, we have common cause."

"I killed Mortus," Alaric said. "It was right that I should ultimately suffer for it."

"Far be it from me to argue when it suits my purposes so perfectly." The companion laughed again, the booming sound an affront to the senses. "You protected my investment, and for this I am grateful." The companion paused before a tray of shiny metal implements and picked one of them up, a piercing thing that looked oblong and sharp in several very wrong places. "Perhaps I'll have Boreagann not use this one today. It looks painful."

Alaric would never give him the satisfaction of knowing that so much as one of the implements was anything but a sunny day by the shore. "Whatever you wish."

"I like that phrase," the companion said. "I should like it to be spoken more." He honed his red eyes in on Alaric. "You kept him alive for so long, against so many odds that they strewed against him. I don't even know if they have any idea how much the two of us unwittingly conspired to keep him from dying. You to make him do things to your purpose, and I to make him do things for mine."

"Cyrus Davidon is his own man," Alaric said, keeping himself even again. The temptation was to lash out furiously, but that would only spike the bastard with malice, knowing he'd gotten under Alaric's skin. No, cool indifference was the order of the day, pronouncements delivered with all the feeling one might give to speaking about the year's harvest.

"Yes, his own man," the companion guffawed once more. "Did you know that he just led an expedition into the heart of Saekaj? Killed poor Yartraak." The companion mimed sticking the sharp implement into his heart, and Alaric wished—oh, how he wished—that he had done it truly. He leaned in toward Alaric and lowered his voice a hair. "What was it you made him promise not to do before he left the shores of Arkaria? I forget." A loud laugh split the air. "And apparently he has as well!"

Alaric waited until the laughter came to a halt. "Will he be punished for this transgression?"

"You needn't worry about him joining you anytime soon." This came with the wave of a steel gauntlet. "Vidara, in her infinite silliness, is protecting him, spinning a story about how Yartraak abducted her out of her own realm. It has the others in such a state they have yet to question why they should let someone who has had a hand in killing two gods continue to walk the face of Arkaria."

"Some of them must suspect that you are involved," Alaric watched the red eyes for reaction.

"They are fools who would scarcely know that I move against them even as I twist and pull at their very flesh," the companion answered. "There are a thousand carrion birds swirling them right now, you should know better than anyone. So many distractions, so many things to consume their time. The pantheon is divided." Alaric could hear the grin even though he could not see it. "And I will continue to use Cyrus as a wedge to divide them further."

"He will not follow your path, Mathurin—" Alaric began.

"Do not call me that," the companion said with more than a little ire. "You do not … call me that. No one calls me that."

"No," Alaric agreed, "they do not. At least not anymore."

"But he will follow my path," the companion swept quickly back to that point. "And as Cyrus goes, so goes the Army of Sanctuary." The armored figured paused, his back turned to Alaric. The satisfaction brimmed out of him. "*My* army."

"You will try to turn him your way," Alaric said, causing the helm with the red eyes to swivel his way, "and you will fail. You will throw manipulative tricks at him and he will resist. Try as you may, he will not bend to become your flawless servant, not yours, Mathurin—"

"Do not call me—!"

"Bellarum, then," Alaric said, and the red eyes glowed nearly to burst with flame. "He is not yours."

Bellarum—Alaric hated to think of him that way—strolled back to the table of implements. They were all of them sharp, at least on this tray. "Use all of them today, Boreagann. Twice." Bellarum turned to leave, but before he did, he leaned in close to Alaric's ear, and Alaric could smell the breath of the God of War. "You can't save him, Ghost of Sanctuary. That's what you call yourself now, isn't it? It's what you are; invisible to the world, unable to grasp or affect it." There was nothing but malice in the words. "You can't save him, you can't sway him from here. He is mine." Bellarum straightened up, looking down with those red eyes, those merciless eyes. "My servant."

"He is his own man," Alaric said back, in a voice that scratched its way out of a dry throat.

The God of War hesitated, and Alaric could see the desire to strike warring with the need to not stoop to such things; his haughtiness won out and Bellarum strolled from the room, armor clanking in time with his steps as surely as if he were still a raw soldier.

Boreagann started his work shortly thereafter. Alaric imagined Bellarum—he still hated that name—lurking outside the door, waiting to hear screams. He kept them to himself for what felt like hours, years, maybe centuries. Every time the pain would rise, he pictured them in his head, the vision he had seen of them in the tower.

She is with him ... Vara is with him ... they are together ... she will save him now ... now that I cannot ...

When he finally broke for the day, the screams tearing through the chamber of Alaric's torture, it was the knowledge that this last thing would remain secret that allowed him to go on.

But this was the very last thing. The secret he kept to himself. The one thing that Bellarum did not know.

The thing he could not take away.

The screams came in a torrent, flowing like a river past his ears. It was another day of torment for Alaric Garaunt.

The Ghost of Sanctuary.

NOW

Epilogue

Cyrus stirred from his place by the window. The diary was heavy in his hand, the weight of all of Vara's words pulling him down. The fire still crackled, the torches still burned, but the odd warmth that Cyrus felt was unrelated to the flames.

"What are you going to do?" Vaste asked, and Cyrus turned to look at him.

"I might read for a bit," Cyrus said, thumbing through the journal. "If that's all right?"

Vaste made an impassive face, a gesture that indicated he gave little care. He had a journal of his own—Alaric's—and seemed to be making steady progress. Cyrus turned back to Vara's clean, swooping letters and paused on a passage that he knew came in the wake of their dive to the Mler temple, where he had drowned in the dark water, alone …

I watched him, dead, flopping about without a hint of life as they pulled his corpse from the water, and I felt things. Annoying things. Emotional things. I had seen him die before, of course, but it bothered me on such a level to watch him dragged up from the depths below, thrown upon the deck of that infernal ship, waterlogged and near-naked. I was forced to stand back, to watch as they ministered to him in all the terrible ways it took to bring him back to life.

I stood and I watched. And my eyes caught the thief's.

The horror was not quite it should be, in my estimation. I knew how I felt, of course, and not being his intimate—whatever—my concern should have been different from hers, yes?

I am completely convinced that I felt it on a much deeper level than she did. Of course, I did not show this to anyone. But neither did she; her appearance was like that of someone stricken, someone who has watched something unfortunate. Part of me wanted to cross the empty space between us, slap her cheek so the salt air burned it, and tell her to feel something—anything.

It is anyone's guess whether I really wanted to do that to her … or to myself.

He blinked. The signs had been there, hadn't they? All along? He'd missed them, every one. Aisling had seemed so … interested. He felt the ache of his bones now, but remembered the hot blood and how it had called to him. He turned his eyes down and found another passage, this one about hot blood of a different kind.

I do so try to avoid a catfight where possible. At least the sort that do not involve swords.

This one most certainly did not involve a sword, though only because my restraint was so great as to keep myself from bringing it into the proceedings. I had plenty of cause. Justification, really. If the dark elven harlot had lost her head to my blade, I am assured that few would have wept. Or been surprised.

But he might weep, and that keeps her head firmly attached to her shoulders.

For now.

It was an innocuous start to a conversation; I was meandering about the grounds, which is something I do from time to time. She saw me, doing some meandering herself, presumably, or else she came actively seeking me.

I would actually lay my odds on the latter, at least in this instance.

For you see, her verbal tirade came in the morning hours after I left her and the object of her intentions—good or ill, I have yet to determine—in the Waking Woods, in the dark, ghouls still about. Not exactly in near proximity, but they were certainly still there, and with the noise that those two make while rutting, it was not a stretch of my imagination to think they might be devoured by the boney weaklings.

Well, perhaps I was more hoping for that, at least in her case.

"You're a bitter, jealous shrew." That was her opening. Sun shining down from above, brisk breeze out of the west rustling my hair, dark elven whore spitting rage in my face.

"And a fine morning to you as well," I said.

"You just can't let him go, can you?" She folded her arms over that leather armor, which she had probably worn during sex on so many occasions as to completely beat the squeaky sounds out of it when she moved.

"If you're referring to last night," I said archly, "I tried to discourage him from coming with me—"

"Maybe you're too old for him," she said a little haughtily, trying to assure me of my inferior place in the equation. As the last born of the elves, it would take

more than a blue-skinned trollop to convince me of any such thing. "I'm twenty-five, after all."

"And you are a dark elf," I said, establishing the facts. "I am thirty-two, and an actual elf, which makes me practically a fetus next to you."

"Maybe that's it, then." She seemed to take little interest in my insult, but I suspected she was trying entirely too hard. "He's looking for a mature woman, someone more confident in herself."

I refrained from slapping myself upon the forehead then stopped myself from giving her a similar treatment. I was not so successful in holding off my glare of ice. "Your maturity astounds me. Why, I stand astounded in this very moment."

She headed off at a brisk pace at that. I presumed it was that she could not find a way to land that ever-elusive insult that would crack my facade.

If only she'd known the truth.

Cyrus paused, regarding the neatly written break; the passage that followed was a simple continuation of the same day's entry.

I entered the foyer after my encounter with the slattern, milling about in a somewhat confused state. It was not long, of course, before Erith—this woman is a monumental pain in my arse on every occasion—approached, begging my help for some task. I accompanied her against my better judgment, and it was there that I was introduced to Administrator Cattrine Tiernan.

I could think of a few things to say about her. Goddess knows I'd heard enough about her before 'ere I laid my eyes upon her face. I would have been prepared to hate the woman.

But I could not.

She was graceful in her introduction where I was not. I thought at first this was simply her high-born manners, but she wore pants, not a dress, which was an immediate mark in her favor. And then we went into the meeting, and she turned out to be intelligent and self-sacrificing, honest about what her community needed and grateful for the help we had provided.

I know, I know. If this sounds like uncharacteristic gushing, I freely admit to it. But she was kind, and she was decent, and she asked me to escort her to the door, to her waiting wizard. I expected something of the sort that Aisling regularly threw my way, those looks when passed, the under-the-breath comments of someone who felt a need to compete for something I wasn't even fighting for at this point. He's yours, fool. Take him with some grace.

"You are exactly what I expected," Cattrine Tiernan said as we made our way down the long hallway toward the foyer. "Tall, beautiful, full of grace and composure—"

"Aren't you a honey-tongued one?" I replied.

"You're everything everyone described," she said, looking me over once more. Then she lowered her voice. "It should have been you."

I froze, and it took me a few moments to remember that I was supposed to be walking with her. I caught up and forewent any attempt to claim I did not know what she was talking about. "It is just as well," I said instead.

"No," she said, "it is not." She halted me there and looked me in the eyes, and I could tell that whatever she was about to say, it was going to be one of those things I am usually quite uncomfortable with—a 'just us girls' comment. "I don't know what her angle is, but I know what yours was, and I know what mine was."

"And what was our ... 'angle'?" I wanted to hear her spell it out. Perhaps I didn't quite believe I was hearing someone be quite so blunt about it.

"We actually cared for him," she said, and I saw that cleverness that I had admired. "Don't you tell me you can't see it? The way she looks at him? The ways she tries just a little too hard? Like she's not quite sure how to get what she wants, so she overshoots the mark by a mile or two—"

"I have noticed that, yes," I said. "But there's precious little I can do—"

"There's precious little any of us can do," she said softly. "He's made his choices. And I'm fine with it, really. I am. But whatever lingering feeling I have ... I think it's mainly regret that I know he didn't at least pick someone else who genuinely cares for him."

With that, she started off again. I did not quite manage to speak the thought which was on my mind: I agree completely.

Cyrus ran a hand over his face, blinking through a fatigue that had settled deep on him. He imagined the two of them standing together, talking, Cattrine and Vara. It gave him more than a moment's discomfort.

We battled trolls, dark elves, watched a bombardment that was nearly the stuff of miracles fall upon our field of battle like some magic so grandiose I cannot conceive of a spell caster who could unleash it, and then we got a glimpse of Terian—yes, that Terian—staring at us from across the battlefield on the side of our foes.

And then, after all that, I went to deliver a private word of congratulations to our triumphant General, victor of the battle at Livlosdald, and found him in his tent bedding his dark elven ... pick an unflattering term to describe her, as I'm running out.

It is not as though I am naïve about these sorts of things. I am fully aware that Cyrus Davidon is a man who is possessed of all the appetites that a man is possessed of. But knowing it and once again having it driven home—this time in the form of his dark elf's caterwauling, matched with his own shouts of lust—are two quite different things.

I thought about tossing some cutting remark toward the tent as I passed, but I decided not to give her the satisfaction. How could I trust a man such as this, so weak and so prone to driving himself toward ... her ... to run this guild?

I wandered off into the night, seeking my solace. It is simply better that I be left alone.

The tingle ran over Cyrus's flesh as he imagined the moment, pictured her outside in the dark, staring at the tent, listening to the sounds. He made a shudder as he pictured that moment with their roles reversed. Revulsion washed over him, profound and heavy, and he hurried on to the next passage.

I felt bad for him in the swamp. He tried to explain his dark elven dalliance, tried to blame it on—goddess, everything. The dark of night, the unthinking mind, the blood flowing to the wrong portion of his anatomy—well, that last part appeared obvious on the night in question—but it didn't take away from the fact that I felt bad for him.

He stood next to the grave of his father and realized there was nothing left. How heady a feeling. I am a bit familiar with it, since there is now a marker outside Termina that bears my mother's name. It is one of countless names on said marker, but it is there. I found it once, on a recent visit. It stands there and declares to the world that Chirenya was lost in the defense of the city. Right there next to the soldiers. It's a monument. It stands in place of her, because she is no longer here to stand.

His father's grave was empty stones, fallen to time and weather. Then he faced me—after he'd caught me following behind them—and tried to explain away his mistakes. Unfortunately for him, they've left a rather large monument in my mind, and it is not an empty one. It is filled with the sounds I have collected in my memory on various nights over the last months. A catalog of all his so-called "mistakes."

And there are so many.

Then we came to Gren, and he laid his fury upon them on the main street. They were duly impressed. I can't say I wasn't impressed, either. This was Cyrus Davidon in the heart of the battle. He runs on a fairly even keel, always thinking, pondering, considering. I wonder sometimes what goes on behind those eyes, especially during battle.

But then, every now and again, he lets loose of the leash, and I find myself wishing I didn't know what goes on back there.

What he did on the main street was ... understandable. Dramatic. He puffed himself up and scared them all off. Sent the trolls running.

What he did in the slave market, though ...

Well, that's another something.

They sent for me, for reasons I could not fathom at first. I was at the other end of town, tying up my own loose ends, supervising the freeing of more dirty, ragged slaves than I could rightly count, and then Nyad appears—have I told you that her choice of a last name drives me absolutely goblin-shit mad? It does. But that's a story for another time. She appears, wild, clearly having fatigued herself with a sprint across the splattered waste that is troll town, outhouse to the balance of a race with the largest bowels in Arkaria, and she pants something about me needing to follow her.

I protest. She ignores it and reiterates her demand I accompany her. I tell her in a moment, cool irritation with her infantile spewing of breathless emotion and she splatters out the words, "CYRUS IS GOING TO KILL THEM ALL!" as though it were an unusual thing, the man in the black armor dealing death.

And yes, before you ask, I sprinted across town faster than the elven princess could keep up. Apparently she used the important word, the one that would get me moving, somewhere in there. I maintain that it was 'kill,' but an impartial observer may come up with another, more likely candidate.

I brushed past Larana, staring at Cyrus in mute helplessness, to get close enough to him to speak. "Cyrus ... don't," I said, imploring him. I have seen him vengeful before; his career puts him in a position to lose friends at a rate a blacksmith or farmer or waterman is unlikely to know. "You are better than simple vengeance." I almost felt the voice of Alaric urging me as I said it, repeating back what the Ghost of Sanctuary had told me in the days I desired to strike down Archenous Derregnault, the bastard.

I watched him pull back from the abyss, watched it unfold before my very eyes. I watched him calmly bury what was left of Cass Ward, putting his frustration into every thrust of the shovel.

And I felt bad for him. Truly, I did. In that moment, I felt a sense of being alone more acutely than I ever have, and it bothered me most because ... I felt it solely because I knew he was experiencing the exact same thing.

Wistful. He imagined the look on her face as she wrote about Gren, imagined her detailing her fears about being alone, about losing control to the vengeful. He remembered her as she had been in

Enterra, when she'd seen his mercy. The look on her face had been ... he blinked a tear away.

I didn't know how badly he was hurt until he agreed to go to the back of the lines. That was when I suspected, but truly, I had no idea even still. Then he staggered forward in his foolish charge, and I watched him go, unable to stop or support him. I tried to use logic to keep myself back as others followed him. I was still ... if not bitter over the Guildmaster election, at least twinged with annoyance. It was not exactly a shocking result, but it stung nonetheless, all protestations and pledges of loyalty to the contrary. I am a sharp blade, and I cut wherever I go. Cyrus is a ... I don't know. Perhaps he's a loaf of sweetbread, desired by all, and something I wish to eat when—

Never mind.

He went into the heart of the battle, bleeding from the wound that infernal bitch opened in his back. I have known many women—they comprise probably half the people I know—and yet I had always seemed to associate backstabbing with men up until that day. No more.

Even seeing her as treacherous, I could not fully imagine that she could devastate him so. Manipulate him for her own gain? Certainly. Enrich her own purse through him in exchange for the relief of his needs? A tale as old as time itself. Curatio could probably tell it.

But stabbing him in the back with a black lace dagger and letting him bleed to death while he tried in vain to do his duty?

No.

Oh, no.

I did not see that coming, not even from a woman who I have run out of terrible names for. Well, I suppose I have one left, but I would rather save it for a less auspicious occasion and less polite company.

If there was one thing I would not have been able to predict even more than who would lay him low, it was who would save him when death was assured.

Terian Lepos.

I didn't entirely trust him, of course, but I was grateful for the help. It's not as though I was blind to it, after all; I was there on the field of battle when he raised his axe to Cyrus's aid.

But I wasn't there when he'd turned his weapon against Cyrus, and part of me still found that unforgivable for some reason. Silly, I suppose, but I felt it nonetheless.

I saw Cyrus when they stripped him of his armor. His mouth gaped open, his dark hair hung in wet strings. I watched, watched as they did their work upon him. I saw the scar in his back and remembered the one in my own. In roughly the same place, no less. I thought it odd, at the time, and still do ... but at that moment, I saw another way—annoying as it might have been—that Cyrus Davidon was like myself.

A single, long chuckle from Vaste broke Cyrus's concentration. He stared at the troll, but Vaste had not moved. His head was deeply in the book, on the pages before him. *Learning the answers to some burning questions he's had for a long time, I'd wager ...* Cyrus turned his attention back to the diary in his hand, and read on.

I was sure he was dead, and I was as vengeful as Cyrus Davidon had ever been. I came at Yartraak with everything I had, sword aflame with fury so righteous it burned the air itself, strength given to me by my armor. I watched Cyrus flung through the air by the swing of a god, and was fully intent on slicing that grey-skinned devil apart.

Or die trying. I was far enough gone that I found that an acceptable alternative, oddly.

"You cannot think you stand a chance against me," the God of Darkness hissed. "I have already destroyed your—"

"Shut your gap-toothed mouth!" I slashed him across the arm and pounded upon him with a fury of blows. I opened his flesh in more places than could be counted by most peasants without resorting to their toes and blasted him back with spellcraft. I leapt into the light and was—more than a little—surprised to find Cyrus waiting for me there, battered, but still holding his weapon.

Then he was struck again, the idiot, this time intentionally—why, Goddess, why must his bravery occasionally outweigh that intelligence I claim he does not have? It's as though he's acting stupid to spite me. Once more, the fool was blasted out of the room, except this time, thanks to the presence of two torches, it was clear he was still completely held together.

"What the—" Yartraak said.

I blasted him in the bloody back with a spell. Just pounded him. Did not wait for him to turn around, simply sent him flying through the doors behind Cyrus.

No, it was not at all paladin-like, but—and I presume that the elven paladin masters would agree with me, were they asked very specifically about my case— when battling a god, the rules go right out the nearest bloody window.

I followed them out at my leisure—oh, who's kidding whom, I ran like mad, through another room, over a bridge, out a gate—and found that Cyrus had now lost his weapon. You know, the one thing that allows him to move faster, strike harder, stand up to the gods—yes, he drove it into Yatraak's back and failed to retrieve it, the fool. Made me reconsider his intelligence yet again.

I caught up with them on a major avenue outside the palace. Soldiers were assembling. Cyrus was dangling loosely from the Sovereign's grasp. And I spat out some fiery challenge, ready to have it out with the bastard once and for all. Of course the coward used him as hostage; I'd been driving him back all along. I could smell the fear on him, it hung like the darkness when he had a chance to gather it about him.

The battle went on, mad, swirling, my blade against Yartraak with only a minimal amount of help from the supposed hero in the black armor. Oh, he certainly fought against those army fellows that charged in, but I was battling something ancient and evil. And then, when he finally inserts himself back into the fight, he does so to grab hold of his sword and get flung to the ground.

I saw him drop, and ... my heart dropped with him.

And then he flung his sword at me.

I could feel it the minute it touched my hand. Through my gauntlet, the power flowed. I was righteous before, but this made me invincible, and I could see the look on that bastard's face as he realized it, too. He tried a goad, and it failed. I swiped his head clean from his body. He said something to Cyrus before his face had the good grace to realize it was dead, but by that point ... I was good and done. I did my best Cyrus Davidon impression and sent the locals fleeing. Watched them run down the street as though they were trolls and I was ... well, him.

And then?

We loosed the Goddess of Life from her chains, set Terian about the business of freeing Reikonos from the dark elven hordes, I had one last opportunity to call the dark elven harlot a slattern (as opposed to the other word, which I will not use), and then ...

... and then ...

Cyrus Davidon did something countless crusaders have pledged to do over the years and steadfastly done not a damned thing about.

He freed the last slaves of Arkaria.

Her admiration was worth the price every resurrection spell had ever exacted on him. He stared down, looked the pages, looked at the ink, spotted with age and exposure to the elements. He felt elements of his own—water, fresh from his eyes, added unto the ravages of time, and he hurried to read the last bit. He'd read it already, but it was his favorite passage.

The day that J'anda Aimant returned to us will be a day I cannot ever forget, for more reasons than one. The party stretched into the night, of course; since the day I joined Sanctuary, they have been a joyful lot. They celebrate at the slightest inclination, and adding that wine-sodden (though now quite sober) idiot Andren to the mix has increased our proclivities in that direction.

I, of course, have a very low threshold for the amount of merrymaking I can withstand. Oh, it all starts out to the good—there's a freeing sort of spirit on the event, a happy chatter that precedes such an occasion. But it inevitably sinks into idiocy, into maudlin sentiment, and these are things I cannot abide. These and leather clogs.

I had safely made my escape, retreated to my haven in the tower, when the knock sounded upon my door. Naturally, I was not expecting anyone, because ... well, I never expect anyone, especially during festivities of any kind. Who enjoys being in the company of a misanthrope during a celebration, after all?

I opened the door to find J'anda waiting outside. I have known J'anda for some considerable time. For as long as I have known him, he has worn many faces.

Since he returned from Luukessia, I have only seen him almost exclusively with one: his own, considerably aged, face.

I didn't really know what to say. I invited him in, of course, and he accepted. "You should be at your party," I said weakly, aware of the hypocrisy inherent in such a statement.

He looked at me with those deep eyes of his. Another thing I have realized in my long association with J'anda—in spite of his charm and the interest of countless women in him, his proclivities run in a different direction than I or any other woman of Sanctuary might provide. "I come back to you now for whatever time I have left."

"Here to Sanctuary, I assume," I said. "Not here to my chambers? Because I am ill-equipped to handle dying."

"Aren't we all?" he asked with that faint, charming smile. There is little about J'anda that is not charming.

"Why are you here?" I asked. "In this room, I mean. Obviously ... coming back to Sanctuary for the time you have left ..."

"I have had a great deal of time to think of late," J'anda said. "And I realized I have never cast a spell of mesmerization upon you."

I froze. I've heard about mesmerization spells, about what they do—what they show you. "I ... I don't really have any interest in exploring my heart's desire, whatever that may be—"

"It's a curious thing," J'anda said, "in the nature of people. Anyone who learns what a mesmerization spell is, they come to some point their life when they come to me. They seek answers. Answers to questions they may struggle with. Many times, we wander through our lives without knowing exactly what it is we want." He leaned in and looked me in the eye. "Of course, there are also those who fear to know what they want."

I have had these conversations before. Well-meaning, always. Good-intentioned, doubtless. But it is the same conversation, every time, whether it is my sister or the newest warrior applicant who broaches the subject. Even Arydni—who has born the brunt of my tirades about the expectations of the Life Mother upon my female parts more than once—has tried to bring up the topic of Cyrus Davidon with me.

The same damned conversation.

And here is what I do. I smile. It puts them at ease, I think. Or terrifies them, perhaps. I don't care, honestly. I count to five because to respond sooner would guarantee that the flames of Enflaga himself would burst from my mouth and consume them wholly. That's not polite, my mother's voice tells me. And then, in the lightest tone, I begin my counter-argument.

"J'anda, Cyrus is a human," I said, well practiced, well rehearsed. These are the words of my mother, given life by me years after her death. "I am not. I could live for six thousand years—"

"You could die tomorrow," J'anda said with a certainty that made me rattle slightly. "And what would you have? What would you leave behind you but an ocean of regrets?"

I did not quite flinch at that, but ... I will admit to perhaps blinking a few times. "I ... also have a reasonable collection of leather shoes."

"I saw the desire of Cyrus's heart on the day I mesmerized him some years ago," J'anda said. "Through land and sea, death and life, errors ..." he made a face, "... numerous errors ... I know that the desire of his heart has not changed." He laid a hand upon mine. "And I suspect all this work you do, the two of you, keeping yourselves apart ... it is a tireless dance, but one that I have grown tired of. Life is uncertain. Death is uncertain." He looked me directly in the eyes. "If there is something in your heart that you are certain about ... it would be exceedingly wise not to waste the rest of your days adding it to the pile with your list of regrets ... and your collection of leather shoes." He shrugged at the last part. "I am sure they are very fashionable."

"Damned right," I said, *but the certainty I had felt a moment earlier had faded. I had known the desire of my heart all along. It was obvious as the nose on J'anda's face, when he wasn't hiding it behind an illusion.*

"You don't have to be alone," he said, and it forced me to look around—to really look around. My quarters were nearly bare, the product of a life that had been lived in a whirlwind, moving from place to place several times. Uprooted and starting over again. Being left to die. Learning to trust again.

I had lost Alaric, lost my parents, lost my trust at the blade of a knife. I looked down at my hands, bare, as I had left my gauntlets on the table when I had come in. They looked lonely, each finger without another to intertwine with. I stuck my hands together self-consciously, and though they matched, it did not feel right.

"Do not enslave yourself to your past," J'anda said, moving toward the door. He walked with a slump to his shoulders and disappeared into the hall, shutting the door behind him.

I sat alone for another ten minutes, thinking over what he said, staring at my bare walls, and feeling the strange absence as I interlaced my fingers in a spectacle that would have looked bizarre on anyone but Malpravus. I should be proud that it only took those ten minutes—well, ten minutes and however many years—to make my decision. I am an elf, after all, and my life is long. Ten minutes to realize that I didn't want to spend it alone is practically a snap of the fingers. I left my empty quarters behind and ascended, searching him out. I felt like I was climbing toward my destiny—

Cyrus snapped the diary shut, the emotions bubbling over. He pushed them away, forced them down, cleared his throat, feigned a cough. He looked out the window, sparing only a glance to look back at Vaste. The troll's head was still down, still on the pages of Alaric's journal.

Cyrus walked, slowly, across the floor of the Council Chambers, avoiding the shattered debris that littered the room. He passed Vaste and walked toward the stairs, stopping when he heard the voice call to him from behind.

"You aren't alone, you know." Vaste's tone was crisp, clear.

"I know," Cyrus said and began his descent.

The foyer was still a disastrous mess, stone and rubble strewn everywhere. He passed through the doors and onto the grounds, the scorched grass stretching out from the stone steps. He marched toward the remnants of the curtain wall, passing under the remains of the gate only moments later.

He stood and looked across the plains, empty, desolate. When he had passed this way days earlier, the spot upon which he stood had been a crater, a jagged, lifeless hole in the earth.

Cyrus turned his gaze to the monument, the only sign that had marked this place other than the crater. It was massive in its own right, a headstone as wide as he was tall. The story it told across the top was one he was all too familiar with. He ran a finger over the text, giving it only a cursory glance.

And then he reached the bottom, the list of names that ran columns wide, row after row.

The dead.

The fallen.

He had read them all before, every one, and on each occasion he did so, it felt like he drowned in his own despair, as though he'd fallen in deep water and no one had reached a hand to help pull him back out again. It was cold and crippling, as icy as Reikonos air in the heart of winter.

Cyrus stood before the stone, his heart barely contained. He kept his eyes closed for fear of being seen and subtly looked back toward the gates. They were empty, a clear path all the way back to the foyer. The gaping darkness loomed inside Sanctuary, a mouth of despair that threatened to swallow him whole.

But not just yet.

He read the names, starting at the top. He did it stoically, containing the emotion that threatened to burst loose of him. He did well in this, he had to admit. The grey skies threatened to open up on him—again—but he kept his own emotions bottled through every single column, every single row.

Until the name at the bottom.

He let his eyes drift to it as a man seeking pain picks at a fresh scab. It gave him the desired result: sharp agony, fresh, dredged back to life.

Cyrus Davidon felt the wobble run through his legs and hit his knees, the shock of the impact rolling up him, all the strength gone from a warrior who had challenged the gods.

Fought death itself.

Plucked the eyes from dragons.

Freed a land.

Five words, carved in stone, were enough to render the warrior in black armor weak beyond measuring. They brought him low without fail, took him down, ripped from him whatever he had left.

But as Cyrus stared at the words, unable to take his eyes off of them—perfectly carved as if a quill had etched them into the stone—he had to concede that … there simply was not anything else left to take. His eyes drifted over them once more, and the stabbing, searing pain clawed its way into his heart again at their mere sight:

Vara Davidon

Shelas'akur

Beloved Wife

The wind howled over the Plains of Perdamun, over the monument to the fallen, grey skies dark over the lonely and abandoned towers of the Sanctuary guildhall—a perfect match for the man in black armor who knelt at the foot of the stone … and was lord of all the emptiness he looked over.

And Now For A Word From Your Author

(Because the last 177,000 were not enough, apparently.)

So…was that my most emotionally brutal ending ever? Discuss. But not here, because you'd basically be yelling at your e-reader (if you've not already thrown it).

If you're fighting the temptation to throw it, let me reassure you – I've just revealed something fairly huge (obviously). This is book five of eight (main volumes; when you count in 4.5 and 5.5, I guess it's a ten book series. Unless you add in the tales…). Point is, the story is NOT over.

Bear with me. I think, when we get to the end of this, you'll be happy you read. It's gonna take a while longer to get to the end, though. After vacillating somewhat (and realizing how much is left out of the Saekaj storyline by the fact that Cyrus couldn't be present for the revolution), I've decided to go ahead and write Fated in Darkness: The Sanctuary Series, Volume 5.5. It'll cover what J'anda, Aisling and Terian were doing during the events of this book and bring Terian and Aisling's stories as started in "Thieving Ways" (available in Sanctuary Tales) and "Thy Father's Shadow" (Sanctuary 4.5) to their respective closes and fold them back into the main story. After that, I will not be writing any more half-measure volumes, it'll be volumes 6, 7 and 8 to finish things out for this series.

That said, it's still probably going to be a couple years to finish this thing. I wrote ten books in 2014, and I'm aiming for ten in 2015. I even managed to squeeze in three Sanctuary books this year, not that most people noticed. (Sanctuary Tales and Volume 4.5 did not do all that well, comparatively – which is fine. As your author, I want to give you more of what you want. Except for that scene that just happened in the epilogue. You obviously didn't want THAT.) I'm aiming to get Volume 5.5 and 6 out in 2015, and I think that's very possible, though Warlord (Volume Six) could be as big as Crusader (about 1.5x the length of this volume). We'll see.

To bring this ramble to a close, if you want to know when the next book(s) become available, take sixty seconds and sign up for my NEW RELEASE EMAIL ALERTS on my website, www.robertjcrane.com. Don't let the caps lock scare you; I don't sell your information and I only send out emails when I have a new book out. The reason you should sign up for this is because I don't like to set release dates (it's this whole thing, you can find an answer on my website in the FAQ section), and even if you're following me on Facebook (robertJcrane (Author)) or Twitter (@robertJcrane), it's easy to miss my book announcements because…well, because social media is an imprecise thing.

Come join the Sanctuary discussion on my website: http://www.robertjcrane.com ! It's more fun that ranting at your e-reader.

Cheers,
Robert J. Crane

Return to the depths of Saekaj Sovar
and witness the revolution firsthand in

Fated in Darkness

Coming in 2015!

Cyrus Davidon will return in

Warlord

The Sanctuary Series, Volume Six

Also coming in 2015!
(I hope.)

Acknowledgments

My thanks to all these people.

Jo Evans, Nicolette Solomita and David Leach each did a read or twelve (David) on this book, helping improve it in the process and making sure the author didn't lose his damned mind and slip into insanity.

Kari Phillips long ago gave me a great idea about using a goddess to create an infinite number of soul rubies, so thanks to her for that one. And more. Probably more, too.

Karri Klawiter once again provided a flashy and eye-catching cover.

Sarah Barbour provided editorial guidance and helped keep me between the lines on this crazy roller-coaster ride of a novel. It ain't easy producing a work of this size, but it'd be impossible to do it this cleanly without help like she provides.

Jeff Bryan gave this book a final read-through that helped me stamp out some persistent errors and made it a better read.

My kids helped push that sanity dial in the other direction. I love them anyway.

My parents helped keep the kids from pushing that dial too far. They came and stayed for a week during which I managed to write at least a quarter of this manuscript, which was a huge help in getting it back on track.

My wife helps me hold it all together. She's kinda of the crazy-glue for our operation. Minus the crazy. That's my dominion.

About the Author

Robert J. Crane is kind of an a-hole. Still, if you want to contact him:

Website: http://www.robertjcrane.com

Facebook Page: robertJcrane (Author)

Twitter: @robertJcrane

Email: cyrusdavidon@gmail.com

Other Works by Robert J. Crane

The Sanctuary Series
Epic Fantasy

Defender: The Sanctuary Series, Volume One
Avenger: The Sanctuary Series, Volume Two
Champion: The Sanctuary Series, Volume Three
Crusader: The Sanctuary Series, Volume Four
Sanctuary Tales, Volume One - A Short Story Collection
Thy Father's Shadow: The Sanctuary Series, Volume 4.5
Master: The Sanctuary Series, Volume Five
Fated in Darkness: The Sanctuary Series, Volume 5.5 (Coming in 2015!)
Warlord: The Sanctuary Series, Volume Six* (Coming in 2015! Probably.)

The Girl in the Box
and
Out of the Box
Contemporary Urban Fantasy

Alone: The Girl in the Box, Book 1
Untouched: The Girl in the Box, Book 2
Soulless: The Girl in the Box, Book 3
Family: The Girl in the Box, Book 4
Omega: The Girl in the Box, Book 5
Broken: The Girl in the Box, Book 6
Enemies: The Girl in the Box, Book 7
Legacy: The Girl in the Box, Book 8
Destiny: The Girl in the Box, Book 9
Power: The Girl in the Box, Book 10

Limitless: Out of the Box, Book 1
In the Wind: Out of the Box, Book 2* (Coming December 30, 2014!)
Ruthless: Out of the Box, Book 3* (Coming Early 2015!)
Tormented: Out of the Box, Book 4* (Coming in 2015!)

Southern Watch
Contemporary Urban Fantasy

Called: Southern Watch, Book 1
Depths: Southern Watch, Book 2
Corrupted: Southern Watch, Book 3
Unearthed: Southern Watch, Book 4* (Coming Early 2015!)
Legion: Southern Watch, Book 5* (Coming 2015!)

*Forthcoming

Printed in Great Britain
by Amazon